The Right Hand Man

By

Lee Cooper

'Fighting's in the Blood' series
dedicated to
My Mother, Grandmother, and friend
Leigh Henderson.

Special Thanks to:

Martin Catlin for a proof-read.
Alan Stephen and Rhonda Cooper for editing.

"Chastise your son, for in this there is hope, but do not desire his death. The man of violent temper pays the penalty; even if you rescue him, you will have to do it again."

Proverbs 19:18 – 19 NAB

Part One

Guilt

Chapter 1

Cutting The Last Tie:

The wait was over, the moment had arrived.

I stormed towards the door with my sleeves rolled up, tingles of nervous adrenaline pumping. Preparing to do the unlawful, my heart beating like a possessed wolf with a desire to bring a terrible end to him, my own blood. Keeping calm before one last violent eruption, to neuter that pathetic cowardice he had as a weak child and watch him whimper in my sight. The prolonged build-up to this moment made my nostrils flare and images swirled through my head like a hunter sniffing out his prey, wondering what I was willing to do when we exchanged uncontrollable looks of disgust. Would I kill him? I didn't know. Was I prepared to? Fuck, yeah.

All I wanted was to escape from a world of solitude I became trapped inside and that's what brought me within moments of my disowned son's door. Sixteen years ago, inside the Fountain Bar in Aberdeen, his vengeful eyes longed to tear me apart; now the feeling had rebounded. The last time I saw him, I helplessly witnessed him viciously kill The Reaper, my protégé, his brother and the only son I held pride for. That chaotic night punctured a hole in my soul and left me with unfinished business. My sons didn't know they carried the same blood, brought together on a bitter night by the law of fate. Ending up in a colossal battle, in a fight laced with a legacy that would never be forgotten by the gathering of deplorable men who watched in admiration. Two men who were on a steroid-fuelled quest to be crowned the greatest bare-knuckle fighter of their generation, as I was, once upon a time. Men who lived distant lives from each other, but so closely bound and so unaware of their connection.

This corner of Scotland, I doubted I'd ever visit again, but needs must, and my connection to Joe was the last tie to my past, and the only dangling branch before my exit. I was so blindly close to getting out of the game with more siller, hard cash, than I knew what to do with, but my fortune suspiciously vanished and somehow, Joe was to blame, I knew it.

Usually I stuck to a compact set of rules, rules that kept me alive, in the shadows and free from jail. Being at the top of Britain's most wanted list has that effect. I'd be breaking the rules by visiting my past but fuck it, it had to be done.

As soon as I made him suffer and harvested some answers, the first ferry out of the country was my next port of call. Airports were too risky. A ferry, I could drive in by car in disguise using one of only two passports I had left.

There was a collection of people burning to bring me down and end my reign, authorities that wouldn't rest in their quest to get me behind bars for the rest of my ageing life. And I wasn't prepared to be thrown into the IRA's torture process, before the standard bullet in the back of the head finished me off. I always told myself I'd get out on top, but I'd gotten too greedy and paid the formidable price. Getting out on top now, meant escaping with my life.

The long festering pain of regret and grief I'd dragged around was about to end as I quickly made my way towards the door. Years of selfish, abusive living had been brutal to my body, the torturing pain I carried in my knees had run me down and could be seen in my scowl that always had an aggravated look. The bones in my hands were brittle, my skin hardened, my head overworked and pounding with my serious addiction to painkillers.

With both fists clenched tight, I psyched myself up and remembered The Reaper's death. The anticipation of seeing Joe's pitiful face conjured up hatred that swirled like a whirlpool. My jaw bones clenched, goose bumps ignited and nostrils flared, the forthcoming confrontation pictured in my mind. His weakened body beneath my stance, his face mauled and begging for mercy. After I left his life, he became a hardened man, feared and respected by tough criminal men, but the fear he had for me would always swill around his brain like a sieve that wouldn't drain. His abhorrence for me would cause his belly to weaken and turn gutless. My face in his would be the last thing he'd expect.

I kicked the low gate off the hinges and ran over the footpath to his door. I used the side of my fist to pound two intimidating knocks. I waited. No answer so I pounded again. My paranoia made me gander over my shoulder, onto the street. Checking my back, as I had to, every minute.

The door opened. Joe answered with a jubilant face, looking like he was enjoying his late Sunday afternoon. Wasting no time, I stepped in and gripped his throat, lifting him onto the tips of his toes and backwards till he slammed into the banister. His stupid, happy face turned to terrified panic as he realised who it was.

"Alright, boy." His eyes burst open and his mouth gargled as he struggled to speak and breathe. I could smell a barbeque, and hear sounds of laughter and chatter from the back of the house. I squeezed harder while his hands gripped my forearm, looking for that strength to break free. I gripped even more tightly, watching his face turn purple.

"What's wrong? Nothin' to say?" I laughed at his weak struggle.

 I relaxed enough pressure so he could answer, but kept enough so he couldn't break loose.

"What the fuck you doin' here?" he gargled, unsure if his eyes were telling him the truth.

"Came to say hello, son!" His whole body squirmed with fear and rage, his girlish grip on my forearms mustered all the strength he had, as all he wanted was to lay his wrath on me.

"Seen yer last fight boy." He began to stop struggling and the rage appeared to turn to shock as he looked at me dead-eyed.

"What?"

"I was there, watchin'." Now an irritation flooded his eyes. "Fuckin' prick!" he replied.

"That's no way to speak to yer old man," I said sarcastically, knowing that would anger him more, "I never did get the chance to tell you about yer brother."

"Who?" Joe asked, as he attempted to pull my hands away.

"He used to be a fighter, like you. We called him The Reaper." His body turned limp, his eyes turned stony and broke contact as he gazed past my ear, onto the street outside, attempting to work out how that could be possible. A few seconds of stillness passed before he got some inspiration.

"It's you who should've died, you pathetic cunt!" His revulsion at his own hopelessness to free himself made his aggression levels rise again, as a stream of saliva rolled from the side of his mouth and spit spluttered into the air. I pulled my Walther PPK from my jacket pocket and jammed it into his eye as he stared at my mangled hand with missing fingers.

"Ye're a fuckin' coward, you always have been son. Who's out the back?" I asked.

"I've proven I'm no coward. You're the one that ran, you fuck!"

"Less of yer backchat, boy! I said who's out back? And don't make ma ask again. You know what I'm capable of wi' ma finger restin' on the trigger."

"You can pull the trigger if you want, but the man behind you might pull his."

I heard a gun cock and press into the back of my head.

Chapter 2

A Father's Troubles:

 The trouble with being a mean motherfucker is you must be able to live with a deceitful conscience and the nasty bastard things you're prepared to do in life, in building a legacy that will float through time like a lasting whisper. You need the ability to trust your instinct, judge when it's the right moment in time to get out of Dodge before the greed for siller and the thirst for notoriety lands you deep in a pile of contaminated shit. That seemed to be a mistake I'd repeated over the years.

 They say there's seven deadly sins in this world; well, I lived them all and probably invented a few more to add to the list.

 Being a hard man was all I knew. From my earliest memories, a terrible upbringing guided me onto my criminal path, growing up living in fear and ironically, living on people's fear of me.

 It's safe to say my journey started as soon as I could take a punch, but the real push towards it began in 2002, when I crept into my forties.

 Davie Rhodes was my name; I'd made the granite city of Aberdeen my home for the past twenty years, where I adopted some of the unique north-eastern tounge but I'd seemed to be able to do that in every area I passed by. I kept my problems to myself and didn't talk of my family in public. I married a sweet woman called Jessica Marks and fathered a son, Joe, then twenty years old. To say I was a good husband and Father was a far cry from the truth. I'd pissed off a lot of people in my life but always managed to wriggle out of it, one way or another.

That day in 2002, a warm summer's weeknight inside my local, the Fountain Bar in Woodside, Aberdeen, starts the story of how I managed to be disowned by my own son, having just returned home from a two-month stint in Liverpool, carrying out some unscrupulous work for a friend. After a brief visit home to our flat in Tillydrone to see Jessica, I visited The Fountain, a pub where I'd spent most of my free time, drinking, speaking nonsense and filling out betting slips for horses that would never win. It was a close-knit pub that didn't welcome outsiders and only the brave would enter.

As I was enjoying a well-earned whisky and can of export with a couple of acquaintances at the bar, Joe suddenly burst through the double doors and before I could utter a word, he landed a barrage of fists onto my face, sending my chin bouncing over the room. His fury-filled attack took me by surprise and sent me to the filthy parquet floor. Joe was a highly emotional kid and a talented boxer with defined muscle and the fittest man I'd seen inside the gym, but he lacked the killer instinct, that would always lead to his downfall.

After beating me to the floor, he continued his savage attack, only to be dragged off by my two acquaintances. Once I came to my senses, I brutally launched my own attack before slamming him into the slot-machine and onto the floor. As I looked down on him, lying in shards of glass, battered, bloodied and broken, he began to revive. He had tried to take on his old man and once again, failed in a blaze of glory. I had to give him credit for the size of his balls and on that day, the killer instinct was ablaze inside him for an understandable reason.

I had never before seen such a look of pure hatred in his eyes as I did that day. My six-foot four size, unforgiving nature and raw power overcame him as he wriggled about like a snail underneath me. His sudden ferocious burst of aggression was for a reason though, a reason I wasn't prepared for, and that reason would lead to my end in time to come. Towering above him, I snarled and gave him a cocky wink to let him know my thoughts, talking through my wounded jaw that clicked in and out of place from his powerful punches.

"See, ye're still no' man enough yet boy." He turned his head to mine and gave me a hostile glare, like he would do anything to rip me apart, so I took a small step back. "You don't know what you've done, do you?" In a terrible rage, the words spat from his mouth and grief heightened his emotions.

"What the fuck you on about?" I asked him.

"Mam, you fuck! She's dead, she killed herself!"

I kept staring at him, shocked, "Don't talk shit, you lyin' weak bastard!" As I said that I grinned, but prayed it was a vindictive lie as he attempted to get another reaction from me.

"Go home, you'll see. She's dead, she killed herself." His palms scratched across over the broken glass as his legs slithered behind him, desperately trying to stand. Blood dripped from cuts to his face, poured from his burst nose and coated his clothes while his fury turned to vengeful tears. His emotions a mix of anger, hatred and frustration that he was beaten so badly and unable to stand. He eyed me with rage and only wanted to rip me apart. I understood that. The love he carried for his mother couldn't be questioned.

I lifted my head pausing in deep thought, and across from me I was reflected in a big square pub mirror with decals of a whisky brand on it. My tough-skinned triangular shaped face and normally tidy slicked back alabaster hair reflected a cold-eyed monster who had brought his wife to suicide and beaten his son to within inches of his life. It was then I realised that years of outbursts of supressed pain had ruined the life of a woman I once loved and couldn't take back. My wife was dead!

I switched my head around to the regulars in the bar, but they scowled at me with disgust. With no other thought, I bolted out the double doors and headed straight for my banged-up Vauxhall Cavalier, jumped in and sped away from the Fountain like a maniac, in a state of shock from what I'd just heard.

I messed up, I knew that. Joe had entered the pub to kill me, there was no doubt. I could see the fury leak from his enraged eyes and felt his wrath in his fists. There were high hopes for the boy growing up, being a talented boxer, but as I said, he lacked the killer instinct time and time again. He could have made it to the top and that's why I raised him with an iron fist, praying that he gained the cut-throat nature in the ring that would mould him into a champion. Having a hand in training him over the years, I only hoped he'd gain the edge that I had due to my up-bringing. I don't know quite where I went wrong with him. Not being around as often as I should could've been the cause. I tried to make sure he became something, something of a legend like his dad, but I failed and came to a brutal realisation: it was his mother's suicide that gave him the killer instinct. The same instinct that was needed to kill The Reaper.

In the city of Aberdeen, I was looked upon as a man to be feared, with a violent temper and a short fuse that exploded on more counts than I can remember. However, the ugly ogle of pure disgust from the regulars in the Fountain that day filled me with a terrible shame. Due to my violent nature, my wife of

13

twenty years had taken her own life. Not knowing the facts about how but inside I knew it was true and my fault. The anger in Joe's punch told the story.

 The only thing I could do was get out, do a runner, as I had done from Glasgow in the past. There was no time to fuck about or grab belongings or say goodbyes. I had to leave.

If Joe was anything like me, he wouldn't rest until he could squeeze every last remaining breath from my lungs. He loved his mother more than I could ever imagine and love like that can drive a man to exact the retribution needed to live a life with a peaceful soul. I felt ashamed of my actions, and my past. My gut was laced with a cold withering flow of guilt, something that couldn't be undone or taken back and I had to learn how to live with it.

 As unforgiving as I was, there was a time I think I loved Jessica, a typical hard-working housewife of Aberdonian up-bringing, but I'd pushed her too far. I say 'love' but it was convenience more than anything. Someone to share time with, cook my supper, wash my clothes and share my bed. Staying in the granite city wasn't an option; my reputation took a hit there was no return from. The filth would be on my back and that, I couldn't be arsed with, being number one on their list of villains to put behind bars. Later in life, I'd become number one on every authority's list across Europe.

 The main reason to leave was the shame. I couldn't live with it; the locals would lose any kind of respect they had for me. I'm not sure if respect was the right word really, they were more fearful than anything.

 The pocket full of cash from my job in Liverpool would have to do for the time being. I didn't own a bank card. The money I earned in life came through a variety of illegal channels. Thieving raids throughout the city: household goods, vehicles, industrial yards, copper - you name it, I stole it. I had no claim to a National Insurance number, a tax code or a pension plan. It was fair to say I'd never worked an honest day in my existence and it would stay that way.

I was a free agent for anyone to hire, wherever it would be, tracking bodies down who didn't care to be found, sorting out feuds for people or families who needed a bit of muscle, the occasional drug-run or bare-knuckle scrap. That's what I became renowned for. I'd grown up with it, fighting, that is. Taking and throwing punches for as long as I could remember, from primary school till now. I didn't have the prettiest of upbringings but it moulded me into the man I am. If I'd lived a thousand lives before this one, I would have been the same person in each one of them, a modern-day outlaw you could say, but proud I'd never felt the pain of defeat in my adult life and held a reputation as the toughest scrapper up and down Britain. I'd taken on the best and beaten the best. Times, I think I rolled on the edge of death, but my will not to be beaten brought me back to be victorious in whatever way I could. When the fights became personal, and I tried not to make them personal, my true nature gave whoever was standing opposite no chance, like the time I killed Carl Jenkins. He had set me up and I'd gotten stabbed five times, outside The Fountain of all places. He wrote his own fate as far as I was concerned, but it broke the minor ounce of humanity I had left and changed me for life.

They say everyone in life has a talent and mine was fighting and the remarkable gift for avoiding punishment for my crimes. Since I was a tearaway teenager, I'd been a rogue, breaking the law, shoplifting, thieving, vandalising, assaulting, and taking many illegal fights in the darkest of surroundings. But I'd managed to avoid jail time, being blessed that way, as if fate kept me away from jail, and death so it happens. Many times I cheated it and shouldn't have lived as long as I have but that was me - lucky in the eye of death. If there was a nuclear holocaust I'd be left foraging the world by the cockroach's side.

Chapter 3

Jack Gallagher:

There was only one place I could go.

I'd spent the past fifteen years or so mingling between Aberdeen and Liverpool, working for a man called Jack Gallagher. It was a good earner, carrying out jobs he didn't feel capable of carrying out himself. Being a reliable candidate for him, willing to travel down at the drop of a few hundred quid and it was a convenient arrangement for me. I enjoyed escaping Aberdeen whenever I wished, welcoming the change of scenery. To me, Liverpool was a different world from Aberdeen. Taking the entire population of Aberdeen, you could pick out the unsavoury characters and fit them all into one room. In Liverpool, there was an unsavoury character in every bar, club, community, street corner and local titty club.

I wasn't well known to the local filth in Liverpool and could easily disappear when the job was completed. Most of the time it was tracking down Jack's runners who wouldn't pay their narcotic's bills or up and coming so-called plastic gangsters who wanted a slice of Jack's pie, or anyone he requested be taught a lesson. Sometimes I'd be down there for months on end, having bare-knuckle scraps to fund my pocket, but it was never about the cash. The rush of being the hard man, I lived for it. You can travel the length and breadth of the world, meet many people, unsavoury or humble, but on the bell of an illegal fight you'll find out their true character, along with your own. I took down every man I faced in my adult life and only lost to one as a teenager. He was hard as nails and losing seven fights to him, served my apprenticeship. My bare-knuckle days were behind me, in my early forties and too old but nevertheless, I still walked the path of a man with a fearsome reputation, wherever it might be.

Liverpool was my only option at that time and it would become my new home, but little did I know, that journey to Liverpool was the beginning of a journey that couldn't be predicted. Racing down the motorway in my car, I knew I'd have to stay off the radar for a few weeks in case my whereabouts were discovered. Knowing I wouldn't end up in jail but I needed my location to be kept secret from Aberdeen and Joe.

I called Jack to inform him I was on the way.

"Davie! How's things?" Jack asked in his placid and mellow Scouse accent.

"Got a bit of a problem Jack, I need to lie low for a few weeks," I sounded desperate in my tone, my mind remorseful and belly churning from guilt.

"What's the problem?" he asked, and sounded intrigued to hear about my predicament. Asking Jack for help was something I'd never done.

"Doesn't matter just now, can you sort me up wi' a hideout." He went quiet, thinking.

"Sure, I can locate one. I'll have a look to see if any of my flats are spare."

"It's got to be off grid Jack." Anywhere public wasn't an option, I needed a quiet place to hide my shame.

"Give me a bell when you're closer."

"I'm just passin' Dundee so I'll be a while yet."

"Alright Davie," he said, lengthening his 'r' as a Scouser would "I'll look into it."

"Cheers Jack. I'll be in touch."

Jack was the face of the Liverpool underground, a highly respected and feared man. An uncharitable character, a calculated and resourceful criminal, who ruled his empire of prostitution and cocaine with a hand of steel. He built himself up from a family man who had nothing to having everything - he wanted for nothing in life. He ran brothels and owned a club, McCartney's, on the famous Hope Street of Liverpool. He had a vast empire of properties around the city, using his flats to house his eastern European hookers and warehouses to store his goods. What made him rich was his cocaine empire. In all the places I'd been in my life, Liverpool was the most ridden with the drug. Everyone was on the stuff, prostitutes, the high-end footballers, school kids and even politicians. There was hardly an area of Liverpool that didn't offer you a gram or two, and it was probably being sold by one of Jack's street dealers, his runners, as he called them.

If the name Gallagher was mentioned in the streets, people knew which family was being talked about. In his past, Jack had a short fuse that burned out often and a well-known murderous streak for snitches. Nowadays, he paid other people to run gear and sort squabbles. He preferred to sit behind an office desk living the easy life. A self-made millionaire with plenty cash and employees for different parts of his operations. He took pride in his style, everything from his gold-plated cigarette case to the products used on his jet black shoulder length hair. Always dressed to impress, it was part of his style. Despite most of his earnings being illegal, he thought of himself as an entrepreneur. He was also the tightest gangster around, renowned for his book-keeping and penny pinching.

Jack was a conniving criminal, one who liked to follow carefully designed plans with unhappy endings if required. I thought with my fists first and brain later, but that combination would change in time as I had to become a ghost.

Approaching Liverpool, I gave him another call.

"Davie, I've got things sorted, my flats are occupied at the moment." He added reassuringly, "But there's a row of abandoned houses on Rhiwlas Street in Toxteth. Enter number eighteen from the back gate. I've left some supplies, a mattress and blankets too. The area's dead just now so you'll be conveniently hidden."

"That'll do for now, spot on," I said thankfully, "You'll come round in a day or two?"

"Sure, give it a couple days and I'll pass by, discuss a nagging dilemma I need resolved."

Jack always had problems and I was constantly sorting them out like some kind of right hand man. Since he paid well and was doing me a solid favour, I had to oblige.

I parked the car a good distance from the street and left the phone on charge in the cigarette lighter. Something I had to do every day while hiding in that house. As I got to the area, he was right. It was a ghost town, only a heavy silence hung in the street mixed with the faint background noise of the city as it began to awaken at six in the morning. Signs were plastered up explaining the terraced housing was due to be bulldozed in a few months. The street was a line of crumbling brick-built houses painted in a mixed match of burgundy, dark red and faded white, windows and doors boarded up with steel sheets, covered in graffiti. The houses at the ends of the block were decaying and falling apart as you could see into the top floor bedrooms.

I didn't think there was a massive necessity to hide, since Joe knew nothing about my life in Liverpool, but it was the remorse that drove me indoors. I located number eighteen in the middle of the street.

I walked down a secluded terraced lane, entering the back garden through a high gate, built into the brick walls that hid me from outsiders and into a house stripped down to the bare bones.

Echoes of junkies lay in the house as used needles, tinfoil and open empty bottles lay on the rotten kitchen work tops. The walls were mouldy and decaying with small pieces of old wallpaper clinging on with their final breaths. It stank of rat piss and that smell would become embedded into my memory bank.

Into the sitting room, pitch black with the boarded window blocking any light, I flicked my lighter and fumbled my way around until I walked into a pile of plastic bags containing a decent supply of food and drink. A single mattress, still wrapped in plastic and a blanket lay beside the peeling gas radiator under the window. A selection of reading material, newspapers and boxing mags, lay amongst packets of stick candles and a fold up chair. He'd done a good job.

The first thing I did when arriving was crack open the bottle of whisky and devour half of it, letting the alcohol blot out my memory banks, lifting the heavy burden of guilt. What I'd done was life changing, not just for me, but for Joe too. It would come to define both our lives. I filled my scratched worn Golden Virginia tobacco tin with what was left in my pouch and rolled a few. I was emotionally shattered from remorse and the night drive, the whisky sent me to sleep in my clothes.

Little did I know at the time, working for Jack would be the beginning of a new legacy I would build for myself, one that would see me become a notorious outlaw.

Chapter 4

Regret:

Three days into my house arrest the alcohol and tobacco were devoured and I awaited Jack's arrival with more. The impatience drove me crazy. When I needed something, I had to have it. There was no electricity or running water and I resorted to shiting in a pail and pissing outside in the little patio garden. I left the house once a day to charge my phone in the car. Other than that, I spent most of the time sitting in the slabbed area hidden by the high built wall, taking in the summer sun, allowing a destructive idea to brew as to how I would occupy my time down here. Then my wife's suicide filtered around my head, encouraging my continual drinking.

Guilt's not an easy sin to deal with. Every night, nightmares of Joe catching up with me woke me in cold sweats. In your subconscious, there's no running from your troubles. The tobacco ran out because I repeatedly smoked rollie after rollie, giving my fidgety hands something to do. Usually when I'd done something I wasn't proud of, keeping busy to occupy my thoughts was a must, but there was only silence and an unsolvable boredom. I talked to myself in the third person and once pissed, I shouted, punched holes in the rotting walls and broke out in sobbing fits of tears I'd tried to keep imprisoned. All the overthinking resulted in my reminiscing about the one man I had feared in my life, and it was him I blamed for who I had become but the reality was, I was the master of my own actions and I had to find a way of dealing with the regret.

Thoughts of Joe, probably on the hunt for me, didn't help either. In a way, it was a bit like life repeated itself in our family; I loathed my father and now Joe hated his.

The only thing that could lighten my conscience was the whisky and something else that bothered me, my failure to raise a real man; instead; he was weak and fluttered around his mother like a love-sick child. There was no real mean side to him. People would walk over him in life. My thoughts raced and the sooner I could leave here, the better.

Jack finally appeared after lunchtime that day when I unlocked the back gate and let him in.

"Jesus man, you leavin' me to waste away out here?" I moaned, "You pick up some baccy?"

He turned up impeccably dressed as usual. Pressed trousers neatly hung over shiny pointed brogue shoes that clumped, slowly across the floor. His regular waistcoat covered a well-tailored shirt on a trim, five-foot eight body. A relaxed look, with his top buttons open to the summer heat, showing his withered chest hair and 24 carat gold chain. A lumpy pale face with heavy wrinkles and red-rimmed eyes. His thick jet-black hair hung to his shoulders that sparkled like it was hair-sprayed, making his lined forehead appear larger than it actually was.

"It's all in the bags Davie." He handed over the shopping bags as I walked him inside the house. The first thing I did was frantically tip the contents over the floorboards, pick up the baccy and started to make a rollie before breaking the seal of the blended whisky bottle and downing a couple of gulps.

"Jesus man! A deprived junkie would look less desperate than you!"

Jack referred to the state I was in, rummaging through the bags and the mess of my clothes. My jeans and t-shirt, which I was still wearing since my getaway, were as dirty as the floor.

As I made my rollie, I could almost hear his pondering thoughts debate my random arrival as he held a wondering stare towards me.

"What's the plan here Davie?" he asked, with his shoulders loose and hands tucked into his trouser pockets.

"Plan! I'm stayin' here and lyin' low for a couple weeks."

I sparked up and waited for him to enquire further as his inquisitive nature needed to know more and the sound of his own voice made him feel all self-important. He moved the fold-down chair closer to me as I leaned against the boarded window, wiped it clean with an empty plastic bag and sat down, crossing his legs. There was a lingering wonder about his fixed stare before he decided to change the subject.

"Well, there's a problem with Donny Casper I could use your assistance with," Jack said bluntly, while tilting his head ever so slightly to the side.

"Donny? What problem?"

I knew Donny. There weren't many men I wouldn't think twice about crossing but he was a cut above normal. He ran a biker's club, off the M62, called Devil's Angels, and spent his entire life growing up around the bike scene. Hard-boiled and seasoned from the years it took him to climb to the top crew, The Rogue Riders, a gang that dabbled in protection rackets and gun-dealing and was well avoided by Jack. If you wanted a firearm around the city, Donny was one of two men you'd go and see. Jack and Donny were rivals and crossed swords on many occasions, miraculously without blood being spilled.

"Jimmy's the problem. He's got himself into debt again and this time, with Donny, and I can't find the little cunt."

Jimmy was Jack's son who could only be described as a free spirit and loose cannon. He had a fluctuating gambling habit and was well known to dig deep debts with certain individuals in card games. He was better known on the streets as Ringo, as he copied the look of a seventies Ringo Starr with long loose ash brown hair down to his shoulders and a seventies style moustache. He and Jack weren't exactly the picture-perfect father and son. In many ways, Ringo was the exact opposite and quite jealous of Jack but nevertheless, he was family, his only child and carried the same Gallagher blood.

"Aye, how much?" I asked.

One thing about Donny, I liked the guy and drank in his club a lot. We had the same outlook on life, living by similar morals.

"Lost ten grand in a poker game, as I hear. Donny won't take his lack of respect. He'll dump him in the Mersey if he has to. There's no point me approaching him. He likes you, you'd be better sorting this out."

That was Jack down to a T, passing the buck so he didn't get his hands dirty, but he was doing me a solid favour and I suppose I had to repay him.

"I'll go see him when I'm out of this shit hole 'en."

Ringo managed to get himself in debt time after time over the years, but most of the time, he managed to wriggle out of it with funding from his own narcotics operation. He kept away from Jack's customers and sold out-with Jack's territory, avoiding his dad's wrath. As well as gambling, he had another flaw, much to Jack's displeasure; he lived the life of a gangster's son, powder filled his nose and alcohol wet his lips every day.

"Good. I've no idea where he is, as usual. You might want to track Ringo down before you talk to Donny, if you can locate the snake, that is. I'll let you know if I hear anything that will lead you to him. He should re-surface somewhere."

Jack was a man with numerous contacts throughout the area, everyone from the guy who swept the street outside McCartney's, to the doctor's patients list. Politicians and council members were also embedded deep in his pocket. He used the council members to obtain cheap properties, fixed them up and sold them on for a handsome profit. It was only a matter of when, and not if, he would locate Ringo.

Jack was still curious about my arrival, itching to know my reasons and couldn't help but ask again.

"So," he opened his palms, "What's the panic about lying low?"

Jack liked to know everything about people he worked with, giving him the power to manipulate them to his advantage. I wouldn't enlighten him of my reasons for being in Liverpool. There are some things that are better kept to oneself and besides, I was too overwhelmed to admit it.

"Just a little trouble I got in, nothin' to worry about."

Again, he fixed his tense stare in my direction for a few seconds, flooding me with an uncomfortable vibe, wanting to hear more of my reason, but that was all he was getting.

"Ok Davie, so be it. I've got to head off now, got an important meeting to attend. Give me a call if you need anything."

Jack rose from his seat, tucked his shirt in properly, trying not to get his cufflinks caught in his waist band, took a white coloured menthol from his extravagant cigarette holder, tapped the end down, placed it into his mouth and lit it with a flameless lighter.

Just before he opened the back door, "One more thing Jack. Max, where is he?"

He stopped sharply and after a couple of tense seconds, he tipped his chin down to his shoulder while keeping his back to me, not keen on the question, "not sure."

"I need to know," I said, while he paused before answering.

"I'll look into it."

With that, he left through the back gate and I padlocked it behind him; he knew exactly what I was thinking.

Chapter 5

Patience:

Over the following few days, an idea melted over in my head and I decided it was the only way. All I needed to know was Max's location and I was relying on Jack for that. Nothing I could do about it, stuck in that vile house. The days inside the house were sticky as the humidity made it uncomfortable. All I had were my thoughts and the out-of-date racing pages of the paper to scowl through. Most days I stripped down to my boxers, sat outside, devouring the drink Jack dropped off for me. Lingering around like a lost soul, biding my time to be released. Mostly, I felt lonely. The solitude of my own company and thoughts I didn't like. I wasn't smelling like the healthiest man either and hadn't shaved in a while; I liked to do so every morning with one of those tough Bic razors. I gave myself three weeks and there were still two left. I needed to get out of this prison.

While I was outside catching the rays, my phone rang. It was Jack.

"Davie, I've got an address for you."

"Go on 'en."

"230 Denton's Green Lane, St Helens. He stays with a couple called Henry and Lorraine Jackson. He owns an accountancy business and she's a housewife."

"Nice work Jack. Anythin' else I need to know?"

Once again Jack had come up trumps.

"Not particularly. They're not connected to anyone I know. Just make it quick and clean and wait till it's dark, will you?"

I had never told him of my plan but he figured it out for himself, being an intelligent individual. There wasn't much that got past him.

"Aye Jack, I will." I'd do it on my terms, not his, "I need another favour…"

"You're pushing it Davie! What now?"

"Relax Jack. I'll sort yer problem wi' Ringo and Donny. I need some clothes for a thirteen-year auld, football magazines and some sweats, that kind of stuff. Will have to make him semi-comfortable in here. I need some kind of groomin' kit and a set of handcuffs…And a lock fitted on the back door, preferably the day or the morn."

Jack sighed and paused for a few seconds, thinking this was a lot of unnecessary work for him, having plenty of other business engagements to occupy his time.

"What you think I am? A fucking shopping centre?" He was like an old man, the way he moaned and groaned sometimes, "I'll sort it out," he replied firmly.

This plan I had hatched was almost in place. But, I needed a driver and there was only one man in my contacts list who would lend a hand and a van.

"Donny, it's Davie. How's it goin' brother?"

There was a chaotic noise of hard rock music in the background; he must have been at Devil's Angels, as he always was.

"Davie! Alright man, what can I do for you?" he spoke with a deep Scouse crackle and seemed pleased to hear from me.

"I need a hand wi' a little job. You've got a van, have you?"

"Go'ed fella, I've got a van. What's the job?"

He didn't need to know the complications about the job but I knew he would help.

"Nothin' too illegal mate. Can you get to Rhiwlas Street in Toxteth at eight?"

"The Bronx!" he mouthed, "No bother. On my own?"

"Aye, brother, on yer own. And change yer plates before you leave."

There was no way I could do this on my own, I needed transport and a driver who knew the area. Donny was the man for the job. Plus, I could talk to him about Ringo.

The afternoon slowly ticked away with my plan growing legs.

Chapter 6

Abduction:

Once all was in place, I was able to get the ball rolling. It was eight on a sticky Wednesday night and Donny picked me up in his Transit van. This was by no means a settling adventure in my stomach, but one I felt I had to do and I'd never done anything as remotely savage as this. It needed to be done quickly and cleanly to avoid attention from the neighbours.

"So, what's this job Davie?" Donny curiously asked as I jumped in the van.

"It's time to pay Max a visit." Donny knew about Max and my past with his mother.

"Max?" he queried, bobbing his bald egg-shaped head up and down. A man built like granite, sitting wide-framed in the driver seat with a tight t-shirt on, arms bursting out and heavily tattooed with biker ink showing motor-cycles and skulls. A hard motherfucker Donny was, there weren't a lot of men around who would take him on, hence why Jack asked me to deal with Ringo's dilemma. He ran his biker's club with an iron fist and looked after his crew as if they were family.

"What's the plan?" he asked.

"Snatch and grab," I answered blatantly.

"So there's no plan, that's what you're saying?"

"Trust me, it'll be easy." I was confident I'd get in and out of the house quickly. A couple of working class peasants wouldn't stop a man of my calibre, I was sure of it.

Donny drove slowly to St Helens as I prepared myself for the grab. I took the time to ask him about Ringo's predicament.

"What's the crack wi' Ringo 'en? Heard he's massed a debt with you."

"I wondered when you'd bring that up. The wee cunt's due me ten grand. Hes had two weeks to pay up but he's done a ghoster."

I could tell he was pissed from the way his eyes switched from me to the road sharply.

"Ten, what for? Poker was it?"

"We had a no limits game at the club a month ago and he'd already lost twenty grand of his own dough. He needed ten big ones to see me. I had four tens, I knew the hand was mine. We debated then agreed before turning cards that I'd give him two weeks to pay. He had a good hand, give him that, flapped over a full house, he was fucking gutted!"

"Have you any idea where he's disappeared to?" I asked.

"Not a clue, yet. But, I'll get my dough, believe me. I'll squeeze it from the cunt's snarly neck if I have to. I couldn't give a fuck who his father is." Donny wasn't a fan of Jack.

Another thing about Donny, he had similarities to Jack in a way - he hated getting done over and wouldn't rest till he got his cash. As a favour for Jack, I had to help Ringo. Donny was someone who didn't like to show weakness and neither did I.

"Let me find him and have a word Donny. I'll get yer siller for you."

It would make Donny look weak if he didn't get his debt back, but even weaker if someone else claimed it. He kept his eye on the road as he thought about it.

"Listen, I'll owe you right?" I said.

He slid his head around sluggishly as he stopped at traffic lights, "I'll give you some time Davie, but not long. If I get my hands on him first, he's toast."

Not much I could do but wait till I was out of Rhiwlas Street.

I wondered what Max looked like. It had been a few years since I saw him last. It was coming down a little dark when we got within a couple of streets of the house.

"Right, park the van, as close to number 230 as you can and wait. This won't take long."

Donny nodded and let me do my thing. I threw my rollie to the ground as I exited the van and fixed my eyes on the house. I looked shifty alright, my face heavily grizzled with stubble, manky rough clothes and a black bomber jacket that I seemed to have had for years. I rolled up my sleeves showing my forearm tattoos of the rampant lion and boxing gloves and started striding to the door with a purposeful walk, heart beating rapidly and skin with a tingle of adrenaline that covers you in the heat of the moment. That was a normal feeling when you were about to do something so off the scale as this.

I got closer to see a boy in the window, shifting through a pile of computer games on the sill. It was Max. I peered right at him as I passed the window with him returning my look. I kicked open the gate and thudded a couple of knocks on the door.

Within a few seconds, it opened.

"Hello, can I help you?" the short, built-like-the-gable-end-of-a-five-pound-note, glasses-wearing Henry Parker spoke.

"Aye, you can as it happens. Is this the residence of the Jacksons?" I could tell my aggressive speech and raw Scottish accent made him cower.

"It certainly is," Henry said, as he observed me up and down like a second-class citizen.

Without a single thought, I stepped inside the hallway and used my trademark move of gripping his neck either side of the windpipe, just under the glands and squeezed, watching him contract in an upheaval of struggle as his arms flapped to the side like a bird trying to take off. Behind his back, Max watched openmouthed, standing in the sitting room doorway. Henry's face grew brightly coloured as his eyes went squint, I felt the life drain from his body. As he went limp, I turned him around and dropped him over the landing, his body on the concrete base and feet poking in the door. The petite Lorraine, wearing an apron and holding a wooden spoon, opened the kitchen door. The spoon fell to the floor and her hands covered her mouth. "Oh my God! Who are you?" She looked in fear at the sight of her husband's feet protruding over the threshold. She rushed to the sitting room door and edged Max into the room.

Taking three steps towards her, I slapped her across the face as the sound reverberated around the hallway. She collapsed over the laminate flooring, head landing at Max's feet as he looked petrified.

I stepped over her body into the front room, as Max walked backwards with fear and disbelief written over his innocent face, stunned at what was happening in front of his eyes. He had grown taller than ordinary for his age, copying my square jaw and pointed wide shoulders. He looked harmless, holding a computer game case with his feathered deep brown hair flapping over his eyes, that were so dark they looked black, the same as mine when I was a kid. I wasn't sure if he clicked it was me.

After standing idle with only a silence hanging for a few seconds, his manner was still, mouth shut and face without reaction until I grabbed him, picked him up and carried him like a second-hand carpet out the door.

"Let me go you bastard, let me down!" He screamed, panicked, kicked and punched the bottom of my back.

"Keep fuckin' quiet boy!" I needed him in the van as quickly as possible, the neighbours across the street were ogling from their front windows.

He screamed, "Get off me! Leave me alone!" He continued to panic, as proudly, I realised he had a bit of fire and refused to accept the situation. I got to the van, slid the side door open and threw him inside.

"Lock the back doors!" I shouted to Donny then jumped into the front.

"Right, move it!"

Max kicked the side door and the wall between us and the rear of the van, still scowling like a hyena broken from his pack, "Let me go, you bastards!"

"Fuck me Davie, that was a bit savage?" Donny said, as the tyres squealed, speeding away from the house.

"Had to be done brother... had to be done."

Chapter 7

Nowhere To Run:

We arrived back in Rhiwlas Street and Donny sped away in the van.

Max, dismayed, trembled uncontrollably in distress as I dragged him by the scruff of his neck down the back lane with his legs tripping over each other. I threw him in past the gate and padlocked it behind us. By now, he only glared at the ground, petrified. Into the kitchen, as I locked the back door, his hands were paralysed in his pockets, chin tucked into his chest and his eyes ogled the back door, thinking if trying to open it would be an option, but he saw me lock it. There was only one thing he could sit on in the filthy kitchen and that was an old juice crate.

"Sit down boy."

He scowled down at the crate and the broken-up, peeling linoleum flooring as I lifted him by his jumper and sat him down. With his head between his knees, he continued to tremble and held back the tears.

As I walked into the sitting room, his head rose and his teary eyes followed me. I bent down for a plastic bottle of coke from the supplies, grabbed a few candles and returned to the kitchen, lit the candles then glued it to the counter with the wax. I held the coke bottle in front of his face.

"Here boy, drink some juice." He still wouldn't take it so I prodded his forehead with the cap end of the bottle, "Here, take a drink boy," I said forcefully.

He grabbed the bottle without lifting his head. I settled back leaning on the counter, taking my tobacco tin out and made a rollie.

36

Again, he looked into the front room, this time making a more thorough examination, spotting the mattress and the homeless-like mess the place was in: empty bottles, tins and fag butts strewn all over the place with candles melted to the chipboard floor. His hands shaking, he opened the bottle, dropped the lid, letting it roll over the ground to my foot before gulping the contents down in a oner, finishing with squeezing the plastic with his life.

I could guess what must've been going through his mind. Why was this man back again?

As I leaned off the counter, took my lighter from my pocket and lit my rollie, he twitched, thinking I was about to strike him. As I took a step in his direction, he leapt up and thudded his back against the wall. His eyes made contact. Grimacing, he closed his legs and placed his hand over his crotch. When the tears started, I saw his green jeans soak with urine.

"Fuck sake boy! Get outside if yer goin' to do that." I gave him permission to move but he wouldn't.

I unlocked the door and told him again. Taking notice this time, he shambled out onto the slabbed area, overgrown with weeds, made his way to a corner and unzipped his jeans. But his business was already finished. He turned from being petrified to ashamed.

"Come inside," I waved my hand out.

Once in, I locked the door again and stuck the key in my pocket. I led him into the front room and closed the kitchen door. It was pitch black before I lit some more candles.

"Have a seat Max."

As I said his name, his neck lifted and he leered straight at me, realising, yes, it was the same man who had visited him over the years.

"Go on, sit down!" I raised my voice as he twitched and sat down.

I looked out some of the spare clothes Jack had taken round, handing him a brand new tracksuit.

"Well, get changed 'en," I said.

He headed into the kitchen to change. I heard the back door-handle being violently yanked. He wasn't going anywhere. My plan was to keep him hidden from the public for a few months while changing his appearance. His face would be plastered on the local and national newspapers. He would be on the news, there'd be posters stuck up all over the city and the police force on a mission to find him and be crowned local heroes.

That first night must've been emotional torture for the kid. There was a part of me that felt sorry for him as I also knew the reality of living with an animal and to be scared out of your wits. He had to adapt to my way if he was going to survive.

I wasn't a total bastard; giving him the mattress to sleep on but handcuffed him to the radiator pipe under the window. Max lay on the mattress, blanket covering his body and with a stuttering tremor, he drifted to sleep. I'm not sure how well he slept that night but I relaxed, opened a few tins and munched on a cold pie, sleeping on the seat and using the juice crate for a footrest.

The following morning, he didn't struggle when I uncuffed him from the pipe. He didn't speak either and eye contact was minimal. I gave him some food, the last cold pie and a just about drinkable pint of milk then took him up to the bathroom, sitting him on the stained dry tub. He glimpsed at me, looking ashamed and sorry for himself.

I bent down to his level and pointed my finger in his face.

"I never want to see that look again Max, never!" He looked lost and confused as to what he should do,

"Never show pity!" It would take time for him to come around to my ways.

I used the grooming kit to cut and shave his full head of hair. The first stage in changing his appearance. There was no struggle from Max; I guess he knew there was nowhere for him to go.

Chapter 8

New Job Role:

The next week wasn't as boring, Max got my attention throughout every day. I could tell he was developing a deep loathing for me. When I spoke to him, instead of replying, he would lock daggers with his darkened brown eyes where I could see something callous, something that ran in the blood line. I repeatedly tried to get him to talk, but nothing. I was aware there'd be a massive on-going search but with no contact from the outside world, I wasn't able to keep tabs on it. Spending time with Max took my overthinking brain away from my wife's suicide and Joe. I welcomed the distraction and began to put the past behind me.

On three occasions that week, Max managed to steal the key for the back door from my pocket while I was comatose with drink. On the first attempt, I caught him as the back door opened but at the second attempt, he managed to run to the gate which was locked, he'd forgotten about that.

He tried to climb over the seven-foot-high wall while I stood and watched him struggle to clamber to the top before yanking him down, trapped him in the corner and treated him to the belt for punishment.

The third occasion, he grabbed both keys and made his exit. I woke in the camping seat after hearing the gate slam shut. I had zero hesitation, ran like a champion sprinter out the house and caught him after a couple of minutes, dragging him back by his hair and handcuffed him to the radiator again. Three days I kept him tied up, only letting him loose for toilet privileges. I think he learned a little lesson from that.

He was introduced to Jack when the latter dropped off food and drink and refused to take him on. There was a stubborn streak in the boy, just like Joe. Before Jack arrived that night, I told Max we were leaving the house.

"Max, we're leavin' the night."

His head keenly rose from his chest as he sat up on the mattress,

"Home?" he asked, as a moment of hope flooded his youthful face.

"No Max, off to a new home." He retreated into his silent shell.

We waited in complete silence until Jack turned up late into the night. I left the house a bigger tip than it was when I arrived, and led Max out the back. This time he didn't need to be dragged and willingly walked by my side. At the end of the lane, Jack's blacked-out BMW awaited. I opened the back door, placed Max inside and took the passenger seat.

"Where we goin'?" I asked Jack.

"I've cleared a flat in Everton. Got a few of the girls to give it a once over and a stock up on food. It's on the top storey so you'll be conveniently tucked away up there."

"Nice one Jack. Any word where Ringo's hidin'?"

"I know where he's hiding," he replied in his assured tone, "The Collins' place in Belle Vale. Pay the bastard a visit and get this situation sorted. Donny sent a couple of his dogs sniffing around the club the other day, asking questions. He's itching to get his hands on Ringo and I could be doing without the fucking hassle just now. I'm heading to Bolivia to organise the next few drops."

Jack regularly flew off to Bolivia to arrange orders of the finest gear. That's what separated him from his

41

opposition, his dedication to making money made him a bit of a perfectionist. The Collins brothers were opposition from the past that failed to oppose. Over the years, they had tried to cut Jack's feet with clients.

Years ago, there had been a raid on one of Jack's warehouses that was supposed to stash his gear but it was misleading information to the Collins brothers from a man on Jack's take, one of his street dealers. He met an uneasy end. Jack lit the match, burning the guy to death, covered in petrol.

Every time Jack did away with someone, he used different methods to kill: chewed up by a pack of rottweilers that he used as guard dogs, freezing them to death in a bath of sub-zero temperatures, left hanging upside down until all the blood ran to their heads and one time, used a funnel to pour quick dry cement down a guy's neck. It didn't matter to Jack how they died. A brutal death was punishment for their disloyal ways.

The Collins brothers, who were behind the raid, had their legs broken with a two iron from me, the bare minimum punishment considering Jack's other unique methods, but he had a plan to utilize the pair. They did however get the point, because, ever since, they hadn't bothered Jack again and stayed away from the distributing side of the business.

Jack kept them alive for one reason. They became his chemists, having the required knowledge of how to cut up cocaine and Jack was in the market for just that. Paying them minimally, next to insulting, showing them their life was a gift from that day forward. The Collins were petrified of Jack and me and stuck to the deal. It was that or nothing.

"The Collins!" I said, "Pair of degenerates 'em two. I'm sure they'll be pleased to see me."

"Oh yes Davie, I'm sure they will." His eyes sparkled as he turned to give me a cold, mellow smile that was rare for him.

"Once we're in the flat, can you get one of the girls to watch Max while I nip round?" I suggested.

"Sure, I'll send Danielle. It's been a while since you two have seen each other."

"Danielle! Aye, send her round."

We carried on chatting as Max listened keenly from the back seat, taking in the conversation. His need to consume his new surroundings seemed to drown his anxiety and fear. He seemed intrigued to hear what kind of world he was entering. One without laws and living by a certain code that most followed, bar me from time to time, if it suited my needs.

We arrived at the L-shaped block of flats in Everton. Five storeys high with a long balcony on each level. The area around the flats was semi-rundown and the block was past its best days, slightly decaying with vandalism and graffiti. Jack led us to the top storey and into the flat.

I locked the door and placed the key in my pocket for safe keeping. The door opened into a small, poorly decorated kitchen with another door into the bare sitting room, furnished with one long pecan-coloured, three-seater crumpet sofa sitting across from a relic of a TV and an old stained coffee table in the middle. The once white patterned wallpaper was more of a stained yellow with damp patches blotting the surface and a big rectangle window with peeling paint overlooked the gloomy horizon of the city.

Jack led Max into the narrow hallway to his room and signalled him inside. The room was decorated specifically for a young teenager, courtesy of Jack's decorators by my request. Everton football posters on the wall, new toys stacked on the floor and a PlayStation with a rack of games to choose from. Max looked into the room with elation and relief - he had a proper place to sleep.

Jack egged him on with a furtive nod and a nudge. Once Max was inside, Jack closed the door and joined me on the sofa for a whisky and fag.

"After you sort out this Ringo problem," he sighed and looked away, "I need someone to take control of my runners. I need someone I can trust and doesn't fuck about. These street dealers are a pain in my ass, disloyal and most are unreliable cunts who are looking for a one-way street to an easy existence."

I'd never delved into the world of dealing narcotics but I guessed it was a forgone conclusion. In Aberdeen, I'd been hired to make short drug runs but this would be slightly different to that. I knew exactly what was involved. I'd been buying for years but never on the other side of the fence as such. Bearing in mind I was near skint and needed income, there was no second thought about it. Jack saw me as a man who got things done, quickly and efficiently, and had probably been thinking over his proposal since my arrival.

"What's yer prices?" I asked, getting straight to the point.

"I bring in substantial quantities of cocaine, more than any other in this country, I'm led to believe. Works out to be a much bigger profit margin that way. You take five grand once a kilo's sold. I'll hand you the gear, already cut and bagged, and it's your job to dish it out to the runners and pick up the cash."

Sitting po-faced, I mulled over the mathematics of the project. It sounded a sure thing. I was ageing and needed to start thinking about a retirement fund, and this sounded like a solid start.

"How long does it take to shift a kilo?"

"Usually a couple kilos, within a week. I've got a large client base, ten runners and sometimes sell in bulk to certain individuals. The runners can sell the product at whatever price they wish. Once it's in their hands, it's their product, not mine. They get a week in play. That means if they're taking the gear as a lay on, then they have a week to cough up. If they don't, then that's your problem," his speech was firm at the end of the sentence as he pointed his finger.

Five grand for every kilo shifted. That would do me nicely.

"Aye, alright, I can do that. How do I get paid?"

I was ruled by money. It was the start and end of everything in this world.

"At the end of the week, you pass all the profits to me and your pay will come from that."

Finishing his drink, he plumped his glass onto the coffee table.

"You in?" he asked.

"Aye, I'm in."

He unbuttoned his waistcoat and relaxed back into the sofa, pleased I'd agreed.

"I've got a diary for you to keep on which runners get what. You'll write in a code we both understand, just in case it falls into the wrong hands. You'll have to keep a keen eye on these kids, some of them would sell their mothers' ashes for a quick quid. You can keep track of the amount each runner gets on a nightly basis."

Fuck me, it's like being back at school.

"Here's a burner. I'll pass your number on to each runner and you take it from there."

"Aye, alright."

I thought Jack was a bit too business-like. Phones and recorded sales were too much evidence to leave around, but that was his way. He needed to know where all his pennies came from.

"Another thing, I'll call you if I get any orders and you can add that to the diary. My operation is growing significantly; a big order's on the way from Bolivia, so you better keep an eye on your back. I don't want any unwanted attention from the bizzies. And I have another job for you. I need a bit of muscle. I'm selling off a large quantity to a man called Bobby Munroe from Glasgow. I want to make it a regular deal, make a quiet profit, so to speak. I've heard some good and some bad information about this man. It's best to be suspicious of him until I know how he operates."

His orders from Bolivia came into Europe through the Rotterdam docks in Holland. The container would be moved onto another cargo ship destined for Southampton. Once there, the container that held the cocaine was transported up to Liverpool where Jack himself religiously picked it up and relayed it to his secret hideout.

Jack dealt with all the uncharitable characters up and down Britain and Bobby Munroe was an upcoming name in Glasgow. An unpredictable man known to kill for fun, who wanted to garner the name of the new Godfather of Crime in the city. He involved himself in any business that led to gaining momentum and Jack was a high-end name; Jack was respected by most and feared by many. His quiet, self-confident business-like approach would fool the uneducated man into thinking he was maybe a bit placid, but his past could tell you otherwise.

Chapter 9

Pick Pocket:

About a month after that meeting, one morning, asleep on the sofa with the TV still on, I'd never made it to bed and a half drank bottle of whisky sat on the table. I was kinda half awake, hearing footsteps around the flat. I felt something brush the top of my thigh and woke. "Get out of there boy!" I yelled at Max and leapt up while he tried to slide the door key out of my pocket.

He took a panicking jump back and held his fist tight by his side.

I moved in his direction, gripped his spindly right bicep and gave him a backhand across the face, followed with a slap on the other cheek with the same hand, instantly reddening both sides. If I wasn't holding him so tightly, he would've propelled across the room. "Never do that again, you little shite! You hear boy!"

He cowered back into his shell, head down, sucking in deep breaths of rage through his nostrils, with his chest puffing in and out in unison with the air he was furiously taking in. He couldn't do anything; if he was ever going to attempt a fight back, that would have been the moment. I paced around the room, burning a hole through the musty brown carpet, thinking what my next move would be, all the time Max still had his fists clenched.

Entering the kitchen, I turned the kettle on for the morning coffee. It was approaching the end of the hour and I heard the local news on the telly.

Max's picture and story was first to air on the news bulletin. I calmly strolled back into the living room and switched the telly off.

Max's face was still beaming bright red from the impact of my fierce slaps and his eyes were glued to the box. He never took me on and I returned to the kitchen; opening a cupboard and spotting some cereal.

"You want some breakfast boy?"

A silent response, but he was still raging, with his focus returning to the floor as if he was looking for something and he probably was: a way out.

"Take a seat. I'll bring you some cereal."

I dished up a large bowl and returned to the sitting room. I held it out within Max's grabbing distance. I could've placed it on the table but I wanted him to take my offering.

I stood idle for more than ten seconds before he scowled at me and grabbed the plate, taking a seat in the corner of the sofa. As he tucked in, I drank my coffee and sat at the opposite end of the sofa.

"I've got to go out today son." As I said 'son', he lowered his spoon and gave me a check, "Got to see a man about a dog."

His eyebrows scrunched together, the first time he'd heard that expression. He was preparing to say something as the spoon hung halfway between his mouth and the plate.

"You're my Da'?" Finally, some words.

"Aye son…I'm yer Da'." His eyes expressed a look of surprise and this time, I felt awkward.

"How?" he asked.

"Long story son. I'll tell you another day. I'm away to get cleaned up. Make yerself at home, there's plenty food in the cupboards, help yerself."

I wanted to give him a bit of freedom in the flat, allow him to relax a little. That's what the PlayStation was for in his room.

48

When in the bathroom, the first door on the right after entering the tight lobby, I held my ear to the door. Max tiptoed down the corridor then a louder tread back with his trainers on. There was a moment of quietness before I heard him trying to yank the door handle open to escape, but the key was still in my pocket.

I continued to listen, heard the TV go on and channels change. I could relax and have a shower, but I had to be quick, didn't want the news coming on with his face appearing on the screen again.

As I finished up in the bathroom, there was a knock at the door, so I rushed out to open it.

"Well well, Danielle. Lang time no see."

She was one of Jack's girls, a good looking one at that. Dirty blonde choppy hair with dark roots, medium dumpy height at five-foot four with bewitching blue eyes. She had that easy going vibe around her. Dressed in tight jeans that gripped her arse and knee-high boots, she was always a welcome sight for me.

"Davie, I would say nice to see you, but I'm really not sure about that."

She had come around to watch Max, allowing me out to fix the Ringo situation.

"Rubbish, of course it's nice to see me."

I nursed her into the kitchen and whispered, "Listen, when I'm out the house, don't let Max see the news. Don't leave the door unlocked and do not let him outside for any reason, got it?" I was very firm on this.

"Sure, orders received Mr Rhodes," she replied, giving me an army salute.

"Don't be sarcastic, doesn't suit you. Ooh and no stories from the past."

I let the two of them get acquainted while I grabbed my bomber jacket.

First stp was the Collins brothers.

49

Chapter 10

The Collins:

The Collins brothers were a pair of second generation Rastafarians of Jamaican origin who spoke with a hint of Scouse under their Reggae like tongue. They ran a shoe repair shop in the Belle Vale shopping centre that they had inherited from their father. Despite their past illegal activities, they took to their daytime job as serious shoemakers and repair men, being accomplished in the trade, I admit, but they didn't hold the intelligence needed to be operating a narcotics operation. Well they didn't in the past, hence why I had to inflict some harm. To the everyday citizen and those who knew about their past, they held a street rep and could strike a cold sweat, but I could see right through that false act.

The last time I was in the pairs company, a year prior, I mocked them, whilst standing over the broken legs.

I strolled into the store, relaxed and loving the fact they feared the sight of me. I adored the smell of the leather and fresh polish that filtered around. They weren't filled-out men, both lean and tall.

Marko, the younger of the two, was behind the counter in front of the out-of-date shoe repair machine, finishing up with a female customer. Standing calmly behind her, leaning against a rack of shoes with my thumbs clasped over my faded blue jeans, I waited for her to move so I could catch Marko Collins' reaction.

The moment we looked daggers at each other, Marko flinched, shuffling backwards and his bottle green eyes burst open then immediately, he went into survival mode. What I mean by that is, the fear kicked in, wondering why I was standing in his sight, thinking my random appearance would be there to dish out another beating.

"Davie!" he stated, "What can I do for you for man?" He stood tall with his shoulders pulled back, forehead lines squashed under his balding flaky hair.

I was in the mood to play, "Here to finish you off Marko. Where's that bastard brother of yours?"

His head started to shake from side to side, along with his frizzy untidy goatee that hung from his chin like an unfashionable musketeer, his face could do nothing but glow with anxiety.

"Davie, I t'ought 'dis trouble was behind us man. I told Jack we aren't dealing, he knows dat. Honest, there's no need." They would be stupid to start distributing again, considering they were Jack's chemists.

"Shut it Marko! Where's he hidin'?"

Just as I spoke, Colin Collins strolled in from the back, through the beaded separator, polishing a shoe, stringed glasses on the end of his wide nose. As he started to converse with Marko, he spotted me, dropping his shoe to the ground. They were of similar build, teetering under six foot and skinny, like a pair of needle users that lacked a layer of fat.

"Davie!" he uttered, taking a gasp of breath.

"Aye, ma name's Davie, good observation by both of you. Now, let's get down to the reason why I grace you wi' ma presence. Ringo! Where you hidin' him? And don't make me beat it from you. The past wee while has been very un-productive and I don't need much of a push for a bit of excitement."

They both viewed each other's reaction and both knew I wasn't in the mood to be messed around. Colin avoided answering as he bent down to pick up the shoe. I bent over the counter and followed his movement, leaving Marko to think it would be wise to answer.

51

"At our place man," Marko muttered quickly.

"Good, that will save us some trouble, won't it?" A long, cocky smile spread across my face as my hands lay on my hip, "And why are you hidin' him?"

"You know Ringo Davie, he's a likeable gezzer, just helping the poor lad out. Said it would be the last place anyone will look."

"I'll be back to see you bums later," I pointed my finger at the pair as I left.

I drove to their bungalow and knocked on the door. No answer, so I carried on knocking then thudding against the door.

Still no answer, so I shouted through the letter box, "Ringo, answer this fuckin' door before I boot the bastard down."

There was no need to introduce myself: my deep Scottish growl, I knew he would recognise.

"Look, I'm here to help you out…I know about Donny."

Still no sight or sound of him. Judging by the way Marko spat out his whereabouts, I knew he was there.

"Ringo, open the door!" I yelled again. Looking in, I could see straight through to the kitchen and a body appeared.

"You better come in," Ringo said, and shuffled me into the house as he checked the streets before slamming the door shut, "Come through to the kitchen."

He was skittish and jumpy, on edge, worrying what would happen if Donny caught up with him.

"What kind of shite you got yerself into now mate?" I noticed his eyes were glazed, nose reddened and face bright, as if his blood pressure was through the roof.

"Donny's going to bury me, I know it. I'm skint, no lemo, can't get a lay on from anyone, nowhere to go, I'm fucked kid." Lemo was Liverpools name for

52

cocaine. If you said it anywhere else in the country, people wouldn't have a clue what it was.

He always called me 'kid', didn't matter I was twenty years his senior or half a foot taller. Wearing long combat shorts and a summery Hawaiian vest because of the heat, he looked like a panicking hippy, if there was such a thing. His head was running at a rate of knots due to the amount of gear that was flooding his nose.

"Look Ringo, I'll sort it out for you, don't worry mate."

Ringo was a topper of a bloke, one of those guys who lived life to the full, very likeable, the reason why he got away with being in debt all the time. Easy to talk to and didn't judge. The kind of person who would take anyone on in a bar.

"We'll just have to find a way of gettin' a hold of some siller for you and we're cool."

"How's that going to happen Davie?"

"How about havin' a word wi' Donny, see if you can work off the debt?" It was the only thing that sprang to mind. Jack wouldn't pay his son out and I had no spare cash floating around, "Tell you what, I'm runnin' yer dad's gear now, so I'll help you out in some ways. I'll give Donny five grand, once I have it, and you can work off the rest?"

"Why? Why would you do that kid?"

"Cuz Ringo, ma friend, I like you, and yer Dad's done me a solid favour, plus there's a little somethin' you can help me wi'."

"Like what?" He looked bamboozled at my request. Ringo wasn't used to getting asked to help someone. He was that unstable.

"It doesn't matter just now. I've got my eye on a wee plan, I'll tell you about it another day." I put my arm around his shoulder. "Listen, just one thing. If this works out wi' Donny, don't fuck him about or someone will be diggin' you a grave."

 Donny spent his life around the complexities of firearms and was a precise marksman. It was his main income outwith Devil's Angels.

 Ringo looked at me, with a little life flowing back into his cheeks as he knew I had his back.

"Let's celebrate kid," he said in an excited pitch, as he planted his hand on my shoulder. The party boy put his hand in his pocket and pulled out a wrap of white powder, "right, one line or two?"

"Ringo, put that shit away. Deal wi' Donny first!"

 He stopped shaking the wrap and thought about it, but chose otherwise. He needed the extra line to take the edge off for visiting Donny.

"Davie, come on, one or two?" He wouldn't take no for an answer.

"Alright, just the one 'en."

 In the kitchen, he opened a cupboard and pulled out a flat square glass sheet, edges right angled to stop spillage, something that was personally designed. Four lines exquisitely cut and formed using a dual purpose, stainless steel sniffer combined with a blade for cutting, taken from his pocket. These items were for the overly enthused cocaine user and that was definitely Ringo. He destroyed the first two lines, sucking them up like an air-vent and slid the snorter over the unit to me.

"Holy fuck, what the fuck is this shit?" An instant rush pumped blood around my veins like a burst dam as I tried to match Ringo's sniffing power by taking both lines. My eyes turned inwards and the veins in my temple heightened. This was the gear Ringo was devouring every day. No wonder he was so paranoid and shifty.

 "Fuck, I need a piss, back in a minute."

In front of the mirror, I could see the effect of the line, as my pupils enlarged, face tingled and my jaw went numb. I splashed water over my face to gain some control. The rush was exhilarating. As I perched on the toilet seat, my head swirled, taking a few moments for the come on to fade before joining Ringo's company again.

"You're looking a little pale there kid." He laughed at my weakness to handle the hit.

"Blew ma fuckin' head off, chalk up another one." I didn't want to lose face.

"That's the spirit." Ringo snorted up the leftover residue from his nostrils and wiggled the end of his nose.

"Where you pullin' this stuff from?" I asked.

"It's Marko and Colin's stuff, probably Da's." Ringo spoke the word Da' like he loved the man, but nothing was further from the truth.

"Jesus! It's wild this shit!" I said.

"What's Da' saying?" Ringo asked.

"Just the usual mate, nothin' but business for him. I think ye're his biggest worry just now."

To be honest, over the years I became a bit sick of Jack's demanding and nagging ways. Constantly ordering me around over time pissed me off and his penny-pinching and book- keeping just irritated me.

"Fuck him! I don't need his concern; I'm doing good on my own."

I eyed him up and down while nodding.

"Sure you are mate, sure."

Chapter 11

Devil's Angels:

With Ringo by my side, I approached the oval bar, the centre piece of Devil's Angels. Heavily decorated in pictures of crews that had come and gone, with stories of the reputable and unfortunate. It emulated the landscape of American saloons and played the same beat. Sleeveless vests and crew threads spread. The place hosted quarrels every week, bar fights were as predictable as an ancient Batman and Robin clip and most knew my face from my appearances over the years.

The Rogue Riders had been enjoying the usual noisy matinee in the bar before they went mute, eyes glued to Ringo's entrance, knowing how much Donny craved his presence.

We took a pew on the stools at the bar with the cocaine intoxicating our bloodstream. Ringo's eyes spread wide and filled with paranoia. I tried to stay cool and appear sober but the mixture of an awkward situation and narcotics put me on edge, as my feet quavered resting on the foot rest of the stool and my teeth clenched together.

"Alright, Donny about?" I asked the young prospect behind the bar, disbelief in his eyes with Ringo in front of him, trying to hold a solid face.

"He's upstairs. I'll go fetch him."

The hovering of bikers, holding bottles of lager nudged closer as we waited. I sensed the hostility coming our way, a gift I'd gained over the years, being educated in dark surroundings and dodgy gyms. Trouble was something I could smell.

"Pour ma a couple whiskies before you go, would you?" Ringo was unusually quiet, the uncertainty of his fate worried him.

Moments later, Donny burst through the door wearing a skull design bandana over his bald head and a plain t-shirt with the sleeves hacked, unevenly off. He swaggered in our direction as the rest of the bikers edged closer. Ringo looked pasty and downed his drink. Donny glided past Ringo with his eyes burning a hole into his back, brushed his shoulder then coolly lifted the flap to get behind the bar while I kept a good eye.

"Davie, how's it going?" He ran the establishment his way, kept the usual clientele, the bikers being their own doormen, acting like family. Jack kept a wide berth of the place.

"Aye mate, all right." I tried to keep the conversation light before the shit hit the fan. The music was hard and loud, voices had to be raised.

"I hope you're here with your wallet Ringo," Donny remarked in a commanding way.

Ringo was silenced with uncertainty and looked to me to take over as Donny eye-balled him.

"Donny, listen, I've got a wee proposition to sort this situation…" Bear in mind, a couple of months had passed since Ringo lost the card hand and that built up a lot of frustration for Donny.

Donny waited for me to continue, standing, discouraged with his bulging arms crossed over his chest.

"I'll pay half his debt, no' now, but in a week or so, and Ringo here," I placed my hand friendly on his shoulder, "will work for you and pay off the rest."

Donny had a swipe around at Ringo, saw his unstable nature through his intoxicated eyes and slack-dressed appearance, knowing full well he was a coke addict.

"You should be on stage Davie," Donny remarked with a hint of sarcasm.

"What?" I replied.

"Should be a fucking comedian. I want cash from this boy, not his help."

"Donny, this is the only logical thing to do here. It's the only way you can get yer cash."

He uncrossed his arms and pointed at me.

"You Davie, can pay his debt, in two weeks time, and Ringo here, will work for me until it's paid off. How's that sound?"

I thought my proposition was a reasonable one; Donny had partly agreed so far but the way the frustration filled his voice, I knew there was another demand on the way. I swivelled on my stool and gave Ringo a polished stare of 'I told you so' before the rest of the deal came to light.

"Aye, sounds fine wi' me mate," I answered.

"One more thing Davie." Here it was, "We're having a fight night for some new prospects coming through. I wouldn't mind another couple of bouts and you fit the profile quite well."

That was the last thing I wanted to hear.

I gave Ringo an aggressive glare showing my annoyance at being stuck in a place I didn't want to be; I was into my forties, no age to be climbing through the ropes.

Donny laid his palms over his mahogany stained bar surface, "One more thing, if the debt's not paid off, Ringo fights."

"Aye, sounds like a good plan Donny." Letting him know my true thoughts on the matter wasn't going to better the situation. He knew, being the man I was, I wouldn't back down. Fighting was something Ringo

58

couldn't take on; if it came to him entering the ring, there was no doubt he'd get a serious beating.

Ringo sat silent, knowing his role, for a change. As the intensity of the confrontation wore off, everyone relaxed while Donny poured the drinks to lighten the mood.

I was still seething about the situation and saw my alabaster hair, untidy from the reflection in the mirror behind the bar. As I placed my whisky on the bar, while reaching into my back pocket for my comb, one of Donny's men shouldered me and spilled half his drink over my shoe. I looked away, speaking under my breath with my temper about to explode.

"Watch where you're going, old man!" he said arrogantly and in a high whined Scouse accent. He was a wee cunt with the stature of a mouse; in his late teens, he wore the threads of The Rogue Riders leather cut over his high-sleeved t-shirt. I played it cool, continued the motion of combing and setting my hair back in place before returning the comb to my back pocket. I picked up my dram and pointed at the over-confident young man with my pinkie and thumb out.

"Do I look like a stable person to you?" My question was returned with a hardened stare, "If you make me place this glass on the bar, every time you look in the mirror after this day, you'll see my reflection, not yours."

I was prepared to decapitate him and send him over the bar, head first. By the way Donny had spoken to me, he thought he had the approval to talk in any tone he pleased.

Donny moseyed over from behind the bar while the wee cunt stood and glared, wondering if he was man enough to take me on.

"Davie, sorry. Fiddle's a little hot headed."

59

Fiddle was half my height; I could have had him for breakfast. Donny was well aware of that. Fresh to his cut and looking to prove himself but he picked the wrong cowboy to fuck with. The silly young bugger still glared at me.

"Look Fiddle, take a walk. In fact, go home." Donny gave him the best advice he'd passed on yet, assisting him to the door. I waited until he left the bar before letting my guard down. Donny returned.

"Sorry about Fiddle, just a thundercat." As he had a chuckle to himself, the rest of the bikers joined in with the joke.

The only person I held respect for in here was Donny; the rest of his crew I didn't much care for.

"If he wasn't standing wi' yer strips on, I would have ripped him apart."

"I'll have a word, the powder must be feeding his balls." Donny was as hard as he looked big, astute and had a history that would scare any man.

"So, how's the boy Davie?"

"He's quiet still, not come out of his shell yet. It'll take time."

"Take him along to the fights. Sure he'd like to see his old man in action."

"Aye, I think I will mate. Who am I fightin' 'en?" That was a question I'd never asked before.

It was years since I had a fight in this manner. Having a scrap in the street was a totally different scenario to bare knuckle. It didn't matter who stood opposite you - you still had the same job to do, whoever it was, Mike Tyson or Daniel O'Donnell.

"I think The Tailor will fit the bill." The Tailor was a man with plenty experience in these surroundings. He was called The Tailor for no fancy reason. The man in his early thirties owned a tailor shop in the city and was the patch man for the club.

"The Tailor it is 'en."

Chapter 12

Orders And Quarrels:

 I spent the first couple of weeks as Jack's enforcer, learning the ropes. I adapted to the role as I had done with any illegal activity in life. Jack gave me a kilo worth of gear, already weighted up and bagged by the Collins brothers. My job was to answer the phone, deliver to the runners, collect the cash and move on to the next one, but it was too busy for my liking, constant calls from Jack with orders and quarrels to sort out. Not only did I have to make the deliveries, I often got called to his brothels to sort out hostile punters.

 Sometimes Jack called, instructing me to pick up a takeaway for him, nine times out of ten, a doner kebab. I was even expected to taxi home the high-end punters from the club. The man wasn't a cripple, he could have pulled his finger out and got his own kebab but no, he preferred to sit in his office in McCartney's, sip his Japanese whiskey and dish out orders. He had become mighty comfortable in life and I don't know if it was because he was lazy or if he liked to play boss, but I assumed it was the second.

 He niggled on my nerves more than usual with the upcoming fight on the way. I wasn't the man I was. I had quit fighting because I knew my role. It was for the young and brave, but now I was older and nowhere near as fit.

 Since I was sixteen, I'd mingled in and out of boxing gyms to my own wishes to keep fit and sharp. Now the only sharpness I got was in the street. Bare-knuckle fights could last for seconds or hours and there was no other option but to be prepared for it, mentally and physically.

The attributes required to be victorious varied from the ability to take punishment, to a cold-blooded streak of heartless violence, the killer instinct. My upbringing shaped my thirst for blood and suited bare-knuckle fighting. There was no room for goodness in your heart and I certainly didn't get that from my youth. If your opponent looked half-dead but still on his feet, you had to continue your assault until he could move no more. There was no point in visiting a gym, pounding bags or sparring. The only thing I could rely on was my unforgiving nature and experience. It worried me, I'd never had this feeling approaching a fight in the past.

In the time I spent out of the house on the job, Max was left in the company of Danielle, one of Jack's girls on the take but nevertheless, she was a sweet one. We had known each other for years and knew exactly what we both were. She took to Max well, almost like an auntie and nephew kind of relationship, and that suited me. I could just come home, lay down the law and do my thing. They spoke freely and shared a bond. Conversation picked up a little between Max and me and one early afternoon, when I got out of bed, he moved onto a topic I knew he would get to eventually.

I did my usual when I folded out of bed, rolled a fag and made a cup of strong coffee. He walked from his room and adopted his usual position on the sofa, cushioned into the corner.

I started off the conversation to break the silence, "Get up to much wi' Danielle last night son?" Sitting with my body open and arm over the top of the seat, blowing the smoke above my head, holding my observation of him.

"Watched a few films. What did you do?" Ah, a question from him, that was a first.

"Just some runnin' around for Jack, nothin' excitin'."

There was an extra spring in him that morning, an indication he wanted to know about me and my out of hours job. The silence returned as his dark eyes gazed into open space, deciphering the next question.

"Where you from?"

"Scotland son, bonnie Scotland," I replied.

"So why are you down here then?"

"I'm down here for you. Here to bring you up as ma son."

That was the door of questions opened.

"What about Henry and Lorraine, my foster parents?"

"You don't ha'e to worry about 'em now. They aren't yer real parents."

I thought I'd get the whole story out there for him; it would stop him from asking more questions and it was about time I said something.

"Yer mum, and I mean yer real mum, wasn't a good person. She was into some bad shit. She died of an overdose just before you turned one. Me and yer mum never got on, that's why I moved back to Scotland. I never knew about you until it was too late, or else I would've taken you with me when she passed. That I'm sorry for, but I'm here to make it up to you."

That was quite a lot to take in for the boy, so I waited for him to respond, let his overthinking mind ingest the information. Doing his thing, he stared helplessly into the space in front of his eyes.

"What was her name?" Max asked.

"Michelle, her name was Michelle McCabe son. Ye're better off without her, trust me, and Henry and Lorraine, forget 'em Max. I'm yer blood, yer real old man. I won't lie to you. I'll make sure ye're looked after in life."

It was hard to tell what went through his head at any time. His dark, deep stares showed no emotion, only an emptiness. After that conversation, I thought it would be good for him to finally get out of the flat.

With his head fully shaved, I had to do a bit more to disguise his appearance. I took him to get both his ears pierced with black studs and bought him a baseball cap. He thought it was cool and was well happy with it. I hadn't seen him smile yet, but it was only time before I cracked that.

One thing I liked to do was have a flutter on the horses, something my old man taught me before I left him and my family behind.

Inside the criminal ring, I had few flaws to an employer for my services, but one flaw was my useless ability in picking a winning racehorse. The bookie would always be pleased to see me walk in. I was a degenerate gambler, a bit like Ringo when it came to gambling, but I knew my limit.

It was a hobby I was fascinated with. It went back to my childhood when my alcoholic father would sit in front of the telly with his betting slips which would be scrunched up and thrown to the floor. He used to fill me with a bundle of information about the history of racehorses and where they originated from, what they were called and what they were bred for. That was the one thing I learned from him in all my sixteen years in that house, sixteen years I'd rather forget, but memories like that, you don't forget.

Entering the bookies would put a conniving smile on the man's face from behind the desk, like it did that day; his ignorant glimmer was easy to catch.

"Davie, what's it today?" the bespectacled bookie asked from behind the perspex counter.

"The Fast Fly for me, fixed price, 7-1." The bookie ran the ticket through the machine and took my twenty-pound note.

"I don't like your boy being in here, he's too young," he nodded down to Max.

"No, he's eighteen, aren't you boy?" I peered down at him, wearing a baseball cap and a brand new black tracksuit with white stripes down the sides. He did his usual shy nod of the head. The bookie knew full well he was under age, but as he enjoyed taking my siller, he let us stay.

"Right son, watch this race. This should be a winner."

The horses were making their way into the stalls and I got that excited gambler's thrill, the same thrill Ringo was addicted to. Sitting on the seat at the back corner of the room, Max was a little taken by the event. I sat beside him as he worked his eyes over the track-listings page, looking confused.

"What's this mean?" He referred to the list of digits before the horse's name.

"That's the positions they finished in on their last outin' son."

I found our horse on the paper and pointed it out.

"This horse here, The Fast Fly, is our one." When I said "our" Max looked in awe as if we were part of a team. "Its last outings have been 444322, so I'm expectin' it to win this one because he's dropped a group class."

"Group class?" he asked.

"Aye, all the races are in a class and he's gone from class two to class three, but he's carryin' more weight in this one, so we'll hae to see how the bugger does."

Spending time with Max like this was taking my thoughts away from the upcoming fight with The Tailor.

My knowledge of horses was never in doubt, but picking winners was rare and I always succumbed to the itch. I was earning a lot of siller now. Even after paying Ringo's debt to Donny, I still had a good bit spare. Working for Jack was filling my pockets in more ways than he realised.

The race began and I stood up, hands in my pockets, flicking my head in and out like I was watching a boxing fight on the telly.

"Come on boy, come on, get on!" I shouted.

Fast Fly burst out the stalls and out in front, leading from the start in the ten-furlong race. Edging closer to the action, I got into the thrill of the race.

"Come on, stay there, come on!" I had an eager excitement, "Come on Fly!" I shouted.

With only a couple of furlongs left, he faded and dropped back.

"No! Get on boy, keep goin'!"

My excitement faded but Max still had hope; it wasn't over until the finish line.

"Fuck sake!" I belted out, then sat down. I saw Max was disappointed and shuffled into his seat. I started to glance over the track-listings and searched for the next pick. I swivelled it around on the table and asked Max to pick one.

"Go on son, pick one for yer old man." He didn't want to, what if it lost? Under his cap, his eyes rolled over the page. Randomly he plumped his finger onto the paper and landed at the Powerhouse Express in the 3.30pm at Haymarket.

"You sure?"

"Aye," Max answered, copying my way of saying 'aye' which sounded strange from his Scouse accent. I scoured the details of the horse, 20-1, not won a race, just been dropped in class.

I wasn't sure, in fact, I didn't want to put the horse on. I approached the perspex covered desk again and slapped my twenty quid down.

"The Powerhouse Express, 3.30, Haymarket."

The bookie never took me on, thinking to himself that I was a fool, but that's the kind of customers he liked to fill his till. The race started the second the slip went through the machine and I joined Max at the corner table.

"If this comes in, we'll go to the shop and buy you some new PlayStation games."

Max tilted his head back to see past his cap then returned his look to the telly in hope. This one was a jump race and lasted for two and a half miles. Half way through, the horse was looking good, sitting fourth, half a furlong back from the leader and favourite. I didn't have confidence in the horse coming in. Max did, his face opened at the sight of the favourite falling at the fourth last fence. I twitched.

"Look, he's down!" Max shouted out.

"So he is boy, come on now!" There was more faith now. Two furlongs left and the horse came neck and neck with the leader. The commentator's voice rose.

One furlong left, The Powerhouse Express took the lead and rallied to the end. I couldn't believe it; I had found my good luck charm.

"Come on you fucker!" Max jumped on the seat and cursed.

"Hey, watch yer language son!" I gave him a little tap on the back of his head.

This time I gladly returned to the counter and took my winnings of £400 from the annoyed bookie.

Outside, I patted Max on the shoulder, "Good pick son. I'll ha'e to take you down here more often." He smiled back.

Chapter 13

Bobby's Deal:

A couple of mornings before the fight, Jack turned up at the flat, too early. As Max let him in, I rose from my pit and joined him in the sitting room that was a tip, empty cans, filled ashtrays and a stale stink of ale that had sat too long. I always let Danielle clean up when she came around.

"Davie, that deal with Bobby is going down tonight." That was Jack's way of telling me my services were required.

"Alright, where and when?"

"Out at a farm I own, around 10pm. It'll be you, me and a couple of the doormen I know. Things should go smoothly, I hope."

"How many men is this Bobby takin'?"

"Just the one he says, but you never know, he could be setting something up. I'll be armed and so will my bouncers. Do you want a pistol?"

"No Jack, I'm no' a fan of firearms."

Carrying a weapon was something I'd never had to do in my time and I didn't see the point in breaking that tradition. Max was again keenly absorbing everything that was said.

"Suit yourself," Jack said with no real reaction, and moved on to another issue, "There's been complaints that some of my gear is of bad quality, what do you think?"

"Don't see why. It's the same stuff you always get. Isn't it?"

"It is Davie, maybe it's a bad batch. I won't look too far into it. It's still making us money and that's all that counts… I better get down to the club and open the doors. I'll pick you up at 9pm."

Once Jack left, I arranged for Danielle to watch Max for the night. I couldn't be assed tagging along to the deal. I had my routine of nightly drops, but needs must. Besides, the upcoming meeting with The Tailor was running around my thoughts. I wanted it over and done with as quickly as possible.

Jack's imports from South America normally had street values of over two million pounds. He saw the big picture in deals, didn't see the point in doing things in half measures. The deal went through that night with no hesitation or complications.

Bobby brought a mountain of a man called Eiffel, arrived in a flash car, deal done within ten minutes, and left.

Jack brought his bouncers and my presence wasn't really required, but Jack insisted I tag along to every deal.

Chapter 14

The Tailor:

A few days later, on a Saturday, time for The Rogue Riders boxing show and my forthcoming scrap inside Devil's Angels, bare-knuckle of course, inside the ropes. Three-minute rounds and fight until the other couldn't continue and by that, I meant until your opponent showed no will or movement to carry on. It was something they did every now and again. There were no counts when the fighter hit the deck. If you couldn't get up then the fight was over.

The new prospects had a big apprenticeship to prove themselves, and part of that was fighting to gauge the size of their balls and how much heart and determination they held.

Tickets sold to certain citizens outwith the club with a certain unwritten rule, it was not to be spoken about in the public domain. The filth weren't stupid; they knew what went on behind closed doors, but it was too much hassle for them to stop it. If they did appear, it would be an all-out war and an overly busy night for them, preferring to avoid the mass of paperwork and bruises a raid would bring.

As me and Max walked in, he was immediately drawn to the occasion. The low-built ring, black canvas and slack ropes in the corner of the decorated bar took his eye. The music loud, with heavy rock blasting out the big speakers. Hovering bikers, heavily pierced and big bellied, dressed in leather pants, bad haircuts and slutty women in short denims and tight tops. Bottles of lager were scattered all around the room and smoke filled the air.

We spotted Ringo leering over a seductive looking woman at the oval bar that dominated the room.

By now, I had paid Ringo's debt off, on the understanding that he would carry out my request of a returned favour, which benefited us both. He was back to his relaxed self, chatting up a piece of skirt at the bar. He seemed to blend in well with these surroundings. Donny made him work off his part of the debt by getting him to scrub the whole place from top to bottom. It took Ringo four full days, but as I told him not to fuck Donny about, he performed as told. Donny took the piss out of him in the couple of weeks it took me to get the cash together. Used him as an errand boy and personal dogsbody.

Something happened in that time, they became pally. Like I said, Ringo was a likeable guy, there was nothing overly complicated about him.

"Ringo, how's it goin'?" I asked.

"Not bad kid. Hey, this your boy?" He held out his hand to shake, "Nice to meet you kid."

Max kept his hands by his side.

"Go on, shake the man's hand." He shook it without as much as a word, feeling out of place in the joint, his body tense, walking and keeping his arms movements to a minimal.

"Quiet one this Davie," Ringo stated, as I saw he'd had his head in a pile of white powder again.

"Aye, it's the quiet ones you have to look out for. How much lemo you got left?"

Ringo was back in the game, another favour from me. I managed to stock him up with some out-of-town cocaine, enough to get him up and running again. Inside Devil's, the drug scene was rife and he offloaded most of his stuff in there, selling it cheap, that was enough for him to be accepted in that environment.

"I'm almost out kid, there's plenty more on my way though."

"Good, don't throw it all up yer nose. You'll need to profit from this."

He was more interested in his slutty company than joining in conversation, as he ogled his companion's half naked body and hand covering her arse.

"Relax kid. Things are good. It's all working out. Chill out for the night, grab a beer, have a smoke and enjoy the show. I'll catch you later on, got to take care of something, if you know what I mean." He groped his girl's arse then led her out of the room.

The man was telling me to chill out! I was doing this for him and chilling out was the last thing on my mind. I had a burning anxiety to get this fight done and dusted.

"Ringo!" I shouted, "We need a chat before I head home." With his back to me, he gave a thumbs-up as he walked away with his chick.

Max and me hovered around the room, him never leaving my side. Watching as people talked to me with an earned respect. Soaking up the atmosphere and quite taken by the occasion. The air in the room was heavily filled with smoke and over-boisterous drinkers. I was left with horrible pre-fight nerves I hadn't experienced in years. A hole in your stomach like someone was trying to take your breath away.

In the past, I had tried not to think about fights too much; instead, I pictured my opponent, cock-eyed and out cold under my stance. No room for doubts in this game.

The upcoming fights were eagerly awaited by the crowd. There was an anticipation in the air, an eagerness almost.

I was the first fight up and Fiddle, the cheeky cunt who tried to push his featherweight muscle on me, was taking on another prospect from within The Rogue Riders.

As we waited, Max became less solid and buoyed up with excitement, like a kid in a sweetie shop, peering around the room at the squad of bikers, loose women and dodgy characters. Having been in the ring on many occasions and used to the raw atmosphere, today, I was more aware than any other. I had doubts over my age. I always preferred to have illegal fights on open ground and always compared the two to sliding open a matchbox. If you were inside a matchbox when it closed, it would be a hard thing to push it open; if you were outside a matchbox, it would be easy to slide it open. The same as pushing your foe around, it was easier on open ground. Inside a ring you were limited to where you could move. Back in my heyday around Aberdeen, I always kept myself fit by visiting boxing gyms around the city. You couldn't be a bare-knuckle fighter if you never kept sharp, but all I had to count on was my raw experience. I had to pull away from the room, get some solitude before I was on.

I took Max into a back room, used to store tables and chairs, out of date juke-boxes, supplies of juice cans and some odd furniture. It was used as the fighter's prep area. As soon as the door closed, the reality hit me. Over the past weeks I had kept busy and used that to keep the apprehension hidden about the fight. But now, there was nowhere to hide my thoughts once the door shut. In true biker's style, there were a few bandages, scissors, tape and a bottle of whisky sitting lonely on a table. Left on my own, that was for sure, only my son for company. Where was Ringo? It was his fault I was here and he doubted how much anxiety I had over the fight. Max sat on one of the chairs and watched me struggle to wrap my hands with the bandage. I had always done it myself in the past but I was out of practice.

"Max, come here and give me a hand! Cut off bits of that tape and stick this bandage down over ma fist."

He jumped off the seat, more than willing to help his old man, ripping the tape with his teeth and sticking it over the bandage where I instructed.

"You've done this before, have you?" he asked.

"Many times son, many times," I said, looking at him deeply as I felt a bond growing. He was keen to help and felt nervous for me too.

"Maybe I can do this one day?"

"One day son, you might, and always remember 'ere's no room for mercy in between 'em ropes. It's you or him, that's it, nothin' more, nothin' less."

He did what he seemed to do best, listened and absorbed. Before entering a fight of this calibre, weird things dance uncontrollably through your mind. A whole load of violence and regret simmers to the surface. The pain that my youth brought, the survival from a knife attack in Aberdeen that should have killed me, even the pain that I brought to others like Joe and his mother. Anything bad that I'd done in life brewed on the surface and then I looked at Max - a young boy who I'd abducted to bring up as my own, to emulate me, but at that moment, when the doubt and tingle of nerves were at a peak, an overwhelming vision that maybe I didn't want him to turn into me broke to the surface. My evil way had turned the boy to respect and fear me at the same time and there he was, idolising me while sticking the tape over the bandage. A dawning realisation hit me that I didn't want this future for him.

Once my hands were wrapped, I peeled my shirt off and started to loosen up. My mind doing circuits, I remembered how I focused in the past, tunnel vision. I placed all thoughts of goodness to a locked chamber and let my past brew like a boiling kettle.

"Max, open that whisky and give ma a drink." Like any other hard to deal with moment in my life, I turned to drink.

I kneeled down to rest and let Max pour the nectar down my throat. As it burned, I shook it off which eased my nerves. What the fuck was I doing? Too old for this shit, but I wasn't about to succumb to defeat, not now, not after an adulthood of being victorious.

"I hope you win Da'." The first time he referred to me as his Da' inspired me with pride.

"Aye boy, just watch and learn." I came across confident but in reality, I'd never faced this much doubt before the dance began, not even when I faced Cluster Sands.

I warmed up, shadow-boxing around the room, focusing my mind for the war as my body shivered with the tickling anxiety of apprehension. I thought of every foe as the hardest man who walked the planet - that way I could be ready for the pain.

Ringo burst the door open.

Max rose. My heart jumped a heavy beat when the door opened as the noise hit me like a gust of wind. I was about to take the walk of death into the unknown.

Donny spoke on the microphone.

"Quiet, you bunch of noisy bastards! Let's get this ceremony under way. Welcome the notorious Scotsman to the ring!"

The speakers blasted a racket of some heavy metal music.

"It's time kid," Ringo said, and Max gave me a nudge with his head.

"Go on Da', take him out," Max said.

"Follow me Max, and stay beside Ringo. Yer about to witness greatness."

Only white bandages were worn over my hands as I could almost feel the pain on my knuckles; I knew what approached. Everything hurt in this game, no gum shield and no referee; it was as raw as it could get. Knuckle clattering off bone, dirty tactics and no mercy - it wasn't for the faint-hearted.

As I walked through the doorway, the noise dimmed in my head. The crowd parted as I paraded towards the ring. The heat of the occasion pierced my skin. The adrenaline made me breathless and I had forgotten the flooding ecstasy this feeling brought. I began to suck large breaths of air through my dilated nostrils, puffed up my chest and released the air quickly. It was the only way I could control the jittery rage that was about to enter my bloodstream.

I staggered between the ropes with a gripped jaw, fists clenched and a burning desire to rip someone apart. My feet hitting the canvas brought the muscle memory back. An instant metamorphosis into the callous man that I needed to be. But what separated me from the rest, was my ability to stay calm and aggressive at the same time. Only experience could teach that.

I entered the ring with Donny holding the mic. Ignoring him, I stood, hands by my side in my corner, only staring at the opposite corner, awaiting my victim. Max stood below me and Ringo behind.

"Right, you all know the man! Welcome The Tailor to the ring!" Donny shouted.

The speakers changed to 'Welcome to the Jungle' and the cheers were vastly more heated than they were for my entrance.

I paid no interest to The Tailor's introduction. I glared into open space, my impatience growing but face glued until he entered my sight and I watched him step through the ropes, calm, like ice, appearing as if he was on a Sunday stroll with a confident swagger. His relaxed way was enough to tell me he was no mug or maybe it was over-confidence. A smooth operator, not letting the occasion show on his face. He knew not to waste energy. He was bulky and big boned on his hairy upper body and arms masked with biker ink, looking the part, wearing jeans as I did. These occasions were raw; there was no dress code to follow, just like the rules.

Max was fixated on the event, the primitive atmosphere and the unique feeling of fear thrilled him. That feeling would become a part of him in time to come.

The bell rang.

Instantly, The Tailor skilfully hunted for my chin, showing me no respect, throwing fast and quick denting punches. I kept an upright stance, tucked my elbows in and tried to parry the incoming assault away with my palms, but he was too quick. My mind went numb as the brain couldn't relay to my body what to do. That was called 'ring-rust', and combined with my age, it wasn't a good combination to carry. I liked to keep my hands to myself in the beginning as it usually annoyed my opponents while I figured out their style. If you didn't use your brain in these situations, you were fucked and I couldn't rely on the sharpness or agility I once had.

I bounced on my toes to regenerate the memory banks. I body-weaved and tried to slip out of the way as we were going through the feeling-out process. The Tailor kept pressuring, he was in good shape and heated up. He had no doubt, heard of my reputation, and wanted to be the one who put that single blip on my record. He broke through my guard too easily, the blows clattering off the end of my pointed chin felt feeble compared to what it was used to. As the hard knuckle registered, the muscle memory began to return. He feinted his shots and made me flinch, my chin pulled to one side and a heavy right split my guard and sent me embarrassingly backwards as the audience appreciated the blow. They lifted their bottles and cheered their man. I could see Max in the corner, edging his head from side to side, poking his chin out as he egged me on. That gave me more purpose. I had to show my boy I was no mug.

As the first round ran on, The Tailor overly tried to impress the room as I soaked the pressure up. His aggressive style looked as if it was gaining the advantage. I started to breathe heavily, my body going into shock, heartbeat couldn't be slowed and pain couldn't be ignored but I absorbed the onslaught as I needed time to think.

The Tailor's confidence grew as he edged closer to me. That would be my chance, too quick to catch, I needed his energy levels to drop and his body to come closer. I purposely backed onto the ropes. First, I needed to rest, second, I needed to invite him in.

Starting to feel comfortable, his head sank into my chest as I rested against the ropes. The tip of his knuckle pierced the bone in my ribs, making me wince like a weakling. It made me sound cowardly and I hoped Max didn't hear. My left hand dropped and there it was, a right hook, numbing my senses. It felt as if he wore brass knuckles as I remembered The Turban inflicting that pain in the past. My legs shifted to the side as I slid across the rope. I side stepped, feeling as if I was walking on wet cement, hoping to find that solid spot so I could stand upright. He instinctively followed, trapping me in the corner and went to work on me. He rattled in a combo of I don't know what, grunting like a man who had seen his legacy begin. I was in a haze and couldn't find that moment of chance to sober up.

Lifting my head in between a barrage of gruelling strikes, I looked for that opening. Two and a half minutes and I hadn't laid a blow on this man; I deceived him into thinking he didn't need a guard. As he broke his, taking a minute step forward, gulping a lungful of air, I fired a short fast left uppercut onto the tip of his nose, watching him grimace in pain and retreat. With my hands down, taking one step forward bringing a hard-clenched piston-like punch straight down the middle, I burst his nose.

The bell came to his aid.

I didn't return to my corner; I watched him turn and stroll to his stool. I kept staring.

Ringo was standing beside Max who picked up a bottle of water, took the step up onto the canvas in the corner and held the bottle out.

"Da', you want a drink?"

I was distracted by his willingness to help me before refocusing on my opponent, letting him understand he was in trouble. It was a trick I'd used in all my bouts right back to my teenage years. It scared them. This was a place where you could only count on number one; no one was able to take the pain away or lend you a hand. Boxing was the toughest and loneliest sport in the world - just you and the other guy. The look on The

Tailor's face changed, his previous confidence taking a huge blow.

Donny rang the ring bell. Round 2.

No charge from The Tailor this time. He looked wary as my trick had worked again. But, I still had to put him away.

I kept my left hand by my waist, my shoulder to his stance and held the right by my chin. He threw a sheepish one, two. I slipped both punches and my piston of a right hand stabbed his ego. He side-stepped backwards and knew then he was dancing with the best. Facial expressions tell you everything in this game and The Tailor could only show shock. I let him come for me again. The crowd cowered down, knew their man was doomed. My heart rate was in overdrive. I couldn't take the adrenaline that now fired though me. Wary of me now more than ever, hesitation entered his game as he couldn't muster how to approach me again, but he did.

As a fast jab hurtled my way, I dipped my head forward and let the blow land on my forehead. It fucking hurt but the crack from his wrist hurt more.

The noise in the room was diminishing. Max looked nervous. Ringo, well, Ringo was Ringo, stood with a kind of half smirk on the side of his mouth as he was probably too wasted to know what was happening.

Now I had complete control of the fight and steadied my breathing. The Tailor's right hand ached, his face stiffened. If he had any tactics for this fight, he just forgot them. I didn't chase and waited for him.

He took his time, slowly making his way into punch range. As soon as he did, I nailed him with a jab and straight right, targeting his nose again, which caused the bleeding to begin.

I mocked him with a smile.

He still had energy to burn. Panicking and taking a leap of faith, he jumped forward and banged a crisp left hook across my jaw. His right hand was immobile. It shook me to the core. For a moment, I blanked out, and came back to feel him pounding me with his left hand. When some senses returned, I was on the black canvas on one knee; as I lifted my head, his knee crunched into my jaw, causing me to bite the tip of my tongue as my teeth clashed together.

It looked as if I was beaten, crouched on the canvas, counting on my palms to stop me from falling. If I did, it could mean it was over. Rules went out the window. The room blanked out from my head. A delayed silence as my senses went all to pot. Numb from the brain down and a puddle of blood formed from my bitten tongue.

He retreated, thinking I was finished and he had won. He was celebrating as the crowd cheered, threw their beer in the air and jumped up to the ring side.

Donny was still leaning under the bottom rope, knowing I wouldn't give up my legacy so easily.

Max walked closer to the ring, looking worried or disappointed in the gap under the bottom rope. I couldn't tell. I gave him a subdued wink to let him know I was okay. My arms flinching but still supporting me from losing. With blood streaming from my mouth, forming a pool under me, my senses returned with a vindictive violence brewing as I pictured The Tailor being slid into a chamber.

He paced around the ring, hands in the air, proud that he had claimed my legacy. Slowly, I bent my leg and used it to raise my body from the floor to my full height. The Tailor slowed like a train taking its dock. I waved him over to me in a gesture of acceptance I had lost the fight. True, he did have me beaten. Donny rang the bell and signalled that the fight was over, knowing exactly what horror was imminent.

The Tailor glided up to me with a confident stroll holding his hand out for it to be met with mine. I sniffed up the blood that caught in my throat and spat it diagonally across the air, missing his approaching shoulder. I rubbed off the blood that ran down my chin and torso, slapping my hand on his shoulder and mouthing the words in his ear.

"Ye're fucked, brother."

I head butted him on the bridge of his nose and punched hard into his throat. Blood spattered from his flaring nostrils. I held him up by his sweat-soaked hair and riveted punches in his face until he collapsed to the floor. Blacking out with rage, something that happened a lot, I only saw red. The wrath cascaded as I continued rapidly pummelling his face. He was out cold and on the canvas. I dropped to my knee but I couldn't stop.

I started to drag him across the canvas by his armpits, towards the edge of the ring. The rope stopped me. I passed under the top rope and continued dragging him until his head hung over the edge. I lifted my boot and showed him the sole. All I could imagine was his neck bone detaching from his spine. I lifted my leg a little higher to inflict as much pain as I could and as I was prepared to decapitate him, Donny and another couple of men pulled me back inside the ring, followed by five burly bikers.

Luckily for The Tailor they did. I was going to detatch his neck from his spine.

Chapter 15

The Dawn Of Time:

The aftermath of the fight brought a new reality, I knew my days in this world were of a finite amount, calendar material, as my old foe, Sam Bryson, would say. It wasn't for me anymore; there had to be a time to get out and our time wasn't far away.

My body was left wrecked from the fight, taking over a month of painful recovery. Bruises covered my stiffened body from my ribs to head, my bones felt brittle, jaw left with an annoying click every time I chewed and my brain left concussed. The new reality dawned after that fight, the trouble and hassle that went hand in hand in this world would see me a corpse one day.

This was not the up-bringing I wanted for Max.

For the next year, I carried on as I had been, with the intention of vacating this city with Max and a bag of notes. There wasn't one night that year that I remembered getting an early night. My retirement fund was building nicely and when I got pissed off carrying out Jack's mundane tasks, I had to remember that. That was the only thing stopping me from telling Jack to fuck off every now and again.

I was earning solid money that I had to maximise by keeping the siller flowing into my pockets and my desire was to get out on top. I'd heard too many stories of how life caught up with the big timers: the Krays, who needed no introduction; my old mentor, Arthur Thompson, the Godfather of Glasgow and the most feared hitman in Britain or even the notorious Pablo Escobar, the biggest cocaine dealer in history. They were all top of their game and didn't know when to cut ties and get out. The lust for power and greed conquered most and I didn't want my name inducted into that particular Hall of Fame. I just wanted to live the rest of my life without having to check who was preparing my death warrant.

My whole life I'd been earning pay cheques in blunt and deceitful ways, capitalising on my cruel sadism with nothing to show for it but a bundle of unique memories and brutal tales. Now my aging body could no longer keep up. The long shifts and early morning returns home, scraps and seven days a week drinking. It was then that I succumbed to accepting why Jack chose to be the business man, instead of the street thug.

There was a younger generation coming through the ranks, youths like Fiddle, with no respect or a hardness that we old school guys battled to gain, which they knew nothing about or quickly forgot. People like Ringo, who could party all night and work all day, have no worries about life and that life many fantasised about, a life I used to lead once. I couldn't show this weakness - I had to be the battle-hardened outlaw everyone knew me as.

After the fight, Max began to show me tons of fresh respect due to my ruthless disposal of The Tailor.

I debated with myself and then decided to induct him into the loathsome world of narcotics dealing. I had to. Jack kept adding more tasks, having me pick up cash from the brothels on a nightly basis, meaning more money to handle and even later returns home. I needed assistance, someone close I could trust: Max was definitely becoming trustworthy. I left him in control of handling the cash and called him my cashier. It gave him purpose and he took to the name. I took him out on the tax run, as I called it, around the city and put him to good use. I would drive close to wherever we would be meeting a runner and send Max from the car to meet with them, always keeping a close eye on him.

Liverpool was full of so-called hard men. Youths who would stand up tall and mouth abuse, spout their connections to the underworld and think whoever you were, they could beat you down. Disrespectful vermin, I thought of them.

Putting myself in the runner's position, if I had seen a young boy approach with an order, looking shady in a cap and tracksuit, I'd pretty much keep the cash and tell him to do one. I watched because if they held a streak of stubbornness about handing over payment, it could well be in their arsenal to give Max a slap, and I wouldn't have that. It was always a nervous time and I had to calculate it in my mind how each deal would roll. It would depend on the individual. How respectful was he? Was he a user or just a dealer? Or did he carry an unreliable rep? I had to take all this into the equation before each drop.

Max could point in my direction or mention my name if he sensed the deal wasn't going to plan. Relying on your instinct in this game was a must, and I passed that on to him. A good instinct you could only acquire in time. Mentioning my name usually worked and I always knew when it did. They would present a face of acceptance then hand over the cash or their heads would survey the scene, searching for my mean face in the shadows. If they spotted me, a wave from me in their direction was customary. Needless to say, on a few occasions they didn't spot me, a large set of balls was grown and thinking they could act the big men, they mocked and taunted the boy.

As soon as I saw Max in any trouble, that was my green light to demonstrate my reputation and leave my name imprinted in their memories, teaching them a

86

lesson, men or women, they wouldn't forget. On these deals, Max would learn how to live on the streets and analyse situations to benefit him later in life, provide him with an instinct that was so important in this game. The major problem with conducting business in this environment was the fact you mingled with criminals and every criminal had a slice of dishonesty, it went hand in hand. I passed on my knowledge and code of street smarts and he soaked them up like a sponge. The most important thing I passed on was the four rules I lived by: always look after number one and never show fear; keep your manner solid and give nothing away. This was business, not pleasure. It was a world not for the weak, but for the ruthless and unkind.

Towards the end of 2005, Jack had a temporary issue. His stash of gear had dried up with complications in South America and Ringo took full advantage, seemingly having an endless supply. He adopted the company of The Rogue Riders and spent most of his time in Devil's. Jack was waiting for his next shipment from Bolivia and expected delivery soon, with the usual cut being sold to Bobby Munroe. It didn't please him in the slightest, but it aggravated him more that Ringo was able to keep stock when he couldn't.

Dealing with Jack in Liverpool was alright when I stayed in Aberdeen, knowing the option to return home was there whenever I pleased. Too much time in his company meant too much work as he liked to take advantage of my presence. Now I owed him and that wasn't good, being in his pocket, as he'd abuse that. He felt he could order me around as he saw fit. It was quite fucking annoying, especially since he did nothing much himself.

Danielle became a regular sight at our flat and I started sleeping with her. It was convenient for me and Max took a big shine to her. He needed a mother figure and she suited the role fine, having practically moved in with a chest of drawers to herself and a pile of makeup lying around. She was still on the take for Jack, but her shifts were few and far between.

My past life in Aberdeen was a rare thought in my head now. The guilt still wallowed occasionally, but the more time I spent with Max and Danielle, the less I remembered and the more I could make things right in my own way.

One rainy November night, as we were on the way home from picking up a pizza, Jack called my mobile. "Davie, where are you?" Jack asked in an abrupt manner.

"Out gettin' supper. Why?" Another demand was approaching I suspected.

"Can you get around to Netherfield Road? A couple of your friends have just entered the brothel. My man on the door hasn't turned up tonight. I'm not sure what their intentions are. I've repeatedly told them to stay away from my premises."

I knew he meant the Collins brothers, a constant pain in my ass.

"I'll head round, see what they're up to." I was more interested in returning to the flat than dealing with this pair of degenerates.

"Good, give me a call back."

It was chucking down with rain that night, the type of rain that hits you like someone's shooting you with a machine-powered pea-shooter. Netherfield Road in Everton wasn't far away from the flat and I hoped it would be a quick stop off. I jumped out my motor not knowing why these two were in the brothel, apart from the obvious.

We were buzzed in, Max walking in my shadow. The corridor was cramped, but in a cornered-off area to the right appeared two hookers. Sitting relaxed around a heavily stained glass-topped table, clogging the air with smoke, talking fast in an eastern European accent, wearing only cheap lingerie and makeup. Max ogled them, probably his first sighting of a woman almost naked.

"Ha'e a seat son," I pointed to an arm-chair in the corner of the alcove near the table.

"Dominique, where's these two degenerates?"

Dominique was middle-aged with a hard face, yellowing teeth, tall, overly skinny with her bones poking through her rib cage and well past her prime.

"They left, just before you come," Dominique answered, her fag hanging from her mouth.

"What did they want?" I was always curious when the brothers were about, they always being up to something suspicious. I had also told them to stay away from Jack's premises, but as per their CV's, they were stupid.

"Nothing," she spouted. "Just come in, make noise, waste my time, then fuck off."

"That's it, nothin' else?"

"Yes, stupid pigs." She was bitter in her trade, always referred to punters as 'pigs'. If Prince Charles walked in, he would receive the same ridiculous abuse. While I was there, I thought I'd better make the most of it.

"Is that young Bulgarian still here?"

"Yes, she is free upstairs, room four, go up. I look after boy."

"I'll be back in a minute son, sit tight."

Max sat tight in the seat beside the two girls. The area lit by a low hanging red bulb in the compact space made it look dingy and cheap.

I clumped up the uncarpeted stairs to room number four, knocked and was shouted in. I heard the downstairs door-buzzer then voices of drunken men enter.

I took out my wallet to pay the Bulgarian, who was way too good looking to be a hooker; she could have been on the cover of Vogue and the last thing I wanted was to head back down stairs with this beauty in my eye.

Un-buckling my belt, sitting on the edge of the bed, I heard the voices starting to sound hostile with mocking laughter and listened to Dominique ignite in foul language. Being annoyed by the voices, I found it hard to relax and leapt up, buttoned my jeans and thudded back downstairs.

"Jesus kid, you're a bit young to be in here!" Was what I heard when I got to the bottom of the stairs, hiding behind the door-less frame and a hanging beads curtain.

"I'm working!" Max replied sharply.

I walked through the doorway to see Colin Collins' skinny body mocking my son - big mistake.

Max was hostile towards the two.

"Working man!" Colin mouthed, "What's a runt like you doing in here?" Now Colin spoke in a condescending way. His brother, Mark, spotted me, tapped Colin on the shoulder and nodded his head vaguely in my direction, signalling to Colin that I was standing tall behind him. They both took a couple of steps back.

"Stupid pigs!" Dominique spouted.

Colin wanted to reply with some more mouth but with my presence standing in front of him, he knew best to keep quiet.

"What the fuck are you pair of bell ends doin' in here?"

My fists were clenched by my side, flashes of their blood on the walls rushed through my head. I had told them not to go near any of Jack's establishments.

"Just having a browse Davie, dat's all."

"Fuckin' browse? Sounds like ye're mockin' ma boy?"

They both turned their heads in disbelief, the kid they were taking the piss out of was my blood. How ironic was that?

"Sorry Davie, we never knew, honest."

I was waiting for one of them to apologise to Max, but they stood in silence as I felt my temper boil. I stood as tall as I could, eyes opened and chin tense. I was about to blow.

The first unlucky man was Colin. I stuck the point of my boot into his shin and his body buckled, bending from the waist. Without a chance for him to register what was happening, I pulled his head down to rapidly knee him in the face and he dropped to the ground like a sack of sand, frantically groaning in pain, his hands cupping his face.

Mark, watching my vicious outburst, retreated to the door and tried to escape. My attention turned to him. I stepped over Colin without removing my glaring eye from Mark and lumbered down the corridor. Mark's face glowed with anguish, petrified at the door. He yanked the handle desperately, not realising it opened by a push button release. Trapped by the tight corridor, watching a barbaric maniac approach with nostrils flaring and mouth gripped shut, he looked for pity: that wasn't my style and nobody fucks with my son, these boys had to learn that.

"Look, there was no harm meant, please." His plea for mercy was feeble in my eyes. His face already clinched before the first punch landed. The barrage of the attack kept him on his feet, trapped against the door before sliding down to meet the wrath of my boot.

Like a corpse, he was dragged by his feet down the corridor, leaving enough room to open the door. Both Collins were towed outside into the soaking wet street and left in a big puddle beside the kerb, grovelling.

Standing proud over my beaten prey, with rainwater running down my gratified face, I noticed Max standing in the door. The savagery terrified him, but he looked proud that I would protect him in such a way. Made to feel small and a fool by the Collins brothers, there was his own sense of pride to consider as the men lay broken, beaten and humiliated in puddles on Netherfield Road.

Chapter 16

Acceptance:

A few mornings later, Jack phoned too early at twenty minutes past ten and got me out of bed. Said he wanted to see me urgently. Bollocks, it couldn't be that urgent. He'd have some kind of moan or stupid task for me to carry out.

I walked into the sitting room, Max sitting with Danielle on the sofa watching the telly in his usual position. I gave them both a nod through my glazed, sleepy eyes, then plodded to the kitchen for my morning coffee. I stood by the kettle as it boiled, trying to register the morning. Not quite tuned into the world and still half asleep, I heard the local news programme air on the telly.

The first headline:

"The twenty-month search continues for fourteen-year-old Max McCabe. The police haven't been able to find any leads with the information so far received."

The newsreader carried on with the story before it clicked.

The spoon I was using to stir my coffee was yanked out of the cup and stained my t-shirt.

Into the sitting room, where Danielle panicked and tried to change the channel with the remote but the batteries needed replacing.

Max stood up, switched his head from telly to me with an open mouth, knowing I'd be furious, astonishment written over his pale face as his picture appeared on TV. Henry and Lorraine Jackson sat in their latest press conference, crying and pleading with the public for any information regarding the whereabouts of the beloved boy whom they had their hearts set on adopting.

With my hair ruffled and coffee spilled over my t-shirt, I watched as Max stared at the telly.

"Max, switch that off! You don't need to see that!"

He looked at Danielle as she waited for my outburst.

"Switch it off love," Danielle said, Max glued to the spot.

"Switch the fuckin' telly off son!" I raised my voice and saw that Danielle felt awkward. Max ran around the table and headed straight for the socket, switched it off and stood still, a shocked look on his face. I sat down on the sofa, with a tension lingering, staring at Max while Danielle waited for someone to speak.

"Listen boy, those two aren't yer parents. I am, that's all you need to know. I'm lookin' after you, aren't I?"

He nodded with acceptance.

"Aye, you are Da'." Just the answer I was looking for.

"I've got to nip round to Jacks, you want to tag along?" He nodded his head, "Go get yer trainers on 'en."

As he left the room, I turned to Danielle, "Have you said anythin' to him?"

She was as fearful of me as everyone else when I reached the end of my tether.

"Haven't said a thing Davie."

"Good, keep it that way!"

Chapter 17

Exchange:

As time passed, the life in the underworld became normal for Max and the need to keep an eye on him drifted as he was able to conduct himself as he liked, now teetering on his sixteenth birthday.

Danielle moved in permanently. I welcomed her, the flat was kept clean and the cupboards stocked. She was no longer on Jack's take and seemed more than happy with that. I kept her purse full and she kept her questions to herself. She knew what kind of man I was and what kind of impractical life I lived.

My retirement fund was stocking up nicely, hidden in the flat under the floorboards in my bedroom cupboard. I figured if I worked for another month, I could get out of there and take Max with me. Danielle would be what I called collateral damage, I'd leave her behind. Where we were going to go, I didn't know. Isle of Man, maybe, or a similar quiet location. I never gave it too much thought. I was only interested in jumping in the car and fleeing.

I was utterly sick of Jack's demands; he treated me like a dogsbody. What I looked forward to the most was not hearing his moaning voice every day of the week.

That night was the latest exchange with Bobby Munroe. Jack didn't need me to tag along, things always ran smoothly, but he always wanted my presence anyway. He would pay a little extra for tasks like this and I welcomed the pay. He always picked me up at 9 pm and mostly returned just after 11 pm.

Me, Danielle and Max were in the flat, watching telly. Danielle was half way through a bottle of wine, and I drank export from the can before being picked up. Max had a can of coke. I didn't want to introduce him to drink yet and he never asked. Usually kids his age would ponder over what alcohol tastes like but he seemed quite content.

"Getting picked up at nine again?" Danielle asked.

"Aye, same story, same deal. I'll be home at elevenish."

"Do you fancy going out when you're back? Head out to Devil's?"

 I could tell she was itching for me to take her out for a night. The way she looked at me with those sea blue eyes, it was hard to refuse and the fact I'd be ditching her played on my conscious. Now that Max didn't need supervision, there was no problem leaving him on his own.

"Sure, I'll drive out when I'm back. Donny can give us a bed for the night, make the most of it."

"What about me?" Max nagged.

"Ye're no' comin', too young for that place son," I answered.

"I've been there before." He was right, but as any parent will tell you, sometimes you need a break from your kids.

"Aye, no' on a Saturday night though."

"That's shite! I'm not staying here on my own. Donny won't mind me kicking about."

"Listen you little shite, you'll do as ye're fuckin' told. There's a lot of work to be done the morn so rest up." Sometimes he still needed to be put in his place.

 Approaching nine, I got suited up for the frosty November night, a woolly hat, thick coat and gloves, before going down to meet Jack in his heavy blacked-out BMW.

 He approached, the boot stocked with cocaine in brown leather doctor holdalls. The passenger was Billy Beats, a man who was a rare sight. An American, who owned a gunsmiths in the area. Besides Donny, Billy was the other man you approached if you wanted a firearm in the city. What the fuck was he tagging along for? A man who had served time in the army completing a tour of Desert Storm. I jumped into the back seat, expecting to see two of his doormen, who usually tagged along, but they weren't there.

"Davie," Jack said, "Baltic tonight, eh?"

"I'm fuckin' freezin'! It's like being back up north. Hey, where's the two bouncers?"

"They're away on some romantic stag do, somewhere a little more exotic than here I suspect. This is Billy. Have you two met?"

Billy struggled to swivel round and slide his hand between the front seats to shake mine. He was a little podgy and short, but looked overly filled out as if he was wearing loads of clothes. I gave him my hand to shake, something I didn't like to do.

"Alright there Billy."

"Davie right?" he said in an annoying heavy American drawl, the kind that made him seem he was right in your face.

"Aye, Davie," I replied, and he let my hand go, "Same set up tonight Jack?" I appeared as if I was interested but I couldn't have given a fuck really.

"Not exactly Davie. Bobby's throwing a few shotguns and Glocks into the deal to make up for a cash flow problem he has. That's why Billy's tagging along. I'll get him to inspect the guns before we make the exchange."

Great! Fucking guns - I hated guns.

We drove off chatting about the street gossip firstly, then moving on to an issue that Jack continued to moan about: the rumours of his shoddy coke filtering around, he couldn't figure out how. He must have the best powder in the country and was still making the same amount of profit, so I didn't see where his problem was.

We waited outside a farmhouse for Bobby to arrive. Usually we went inside to conduct the deals, count the cash and weigh the goods. Jack was quiet and deep in thought. Billy Beats came over slightly anxious, lifting himself up and down on his toes like someone would do if they were choking for a fag. I put it down to the cold night.

Being a military man, needless to say, Billy was armed with a pistol, an all-American made Rugger Sr1911. Stainless steel silver with wooden grips. Jack was armed with his usual, a Walther PPK, which fitted into his shrimp hands elegantly. I filled the time by standing unarmed making a rollie, relaxed as ever in that deal.

The farm road lit up as a vehicle approached.

Billy pulled up his polo neck jumper and removed the Rugger from his gun holster, revealing that he was wearing a bullet-proof vest. He checked the safety was off, slid it down his trousers behind his back and then slid on a pair of leather driving gloves. It was then I thought of this man as a bit of an over-serious tool. Jack checked his safety and slid the gun into his pressed trouser pocket.

"Let me do the talking, this should be done quickly," Jack said, as Billy nodded and I stood disinterestedly between them, under the floodlight above the front door of the house.

A white transit van drove past us and stopped, which was strange - Bobby usually turned up in a long Jag. From the passenger door exited Bobby, a short, fat man with a belly like a monk's, in his mid-twenties with square Italian Mafia-like tinted glasses, wearing trousers that were too long, dragging in the dirt, and a polo neck sweater. The driver was a Danish man called

Eiffel, built like Goliath who I'd never heard speak, brought along for face, leaving footprints the size of a T-Rex's, with permed hair and a boxed beard. Even I admired his stature.

"Bobby, fine evening for a meeting." Jack was being sarcastic about the situation and shook hands with Bobby. They were both relaxed.

"Aye, no' bad. How's the family?" Bobby's accent was pure Glaswegian. I understood it, being from the Glasgow Gorbals, but Billy had to fine tune his ears.

"Just fine Bobby, just fine."

Eiffel's hands crossed over his solid frame, an unfazed look on his face. Paid for his size, not his reactions, as he kept a solid focus towards me. There was something about men who were bigger than me. I had the urge to overpower them, I didn't like being intimidated; it played with my temper and that wasn't a nice game to be part of.

"Let's get down to business Bobby. The money and guns?" Jack said, with his hands in his overcoat pockets and collar pulled up around his neck to block the cold. I think he wanted this deal done as quickly as possible to get back inside the warmth of his car.

"In the back of the van. The gear?" Bobby asked.

"In the car Bobby. Can I see the cash and the guns first?"

"Sure, no bother," he indicated for Jack to open the back doors of their van with a tilt of the head.

"Davie, check the goods."

There it was again, another order. I took a spiteful glance round before walking to the rear of the van with my rollie hanging out of my mouth.

Eiffel shadowed my walk, keeping a certain distance between us. I peered over my shoulder, screwing up my face at the lump ogling me. With both hands, I swung the doors open.

"Mr Rhodes, lang time no see."

Mute at the hearing of my past, I thought I'd never see this man again. My rollie hung momentarily immobile in my mouth before slipping off my bottom lip.

He was still as stocky and dapper as I remembered but now wore a glass eye. I turned around to see Eiffel's fists clenched, ready to strike. Billy Beats slipped his gun from his back and pointed it at my head. Jack walked around the rear of both Billy and Eiffel, pointing his PPK, blocking off any exit route for me, standing out at the ends of the open doors.

"Fuckin' cunts!" I said, running my head across the three men blocking my route away. I was proper fucked here.

Sam Bryson sat on the crate of weapons leaning his elbows over his knees, fingers intertwined, looking straight from the back doors at me.

"I've waited a lang time for 'is special moment atween us Davie," he said, with relief, sharply dressed in a clean white suit, more fitting for a Columbian drug lord but nevertheless, he still pulled it off.

Enraged, having no hope, there was nowhere to run and an attack on anyone would leave my body with bloody holes.

"Jack, you fuckin' snake!" I snarled, as he watched me with a brash smirk.

"That's hypocritical of you Davie. I know you've been ripping me off. You look surprised. Surely you didn't think I was that stupid?"

"Aye, for some time I did Jack."

The complaints about Jack's gear were true.

Jack, using the Collins as his chemists, gave me an idea and I struck a deal with them. Paid them handsomely enough to cut the gear that Jack handed them to double in quantity. They needed some gentle persuasion in the right direction and it became easy enough to get them on board.

Each kilo Jack handed the Collins was cut and the bags returned to him after being laced with cutting agents like extra boric acid, laundry detergent and a mixture of legal-high products. The cocaine came in sixty-five percent pure and left the Collins lab at around twenty percent. I handed a kilo's worth to Jack's runners and whatever was left, I handed to Ringo and we split the profits. The runners had to sell the product at cut-down prices and complained like old pensioners about the 'stodgy lemo' as they called it. I continued to run them down over complaining, but they always had something to say. It was take it or leave it, I insisted. Ringo used his profits to live his party lifestyle and I put all mine into my retirement fund. Now that fund was fucked and left inside the flat.

It was a fucking beautiful set up while it lasted. Only a month away from doing an exit, I wished I'd left before that moment. From the first second Jack asked me to deal for him, I thought about maximising the situation and once I found out the Collins were Jack's chemists, the deception begun. The five grand he offered for each kilo just wasn't enough for me. Like I said, I was thinking of my retirement. Jack didn't care too much about the complaints at first. He still made the same money. I guess his penny-pinching mind kept overworking, causing him to investigate the problem. I suspected he visited the Collins and they buckled under the pressure.

"It took me a long time to figure it out, but I got there," Jack said pleasingly, "Your friends, the Collins, at this moment will be taking their last breaths. Cutting up my

101

product to double the amount was a good trick, well played there."

"You've figured that out, good job." Sam had exited the side door and joined in at the rear of the four men.

Bobby pulled out two chunky cigars and shared one with Sam, cocky smiles from ear to ear. The connection to Sam Bryson must have been made through Bobby Munroe. Bobby was a ruthless contender; there was something extra put into this deal for him.

"I can only assume you were going to milk me dry then do a runner?" Jack was calm and assertive, as he always was under pressure. Loving the fact he got one up on me. I had taken advantage of the Collins' fear of me and made them cut up the coke. I knew they had the knowledge to do so.

"Well, let's say I wasn't goin' to be stickin' around for the scenery Jack."

"I thought different of you Davie. I've never been so sad to do something of this calibre before, but you were a friend and I can only express my disappointment." What Jack had prepared for me was scary.

"Somethin' like what?" I asked.

"Don't get me wrong Davie. I had a bullet in this gun with your initials on it, but then some knowledge came across my desk and I thought this would be a more, let's say…ironic end for you."

Ringo's name wasn't taken into the equation at all. I don't think Jack knew of his involvement, but neither did Ringo. He had no idea the gear I was supplying him with came from his dad's stock. I told him I was getting it from out of town and it was our own little arrangement. He was a reckless character, not stupid, and I think on some level he must have known where the gear was really coming from, but I think he was in the clear with Jack.

102

I was, how they say, FUCKED. My nemesis, Mr Bryson, had something planned for me and if Jack had anything to do with it, it would be painful.

My body burned to throw a couple punches, not being the type to lie down. Billy and Jack retreated and from a specially made pocket in his combat trousers, Eiffel slid out a smiling shark, a long baton with a torch fitted on the end. Mostly used by the police force, and with a lacklustre stretched grin, smashed it over my head...

Chapter 18

The Gorbals In The Late Seventies:

 The Gorbals during that time echoed stories of the criminally famous and ruthless. Since the turn of the First World War, the area was overpopulated and filled with uncontrollable violence. The constant spat between Protestants and Catholics brought an argument that would never settle and a war that would never end. Looking after number one in the city was a must, and that was something I managed well.

 Walking down the grim streets, I savoured the stench of blood in my nostrils. The area was undergoing major reconstruction but the past would never change, people would still carry blades and men would still beat their wives.

 Using your knuckles was like working a knife and fork. Organised scraps were a weekly event, and the Gorbals had its own version of rules. There was no lack of interest in exchanging fists, the area was engulfed in crime, the passionately religious and the men who held no morals. The weakest human in the area would stand tall somewhere less vicious. Surviving in the environment was like walking off Dunkirk beach with your balls still attached. The youth were brought up witnessing their mothers and siblings being beaten by their heavy-handed husbands and fathers. Naturally, that brutality was passed down to the next generation.

 My vicious father was no different.

 An ex-Navy man, he had been enrolled in conscription during the start of the Second World War in Northern Ireland. The Derry man was based on the destroyer, HMS Harvester, when it met the bottom of the Atlantic

Ocean on 11th March, 1943. By that time in the war, he'd been hardened into the man who managed to be only one of three survivors from the sinking ship. The sea was masked with gunfire, flames burst all around, the destroyer had been torpedoed by a German U-boat, the men were deafened and temporarily blinded from smoke.

Coming around after being knocked out from the bombardment, he stood to reload his gun. A squirt of red leaked from his arm; on looking down, he discovered he had no arm. He saw the ship tilt dangerously and realised it was going down. His head was light and he knew he should've died that day, there was no question of that. But David Rhodes Senior didn't succumb to defeat; he wasn't prepared to come to his end. Through stubbornness and toughness, he kept himself alive. David held on tight to the edge of the boat while the lump of steel sank into the ocean.

Leaping into the sea and grabbing some debris, he paddled his body over a mile to the next allied vessel. After he was hauled aboard, he instantly passed out and woke in a hospital bed on the Faroe Islands.

A good-hearted man died that day he woke. Fighting infection and gangrene for the next few months made his suffering even harder. Hailed as a war hero, his tale of true grit filled the news feed and papers. He was even privileged to receive a personal visit from Winston Churchill, who vowed to make sure the man was financially secure for the rest of his life. That didn't mean necessarily he would receive a handsome pay out, because the country was hard up and in turmoil.

Returning to his own land frightened him, not knowing how life would be without his limb. A hero's welcome, a parade for his return with a weakened brave face, a face that would be put on for the rest of his life.

Winston Churchill was a man of his word. After the war finished, Mr Rhodes was offered a job in the design department of naval construction in the Glasgow shipyards.

His home in Derry wasn't the same to him as when he had signed up four years before; the things he used to do, he couldn't now. Frustrated and depressed, all he had done since his hero's return was bury his head in a bottle. There was no other way to deal with the emotional impact of his accident. He did, however, find some happiness in his post-war life.

The Government moved him into a house on Cavendish Street in the Gorbals. The area reflected his scarred memories, bitter, poorly sanitised and poverty stricken. He married a local lass, who took pity on him, but loved him nevertheless.

My mum, Grace, made him forget, and that's what he needed more than anything.

Chapter 19

True Story:

 Throughout the years growing up, from my first memory to my last in that house, life was emotional and physical torture.

One night when I was on the way out of the house he yelled from the livingroom, "Hey, boy, where the fuck ye' goin'?" I was the youngest of six, and seemed to get the worst treatment of us all.

 Sitting in his Dijon mustard-coloured arm chair in front of the green and white patterned wallpaper, my father was rubbered with drink as usual, Wednesday night was as good as any for him. His left arm lifted his half-filled nip glass from his side table, sending what was left down his foul mouth as I reached the door.

"Out!" I shouted.

"Ye're going fuckin' nowhere boy! Here!" he grunted, calling me like a dog and at sixteen years old, I obeyed.

 My father stood up from his chair and looked me in the face, swaying from side to side, with his lazy eye half shut and his right sleeve tied in a knot.

 "Ye cleaned yer room?" He talked to all his six children as if we were stupid and simple. When he was pissed, he became hard to understand as his Irish brogue came alive; sometimes we just nodded our heads in agreement and hoped for the best.

"Aye Da', I've din' it." My mum sat on her plastic covered two-seater, fully aware of what her husband was thinking.

"Ye're away to fight dat fuckin' Turban, aren't ye'?"

"Naw, am I fuck."

"Fuckin'…." he cursed in my face and the usual left hook bounced me across the room, causing me to fall over mums lap.

"Don't fuckin' use dat language wi' me cunt!" When he flipped, the man completely blanked out with rage to the point that he could easily have took a life. Mum gripped her hands round my belly.

"David, no, no' again!"

He slapped her across the face, "Fuckin' shut it woman!" He pressed the tip of his finger into her forehead as the fumes from his breath went through the air like smoke.

"Get up ye' smart cunt!" He dragged me away from mum, my eyes watering with pain as his grip on my hair intensified. Rooted in the middle of the room, there were continuous boots to my shins and knees while cupping his hand into a fist, pulling hair from my scalp. I was used to this treatment, learned not to beg or cry: it satisfied his vicious nature.

"Stop, stop!" Trying to get in the middle of us landed mum with a Glasgow kiss in her eye.

Then, I was well over Dad's height, three inches of it, but still afraid of him. His rotten eyes closed me down, backing me up against the wall, when a whip of a fist trapped my face to the wall and I slid down.

"Ye'll get more blood on ma carpet boy!"

By now, his caustic rage controlled him, boots into the stomach finished me off, leaving me battered on the floor.

Mum sobbed on her knees on the shag-pile rug, in disbelief of what had become of her life. My two sisters could be heard creeping down the stairs, peeking in the door, feeling sorry for their brother in need.

Every child received the same treatment over the years. Post-traumatic stress syndrome psychologically damaged the troubled man, and turned him into an abusive alcoholic. I got the raw end of the stick, became a rogue, continually stealing and scrapping, pushing him to the limit. Baseball bats, a crocodile-shaped ashtray carved from hardwood, his belt, cups, or even the thick wooden chopping-board, were all weapons of choice. This upbringing transformed me into the barbaric street fighter I became, earning a reputation as a fearsome bare-knuckle fighter, but never able to stand up to my father's wrath. He had a tight hold of my fear. Dad was right though: there was a fight that night.

I hated the sight of The Turban and the feeling was mutual. We could feel each other's presence without sight, the hatred was that strong. Every month we had a fight for a fiver - it was up to each other to raise the cash, the consequence of any fifty pence missing from the pot was a free hit of the jaw before the fight broke out.

The Turban was a lad of Indian descent and fought for his big community of immigrants settling in Glasgow. He came from a peaceful family and was tortured by discrimination threats. Moving to the city at the age of ten, his parents held fruit and veg stalls in the market and ran a restaurant at night. Their son, Rajeed, soon hardened his way to contend with the other occupants of the Gorbals. He was equally as hard, well-dressed and well-educated, but lived with the need for notoriety, caused by constant racist rants toward his family. Personally, I never mocked him because of his background, I grew up with a father that had no arm and learned that mocking someone because they were different was neither hard or necessary.

Our previous fourteen fights, one every month, left the record at seven-all. When we had our first fight we were mere boys that liked the thought of being hard men, but by the fifteenth fight, we were toughened young men. We grew into an early adulthood together and it may sound strange but on some level, we respected each other because we never gave up.

Our fights were held inside a lorry storage-yard disguised behind a tall wall and rolling gate. Already beaten that night, the option of not turning up didn't enter my mind.

Chapter 20

The Turban:

That evening would be the final bout between us, and the usual pre-fight tingles that became as normal as a heartbeat, ran through my veins. Once the first exchange took place, the nerves vanished and our true nature of surviving would unfold.

These fights attracted attention: their infamy was legendary in the community, often pulling in massive crowds and even the filth attended once or twice. We decided this was the last, the victor gaining the final word and crown of the toughest man in the area. Word also spread to the Godfather of Glasgow, Arthur Thompson, who attended that night along with his godson, Sam Bryson, who was documented as an unlicensed boxer and worked for Thompson. It wasn't rare that men from the area were scouted and taken into the world of unlicensed boxing. The routes out of the Gorbals were short and limited: boxing or football were two tracks that filled people with hope. The other was through a maze of criminal activity that held a risk of death or prison time.

Daunting floodlights beamed down on the lorry depot and I could see The Turban remove his thin shirt and undo his turban. He stood with his fellow ethnic crowd, only eight of them, compared to the rest who were all of local descent. I did the usual, tucked my trousers into my socks and took my shirt off. I didn't have many supporters or friends, that's how I choose to be. The only person you can rely on in life is yourself.

The usual ten pounds was held by a stranger awaiting the winner, but neither of us cared about the money - it was the legacy we would leave behind, well, at least that's what I wanted.

The night was warm and the atmosphere tense with a dull clatter of voices in a circle of anticipation.

The Godfather looked on. He wasn't a stranger to a scrap or two; neither was his twenty-nine year-old godson, Sam Bryson.

The rules of the fight were three-minute rounds, if you were knocked down you had to get up before the round ended. The scary thing about this environment was any tool you carried on your body could be used, but me and The Turban shared a mutual respect, well, I thought we did, up until that night. It was time, only the toughest could win.

The Turban had dark determined eyes, a slinky frame and a rapid punch. Hiding my inner pain from my father's beating, I wasn't in the best shape to be scrapping. We shared almost identical frames, but my shoulders were wider and The Turban modelled a turtleneck.

There was no hooter of bell. We walked in a circle, eyeballing each other, wondering who would be victorious. We squared up in the shadowy light for the first blows. I felt tense, already in pain and tried to loosen up. Our clumsy footwork finally saw us come to blows as The Turban landed a sharp punch to my face, sent from his rear shoulder, then awkwardly, he tripped over the tangle of our feet. Instantly enraged, I capitalised on his half-slumped body, angling a left knuckle down onto his chin. Both of us scuppered away from each other and re-grouped. The scallywags in the crowd roared with satisfaction. A couple cagey minutes of tit-for-tat exchanges led to the end of the round. I chose to stand and wait on the spot, The Turban returning to his clique for a drink. I stood and waited to show I wasn't fazed and pretended I held no fear, but the truth is for any fighter, fear was what kept you alive.

We both knew a lot about the other's skills. The Turban knew I was ruthless, aggressive and hated life. I knew my opponent was determined, burned for respect and had great speed of hands. Raw power was possessed by both of us and each earned the reasons for our notoriety in the Gorbals.

Wrestling in a clinch at the start of the second round, I opened my jaw and bit into his shoulder, spat the chunk of flesh out at his feet, head butted him and stood back. I gloated with a confident smirk while gore layered my mouth line. He howled, padded his wound and noticed the chunk of skin on the murky ground. The Turban wasn't shocked, just disgusted someone could do that. The sight of his wound outraged him, as his eyes flashed with fury and awakened his dark side. Riveting me with a hostile spit of disgust, he pounced furiously on me, throwing his unschooled arms in a flood of aggression, pinpointing my badly pained stomach and after wincing from a blow, still livid, he punished my wound until I met the hard ground.

I suppose I had that coming. Leaving me wounded on the ground without inflicting more pain was a mistake. Momentarily I struggled for breath and managed to stand before the welcome shout of 'Time.'

One thing I specialised in was the ability to absorb pain. I'd been consuming it from an early age and it became a part of my life.

The Turban knew only too well I was a hard motherfucker, prepared for whatever came my way. His clan looked nervous and didn't understand their man's need for this crown.

113

The shout for the third round brought a roar from the crowd, equalling that given to the men in green and white walking onto Parkhead, Celtic's football ground. I operated alone, between rounds, strode back and forth, hands staying clenched. That way would become legendary in the stories told about me. The round saw knuckles clatter off jaws, with both of us hitting the deck. The Indian warrior was strong and stubborn. Near the end of the round, a wild uppercut hit the butt of my chin and crashed me to the deck.

Rising sheepishly, uttering the words, "No' good enough ma Indian friend, try again." I reached my full height, long limbs by my sides, then The Turban slipped his hand from his pocket and a heavy clump smashed my face and my world went black.

A couple of minutes passed before I woke, vision blurred and confused. The Turban was placing his shirt back on. At first, I figured I was dreaming, having no idea why I lay on the manky ground, chin feeling feeble and body powerless. Mr Thompson went past my blurred sight in slow motion, heading towards The Turban. He demanded the knuckle-duster from his pocket.

He reluctantly handed it over, thinking the Godfather intended using it on him. He spoke quietly and calmly with his back to my disorientated body. Rising to my feet without aid, I saw The Turban glance at me and remove his shirt. Blood from his shoulder running down his body and his remorseful face showed he wasn't proud of his actions.

The Godfather ambled across the middle of the stage. "I've convinced The Turban tae continue." Punch drunk, my feet were unsteady and I was head weary, "Tak' five minutes to yerself."

"What? Why?" I didn't understand the reasoning behind it. The Godfather was feared more than any in the country; back in the day, even the Kray twins were scared of the man. He had seen the unfair use of the knuckle-duster and wanted me to show my worth.

"Mr Rhodes, it wis an unfair use o' the rules."

Now it clicked - the duster! "Fuckin' sneaky cunt!"

Arthur saw the rage flow into my eyes like a cascading waterfall. The surrounding bodies were mute during the events, no one dared talk in argument with the most notorious gangster in the land.

"Aye, now it's up to you." After sending a wink my way, he returned to his godson, Sam Bryson, "A few minutes 'en we'll start again," Thomson uttered from the crowd.

The Turban was annoyed; the Godfather gave him no choice.

Now I wanted the fuck killed, buried in the Gorbals cemetery. The Turban had dug his own grave. I took the time for my senses to return before I heard The Godfather shout

"Alright, get on wi' it an' keep it clean!"

The Turban walked out, looking confident to finish the duel. Enraged, I was about to pile-drive him back to India. There was no clumsy footwork; toe to toe, we scrapped like wild cats. The Turban retreated with faltering steps - the pressure broke him down and my vicious nature took him apart, mentally and physically. I had no mercy. Clinching together while he locked me in a bear hug, I sank rapid, un-controllable head-butts into The Turban's face.

Before he knew it, punches that he was blinded to, sent him falling, where I continued to clatter my knuckles across his wounded face leaving it in a mask of blood, sending him to hospital and eventually his family back in India.

Chapter 21

Enforcer:

The Godfather saw my potential, culminating in me leaving home and being set up in one of his flats on Baker Street, near the centre of Glasgow, a far cry from the Gorbals and a welcome change in my life.

I started as an errand boy and driver before soon becoming Arthur's debt collector, having to learn a new way of being an uncharitable character. Some of his clients laughed and spat in disgust at a young lad picking up their dues. I struggled to gain their respect but earned it from my infamous savage ways of squeezing cash from the unwilling and greedy. It became a speciality for me and that impressed Arthur.

I settled in well to my one-bedroomed flat, and took to boxing at a local gym to fill my time.

Arthur was a man I gelled with, both of us had a cold-hearted demeanour and a nasty streak. Sam Bryson was a man I didn't get on with, disagreeing and arguing at every opportunity. We simply never saw eye to eye. We would all hang out together and from time to time, I needed help with the collections, but since we were both vying to be the Godfather's understudy, Sam was jealous of our relationship.

Sam was your typical eighties hard man, spread wide like a gorilla and didn't take any nonsense. Had a ball-ended nose that had seen many blows and a thick, chiselled jaw. He took his training seriously, emulating men like Lenny Maclean and Roy Shaw, wished his name to be mentioned in the same sentence and by what I'd seen of him, he wasn't far away from that dream. The coming together of our fists was a foregone conclusion: it was just a matter of time.

I made things difficult for myself, falling in love with his girlfriend, Nancy Fowler. A devil of a woman, the kind that would have you smitten by her flawless looks and shapely body, who loved a bad boy. She was the only women in my life that made my eyes follow her across the room, like she put me under an intoxicating spell, but she had that effect on every man. What made her alarmingly dangerous was her addiction to attention from lusting males and she played them for whatever she could get. On top of her beauty, I took an extra shine to her because she was with Sam and I became determined to have her, it was that simple. I didn't like the stocky prick anyway. Nancy had a sixties look about her, her carrot hair softy curled and hung long, with big eyelashes that fluttered when she wanted something. Her short skirts and tops she wore to push her ample breasts together drove me crazy. She had that 'je ne sais quoi' you couldn't pinpoint about a woman, a desire, a lust you couldn't control, and she knew it.

"Pass the wine would you?" I asked while both of us lay naked on a hotel bed after we had finished shagging like animals for forty minutes.

"Pour ma one as well babe," she insisted. Nancy was always one who revelled in a bad boy. She must have been one of those girls that had daddy issues. My street cred had taken a goliath rise since I started working with the most feared man in the business.

"Davie, I need ti get away fae Sam," she spoke quietly, locking eyes with me while scratching her nails ever so lightly across my chest.

I was smitten at the time, there was no doubt. She brought out a good side in me that was normally hidden.

"Aye, an' what do you want me to do about it?" I ran my eyes up her perfectly shaped body and sweet

118

rounded breasts, ending in her eyes like a love-sick puppy. The only real feeling of love and happiness I would experience in life was with her. I enjoyed deceiving Sam, like a hobby, mocking him behind his back, but I felt for her all the same.

"Don't know. That's up ti you," she said, while I ran my hard-skinned fingers through her carrot hair and looked into her chestnut eyes, not questioning that what I was doing was wrong. I knew it was.

There wasn't an ounce of respect between me and Sam.

"Well, why don't we carry on wi' what we were doin' an' speak about it later?"

I opened her legs, felt her wetness, pulling back her hair as she groaned with pleasure; she enjoyed pain in the bedroom. We rutted like rabbits and I forgot about her question.

I was sly with the affair. Sam didn't suspect a thing during the six months Nancy and I were having steamy sex sessions. Often in her car, sometimes in Sam's own bed. No one suspected a thing. We kept the dirty secret to ourselves.

At the age of eighteen, I had grown tall, six-foot four, becoming bigger than anyone in my family and fit as a fiddle with the boxing. With my savage ways and brutal street smarts, I was a formidable force. The only man I respected was The Godfather and he took to me and my no-nonsense attitude, regarding me as his apprentice enforcer.

By 1980, I had won a fearsome rep from my intimidating and irate methods. I never did come into contact with my father again, nor with any of my family. It wasn't a regret; I always knew I was the black sheep. I was just glad I wasn't there anymore and God help his soul if I ever bump into him again.

I realised that if news of this seedy affair broke, there would be the chance I'd have to do away with Bryson and maybe even the Godfather. I was that badly stunned with love for Nancy, I was almost prepared to do that.

After a day of debt collecting, working through the diary, I looked forward to getting home to the flat for a meeting with her. The flat belonged to Arthur, one of many in the city. She had told me Sam was out of town, away for a prize fight in London with Arthur. The night would be ours without worry.

As I trudged wearily up the stairs from street level, I was surprised to find the front door of the flat ajar. Entering the sitting room, I saw Nancy tied naked to a dining room chair in front of the open window.

"Mmmh mmh!" Nancy mumbled through the shirt tied round her mouth. She was bound to the chair, struggling to break loose.

"What the fuck, Nancy!"

A clink of a metal object struck the back of my head and should have knocked me out. I turned to see Sam holding a baseball bat in the style of a New York Yankee player, preparing to hit a home run.

"You didnae expect 'at, did ye' cunt?" He wasted no time slamming the bat across my knees, swiping my legs from under me.

"Fuckin' cunt!" he growled, filling his mouth with spit, before spitting in my face as I knelt in front of him.

Throwing the bat to the side, he pulled a Beretta from a gun holster inside his blazer. Spitting with rage, his skin turning red, his emotions heightened, his chest puffed in and out hard, prepared to do the unlawful. The barrel of the gun indented my forehead, with every intention for the bullet to burst open my brains.

"Took you lang enough pal," I said, trying to stay cool in the final moments of my life.

120

"Aye, Nancy here," he cocked his head in Nancy's direction, sitting in apprehension of the inevitable, "Is up the duff, you cunt, and it's no mine cos I canna ha'e kids pal."

"What!" Nancy had played me and used me to give her a child, or maybe it was her way of an offering to get Sam out the way. I was disgusted.

"Noooo!" Kicking and screaming, her eyes popping out her sockets, bound to the seat, I think she loved me as much as I loved her.

"Well I'm no' goin' to waste any more time, ye're calendar material PAL!"

Click. Misfire. The gun was unshackled from his hand. I wasn't firearm savvy, couldn't locate the safety and didn't have time to look.

Sam clocked me on the jaw with a thundering hook, his trademark. The gun flew out of my hand, over the sofa and landed in front of the fireplace. It was now a race to grab the firearm.

I leapt to my feet and returned with my own blow onto his chin, but it had little effect. We moved across the floor, swinging and landing heavy. Sam took the first move towards the gun, lying beside the glass table in front of the fireplace. I saw where he was headed, caught up just in time; as he leaned down, I kicked him through the glass table then went ballistic, stamping on his head and body, breaking the wooden frame of the table in the process.

Sam was a man who didn't stay down long. He struggled, taking heart, grabbing hold of my legs, sweeping me off the floor. We couldn't see where the gun lay any more. Both of us scrambled to our knees, shards of glass wedging into our skin while exchanging blows. We ducked and wove, grounded on our knees. My longer arms gave me an advantage and made Sam look stupid as I swerved away from his punches and made him miss.

In a moment of clarity, I picked up the iron poker from the fireplace and ruthlessly plunged it into Sam's eye, yanking it back, snapping the eye muscles as they hung from his socket. He howled, grasping his wound with his palm as the eye and ropey muscles slithered and hung between his fingers. He dropped to the ground and started wildly rolling around in the broken glass. His howling continued as he rose to his feet, but his cry had to stop; he was making too much noise and that would attract attention. I picked up the iron coal shovel and violently swung at his head, rendering him unconscious. I was out of breath and relieved.

I stared down on my beloved Nancy, into her saddened, watery eyes, filled with pity. I released her gag.

"Davie, get ma out of here!"

The empty stare that met her gaze frightened her even more. She thought her knight in shining armour would whisk her out of the flat. She was pregnant with my child; a child I could have nothing to do with.

"Davie, what you waitin' for? Untie ma!" her voice trembled with distress.

"I'm afraid I cana' do that Nancy." My voice was full of disappointment that she either lied or deceived me.

Nancy's mouth opened wide in desperation, "Don't do this, don't leave ma here!"

Unpredictable and having a murderous streak, Arthur was someone I didn't care to cross, having a violent list of clientele he could rely on, if needed.

"Nancy…I doubt we'll ever see each other again."

I picked the Beretta up, slid it into my waistband and collected a stash of cash from my safe.

"Noooo! Davie, wait! DAVIE!"

Just like that, my life in Glasgow was over, leaving my possessions, my love and my unborn child. That was the first time I'd cheated death…

Chapter 22

Torture:

Stitched up and out-thought by Jack, I had to give him credit, thinking I was getting away with the deceit but I was a fool really. I was so close to doing a vanishing act with Max but I'd gotten greedy, should've cut ties and left long before then.

Tied up and blindfolded, lying on a shiver-inducing concrete base, I could smell stale alcohol and hear Glaswegian accents. Sam Bryson held a streak of vengeance for twenty-five years and was about to get his revenge. I assumed I was in the Glasgow area, judging by the amount of time I had been tied up in the back of the van.

Glasgow was a place I hadn't visited since I fled my flat in a hurry. I guessed I'd been tied up for over twelve hours and left shivering on the cold ground. The tie wraps around my arms cut off the blood flow, legs pained with stiffness and my back strained with my hands strapped to my feet. I accepted my death was forthcoming and an agonising one at that. I figured it was an end fitting for the life I lived. The wait was only extra punishment.

The door opened, two sets of footsteps approached, one set could be felt inches from my head. The cable-ties restraining my legs were cut and I stretched long in relief. A seat was dragged across the floor and I was moved onto it by the two men. The mouth gag slackened and blindfold removed.

Sam bore the look of satisfaction. His dormant glass eye held a glint of a smile.

"Mr Rhodes, comfortable?"

"It's no' the Hilton, but can't complain." The seat was specifically designed for torture, wrist-straps on the armrests and stocks to lock the feet in.

"I see you've no lost that sense of humour," he basked in the glory that his nemesis was helpless.

The second man was of feeble build, with a puny neck and a spine as hollow as a snake, modelling a green Butcher's apron. His head was mostly bald with puffed out wispy hair wafting into the air from the sides.

"How's the eye?" I asked, while Sam kept his sly glare and gloated at my misfortune.

"Ye're goin' to find out exactly how that feels Davie."

He leaned down and pulled a punched bladed knife from his ankle sheath, pushing the point into the hollow space in my windpipe.

The man behind broke the cable-ties on my wrists and strapped them down, leaving me with a feeling of uselessness. Sam spun around my body, feeling my skin tear and a trickle of blood from my neck. His runty accomplice fixed my feet inside the stocks. Not a struggle nor verbal expression was made: I'd accepted the consequences of my past. There was nothing I could do.

"My associate here had an itch to meet you," said Sam, "We call him The Eradicator. Well, I'd love to stay for a catch up, but I've waited lang enough and this kind of gory shit disturbs ma, so I guess I'll leave you two to get acquainted."

After a pat on the shoulder and his famous words, "Ye're calendar material PAL!" he made his way to the exit, "Oh, I almost forgot. Yer daughter," my head spun round to the door as Sam prepared to leave, "is a great lass."

He made Nancy have the child. I thought he would have done away with her, or made her have an abortion. I had a daughter!

The Eradicator opened an A3 size dirty brown wallet across two beer kegs, pulling out a small corroded medieval thumbscrew, a device used to crush fingers and toes, placed under two steel plates and tightened by a threaded handle, accompanied by larger ones in the wallet, designed for knees and elbows. The creepy figure turned with a cheesy grin on hearing my gulp of fear. I could see other objects of torture: a tongue-tearer, shaped like a large pair of scissors, that prises open the mouth and slowly slices the tongue at the same time; and something that terrified me the most, a hardwood handled draw gouge, with an angled razor, cut half circle that sparkled in the light, used to remove eyes.

That moment I regretted my past as The Eradicator prepared my death. Even a man of my calibre couldn't escape from this situation. The distress of imminent terror drove me to panic, twitching my body while bound to the stool. Looking for the way out as The Eradicator crept closer.

He struggled to place my fingers under the rusty plate of the thumbscrew and became frustrated. A bottle of spirits clunked into the back of my head, stopping my squirming. The turning of the squeaky threaded handle filled me with anguish, where I could feel the gritty surface of the plate and minute spikes mould into my fingers before the howling began…four fingers half crushed…it stopped.

Being struck by that kind of pain, my whole body wanted to burst and flap around, but as I had to sit in a pinned position, it made everything more painful.

"Now Mr Rhodes, how are we feeling?" My persecutor was calm, coming over all snide, speaking to me like a patient. The veins in my head felt as if they were going to burst and saliva ran down my chin. I tried to slow down my breathing. Teeth clenched together, sweat dripping from my brow, I needed released from this hell.

"You better hope you kill me, you creepy fuck!" My spit curled around in my mouth and I spat over his apron, venting my rage.

"That antagonistic attitude will get you nowhere. Just relax and go with it."

It was obvious he was experienced in these ways, sickly pleased in his work. He ignored the first thumbscrew, moving onto my right hand, trapping the tips of my fingers down and crushed them until they were on the verge of bursting open, like my other hand. The Eradicator loved watching them flatten like playdoh and hearing my groans of agony as I couldn't hold the pain in.

"Now you're in for a real treat, Mr Rhodes."

My eyes burned with a passion to break loose as the tips of my fingers on both my hands were mangled.

He opened the knee thumbscrew up like a pipe-gripper and slipped it under my thigh, then over the bone. As it tightened, an initial pop of bone caving, as if someone shot a bullet from point-blank range into my knee, made me scream at the top of my voice. My eyes turned cock-eyed as the room went into a haze and my head sagged back on the chair. As I passed out, another knee thumbscrew seized with the first crunch of bone. I was awakened by continuous thudding slaps on my face.

"Davie, wakey wakey! Can't have you taking a nap through this."

My fingers were burning and my knee bones cracked. There was no fight left.

"I'm just going to give them a good tighten now."

He focused on the left-hand thumbscrew and a slow turn of the threaded handle. The bone squashed like a juice-can and blood oozed out in a short trickle. Helplessly, I roared as I imagined Sam was listening in to my end. My body contracted when I hurled up, choked and then spluttered out vomit. The twisted man felt pride and held my spattered fingers under my eye, a collection of gory blood, broken fragments of bone and what looked like melted skin between the plates. He shook the contents onto the floor as my body shivered and twitched with shock, longing for it to end. I felt increasingly nauseous as he pulled a device from his half-circle chest pocket - a vicious looking pair of crocodile shears.

"I'll just get the rest of the fingers out of my way."

The shears made their way to the base of my index finger on my left hand as I hoped someone would awake me from this nightmare. I could feel the sharp teeth dig into the skin. The Eradicator took a grip with both hands and with one sharp movement, it crunched through as I heard the finger plop onto the floor. The same action repeated on the middle finger.

As I was cockeyed and struggled to focus, the drizzle of blood squirted out in front of my eye, landing on the beer kegs, a vision I only wanted to see from a TV screen.

"As soon as this first stage is over, we can move onto the next." He picked up the eye gouge, pointing it as if he was holding a pencil.

"Mr Bryson told me a little story about a fireplace poker, an eye for an eye, as they say," he smiled at his own humour.

My head slumped to the side, the sick on my chin whipped onto my jacket, my eyes blinked lazily, fatigued, terrified and infuriated with the ordeal. Giving my enemy an unrelenting stare, I demonstrated a last moment of bravery before the screaming continued.

"Get it fuckin' done, cunt!"

"Okay Mr Rhodes, as you wish."

Thoughts of my life flashed in my mind, my vicious father, the beatings I dished out to my wife and my son Joe, in Aberdeen, Max who I wanted to raise, but there was no chance of that now. Plus, the news that I had a daughter I'd never seen. I had to accept my end and now numb with pain, I think I did.

The Eradicator returned to my left hand, preparing to cut off my other two fingers with the shears.

A sudden gunshot took him by surprise. A rally of shots then fired and The Eradicator panicked. There was only one door in and out of the cellar, footsteps rattled down the stairs, the door burst open and a bullet straight into The Eradicator's brain killed him.

That was the third time I cheated death…

Chapter 23

Rescue:

The sight of Donny bursting through the door was more than welcome; he saved my life.

"Donny!" I whispered, barely able to speak.

Donny Casper walked into the cellar, splattered in dark red blood over his black Rogue Riders waistcoat. He had killed both Sam and his accomplice. I had no idea how he managed to locate me.

He immediately slackened the threads on the device around my knees. It brought a feeling of relief and a new horror of pain as I hovered around consciousness again.

Donny went into a panic and checked every pocket twice for his phone only to realise he'd pulled it out of the first pocket he looked. He called Fiddle, who was outside in the pickup, and instructed him to drive as close to the front door as he could get.

"Going to have to take you to the 'ozzy," Donny said, while releasing the thumbscrew on my hand.

Fiddle entered the room frantically and halted suddenly.

"We need to get him to the 'ozzy, quickly!" Donny shouted, trying to snap Fiddle from his trance.

They picked me up, their hands under my thighs, carried me awkwardly up the narrow staircase, dropping me a couple of times due to the awkwardness of the tight space and my weight being too much for Fiddle to handle. The movement of my legs swinging from my knees in mid-air made me wonder if I had legs. The bone grinded and scraped together as all I could feel was a terrible feebleness.

Once up the staircase and into an open hallway I managed to lift my head, and in a daze, I saw two bodies lying on the floor inside a decorated drinking lounge. Sam had a blaze of bullet holes bursting into his chest and an accomplice, whom I didn't recognise, mirrored the first image with a gun holstered in his hand.

The men slid me cumbersomely into the back of the pickup, parked in Milngavie, on the northern outskirts of Glasgow. Donny joined me in the rear of the truck while Fiddle took the wheel. My body was completely numb with the intensity of what had just happened, my brain was in shock as I trembled uncontrollably. I tried to stop it, but was powerless.

Donny looked worryingly at me, unscrewed a half full bottle of whisky found behind the passenger seat and held it out, but I couldn't grab it. Index and middle fingers missing on my left hand, tips squashed like Blu-tak on the other two fingers and right hand, a flow of weakness ran through me. I looked at him, blinking tiredly with my head dangling over my chest, as he realised I couldn't grab the bottle. He poured the whisky down my throat as if he was feeding a child with a bottle.

"Fuck me mate, they've done a proper job on you haven't they?" Donny stated the obvious, "We need to get him to the 'ozzy. FAST!" He kept repeating that.

"Glasgow Royal Infirmary is about seven miles away," Fiddle answered. I kept trying to speak and ended up opening and closing my mouth like a fish.

"What you waiting for Fiddle? Step on it!" Donny demanded, and Fiddle put his foot to the floor, speeding through the quiet streets of Milngavie.

"We can't take him to the 'ozzy, it's too dodgy. They'll report it to the scum," Fiddle said.

131

Fiddle was dead right about the hospital, we couldn't go. I needed to stay hidden.

"No hospitals," I demanded in an exhausted strangled voice, cupping my left hand in my right as the blood leaked down my jeans onto the leather upholstery. Donny picked up some clothing from behind the passenger seat and wrapped up my hands.

"Davie, look at the state of you. There's no choice."

"No' an option Donny."

Donny turned in his seat, accepting that I was right.

"Burn ma wounds, stop the blood, slice the rest of ma fingers open wi' a blade. I'll take my chances."

"Are you mad? You can't do that!" Donny was thinking. I slumped my head over the back of the headrest and lifted my left hand up to slow the flow of blood. Fiddle drove like a maniac and it wasn't helping the dire serious agony I was in. "I know where to go Fiddle, drive to the Geordie's. They owe me a favour." Donny knew the Geordie bikers owed him one and one of the members' sister was a nurse. Attending the A&E for help was something we couldn't do. It would no doubt get the police involved and we weren't exactly the most inconspicuous looking characters. Jack would find out what had occurred soon enough and he'd be searching for me to finish the job. It was a long drive, but the only option on the cards, and one I didn't mind taking.

"Donny, how'd you know?" My eyes were closed and head still slumped over the back seat.

"Danielle. She phoned Ringo around 1am and asked where you were. Me and Ringo put our heads together and figured it out." They had driven all night to get to Milngavie. The little drinking club I had been inside was owned by Bobby, who loaned it out to Sam for my demise.

132

On the meetings with Bobby in the past, I had always returned home straight after eleven, and Danielle had been expecting me home so we could go out.

"Bless her, give her ma thanks."

"Davie, she's missing!" My head raised up from the headrest.

"Max, where is he? Call him!" In the torment I was in, I had forgotten what could happen to Max. Jack was cold-blooded when it came to whipping the seed that tried to do him over. He wasn't going to let my boy off.

"Phone Danielle. Tell her to get Max out of town, now!"

"I'll call her again, but there's been no answer."

I heard the ringtone from the phone, "Put the phone to ma ear. "Danielle, it's Davie, what's goin' on? Is Max wi' you?" it took all my energy to muster up the words, and all I could hear for a few seconds was silence.

"Hello Mr Rhodes. I wasn't expecting to hear that voice of yours."

"Jack, if you do anythin' to ma boy, I'll rip yer life from you." My heavy eyes could hardly stay open and my speech slurred as if I was drunk.

"Your boy is going to be just fine. I'm looking into having him adopted again by a whole new big family."

"What have you done wi' Danielle?"

"Me, Danielle, and Max are just fine." I knew he had some kind of sick plan for Max but I couldn't do anything for him in my present condition. "You've gone quiet Davie. I can hear you're in a car. Where you headed?" Jack spoke as if nothing had happened.

"Jack! No' today, or in a week or a month, but I'll catch up wi' you and when I do, it'll be when you least expect it."

Chapter 24

Davie's Step Up:

The healing of my gruesome injuries took time, a horrific time at that, bound to a bedsit inside the Geordie Highwaymen's Club in case my whereabouts were exposed. The nurse who looked after me was thorough. As soon as she arrived she knocked me out with anaesthetic and attended to my hands first, then proceeded to pick out the broken bone fragments from the burst of skin that used to be a pair of knees. Normally, a brace or a knee-immobiliser would have been used to mould my knees back into place, but the only option was to mould a plaster, up to mid-thigh height and leave it on for eight weeks. That nurse attended to me every day, I relied on her and the bikers to help me in everything I had to do, shitting, bathing, and feeding. I felt frail, I was useless, physically and emotionally broken by the whole affair. The damage to my knees needed operating on and re-built, but I wasn't interested. Visiting a hospital, filling out forms and handing over ID would expose my position. My squashed fingers would forever be deformed, having permanent nerve and tendon damage. I had to learn how to live with my disfigurement. Making rollies was my physiotherapy. It was immensely frustrating, but I got on with it. What pushed me on was the dream I would re-unite with Jack one day and hopefully reconnect with Max. When Jack had said he was sending Max to a whole new family, I had no idea what he meant, and I worried for my son's future.

Immobilised for three months, confined to the inside of a disgusting bedsit and keeping company with the over-exuberant club members, pissed me off. Like a weak

134

toddler, I had to learn how to walk again, starting with crutches, building my strength until I could let them go after twelve weeks.

The injuries to my knees left me with a permanent limp on my left leg. During that time, I gained an addiction to strong painkillers and sank massive amounts of ale every day, becoming bitter with life. I felt lost and weak, not knowing what the future would entail and how would I make money? I had the unwelcome feeling that I was an idiot for sticking around longer than I should have. Some days I thought about my father: his life was ruined by losing his arm which affected his mental health and I could almost see his reflection stare me back when I gazed into the mirror. With my injuries, I too had to tackle a life tormented with constant pain and I became determined that I wasn't going to go down the road of being a bitter man; but to do that, I needed a focus, something to drive my thoughts away from the pain.

My planned retirement was on hold. I'd lost everything. The stash of over a hundred grand I'd acquired was left hidden in the flat and had probably re-entered Jack's pockets.

My job opportunities were limited, until Donny pulled up four months later on his fully customised, heavily blacked-out chopper motorbike, oozing more cool than the Batmobile. I was sitting outside on a swing seat accompanied by a couple of Geordies, holding an intense smelling skunk joint at the curve between my two fingers on my disfigured hand. Donny rolled up right beside the seat and removed his helmet, showing the sweat gathered under the base of his bandana. "Davie, good to see you up and around. You look like shit mate."

Gripping the inside of each other's forearms, we exchanged our customary shake of mutual respect. We were both big men, Donny a couple inches shorter, but wider and thicker in the chest than I was. The kind of guy who sat at home, downed tins, smoked weed and lifted weights.

My eyes were glazed red, caused more by my addiction than my stoned state.

"Aye, I know Donny. What's the news down the road?" Donny gave the two Geordies a tilt of the head to vacate the scene. Donny swiped the joint from my hand and sat beside me, hearing the swing chains creak with our combined load.

"News. Jack's losing his grip Davie, he's brought Eiffel down as a personal bodyguard."

I shifted my weight in Donny's direction, "that's good, he must think I'm plannin' a return."

"So, where's Casanova himself?" I referred to Ringo.

"Ringo, Jack beat the poor guy to an inch of his life and disowned him. After he got out the hospital, I moved him into Devil's. Jack and Ringo will never speak again."

It took a moment for me to realise that I had caused Ringo's beating and I felt sorry for him, but there was nothing I could do about it. In a way, I thought that might have been a blessing for Ringo, after all who would want a moaning tight bastard like Jack to answer to all the time?

"No retaliation from you?" I asked, knowing that Donny would have offered Ringo his hand.

"Ringo didn't want any. He just wanted all the hassle to be done and dusted." Donny changed the subject, "What's your plan then?" speaking from the bottom of his throat, inhaling a heavy drag of the joint.

"Fuckin' plan! I have none. I'm a cripple!" There was a massive slab of acceptance in me, that I'd never be the same again.

"I might have a plan."

He got my interest, "Aye? Go on 'en?"

Donny's speech quietened, as he nudged closer.

"Ireland."

"Ireland?" I queried.

"My supplier is short of men, needs a good hand."

I smiled, held up my ruined hands, wrinkled my forehead and leaned towards him and mouthed,

"Supplier of what?"

"Potatoes Davie!"

I didn't find it amusing, just gave him a serious glare.

"Guns Davie, pocket pistols to RPGs, Berettas to machine guns."

I paused, having a draw of the joint, thought to speak, stopped, thought more.

"I don't like guns pal." I had never liked firearms; I preferred to use my fists rather than guns, but that moral in life had landed me in my present predicament. Donny probably knew I was going to say that and had prepared an answer.

"All you have to do is arrange the exchanges and stock the goods." My face opened up, spreading my weight across the seat. "You can't stay here for the rest of your days. Once you're in Ireland, get set up somewhere. I'll give you a couple of grand, keep you sweet until you get paid."

"And who's ma employer?"

"C4 Millacky."

"Aye and I'm supposed to know who that is."

"He's IRA, the real IRA!".

"Is that where yer guns come from?" I wondered.

"It is. He's a man that can get me whatever firearm I ask for."

He removed sheets of A4 paper from the inside of his Rider's waistcoat and handed them over.

"I've spoken to him about you. He wants to meet, talk it over, and it's all on this paper, instructions and directions to an airstrip. He wants you to fly over, have a chat in person like."

Reading from the paper, 'Disguise yourself with the overalls I've provided to gain entrance into hanger B12. Inside, you will meet a man called Rankin. Follow his instructions and board the plane. You will receive another set of instructions on where to proceed once landed. Regards, safe flight'.

"This is a bit James Bond, is it no'?"

"He's on every wanted list in Europe. He's not exactly a man who can nip out for a Sunday lunch."

"He wants me to leave in the mornin'?"

Donny dropped the uniform and a couple of grand onto the seat, "You better get your shit sorted then. Come on, let's have a bevvy before you leave."

I limped into the club with Donny, slowing his walk.

"Where am I goin'? Belfast?"

"That kind of information doesn't come my way but I'll near guarantee, it won't be Belfast."

Inside the darkened club, we sat down at a round table where Donny guzzled a refreshing bottle of beer and I poured a pint of export from the can.

"What's happened to Max?" I asked.

"He got lifted. The scum snatched him from the flat the day after you vanished. Turned up with a riot squad and search warrant. Looks like you were under their radar. Max is in the young offenders now and Danielle, she's still not been seen."

138

"Young offenders!" I said, "Least he's no' on the street. That place will make a man of him."

When Jack had said Max would be introduced to a whole new family, he meant jail. He pulled some strings and had him arrested and Danielle, God knows what happened to her.

"Aye, I've spent plenty nights in the slammers. It's no picnic, a lonesome place where you have to live with one eye on your back and the other on your release date. I suppose it'll toughen the boy up," Donny agreed.

Chapter 25

Chopper Ride:

It was your typical British winter morning, frosty and bitterly cold. I travelled on the back of Donny's chopper without the safety of leathers. Donny was fully suited-up with The Rogue Riders biker waistcoat, thick leather trousers, high boots and a polished helmet with the Rogue Riders logo on the rear, wings of an eagle stretching from the sides of a chopper bike. The ten-mile journey north on a Sunday morning from Newcastle was a long and chilly one. My knees were feeling the brunt of the chill and I wore a pair of heavy gloves that felt distinctly weird. We pulled off the main road, along some bike-tracks, and idled the length of a corrugated fence till he stopped in the shade of a cream-sheeted hangar. I slid off the back of the bike, removing my helmet.

"How am I gettin' in this place?" I asked, as I lit a joint I had prepared before we left. I was never a big smoker of the stuff, but it distracted me from the pain, mentally and physically.

"Bolt-cutters."

There wasn't a soul around the hangar at the start of the incoming runway, miles from the traffic-control tower, hidden from view by the hangar. Donny took a pair of orange overalls from the compartment under the seat, throwing them at my chest to indicate I should put them on. While I did so, he cut a straight line in the fence with the shears, all the way to his head height. Donny untied his bandana, wiping the sweat from his forehead, "You keep well friend."

"Aye, and yerself, brother."

I was greatly in his debt for what he had done for me, saving my life from The Eradicator and getting me on this plane. We held nothing but earned respect for each other, shared a loyalty that most people couldn't understand. I owed him my life and was prepared to repay the favour whenever needed.

"Make sure you keep in touch." Donny knew keeping communication lines open was unrealistic. The world I was about to enter was a dark and lonely place, working with men who lived for power and money.

"Aye, I might call now and again. You'll keep an eye out for ma boy, will you?" Donny would be the only person I could rely on, to keep a watchful eye over Max once I jumped on that plane.

"Not a problem Davie. I'll keep a look out for him once he's out the nick."

It was a humbling feeling, knowing someone would watch over my son; I knew Donny, a man of his word, would.

Saying our final farewells, we held each other's forearms, both squeezing a little extra before a brotherly pat on the back.

"Keep it lit boy," I said, and Donny replied with a departing smirk.

I strolled across the white-tipped frosty grass towards the shed with a hobbling swagger, hearing the roar from the bike's exhaust, taking a final glance around, happy I would be out of Jack's reach and elated I still had something to live for.

Inside the hangar, men were working, wearing orange overalls, under a single small engine, turbo-prop cargo plane. Two were working on the engine and another was polishing the logo on the plane. A picture of a woman in a bikini sitting on a beach recliner, sipping a cocktail, her signature indecipherable except for the initial 'L' written underneath. The polisher glanced to the door as it shut with a thud. Dropping his wrench, a mechanic walked over.

"Davie?"

"Aye, are you Rankin?"

"No, he's on his way and your ride will be ready in an hour or so. Just finishing up some maintenance."

"You've got half the plane stripped over 'ere." Flying was something that didn't tickle my fancy. Anything I couldn't control gave me uncertainty.

"It'll be ready, trust me."

I glanced over his shoulder, examining the plane again.

"Aye, I'll take yer word on it."

"Help yourself to coffee, pot's in the office."

I waited in that dingy office for over an hour, a rollie constantly burning in the melting polystyrene cup I used as an ashtray. As I leaned back in the office recliner with my feet resting on an open drawer, rocking, a nagging feeling came to mind and the rocking stopped.

What if this was a setup? Jack could be behind this?

I trusted Donny; surely he wouldn't stab me in the back? It was suspiciously random, Donny showing up out of the blue, without any contact in four months, and made this happen so quickly. My heightened state of paranoia was caused by three months of smoking mind-blowing skunk and a cocktail of painkillers.

I heard steps approaching the door. My brows knitted together, now I was nervous as to who was about to walk through. I switched my gaze across the office for a weapon of some kind. The door opened, my feet hit the floor, my back straightened and my eyes were on the alert.

"Mr Rhodes I presume?"

Dressed untidily in loose combat trousers, the end of his belt flapping out, Top Gun shades and a striped shirt, half tucked in, the visitor entered. A thick well spoken Belfast accent and the 'H' in Rhodes grabbing my name with the back of his throat.

I gave him my usual one-word response, "Aye," waiting for a crew of heavies or maybe a gun to appear from behind his back.

"Rankin." He introduced himself, lifting his hand, looking for it to be met by mine but I didn't comply.

"Mr Millacky sent me, I'll be your pilot today."

My paranoia faded enough to accept the handshake and get rid of his floating hand, "Where we goin'?" I asked.

"Never mind that just now. I have a passport for you." He tilted down to his left side, dipping his hand into his side pocket at knee level and handed over a Republic of Ireland passport.

Opening it, I read my new fixed abode.

"Danny O'Brien? That's very original."

"It's just a name Mr Rhodes, in case we get a custom check on the other side."

"And where's the other side?"

"County Fermanagh to the west. Once the plane's ready, we'll be on our way."

I dipped into my supply of painkillers, taking a mouthful along with a gulp of the strong coffee.

"Millacky, will he be there?"

"I'll explain everything on the plane Mr Rhodes."

To me, a pilot should have been dressed smartly, in a uniform with stripes on the ends of his sleeves and a fancy hat; this sluggish guy looked as if he had just crawled out of his scratcher.

"My job is to get you to an air strip at St Angelo, just outside Enniskillen, where you'll be escorted to Millacky's position."

Chapter 26

C4 Millacky:

Everything was done professionally by Millacky. The pilot, Rankin, flew me over to St Angelo in the west of Northern Ireland. After that, a suited IRA member drove me east to a safe house in the rural area of Carnagh, in south County Armagh, near the border with the Republic of Ireland. An area referred to as bandit country, a republic stronghold and a convenient place where a quick getaway to Southern Ireland could be made.

The destination was a small vintage picturesque bungalow cottage, on a sparse bit of land in the middle of nowhere. In the drive was a five-door Volvo estate car. The driver instructed me to enter the house while he stood guard outside.

I heard dull voices from a room, having a relaxed conversation, and entering two men sat comfortably at a long rectangular hardwood table, a window looking out to the rear of the house showing an ancient wooden shed with the door ajar revealing a car, covered by a tarpaulin.

At the head of the table facing me, the man introduced himself, "Hello Mr Rhodes. I'm Millacky, this is The General." His hand opened, offering me a seat adjacent.

Millacky had a striking, lean presence. Balding alabaster hair at the sides, leaving a fringe falling down the middle of his head in a blunt point. I was drawn to the indented square wound on the slope of his forehead that suggested he'd been hit by something big.

"Have a seat." He gestured me to sit opposite and I accepted, sliding back the bulky built chair as it screeched across the wooden floorboards.

The General held a stare almost like he felt awkward. His build was thick set and his skin heavily blotched, looking as if he had spent his teenage years picking his spots and bursting them with a gritty razor, but I expected it was some kind of explosion wound.

"Would you like a drink Mr Rhodes? You must be parched after that flight," Millacky asked.

"Aye, wouldn't mind a wet of the lips."

Millacky looked at The General as he swivelled in his seat, taking a can of export from an outdated waist-high cupboard behind him, then planted it down in front of me. Then I knew they had done their homework. It was no coincidence that my favourite tipple landed on the table. I opened the tin, taking a few gulps without pausing for air. I was agitated and nervous about the occasion, exchanging words with the main men of the IRA.

"I can see you have had a little trouble recently, Mr Rhodes." Millacky referred to my limp and my deformed fingers.

"Aye, a little trouble from ma past bitin' me in the ass. And call me Davie." I didn't care to be called 'Mr' or 'Sir' or any of that nonsense. It sounded to me as if someone was trying to butter you up, being so formal.

"Ok Davie. Donny told me you had a brush with death, but I'm not concerned about your past troubles. What does concern me is if you can do a job for us, a very high-risk job, with a lot of cash benefits."

Millacky was notably, proper spoken in his casually spoken voice with hands hidden under the table and head movement at a minimum.

"Carry on," I encouraged him.

Millacky rose from his seat, stepping towards the window, hands slid into his flash slate coloured pressed trouser pockets.

145

"I need a gunrunner Davie."

That I knew. I just had to hear him say it. He turned from the window, fixing me with a sombre look.

The General had his elbows on the table, fingers locked together, continually staring, causing me to feel he was analysing my behaviour and reactions.

"I've recently lost a few good men and have a lack of staff, so to speak. I need someone I can rely on, someone to run my shipments and work to my demands, a gunrunner that's capable of following procedure. I've heard of your predicament with your past and Donny is someone whose opinion goes a long way with me. He says you're the man for me."

I mulled it over. What options did I have? None, was the answer. This arrangement would go a long way to re-stocking my retirement fund. Returning to life in England or Scotland wasn't an option. I needed to stay hidden from Jack so I could surprise him one day and living in this underworld could keep me concealed.

"What's my cut?" I asked straight up. There Millacky turned to The General to step in.

"Your cut will be high, very high," his voice a deep drawl, but he spoke in what was known as received pronunciation, so he wasn't a hard man to understand. I could tell he was a cold character, giving off an aura of violence. Coming across as a gentleman but a gentleman he wasn't. He looked ten years older than Millacky, who still stood casually in front of the window. "Your life will change. You won't be able to enter bars and down ale as you do," The General continued, "You'll have to move around a lot. Contact will be rare between jobs and it'll come directly from Millacky or myself.

This sounded like a solid move in the right direction. I had a habit of falling on my feet over the years and I'd done it again. I did have a small problem though, well, a major one in this trade. I turned from The General back to Millacky.

"I have to say, I hae little to no experience wi' firearms."

I couldn't help looking at the side of his hairline, the indented wound sunk under the top level of his skin. "You may not have much knowledge, but the time I spend with you will give you the knowledge you require in this trade. I'll go over past operations, the way we conduct ourselves, and the people you can work with." He stepped back over to his seat and before sitting down he complimented me, "What you do have Davie is a hardness, and that's rare in today's world."

I hadn't twitched from my position in the high-backed chair, letting the scheme construct in my head. "Your knowledge will grow in time. What's more important is looking after the stock and organising the drops," The General interrupted.

I turned back my look to Millacky who was so relaxed, so smooth, it was obvious he'd been making speeches similar to this for years. I waited until he had finished before asking him the question I needed answering.

"Tell me?" I stood up over the table and slipped my hand inside my jeans pocket, making The General flinch, and his hand slid under his blazer to the handle of his gun. Millacky didn't fluster. All I was doing was grabbing my baccy tin.

"General!" Millacky's tone was all that was needed to tell The General to stand down, "Go on Davie, you were about to say something."

I started to make a rollie. It looked awkward to an outsider. Millacky watched closely, admiring my patience with my missing digits and the way I'd adjusted.

"Aye, what do you lot need a man like me for? Surely you ha'e someone else who could fill this position?"

What I meant by that was I was still in heavy recovery from The Eradicator's punishment. I had little knowledge of firearms and even though my father was Irish, I didn't consider myself to be, and that was my biggest wonder.

"We have plans, Mr Rhodes. We are an underground army and have been quiet for too long. An operation we are planning is using up all of our committed members to the cause from different cells throughout both Northern and Southern Ireland. The political war and Sinn Fein doesn't hold any worth with us. Like I said, we have a lack of men. You're a man that won't be recognised, a man that we can utilise and establish as our gunrunner. If you're able to stay off the grid, you'll be an invaluable asset. Do you think that's you, Davie, or are we wasting our time?"

I tilted my head to the side, lighting my rollie.

"Aye, I think you've found yer man."

Part 2

Inside The IRA

Chapter 27

Fresh Apprenticeship:

The following weeks, a jam-packed programme on the ways of their operation filled my time. Me and Millacky were bound indoors, day and night, having one of his henchmen make deliveries of food and essentials. With there only being one bed, I initially slept on the floor. Not agreeing with me, I chose to sleep inside the 1979 showroom-kept red Ford Cortina in the garage. Here was me at the beginning of a gunrunning career and having to resort to sleeping inside a car. Hardly exotic! I continued my heavy daily intake of painkillers that became a necessity, mixed with Millacky's Irish whiskey at the end of every day, a ritual we followed. Millacky got drunk quite easily, slurred and repeated his words with bursts of predatory aggression towards the British government. His intolerance to hold his ale surprised me somewhat, being Irish, but I suppose that's a cliche. He was gratified to tell stories from the past and his family history. It was all insight for me to assess what kind of man I was working for and what kind of criminal world I was entering.

In 1914, his grandfather had refused to enlist in the First World War, as had many other Irish men. That led to the birth of the original IRA. In 1919, Sinn Fein formed a breakaway government called Dáil Éireann and declared independence from Britain. Later, on the same day, two members of the armed police force of

Ireland were shot dead and the war of independence began. Millacky's grandfather, who carried the same name, Conner Millacky, was one of the men who carried out the killing, which gave birth to the family line of dedication to a united Ireland. One of the primary objectives for the IRA in the rest of that year was capturing weapons and freeing men who had been imprisoned for failure to comply with London's request to enlist. It was enough that Millacky's grandfather was a passionate Catholic Irish man, but extra fuel was poured over his buoyant heart, ignited after his wife's murder by a division of special reserves called Auxies, who were renowned for their savagery and random attacks on civilians. Conner was to oversee the gathering of weapons and gained the title, The Quartermaster.

I always thought the spat between Republicans and Protestants was a religious one, like that in Glasgow's Gorbals, but in truth, it started because men stood up for themselves. Being controlled by another island and having them tell you how to live did not hold well. Strange really, the First World War ended in 1918 and another war started in 1919.

Millacky grew up in Southern Ireland, as he still called it, and acted as a precious marksman for the PIRA (Provisional Irish Republican Army) in Belfast and around Northern Ireland, followed orders with a capacity to be pinpoint accurate and ruthless. He counted his total kills to be sixty-two men.

The Real IRA was formed in 1997 after breaking from the PIRA, and consisted of members opposed to the Northern Ireland peace process. Millacky went straight to the top of the command chain and assumed position at the top table. Ever since, he had been putting calculated plans in place for a rebellion and turned to gunrunning to fund his operations.

At the top of the Real IRA table sat seven men including Millacky and The General. The other five were elusive and I would never meet them. Stationed around the globe, two were notably in America but the other three, I would never find out where they were.

Millacky had The General as his right-hand man, who wasn't needed in my weeks of training, and was left to carry out other tasks. Before he left, I heard them talk secretly about the mission in planning and how everything was piecing together nicely; that's all the details I could ascertain at that point.

Once again, I'd landed on my feet, so to speak, and stepped up the ladder into a whole new world. Looking back over that time spent in-house probably turned me into the perfectionist I was to become. It was a lot to take in, but the figures talked about were beyond anything I'd made in the past in any criminal organisation. Millacky sold guns all over the world. He could buy from a corner shop in Ecuador and sell to an Eskimo in Mongolia, with a list of dependable men he counted on for certain items.

His pilot Rankin, was an information asset, and could pretty much create a new life and identity in a matter of a day. That would be his role in my life over the next years, as and when I needed. He could forge passports with fixed addresses that would link to a searched database, do background checks on any individual, give you a family, a National Insurance number, a dentist's file, a 9-5 job, a station wagon or even a pet parrot. The man was a genius and Millacky spoke of him in an esteemed manner. I was about to learn he was unquestionably Millacky's biggest asset.

The General was the man who dealt with the logistics part of their operation. Bank transfers and money laundering were his expertise. Offshore shell-accounts dotted all over the world, with money constantly being transferred between them to create an impossible trail to follow.

Safe houses for his men to meet were dished out from a contact in an estate agents, a scrapyard dealer could issue cars meant for crushing; there was even a contact for cheap cigarettes and alcohol.

Whatever he needed, he could get through the maze of loyal men at his disposal.

He instructed, after my time in the house was over, we would separate and go our own ways. Contact with each other would be minimal and by mobile phone, demanding that I memorised one specific number, insisting he could be contacted in any situation on that number. He handed me ten burners and explained I had to mix communication between a few of them and every now and again, destroy the phone and sim card.

It was up to me to find my own accommodation and transport; we couldn't be seen together in public. He felt the need to keep my appointment as his gunrunner quiet from the head table of the Real IRA, probably because as I was an outsider, it would be frowned upon. The reasoning for appointing a person like me to this position was the fact the authorities, who tracked Millacky, wouldn't have an inkling as to who I was, giving me free reign in the beginning. I wished it had stayed that way. Through the coming years, it was to change drastically.

Millacky only dealt with certain clientele. Working with any Protestants or members of the government, British or Irish, was an instant bullet in the head, he explained. At the end of the final week, we sat down at the table and shared a whisky before we went our separate ways.

"Your first task will be to meet me at this address." He slid a piece of paper over the table with coordinates to the outskirts of a place in County Donegal, in the north west of the Republic of Ireland. "I'll meet you there on Friday morning, nine sharp." Millacky wasn't a man to be late. I caught on to that quickly through his meticulously run operation.

"What's there?" I asked.

"That, you will find out next week Davie." Millacky stood from his chair and finished his drink, "Davie, do you think I am a man that takes liberties?"

I took a big gulp from my glass, "No' at all."

"Good, then you'll have figured out that I'll know where you are every minute of every day," I gave him a vacant stare back. He was indicating I'd be watched, understandable, considering what he was trusting me with. Opening the drawer of the cabinet, he slapped a thick envelope on the table.

"I know you're a man that's ruled by the coin Davie. There's a substantial amount of money, and it's money for the time you have given me this past week."

I opened the flap and saw the envelope held around five grand in euros. A little incentive for me to do a good job.

"That is only the base of a very large iceberg. If you do a good job for us, that pile will only increase. I'll see you next week, don't be late."

With that blunt statement, he exited the cottage. I knew after spending time in his company there would be no easy exit from this job, but it was my last chance to make some serious siller. Build that retirement fund I failed at last time. I only had to get out on top and use the rewards to set me up in a remote location where I could live a peaceful life. That's what I thought back then, but the hook of addiction this job was to cause would be frighteningly thrilling.

There was something missing in my life though – Max. I yearned to see him, but knew there would be a day when we'd be re-united. When I left Aberdeen and Joe, in time my conscience was able to settle and Max was the reason for that, but this time, it felt different. Even though I changed my mind to Max growing up like a hardened man like myself, I still had a chance to make a real man out of my blood, but that chance was gone now and he was about to walk his own path.

Chapter 28

Hidden Den:

 A week later, as scheduled, I made my way to the coordinates in a rusted Vauxhall Cavalier, bought for £500 through an advertisement in a paper. I also bought a GPS navigator to locate the spot, another £100 down. I spent the week in a well-maintained bed and breakfast in Creeslough, very close to my meeting point, visiting the bookies every day, while fluctuating between boozers. It was the only thing I could think of to fill the spare time I had. I found the Irish people humble and content, who liked a drink, a yap and some good craic. I had nothing against anyone in the debate for a united Ireland. I didn't choose sides; I was my own being.

 The rest of my lonesome time was spent reflecting on what kind of life Max was leading inside the Young Offenders' Institution and the path I was now walking down. Being involved in the most potent criminal organisation in the land was an addictive rush. It reminded me of how life felt working for the Godfather as a blooming teenager. Knowing that I was under Millacky's rule was an ego boost; after all, he was top of MI5's wanted list. I'd never held any abhorrence for the violent men I'd worked under in the past - I think that's why I had fucked up so much. The fear was never alive with the likes of Jack or The Godfather, but any minute spent in Millacky's company sent shivers throughout my body. The same feeling my father dug into me after he erupted. Even the shaking tremor that The Eradicator put me in didn't come close to the unrelenting vibe of savageness that leaked from Millacky like a foul-smelling gas. I don't think the everyday human could sense that, but the characters I'd mingled with over time gave me a gift in judging people's darker sides.

I followed a tourist trail, marked the Red Line, around Ards Forest Park, where plenty of folks were out catching the morning air. Having had to cut off-line and go walkabout through bogs, around bulking oak trees, high grass and hilly ground, I sweated heavily as I came to an intimidating vertical rock face and my checkpoint. I knew it was a remote part of the forest. The area was kind of humble, a getaway where people could gather their thoughts but a hassle to find. I took a pew on a boulder, looking onto a flattened piece of ground, covered over with a cluster of broken branches and a massive chunk of a fallen tree filling the space.

Millacky approached right before 9 am, wearing an open-shirt and carrying his suit blazer. He clumped over some boulders and heavy rocks, that must have fallen from the rock face, with a stern look, trying not to mark his shiny shoes. I couldn't understand why men like him wore suits all the time. It's not as if he worked in an office.

"Davie, on time. I like it," he said, panting for breath as the sweat glistened across his forehead.

"Aye, might be the first time ever?" I raised my brows, optimistic about keeping him happy.

"Better make it a habit then," he said as he surveyed the area. "This is a place you will visit often; you might need to use it as a getaway from time to time, and it will be a place where we meet."

I glanced around, trying to fathom the reason for our presence there. I thought it could be a convenient meeting place to discuss forthcoming jobs without the paranoia of using phones, but why take me all the way out here for that? Another thought entered my head: what if this was an execution? What if Jack had gotten to him, paid him a handsome sum to off me? Why not? This was a convenient location, in the middle of nowhere. But why would Millacky do this himself? Surely he had foot-soldiers he could utilise, and why would he spend that time in the house going over his operation? Maybe it had been a kind of distraction, to get me there at that moment in time.

"Can you step to the side?"

I wore a bemused gaze.

"Davie, to the side!" he commanded, and I side-stepped. Millacky knelt down and chucked a few clumpy stones to the side, lifting patches of grass that had been intertwined. He then shovelled a load of dirt with his shoe and hissed at the residue that stuck, unveiling a round wooden cover, like something that would be fixed over a miniature, abandoned water hole. He removed a screwdriver from his inside pocket and started to slacken screws from the outer edge. He wasn't a man who was handy with a tool as the screwdriver kept slipping. Eventually, after a couple of minutes, six screws were removed and the round lid of wood placed to one side, revealing a hole and a make-shift ladder built from pieces of two by four timber. He nodded his head down to the empty space of black.

"Ladies first."

I poked my head over the dark hole to see if anything was down there. Was this my grave? Millacky opened his hand, gesturing me to enter. I gave it deep thought and switched my look from the hole to his bright emerald eyes at least three times. He stood and waited. Curiosity got the better of me and I headed in, climbing down the awkward ladder, trying to grip the slats. Once inside the cramped area I felt a bouncy ground on a wooden surface, and touched the side walls that were sheets of ply.

157

Millacky joined me inside and started fumbling around the ground before picking up a torch and switching it on.

"Hold this," he instructed, "Shine it up to the hole." He was obviously paranoid about approaching civilians. He reached to the ground and picked up a battery drill. Climbing back up two steps, he slid the wooden cover back, securing the hatch and hiding it from the outside world. I was still holding the torch as he took a set of keys from his pocket.

"Watch your back there."

The area we stood in was a cramped box shape, two metres wide and two metres high. I turned around and bang right in front of my face was a shack door with four steel bars across the front, all with their own padlock. He unlocked them, slid them out of their slots, and opened the door that hung on one hinge. Once inside, Millacky strode down the middle of an underground arms bunker, lighting paraffin lamps that hung from the roof on pieces of wire, illuminating the container. Three homemade shelves ran the length at either side. The shack was around fifteen metres in length and held enough firearms to supply a heavy regiment. Inside smelt rotten with rat piss, the air heavy with festering dampness, immediately reminding me of the abandoned house I had taken Max to. The construction was impressive. It must've taken many hard hours to dig a hole of this size and many more to build such a barracks inside. Standing at the rear with his legs crossed and a hand at either side of the middle shelves, Millacky picked up a gun.

"The M10 45 ACP sub-machine gun fires 1,090 rounds per minute - it's a nice size for such a violent weapon. Sounds tasty, but in truth, you could only use it for fighting in a phone box. You couldn't shoot an elephant off a merry-go-round with this."

I was relieved to note it hadn't been pointed in my direction and I got the feeling I was in for a bit of a lecture. He returned the gun to the shelf and swivelled around to the opposite side.

"This here is the Barret M90. A bolt action 50 calibre sniper rifle. It's old and slow, but it was a good servant to the IRA in the early nineties. I've gunned down many RUC officers with this weapon." The Royal Ulster Constabulary was the police force that acted throughout the troubles in Northern Ireland.

"I've only a couple of these left, but I can't seem to part with them, too sentimental you could say, like a toy you don't want to throw out."

He stroked the barrel, admiring its appeal, but yet again didn't aim in my direction. He started to move down the aisle, sliding small pallet boxes that once held fruit and veg from underneath the bottom shelf.

"Now, these are smoke and stun grenades. Everyone has a fetish for these." He kicked the box back in, moved closer to me and slid another one out, three boxes down. "And handguns."

I looked around at crates on the bottom level and spilling into the centre. There were too many to count.

"I've probably got one of each handgun ever shot in this country."

I continued to pan my eyes over his stockpile of death. Automatic rifles and machine guns spread across the middle shelves, magazines and loose bullets, attachments like chest and ankle holsters, cardboard boxes of silencers, unopened, sniper rifles, a collection of knives, tactical vests, camouflage wear and around a dozen bullet-proof vests. I could see components of guns stripped down and left in pieces. There was little room to manoeuvre and if he wanted to kill me, he could have done it twice already. A lot of cash value was lying in there, yet the stock was a riddled mess, strewn all over the container, much to my annoyance.

"This place needs a tidy up," I spouted, feeling the need to say something. The valley of death I gazed upon and the easy way Millacky was at one with himself, scared me even more.

"Aye, and that'll be your job Davie, not mine." He picked up a general purpose M60, E6 machine gun. The only one in there. A bad-ass looking weapon that ran a chain of bullets. One of those guns you could imagine hanging out a chopper door or on the back of an army truck supported by a tripod. He rested the stand on the middle shelf and slotted in a short cutting of armour-piercing bullets. He lifted and rested the butt on top of his belt, angling it up about thirty degrees. Turning around, he took a few steps in my direction until the barrel was inches away from my chest. He eye-balled me as I froze with horror. In that moment, I took a trip into his world of violence with his one deeply ambiguous fix.

"Mr Rhodes, I thought we made it clear, you weren't to enter the public eye." He chocked the gun. I gulped nervously, all too aware, knowing exactly what he meant. When he made the threat that he'd be watching over me, I needed to make sure he was, and that was the reason I spent the last week visiting pubs and bookies.

"One pint doesn't hurt."

"Ohh, it does Mr Rhodes." I hated being called 'Mr'. It was condescending the way he talked down to me but after all, he was a terrorist of the highest calibre.

"You're working for me now. If you choose to disobey me then that's your decision, but I wouldn't want to live the rest of my life without fingers," he mocked, due to the fact I was down to eight, and confirmed what I already knew: I was under his rule.

"I know everything about you. Your armless father and your time spent working for Arthur Thompson, your reputation speaks for itself with the use of your fists, your son Joe, yes, that one, the failed boxer in Aberdeen, your second life in Liverpool with Jack Gallagher, and your other son, Max. I probably know more about your life than you know yourself."

I took him for an intelligent man but I never expected him to know my life story.

I knew then, this man was a class above anyone I'd ever worked under in the past.

Chapter 29

First Drop:

My opening drop was for two members of the ISU, Internal Security Unit, a name given to the counter-intelligence and interrogation unit of the PIRA, a branch of the IRA. Holding a unique collection of skills that could be employed and adapted to any operation inside the IRA, including character analysis, education in political history, collaboration of material from failed compromised operations, shadowing of potential informants and collecting necessary information, the polite process of interrogation, knowledge of weapons, guerrilla warfare, debriefing of individuals on release from capture and of course, carrying out ruthless killings of those betraying the IRA.

The two members of the ISU had been part of the division for ten years, established an invaluable skill set and acted with distinctive intelligence. They grew up together on Crumlin Road, in one of Belfast's most troubled neighbourhoods, a street where several pockets of Republicans and Loyalists were connected. Since the Troubles were drifting into the past in 2007, these men still needed to make money and making money legally just didn't cut the mustard for them. Millacky would pay handsomely.

Millacky gave me details of their need for 14 Taurus PT 24/7 semi-automatic pistols and 14 AKM assault rifles, along with tactical vests, smoke grenades, magazines and a substantial amount of ammo, all of which came from the arms bunker. The real IRA weren't ones to associate themselves with other divisions of the Republic, but when it came to making money, their morals would relax, slightly. With

Millacky's need to conjure up money to fund his secretive upcoming operation, he had no quarrel in hiring the two men to take control of the job. It wasn't the first time either: they were often used as step-in gunrunners when Millacky thought there was too much heat on his back, or if he was indisposed to make the drop.

The Northern Irish government was transporting a painting, as a gift from the Royal house of Hillsborough Castle, nineteen miles from Belfast, to the Irish Parliament House in Dublin. Ireland's artist Jack Butler Yeats' 'The Wild Ones', had been donated by Sotheby's of London to the Parliament House via the Queen's good word. Bought by Sotheby's for £1.2 million, it was sure to ruffle some feathers. It was foreseen as a gesture of goodwill between the nations, promoting peace and good relations. Millacky was resolute in his struggle to obtain a united Ireland and saw it as an annoyance that the IRA's passion was being ignored by the Republic's government.

The weapons were to be part of a planned ambush of the painting. All I had to do was deliver the merchandise. Piece of cake, really.

Until the deal, I stayed at the same B&B in Creeslough, neglecting my addiction to pubs and bookies. Instead, I turned into a TV couch potato, struck with big bouts of boredom. There was a nervous excitement about my first drop, almost like a kid waiting to play his first game of football, or a boxer who waited patiently the week before a fight. I even caught myself going out for walks, like a tourist, despite the pain in my knees. I continued to drink on my own and devour painkillers, a habit that wouldn't end. I began to use heat packs and spray, anything to offer relief.

After four days, I finally got the go ahead.

The guns and equipment that I was required to transport were sorted into long canvas bags before leaving the arms bunker with Millacky, ready to be picked up. I acquired a wheelbarrow and moved the load in one heavy trip to the car. Millacky gifted me a uniform, the same used by the forest staff, and I lugged the order before the sun came into the day, just having enough light to manoeuvre around the woods. Meeting with a couple of early morning dog-walkers, a welcoming smile and some trivial chit-chat prevented any suspicion. The order stayed in the boot of my car for a whole day before I set off for Belfast and the rendezvous.

The location Millacky sent me to was a car park at the rear of a dingy two-star hotel. No money would be exchanged with only a handover of the goods requested. There was a feeling my every move was being observed, removing a sense of freedom which annoyed me.

It was pitch black and gusty around the hour of ten as I pulled into the back of the sheltered hotel car park, stopped and turned the engine off. With impatience getting the better of me, along with the excitement of my first deal, I smoked a few rollies, expecting a couple of real hard-men to turn up, their reputations speaking for them.

Ten minutes late, ironically, as Millacky drummed it into me how I'd better get used to being on time, a three-door Ford Escort XR3i inched through the open gate, parking exactly opposite my car's rear with our boots facing. Their engine purring, I wasn't sure if I should exit my car first.

With more impatience, I jumped out, with my rollie hanging from my mouth, closed the door and strolled around to lean over the boot. Still they didn't exit. I wondered if they had plans other than collecting the guns. I looked directly through their back window, clocking the driver stretch over and collect a gun from the glove compartment. I was taking their armoury as precautionary, while asking myself why I didn't have a gun. I swapped my rollie to my mangled fingers, assumed a casual stance with a hand in my pocket and legs crossed.

The car doors swung open at the same time. The two men horsed up their trousers and lit cigarettes before joining me between the cars. They both decided to take the same casual approach and lean their elbows over the spoiler. It was then I noticed they were twins. Identically scrawny, pale complexions with baby-faces, of average height, and knotted, mullet, ash brown hair blowing in the wind, dressed in faded jeans and fern-coloured stylish anoraks.

"What's your name then?" The guy on the left of the two who vaguely asked the question was Turk. I knew giving them my name was unimportant.

"Doesn't matter," I replied, catching him wondering what had happened to my hand.

"It maybe does, it maybe doesn't, but it would be good courtesy, wouldn't it?" He rotated his head to Barb, a man of few words, who gave his head a little tilt to the side in agreement, happy for his twin to do the talking.

"Are you wantin' these guns or will I be on ma way?"

"Don't get excited there. I note you're not Irish. Where you from?" He was naturally curious in our first sighting of each other, trying to decipher my identity, but I didn't care to enlighten them.

"No, I'm nae Irish and it isn't important." I leaned off the boot for the first time. Turk and Barb exchanged looks with each other. Barb slid the front of his jacket over, putting his hand into his jeans pocket, revealing his handgun, thinking the stance of my full height was a demonstration of intent.

The Irish were a paranoid breed.

"Well if you're not Irish, why are you working for Millacky?" Turk asked.

"He pays well."

"You know he's a man on the way down, he won't be paying you forever?" I couldn't understand his meaning. The only thing that occurred at the time was they were referring to the up-coming mission Millacky was so secretive about, not the planned ambush they held some knowledge on.

"What are you speakin' about?" Now the tables had turned on the conversation and now I wished to extract information from them. They had blatantly ignored the question, "If he's a man on the way down, why are you workin' for him?" I asked.

"I'm not working for him, I'm working for my wallet, same as you," Turk said casually, "Never mind, show me the guns."

I popped the boot open. Barb, the quiet one, examined one of each gun, the box of ammo, and checked the condition of the tactical vests.

I stood a quiet observer, watching them transfer the load into their car.

Before Turk entered his car, he stopped, looked over and said, "I'll be seeing you around."

They drove off quickly, leaving me standing.

First drop completed.

Chapter 30

Plans:

For the next few months, I had similar drops in and around Belfast, connecting to the heist. Millacky dropped off the goods in various locations where I would pick them up and relay them to the source. Lockers at the train station with combination padlocks were commonly used if the delivery was small enough. It was a dodgy move considering the security there and the fact I looked like a convict. My clothes would often be raw and dirty. Instead of purchasing new clothes, I stole from washing lines, kept them until a change was needed and then stole again. It wasn't easy either because Ireland seemed to consist of men with a shorter stature than me. Times it would take up half a day to locate a decent pair of jeans to fit, but I wasn't bothered because it filled the time.

A4 sized packed envelopes, that I presumed contained detailed plans of the route to taken by the convoy that was escorting the painting, were delivered to a PIRA cell in Londonderry. Another task was to pick up four sets of road spikes. Millacky instructed me to visit a privately-owned newsagent in Belfast, and ask the shop clerk for a certain magazine, that didn't exist, where the middle-aged man insisted I drove around the back while he locked the door. I loaded them into the car and headed off without the slightest need for chit-chat with the gentleman.

The boredom between movements became a problem. My only hobbies in the past were fighting, betting and social drinking, but I couldn't get involved in any of those activities now. I became a thorough reader of The Republican newspaper, learning about the country's past troubles: Troubles that I had no real passion for but nevertheless, I was involved in. In the time spent on these deals, I tried to understand the people I worked with and their dedication to a united Ireland. As far as I could figure by the papers, the conflict was over. I didn't see the need to re-ignite it, but that was Millacky's intention.

Floating around Northern Ireland, I tried to keep my public appearances to a minimum, but it was nearly impossible to live and not enter shops for the necessities in life. Items like toothpaste, who could live without toothpaste? I needed tobacco and food too, petrol, I couldn't go anywhere without it. Often, I would drive around looking for a quiet place to relax, read or drink a six pack. All the time waiting for a call from the boss with my next instructions. His location at any time was unknown, but I had the sense of being watched or could it have been my paranoia? I trusted my instinct, but my past would tell you otherwise.

Jack caught me out without so much as a hint of suspicion, Sam Bryson as well. Those were lessons I should've learned from.

I became a little desperate to fill my time after all the drops were completed, so I visited the arms bunker after shopping for supplies to last me three days and headed off.

After driving around Belfast and Northern Ireland, delivering illegal goods and accessories, I decided it was time to ditch the car and pick up a fresh one. On getting close to the bunker, I pushed it into a lake, making sure there was nothing left inside that could be linked to me. After that, there was a hardy three-mile walk to the bunker. Having to carry three days supplies was hard graft and pissed me off. Every step was painful, feeling the grind of bone in my knees, but that

168

became normal and there was no other choice but to accept that. I knew I'd wake up in pain and knew it wouldn't go away. There was no point in moaning about it, I just got on with it.

When I arrived at the bunker, I opened the hatch, lowered the bags then followed. I unlocked the padlock on the self-built shack and entered, noticing there had been a few more visits as some of the stock was missing. The boxes under the bottom shelf had been rearranged and moved around with three absent. The middle shelves, mostly containing machine-guns, had taken a hit. As I scowled around, I questioned whether I was the only gunrunner Millacky had on his take. Were there other men who came here or could it have been Millacky himself? I didn't know because I was kept quietly in the dark, but that suited if the jobs and siller kept flowing.

Being knackered after the trek through the forest, I made a seat out of a hard plastic gun-case and crouched my back against the bottom shelf.

I placed a couple of the paraffin lamps beside me, opened a tin of export and ate a sandwich, making myself comfortable in whatever way I could muster. Once I'd finished eating, I got stuck into the Republican paper. An hour later, I was bored again. As it was approaching the hour of ten, I decided to get some shut-eye. With no bed, I found some cardboard from under the bottom shelf and foam from inside gun-cases and lay on them, using an old helmet to prop my head against and drifted off.

Surprisingly, I slept over seven hours on the uncomfortable chilling floor and put it down to fatigue after the trek through the forest, and the combination of paracetamol and export. After the traditional morning rollie and a pint of milk, I was suckered with that same dawning of boredom.

Scanning the disorganised mess of weaponry, I decided it was time for a clean out. When attempting to sort out the gathering of weapons, I was coming across so many random components of guns that I decided to try and form as many whole guns as possible. Also, I needed to get into touch with the merchandise I was selling.

Inside the door, there was a waist high cupboard without door handles that never closed properly. Inside it was a maintenance cupboard, where I came across a stack of small booklets and two other small manufactured boxes, kind of like a pre-century old school medical kit box, that contained gun cleaning tools. Bingo! One of the instruction booklets was for doing a field strip of an AK47. Luckily the instructions came in various languages and that enabled me to start.

Firstly, I had to place the safety-catch on and remove the magazine. I had to remove the cleaning rod from the barrel, a simple press down and release, before I removed what was called the receiver cover that housed the middle area of the gun between the stock and barrel. This was easily done by a push of a button and a little manhandling. The revealed recoil spring released a distinct odour of gun-oil. The spring had to be depressed, slid to the side and pulled from the bolt-carrier. Pulling back on a handle and sliding the bolt-carrier out from a set of grooves left the gun much lighter. Lastly, I removed the gas tube from the fore-grip and that was a field-strip of the AK47 done. I couldn't believe how remarkably easy and quick the process was.

The parts sat on the floor, manky from outside to in. Now I had to clean them.

Inside the maintenance cupboard, as I now called it, was a bunch of rags, skewering pads and oil lubricant. The cleaning tool kit contained long pistol brushes, short thin brushes and a couple of toothbrushes. Most of them brand new. I horsed the lube over the main part of the gun, scrubbed vigorously with the brushes and used the rags to pick up the dirt. I cleaned every slot, groove, hole and pole, until they were gleaming, then reassembled the gun. I did this for fucking hours, so long that my fingers and wrists ached, back cramped, and neck stiff. My clothes were covered in lubricant and residue. I knew I'd never get them all finished in one sitting, so I piled the uncleaned guns on one side of the bunker and cleaned ones on the other side. I hadn't even touched the piles of Berrettas, Glocks and other handguns. I organised the shelves and nine hours later, aye, nine hours, the job was done.

I think that was the start of my compulsion to do things properly.

After the mammoth tidy-up was finished for the day and a little stretch of the legs outside, I relaxed having a tin and a smoke with my feet up, proud of my achievement. Sitting down, it didn't take long before I started to drift off on one of my regular everyday naps when the phone rang.

Millacky, of course.

Chapter 31

Not A Forgotten Date:

Millacky required me to attend a meeting back in the safe house in Carnagh in a matter of days. Once I'd located another car which I bought, again as a result of a newspaper advertisement, I travelled over. When I bought cars, I sent the registration documents to Rankin who dealt with them. Stealing cars would bring unwanted attention and I wasn't confident in doing so; buying was the easiest way. If the documents weren't dealt with, eventually the previous owners of the vehicles would realise, contact the police and my description would be taken. Sending the documents to Rankin meant keeping things right and kept me under the radar.

Millacky wanted me at the meeting because my first high-scale job was on the cards and after five months it was welcome. Me, Millacky and The General sat around the same table as before, but in a much more relaxed atmosphere.

Millacky instructed me on my first big drop, "A herring sea vessel is going to transport forty Heckler and Koch MP5 semi-automatic machine guns, 160 magazines, four thousand rounds and waist belts. I've imported them from Sweden, specifically for the needs of Vogue." The guns were the American SWAT team's weapons of choice, but made inside an arms factory in Sweden. A lightweight gun with an angled magazine holding 30 rounds a clip, with a barrel extension fitting comfortably onto your shoulder. The perfect weapon for a surprise assault. Get in, get it done, and get the fuck out. "It's your task to get the shipment on and off the boat and transported to the location requested by Vogue."

Millacky passed a piece of paper with Sinbad's number.

The owner of the herring vessel was named Sinbad; whether it was his correct name, I didn't know, or care. The guns were being delivered to Vogue, the head of The French Hells Angels' biker outfit. As soon as Millacky said, 'Hells Angels', I knew my good friend Donny could lend some information on the outfit.

There was major planning to do. This felt more of a final exam than a job, and it would take a little time. I had Millacky's contacts to utilise and my own life experience to draw upon. On the completion of the talks, Millacky insisted, "Let's have a wee celebration. General, get the whisky out."

A couple of bottles of expensive Irish malt landed on the table along with three glasses. The last thing I wanted to do was get drunk with these unpredictable characters, but it would be rude not to partake. The glasses were filled three quarters full, drunk fast and continually re-filled. I listened to them share conversation for the rest of the night without much input from myself. They spoke of the troubles against the loyalists, the bombings, deaths of family members, and their determination not to succumb to English rule. It reminded me of my youth in Glasgow, the constant feud between religions that made no sense to me. The more we drank, the more passionately aggressive they became and I finally got to hear of the secret operation they were planning. A terrorist attack in three different English army barracks. I had been waiting a long time to hear of this plan.

"The three bombs will go off simultaneously, at exactly 10.43 on the anniversary of The Poppy Day bombing in just over a year's time. Three different English army barracks in Colchester, Aldershot, and Tidworth will have a substantial bomb planted by inside men. Me and The General will personally be there when the bombs light up the Queen's men. We've planned this for some years, raised a ruthless army for this attack and our dream is close," Millacky spoke, with a refined pride in their plan. With the whisky taking full effect, his hands began to point, and his speech became aggressive as he gripped his glass, close to crushing it, "Davie, your position as gunrunner in The IRA is top secret between the three of us" He slurred through the conversation, making me struggle to understand him and thought that man could be Rankin. But what about men like Turk and Bard whom I'd met? They knew who I was. He became so drunk, the words leaking from his mouth made little sense.

I couldn't figure out if it was the whisky, or if they trusted me that much, but I didn't care to get involved in their squabbles and thought their ways were barbaric and unnecessary. I was only there to build a retirement fund. The more they drank, the less I could understand, and any level of respect I had gained for them trickled away. I had drunk the same amount, but unlike them I could handle whisky like water and eventually watched them drop out over the table top. Sometimes my head would spin, mixing alcohol with painkillers was not the given thing, but I controlled it. Sitting there on my own, spotting Millacky's phone on the table, unlocked., I couldn't resist having a look at its contents, then put it back.

I discovered The Poppy Day bombing they talked of happened in Enniskillen on November 8th, 1987, and detonated at 10.43am precisely. Eleven were killed and sixty-eight injured in the attack, all Protestants. The bombing was a counter-attack to a raid on The Royal Ulster Constabulary in Loughgall, County Armagh, that went wrong. A unit of eight IRA members broke into the barracks by driving a digger through the fence; in the bucket was 200Ib of Semtex explosive. Their plans were scuppered by MI5 gathering intelligence on the matter. A team of thirty-six members of the SAS were in hidden positions throughout the barracks, and killed all eight IRA members.

Millacky lost two brothers in the attack and had started planning this counter movement five years ago.

On November 8th, 2008, the twenty first anniversary, the Poppy murders would be re-enacted.

Chapter 32

Drunken:

I didn't wait for the drunken wake, leaving in the early morning. I had my task, but no deadline. The General had insisted a transport of this size required meticulous planning and to be fool-proof. No stone had to be left unturned, and I intended on doing a formidable job.

First, I got in touch with Sinbad, meeting him in a harbour in the south east of Southern Ireland to discuss our plan. He familiarised me with the situation regarding his herring vessel, being run down and requiring many hours' work; the reason he agreed to help Millacky, he needed the extra coin. We concluded we could mimic some maintenance happening on the boat and smuggle the guns disguised as refit parts. He mentioned the electrics on the boat were all to shit and needed rewired. The plan took shape - we could smuggle the merchandise inside a mains panel, a big one. Once I'd seen the size of the guns, I could gauge what size of panel would be needed.

Five days after that meeting, The General came to me with a set of keys and an address to a warehouse in the small village of Crossmaglen, 15 miles from the Irish Border in County Armagh. He also handed over a bag of notes, my pay, and it was a handsome amount, triple what I had received last time. The stockpile of money the IRA held would always be kept secret, but I assumed they were rich bandits by their generous payments.

On arriving in the village I sent The General a text, who replied early the next day, `Delivery on the way, please be in to receive your package`.

The guns and accessories were dropped off in wooden crates packed with straw, by an official delivery company, and that gave me another idea. Once I saw the size of the haul, I ordered a 6ft tall by 1ft 5 wide steel enclosure, the kind that an electrical control panel would be built from. The General paid by bank transfer.

Inside the warehouse there was a Portakabin, already wired up with a heater inside. It became a homely environment for the time I spent there, and I kitted it out with a kettle and microwave. I had to wait three days for the panel to arrive. While waiting, I visited the hardware store for some timber, wood saw, screws, cable ties, a battery drill and bits. It felt like a slow process because of my eagerness to get on with the task. I kept a look out in the newspapers for confirmation of Millacky's planned hijack of the painting. I wasn't bothered when, but wanted to know as soon as it happened so I could stay out of sight afterwards, because the government would easily identify who was responsible.

Millacky had many endeavours happening at the same time and I understood his need for assistance.

Inside the panel, I built ten wooden shelves. To make the most of the limited space, two guns were strapped to each side of a shelf using cable-ties, keeping them fixed in place. The magazines and bullets were packed bubble-wrapped inside a long cardboard-box and strapped down at the bottom. The waist-straps were packed into a separate box, left aside, marked as 'Tool belts'. This took three days as I found it a great struggle with my misshapen hands, but with perseverance, I got the job done.

I requested a truck with fake graphics from The General to appear as a haulage company and he obliged.

177

Once all the guns and equipment were securely fixed inside the panel, I built a plywood box around it. The reason - if anyone wanted a look inside, they would have the hassle of stripping it apart and I didn't expect anyone to do that.

Borrowing a forklift from a neighbouring business, I lifted the box into the truck. Sinbad had explained to the harbour staff that he was expecting delivery of a panel to upgrade his boat. I disguised myself as a delivery man, wearing a t-shirt with the truck logo and a baseball cap that Rankin sorted out for me. He also sorted out the paperwork required to get through security at the harbour.

On the drive to the harbour gate, I was pumped full of adrenaline. A nervous tingle heightened my senses but on the outside, I maintained a sober expression. My head was covered with the make-believe delivery company baseball cap.

The harbour was busy with a queue of vans lined up leading to the entrance point. A security guard was inside a hut, checking everyone's papers and letting them pass. As it came to my turn, my heart beat quickened, I became aware of my breathing, my paranoia soared, I panicked, was this going to work? It all sounded too easy. The panel was strapped down horizontally in the back of the truck. If the security guard wanted a look, it meant dismantling the frame I'd built around it, I didn't fathom them doing that, but the doubt always lingers.

"Hello, delivery note please?"

"Sure, no problem sir." The papers were inside a closed clipboard on the passenger seat, "Here you go."

He sifted through the information, "What are you delivering today?" he asked.

"Some kind of electrical panel to a herring vessel."

"Okay and you have another package, I see here," he pointed at the sheet. I didn't want to answer too many questions in case I slipped up, said the wrong thing. In a momentary fluster of panic, I didn't have a clue as to what he was referring.

"Can I have a look at that sheet please?" I asked, and he handed it over, had a quick glance and I knew what he meant.

"That's the tool belts, here." I picked the box of so called 'tool belts' from the floor under the glove box and showed it to him.

"Okay, not a problem. Follow the signs to the unloading area and Have a good day."

"Thanks sir." That was it. I got through with no problem, and my heartbeat returned to normal. With a gloating smile, I drove to the unloading area.

The heavy-duty forklift unloaded the crate.

Driving away, I noticed Sinbad standing outside the bridge of the boat and lifted my cap to acknowledge the drop had been made.

The cargo would be shipped to a village in the north west of France.

The next part of the plan was to get to France but I couldn't leave for ten days or so. Sinbad planned a fishing trip as normal to add to the ruse of the smuggling operation. Plus, he needed the cash. My impatience about this whole process drove me crazy. Like I said, I wanted the job done.

Not only was I waiting for Sinbad, but I also waited for Rankin to drop off a new British passport so I could cross via the Channel Tunnel with the truck and drive to the village to pick up the load.

During impatient times of waiting like that, I always cast my thoughts back to the past and the twists and turns my life had taken. Most of all, I wondered how

179

Max was handling his time in jail. It had been eight months since I left him and every day I conjured up thoughts of him. In the beginning, when I took him from the Jacksons, I wanted to mould him into a proper man, a hard man, but before Jack caught me, I only wanted to take him away from that world. Now, I could do nothing to help him. He would become his own man.

Calling Donny to ask about the Vogue character would give me an opportunity to ask about the son I missed.

I located a phone box instead of using a burner. Donny didn't use an answer-phone and I left the ringtone going for more than two minutes.

"Alright!" he answered, annoyed.

"What's wrong? Havin' a bad day?"

"Is that who I think it is?" He picked up on my accent straight away.

"It is."

"To what do I owe the pleasure?"

"Just a friendly call."

"Go'ed then, what's the biff?"

"You know a man called Vogue?" There was a eerie pause before an answer.

"If you're talking about a Frenchman, then I know who your talking about."

"And?"

"Let me guess. You're making a delivery to him."

"Correct again."

"Vogue's a dangerous man Davie, and he's not exactly what you would call your typical biker."

"How so?"

"He stays on an estate, wears yuppie clothes an' you'll never see him in his bike gear."

"How dangerous is he?"

"He makes your man Jack look like a grain of rice in a pile of boulders, but if he respects you, then he's a good source to have."

"Talkin' about that vermin, what's he been up to?"

"Not much, the usual shit. Still penny pinching and moaning."

"Aye, and Max, have you heard anythin'?"

"One of my crew's sons is in the slammer with him just now. He's not in a good way!"

"What do you mean?"

"He walks around beaten to a pulp all the time. The screws are having their way with him, I'm sorry mate."

"Well, you need to tell yer man on the inside to pass on a message for me."

"Sure!"

"Tell him, do the time and I'll see him on the other side."

I couldn't imagine what pain Max would be going through in there, but it sounded like he needed hope. If I see him on the other side or not, he still needed to know I was thinking about him.

Chapter 33

Hanging Loose:

The journey through the Channel Tunnel was spent in a pent-up rage. That moaning cunt, Jack, was responsible for the pain inflicted on my son, I knew it. There was nothing I could do about it either. I could have asked Millacky for some help in getting to Jack, but what would he care? It wasn't part of his quest for a united Ireland and anyway, this shit was personal and my hands needed to be responsible in ending his life. Patience, his time will come.

Out of the tunnel, I travelled to a fishing village in the north west of France where I met Sinbad and had the crate loaded onto the truck with little struggle. I typed the address given to me by Millacky into the sat-nav. Driving in the direction of Paris then south, arriving in a city called Olivet. There, I met two of Vogue's men, sat on their Harley Davidsons at a petrol station with a patient aura, helmets on their laps, dressed in heavy leathers and snoods around their necks. They knew exactly what type of vehicle to look out for as they spotted me before I spotted them.

Without much of an acknowledgment, one of them pointed his finger towards the exit of the station then inched out on his bike, waiting for me to spin the truck in their direction and follow. As I drove nearer, they sped away. It was hardly the weather for bikes, creeping below freezing with a murky frost hanging in the early-afternoon.

We drove for thirty minutes and my escorts seemed to take me on many back roads before we arrived at an electric gate, opening through a couple of stone statues and a long eight-foot high wall, secluding the property.

It led on to a track surrounded by a tight run of trees. Outside the line of trees was open grass.

The bikes slowed their pace, due to the pot-holes and narrow tracks but the truck sailed over, carrying on for what seemed like an age before the ascension of a steep hill opened to a magnificent patch of ground, levelled off with cement and a large estate of buildings. To the right of the space were four rows of long, narrow, slate-roofed buildings, with a gigantic house overlooking them at the rear. On the left was a much larger building, a cattle byre.

As we drove closer to the narrow buildings the escorts led me between two, and stopped. Casually stepping off their bikes, one walked into the building through a side white-painted door, and the other stood by his bike. Sitting there, I felt like a spare tyre and wondered what to do.

After a few minutes I exited my truck. With my mind occupied about the deal, I forgot about my knees and landed on the ground, with my left knee, the worst one, buckling, leaving my palm grazing the gritty surface. Feeling stupid, the first thing I did was lift my head in embarrassment to see if the biker had caught sight of me. Luckily he was looking the other way, but unfortunately, Vogue had, as he appeared from a side door, wearing a full length dampened rubber apron over his bare pale chest and yellow wellington boots.

"Are you okay? Looks like you can use some help?" His English near on perfect and eloquently spoken like a rich lord. Below average height, milky skinned, dainty with a hunchback and a triangular sloped face that ran down at an angle, leading to a chin that jutted out.

"Aye, I'm fine," I lied. He turned to one of the escorts and spoke in French. The biker entered the building, came out with two seats and Vogue planted them up against the wall.

"Have a seat, take a rest." I only wanted to get out of the cold; nevertheless, I accepted his offer, leaning against the backrest. Vogue sat sideways, with his arm on the backrest.

"What is it? The knees? They're a weak joint when the body ages David." I fixed my stare into his eyes, wondering how this man knew my name. I didn't like that. Had Millacky passed my name over, as I surely hadn't?

"Aye, an old war wound Vogue."

He clicked his fingers high in the air and the same escort who grabbed the seats walked over with a skinny cigarette, placed it into Vogue's mouth, lit it and walked away. Vogue shouted, "Philip! Our guest!"

"Pardon me sir," he apologised, returned and attempted to place one in my mouth. I twitched my head, grabbed the cigarette from his hands and took my own lighter from my pocket. Vogue, annoyed with his employee, flicked his head for his man to leave.

"Do you like cattle David?" He pronounced 'David' with a 'da' sound that made me sound like a camp house designer. The cold didn't bother his pale skin, but it sailed straight through mine and especially into my knees.

"Cows! I enjoy eatin' them." What was I supposed to say? It's not as if a cow is your first pet.

"Oui, they are a fine meat. Bred and slaughtered properly, they taste divine. Especially when it's hung for a few days. Sometimes the raw smell tempts me to take a bite, but most of the time I resist."

Who the fuck was this man, a cannibal?

"Is that right?" I answered.

184

His two men stood precociously still with their arms crossed over their waist line.

"Come on, I'll show you," He wandered away and I followed.

"Follow me, David."

He walked with a long bounce, his hands crossed behind his back, leaning his weight over his waist and poking his chin out, taking strides longer than the willingness of his feet. We approached the door to the building which he held open for me.

I walked in, followed by him and his two men. One long steel hydraulically-powered rail stretched the length of the building from the left to the right, with hooks hanging from the line. Different stations were dotted up and down for animal slaughtering with a mechanical-powered rise and fall platform, cattle-splitting saw, hide-peeler and a leg-separator, amongst other equipment. The scratched floor was stained with red gore, guts, idle tongues, slithery chunks and strings of white fat, burst open intestines, and cattle heads with their skin peeled off. Piles of the days hides lay on a crate scattered with salt. The shed smelt of uncooked meat, rotten faeces and with no air conditioning, the smell lingered in my nose and I put a hand under my nostrils to block it. My throat retched and belly contracted, but I held in my sick.

"You arrived just in time. I have one special animal left to attend to today."

I stood a good few metres from the start of the line, his men in my shadow. Beneath the first station was a drain, covered over and folded into place was a sheet of stainless steel metal two-foot-wide, on a downward slant that ran into the ground. At the start of the line, black rubber curtains separated it from whatever was behind. Vogue mouthed something in French and through the curtains emerged his special animal that swung morbidly back and forth.

"Do you know how much blood a cow holds?" He gazed at me while gripping a calf, his hand wrapped around the 'special animal' hung upside down, waiting for an answer. I removed my hands from my mouth and slotted them into my pockets. Trying to give the impression I wasn't mentally affected with what I was seeing.

"No idea."

"Fifty millilitres per kilogram. A cow averages one thousand, one hundred kilograms. I won't do the maths but that's a colossal amount of blood."

I still wasn't getting the point he was making and let him carry on,

"Now, David," he said, while walking with his finger pointing to the roof, "Do you know how much blood a human transports around?"

Approaching a stand with water boiling over a stainless steel upright basin, he spun with a cleaver by his side and returned to his animal, as he called it. He placed the cleaver gently on the throat of one of his men, stripped naked, gagged and already beaten to within an inch of his life, his special animal! I recognised this was one of his own men because of the motorcycle ink covering his front. He slit the man's throat so delicately, it looked as if he hardly moved.

"A man of this size, probably has about five litres." He brushed the floor as he shuffled in my direction with his hands and cleaver hanging behind his back, "You would think a cow would survive longer than a human." He kept clumping in my direction, "That's true, of course, but not when you slit the right area. It can take over an hour for him to pass."

He made his way into my space as I noticed the trickle of blood beginning to run down the man's neck then slide over his face until it dripped onto the ground. Vogue reminded me of The Eradicator, having the same smug look, more than at home with his torturing techniques.

"Like your employer David, I hate snitches and there's only one way to deal with them. I had a tip-off that someone knew the location of the deal and with interrogation, I discovered who it was, and changed the meeting place, of course. No time for it, none. I also found out another handy piece of information that could end up favouring us both in time."

All the time he was speaking, the man twitched and struggled while choking for air, each time attempting to cough, slivers of blood shooting out from his slit neck. I didn't have the foggiest idea about the piece of information that would benefit us both and I didn't care to ask. The only thing I wanted was to get away from the vile smell.

A third one of Vogue's men entered the slaughterhouse and nodded to his boss.

"Good David, seems everything is in order with the delivery. You're free to leave now."

Chapter 34

Brian Fitzpatrick:

It turned out the man Vogue slaughtered was a double agent for the French Secret Service and had been a part of his crew for several years. He had been responsible for his men being caught in illegal activities and sent to jail. Vogue had the man under surveillance for thirteen months and nailed him in a meeting with another member of the service in Paris. Needless to say, it touched a nerve with Vogue.

I learned the world I was now a part of housed brutal men, men who had even less of a conscience than I had. The cold nature of Vogue disturbed me, the same as The Eradicator's. Men who could massacre other men with enjoyment, didn't register as necessary in my mind. Even though up until that point I hadn't fired a gun in my life, a simple bullet would suffice, not brutal dismemberment and beatings to near death. I'd beaten Carl Jenkins to death but that was fully deserved, you only had to look at the scars marking my chest and shoulder. Those kinds of people I could never understand. If someone pissed me off, a stern warning or a slap would sort them out; if that didn't work, a bigger slap would be necessary. I would never think of punishing my foe by beating and hanging him from a hook.

My job was done, full marks in my book, and I headed home. Once out of the Channel Tunnel and back into England, I made for Pembroke, in the south of Wales, for the ferry back to Ireland, landing in Rosslare.

On the way to Pembroke, I tuned the radio in; once the pipes struck the hour, I heard some interesting news:

"Yesterday morning, a four-vehicle armed transport unit was hijacked on the M1 near Drogheda. It's thought to be the work of the PIRA. The convoy was transporting a painting from the Northern Irish Parliament to the Republic, in a gesture of good relations between the countries. The move of such a gift was billed top-secret and the convoy taken by a surprise assault. The four-armed Tangi Land Rovers were travelling at speeds of roughly forty miles per hour, when sets of road spikes were thrown down in front of the first vehicle. Metal grills over the bumpers prevented the spikes from damaging underneath the vehicle, but slowed it enough for homemade petrol bombs, mixed with gloss paint, and smoke grenades to be thrown at the vehicles, disabling the convoy. A squad of fourteen masked PIRA members, dressed in camouflage, tactical vests and balaclavas, armed with Taurus PT 24/7 semi-automatic pistols and AKM assault rifles, swarmed the area, attacking the Land Rover containing the gift, while holding the rest of the men at gunpoint. All members of the Police Service of Northern Ireland escaped with their lives, but were taken to hospital where they were treated for shock and a range of minor to serious injuries. Stay tuned for a detailed report right after this break."

That had been the reasoning behind supplying Turk and Barb with the equipment – a PIRA assault with no deaths, and I wondered if Millacky would be happy with that. Nevertheless, the job was done and there were no bereavements. The police officers could return home to their wives and loved ones.

On getting off the ferry, I decided to have some well needed R&R. The past month had totally drained me and I needed to take some time to recuperate. I was no spring-chicken and since starting gunrunning, naps became a daily necessity. In Rosslare, I looked for somewhere to lie low for a while. I passed a pub and being sick of my own company, I decided, 'fuck it! I'm going for a dram.'

"Pint of Export and a whisky please mate."

The smell of stale booze and pub-grub sent a blissful feeling through my body. Every pub I walked into felt like home. It had everything I needed, Export, whisky, newspapers, and conversation that didn't include death, guns and spilled blood.

Sitting there was a joy, I hadn't heard from Millacky since I got back, still had a heathy pile of cash and the fresh ale kept flowing. I was the kind of man who could walk into a pub, sit there, drink all day, and walk out on the same straight line on which I'd entered. I made some friends and conversed my way through the day, explaining I was travelling and working at the same time, picking up any jobs I could get my hands on.

One of the guys was Brian Fitzpatrick. We got chatting and played a few games of cribbage before he offered me some work, fixing some fence gates.

"Aye, that'll do nicely," I said, as I offered him my hand to shake on the deal. He was an old guy, hobbit-sized, mid-fifties to early-sixties. Had a cluster of a ZZ-Top beard, wild fluffy black hair that seemed to poke out in straight lines over his heavily tinted glasses. What would Millacky know? There was no way he could know, surely? Driving all over Ireland, moving from place to place was okay, taking in some amazing scenery, and it filled the time. However, sometimes I just wanted to chill the fuck out, stay somewhere homely and sit on a pub stool. I set up shop for a few days in Rosslare, found a caravan park, paid the rent for a weeks stay, and parked up the truck.

Up bright and early the next morning, Brian picked me up from the caravan park just after quarter past nine, arriving in a low to the ground red pickup. He was dressed in dungarees, covered over with a padded fleece and a thick black hat covering his long flocky bush. I didn't have much wear to keep me warm, as I travelled light with jeans, t-shirt and bomber jacket. I was a gunrunner; travelling light was a necessity. I jumped into the heated truck and rubbed my hands with the comfort of heat.

"Alright dere me lad?" he spoke, with his morning fag hanging from his mouth, both hands fixed on the steering wheel at ten and two.

"Alright. Fuck me it's cold," I said.

"Aye, it's bloody nippy, so it is. Dere's a hat and gloves in the glove box dere."

"Cheers Brian, that'll do nicely."

"You can hold onto them; I've got loads at home," Brian offered.

It was a breath of fresh air being in the company of a normal guy who lived a normal life. After completing the dismantling of a couple of small gates, we headed to a field with a mangled gate to the entrance. Someone had driven into it, writing off their car, he explained. We knuckled down and removed it, having to use a grinder to cut the bolts holding the fence to the frame, due to the warp in the steel from the impact. We struggled together, had some good craic and shared

191

some stories. I had to make a couple up mind. We lifted the mangled end of the steel gate into the pickup. I jumped on the back and struggled to drag it on, leaving the end poking out. I leapt off and we used a ratchet strap to fix it down securely. On finishing, we removed our gloves, taking our tobacco tins out. Standing at the front of the truck, we proudly made rollies. On doing so, he became distracted by my mangled hand. It wasn't the first time he noticed, but since we became friendly, that gave him a reason to enquire. He looked down at his own rollie as he was about to wet the seal.

"Tell me, what happened to yer hand dere lad?"

"Och," I grunted, "Somethin' from a past life Brian."

"Aye, someting you can't talk about then?" he asked.

"No really, but I'll just say, it wasn't pleasant." We exchanged looks as I angled my neck down to his height.

"We all have stuff we can't talk about, it's a part of life. Stuff that'll burden yer conscience like lava that never sets. You hope to forget but…you can't, as much as you try. It's always dere to remind you of a time you want to forget."

I lit my rollie, glancing at him, standing dead faced, fixated straight out onto a grass field, full of sheep, poking his glasses up with his finger. Here was the friendliest man you could imagine, living a humble life as a handyman, but he'd done something in the past that left him with a heavy conscience. What, I didn't know, and I was sure he wouldn't enlighten me. I didn't want to know anyway. Just goes to show we've all done things we aren't proud of.

"Come on, let's get this gate to my house and grab a pint for dinner."

"Aye, good idea," I agreed, and jumped in the van.

Brian went to the back of the vehicle to check the security of the load. I turned the rear-view mirror to see him using the gate to hold his weight, one hand on the frame and another removing his glasses while shedding tears. He had a breakdown for about thirty seconds, sobbing heavily. He took himself to the rear to save himself the embarrassment of crying in front of another man. I understood his pride, wanted to console him, as he was a humble old man. I watched him gather himself after a minute and brush his emotions to the side. He hadn't realised, but he'd squashed his rollie into his hands as he made a regretful fist of guilt. He walked to the driver's door and entered.

"Ok, let's get dat pint then," he said, ignoring that he had just been in pieces.

"You alright there Brian?" I was concerned.

"Aye Davie, I'll be fine." He focused on the road and we drove off.

I changed the subject, asking him what the pub grub was like. We got talking and forgot about his little episode. I wondered if I would end up like him. Old, lonely, and carrying a guilty conscience, buried in your memory banks. I knew that gunrunning would mean I'd at some point be responsible for a family's grief or wounded men, but on the other hand, I'd become a rich man and that, I had to remember.

Chapter 35

Stealing Gates:

I happily aided Brian for the rest of the week, knowing I was doing a good deed for a change, helping an older man with his chores. We fixed another three gates and some fencing, taking us to early Friday afternoon and the end of the working day ritual, a couple of pints in what became a very temporary local. We were happy to enter the warm friendly pub, our feet and hands frozen from the weather. There was a humble satisfaction within me, in completing a hard-working week, probably my first honest job, ever.

It had crept into December and the owner of the pub was half-heartedly decorating the bar. Then, I wondered what Christmas would bring, and where would I go for that roast dinner with pigs in blankets?

"Davie!" Brian raised his voice as I stared into open space, "Your pint!" he insisted, as he slid it over the bar. "Hey, did you hear about the guy that's been stealing gates around here?"

"What! Stealin'?" I thought he meant someone was stealing the mangled gates we took back to the scrap-ridden land at his house.

"Aye, stealing. Do you know who it is?"

"No! Who?"

"Can't tell you who, you might take A-FENCE!"

The five perched over the bar and the barman burst into laughter, taking me a few seconds to click onto the joke.

Brian was clapping the bar in a hysterical fit as the tubby barman turned around, "Don't worry, everybody falls for dat one."

194

I joined in the joke, holding a suckering smile. It felt good, not remembering the last time I had laughed.

"Bunch of cunts!" I said in a banterish way. I had nowhere to go but back to the caravan so I stayed with Brian and got pissed. We ordered food then more ale until it came to the hour of six. A TV sat on a corner shelf, overlooking the bar. I sat at the corner of the L-shaped bar with the TV staring me straight in the eye. The barman, with a towel hanging over his shoulder, turned the volume up as the news aired. The story of the heist came on. There was some new intel received by the G2 as to who was responsible for the heist.

"It was thought that this man," (I choked on my ale as a sketch of my face appeared on the screen and dropped the glass onto the bar) "was responsible for the planning and carrying out of the robbery."

The five men who filled the stools all locked daggers. Starting with the barman, I ran my eyes all the way around to Brian. There were no words as tumbleweed blew past. The barman switched the TV off. Brian took his phone out. The last thing I wanted to do was get violent with this collection of men but if needs must, then I would have to. I started to imagine who I'd have to take out first. The barman was closest to the phone; he was the first target, and then I'd have to block the door, save anyone getting away. They were all weak looking fellows and I fancied the odds but still, I was outnumbered. As the silence threatened, the barman turned, picked up a Post-it and pen, then handed it to Brian as I rose from my seat.

The exit was behind me and I could have legged it but I was always wary about doing that with my fragile knees. Brian then started scribbling on the paper and slid it across the bar, while looking earnestly over his glasses. It was simple to say before reading that piece of paper, my imminent future was in his hands.

"If I was you Davie, I'd be making dust by now. That's an address to a safe house. Keys are buried under a tree stump; you'll know which one when you see it. Dere's food and clothes dere, enough to keep you hidden for a few days." I wasn't sure how to react to that gesture, "You can take me pick-up. That van that you have?"

"Aye, the truck, you mean?"

"The truck, aye, can I have the keys? I somewhat tink you won't need it." I passed over the keys, "I'll have a word wit' the caravan man, make sure he stays quiet. Now, you better be gone."

He turned back to his pint as I gave him my hand to shake. He removed his round tinted frames and graced my offer.

"Thanks Brian, I won't forget this."

"Be gone wit' ye' lad."

Chapter 36

Rat Bastard:

I rocketed out the pub and straight into Brian's pickup. I didn't know how that was possible, my face on the news. As I sped away, I phoned Millacky, and he answered before the first ring could finish, expecting my call.

"What the fuck's goin' on?"

"I don't know."

"Don't fuckin' know? My face is plastered across the news."

"There's no information I can give you at the moment. You better get out of Rosslare." He knew my position! There must have been a tracker on the truck The General had supplied, "You must find a hideout for two weeks, then meet me at the safe house in Carnagh." I couldn't believe his only solution was to hide out.

"If I last two weeks!"

"This will be a test for you, this will blow over, I have no doubts about that. It seems we have an informant in the ranks. My guess, it was someone from the PIRA cell that I hired for the heist."

My head ran off course, not my usual calm self. I was in this game to make money and I'd only been in it for a couple of heartbeats. Already a fugitive.

"Aye, two weeks from today?" I asked.

"Two weeks from today. Destroy your phone and sim card and use the next burner on the list. If there's a problem before that date, I'll be in touch." My silence to his instructions was followed by him hanging up. The past days were as normal as life had ever been for me and were ever to get.

I took the pickup to a small village on the main road towards Dublin. I located the safe house that had a 'For Sale' sign in the garden. On finding the key, I entered.

The house was dead with no electricity until I located the mains switch. My biggest problem was the need for supplies to last me two weeks, as there wasn't much in the house: four tins of tuna and a tin of beans, a kettle and a jar of coffee. I found a shop straight away so I could settle into hiding mode.

I walked in with my hat tucked down to my eye-line and jacket zipped up as high as it could go. The first thing I spotted was a newspaper with the headline of the heist splashed across it. I quickly swayed my eye away from it, thinking the people in the shop were watching. I grabbed a pair of reading glasses from the shelf to aid in my disguise to avoid capture and bought a scarf too. Everyone in Ireland wouldn't be as helpful as Brian and his friends in the pub. Brian struck me as a man that had lived a previous life inside the troubles of Ireland, there was a way about him that led me to trust him.

I kept up to date with the unfolding story, nipping into the pickup every morning to listen to the news.

Apparently, I was hired to construct and carry out the robbery, brought in from overseas, it said. It worried me this story would air back home, worried the son I'd forgotten about, Joe, would see it, and Jack too, for that matter. Jack was acquainted with a Scottish gangster from Dundee, Steve Dean, whom I knew from my prime as a fighter. Steve had a right-hand man named Lukas, an ex-Hungarian police officer from a special division. A special division that was built to find the un-findable. His name carried reputation. Jack would have no second thought about hiring him to track me down if he caught the headlines. He probably already had. My only hope was the story only aired in Ireland.

But hope can land you in trouble. That week was the beginning of me becoming a ghost, invisible to everyone.

After two weeks without a shower and no change of clothes, I stank like a slate of vermin. Another two weeks stuck with my thoughts, I tried to figure out how my sketch got onto the news - it wasn't an up-to-date one either. It had me with short, slicked back, medium length hair which was far longer now. If anything, the picture was at least a couple of years out of date. I kind of figured it hadn't come from any PIRA members that I'd delivered merchandise to. If it was, surely they would have mentioned my disfigurement and longer hair. Like Millacky said, there was a leak. As far as I was aware, the punishment for being a rat in the IRA wouldn't be forgotten and didn't warrant a happy ending. If the IRA couldn't catch you, they turned to your next of kin and they would suffer the retaliation.

The safe house in Carnagh had running water and a shower. That's all I needed and the relief of being able to clean my teeth. My chin had gathered the beginnings of a beard but I wasn't to shave. I needed to change my appearance and a beard would go some way.

I drove through the night for obvious reasons and arrived around 8am. I stormed into the meeting room with the hardwood table. On it was a newspaper, brown envelope, Millacky's and The General's steaming coffee cups. They were waiting, clean dressed and fresh.

I burst in with my eyes wide and annoyance covering my face. That was so out of character for me but that's how pissed I was. I clumped across the wooden flooring, around the left of the table and back of Millacky to the cupboard behind The General. Opening it, I grabbed the whisky and a glass. I returned to my allocated seat, next to Millacky, and started to fill the glass. The last time I'd gone that long without a drink I couldn't remember, and slowly the glass filled with a shaking hand, watching the golden nectar as if I was about to drink from the fountain of youth. Both men watched and witnessed my new side. A side that said, I didn't care whose company I was in, I was Davie Rhodes, and I'd take them on, as I liked. Taking a tight grip of the glass, surrounding it with my shovel-sized hand, I lifted it slowly to my mouth, capturing the moment before swallowing half the glass. The instant relief calmed me down straight away as the whisky burned down my throat. I wasn't finished though; taking my time in making a rollie, refusing to take them on, as Millacky had a cheeky half smirk. I guess it could have been translated as a bit of a tantrum. There were no welcoming greetings and when Millacky decided to break the ice, he wasted no time in getting to the point.

"This is bad for business Davie, we have a rat in our operation and I intend to find him."

"Well, find him you might, but ma face is still fillin' the news," I pointed my finger off the side of the glass while it hung in mid-air.

"This conflict in Ireland is a lasting one. If you stay out of sight, you'll be forgotten. As far as I'm concerned, the authorities don't know my gunrunner. They think you're a hired merchant and so be it, let them assume that."

The General maintained his usual intimidating stare with his neck twisted and forearms resting on the table, brown envelope by his side. His blotched skin annoying my sight. Millacky was calm, arms tucked under the table and shoulders relaxed. I finished the contents of my drink.

"You've done a good job so far. We are happy you've chosen to work with us," The General said, in his dull growl as he slid over the brown envelope full of cash. I stretched out, pulled the envelope towards me and glanced inside. It suddenly drowned out the past two frustrated weeks. Millacky saw my eyes register and felt the drop in tension.

"How much is that?" I queried.

"That painting we stole fetched quite a sizeable amount. Consider that twenty grand payment and bonus," Millacky answered coyly.

"Okay, what's next?" I asked having no clue on where or what he wished me to do.

"We have a change of clothes for you in that bag," Millacky pointed, as I looked over my shoulder and saw a large heavy bag directly to the left under the window, opaque with condensation, "Everything you need to freshen up is inside the bag. I've just had the heating sorted and there's food in the cupboards. This paper here will shed some light on what's happened while you've been away." He picked it up and flipped it over the table. I re-filled my glass and stubbed my rollie out, being far more relaxed after the whisky took away my irritation.

"I take it I'm stayin' here 'en?"

"Yes, things carry on as normal. We still have a major operation in progress and some planning to be put in place. You have guns to sell and money to make. The Vogue drop was perfect." I'm sure he was trying to butter me up.

"It was easier than expected."

"Expect the un-expected and whatever happens, you will be prepared. Your planning was flawless. Do you know how hard it is to find a man that can think for himself as you do?"

201

"No."

"Near impossible."

Chapter 37

Trip To Europe:

Leaving me to my own devices, they vacated the house. In the spare bedroom was a TV, much to my delight. The bag was well stocked with the right size of clothes, a pack of balaclavas, gloves, black combats, shoulder patched black jumpers, black polo necks and heavy duty black boots. There was also a soap bag with all the essentials. Kitting me out properly was a necessity, knowing I couldn't exactly walk into the local River Island.

The Republican paper they left provided me with details about the heist. Twelve of the fourteen involved had been arrested and locked up, awaiting trial. The two missing were Turk and Barb who were still fugitive. Chances of the captured getting off without jail time were slim due to all of them being known members of the PIRA and targets of the police. The capture of the men was considered a stonewall success but they were still after the two missing men, the painting and me, of course. I decided from that day on, when conducting deals and exchanging weapons, I would hide my appearance as much as possible. I also tried to mimic an Irish accent so people couldn't catch my Scots tongue. I had to adapt and survive, as they say in the Navy SEALs.

Time moved on, months in fact, and I lived in the shadows, conducting arms deals, little and large, having several tiny drops around Ireland. There was a trip to Sweden where I travelled across on a commercial airline under disguise: glasses, walking stick, business coat, paper under my arm, loose luggage and clean-cut beard. I arranged a substantial transport of guns fresh from a gun-making factory and delivered them to the poverty-riddled area of Bratislava, Slovakia, using a sat-nav for direction. It was a 2200 kilometre drive in an uncomfortable Bedford army truck. A bent man in the Swedish military snatched the weapons from the factory and contacted Millacky for a body to transport them to Slovakia, the military man making a substantial amount from the consignment.

From the outside, the city looked like a magnificent place with an early nineteenth century castle prominently overlooking a collection of medieval towers, renovated castle ruins and grandiose 20th century buildings, but I entered the slums. There, my eyes opened to a standard of living that can only be described as 'third world'. Mass populated areas of slums and families living in skyscrapers, balconied blocks of flats that appeared as if they had been in the middle of a war-zone and should have been deemed unsafe for humans. Tin huts surrounded with famine and polluted water streams of litter and faeces. It was a far cry from the scenic surroundings of the city.

This was the only job I'd done up until then that I got paid cash on delivery, ten thousand dollars, after inspection of the delivery. A Slovakian, Alexia Janko, the head of an organised crime gang, a hardened stout character with a Desperate Dan grizzled face, dressed all in black with a cheap leather coat and the thickest stainless-steel chain imaginable, accompanied by his right-hand man who was a contradiction to Alexia with unfashionable tracksuit bottoms, zip top and cap.

The handover was done with myself, balaclava on, hiding in the shadows of a secluded corner inside a disused Communist glass factory. I had the truck sitting deep into the bottom floor, instructing them to leave the payment on top of a table, home-made from the scraps of brick and wood. On top of the table was a document the Swede insisted be handed over. An end-user certificate. A piece of paper that was worth its weight in burned charcoal. It was supposed to certify that the buyer was the final recipient of the weapons, and didn't plan on transferring the materials to another party. It was a legal thing, governments required an EUC to clarify the materials wouldn't be passed on to embargoed states or rebel groups. Obviously, they would be, but it was the Swede covering his ass and Alexia Janko had his name on the document.

The payment in dollars annoyed me somewhat, knowing I'd have to exchange the money into euros, but that gave me a little idea. Millacky didn't pester me when I was conducting drops; he had no interest in this delivery, he only supplied aid to the Swede in a dilemma.

The idea of opening a bank account on foreign soil was a solid move, a little safety money, so to speak. Instead of catching a flight back to Dublin, I flew to Luxemburg, used the name on the passport and address provided to open an account with ease.

The money inside that account would be a backup plan. I had to be smart and one step ahead of things now. Usually passports were burned after use, but in this case, I held onto it.

When I wasn't gallivanting, the safe house in Carnagh was my main point of stay. There was an internet connection and I purchased a laptop, something else I had to learn about. I was an analogue man stuck in a digital world - using a computer was alien to me and constant calls to Rankin were necessary in my learning how to use it. It was surreal that a man travelling around Europe, delivering high end merchandise, didn't know how to use a laptop but, hey, I'd never had any need in the past. It frustrated the fuck out of me but I learned, having little choice. I used online shopping to have essentials delivered to random houses around the area, instructing the drivers to leave the shopping at the door, pretending that it was my house. Of course, this meant surveilling a house for a day beforehand to check the occupants' daily pattern, taking a gamble no-one would be at home at delivery time. The life of running guns wasn't as exotic as it sounded. It was a lonely but addictive game to be in. Knowing I worked for the IRA and danced on the edge of getting caught was a thrill.

Smuggling guns, as I was doing, was referred to in the industry as the black area, totally illegal. The big-time gunrunners used legal methods with licences and permits, that being a problem for me as it produced a trail and anyone who wanted you dead, for whatever reason, could find you a lot easier.

Every time a bank account Rankin created was used, it was then deleted and Rankin issued me with new details when needed. I had no idea how he was able do it and I didn't need to know. I asked The General to pick up a drum of petrol and a hand pump. I also asked for tobacco and lighters, and he dropped off around a year's supply. With these things in place, the visits to shops were down to a minimum.

The best thing about the 'net was being able to keep tabs on the news, stories of conflicts in other countries and other gun crimes and so forth. The excitement of the heist between Irish governments died down, and my picture vacated the news channels and newspapers. Millacky was right, it was now old news.

The final stages of planning were coming together for the bombings on three different barracks across England on November the 8th 2008. It was approaching the end of October and I'd been more active than ever in the past couple of months. I looked forward to it being done and dusted.

 I had to face a stern reality, men would lose their lives because of the weapons I supplied, but if I didn't deliver them, someone else would. I took the cash, followed orders, and filled my pockets.

Chapter 38

Black World Of Death:

As another important date, Max's eighteenth birthday on the 31st October approached, I thought it was about time to check in with Donny. I always phoned him from a phone-box and located an isolated one in Armagh.

"Hello," Donny spoke.

"Alright brother, how's tricks?" As usual he picked up on my voice.

"Tricks are good, really good. How's life?"

"Good Donny, can't complain."

"To what do I owe the pleasure?"

"How's ma boy?"

"He's out!" Donny said.

"Oh aye. Where is he?"

"He's hanging around at Jack's, came over to Devil's one day to see Ringo."

"How did he do his time?" By that, I was referring to how the jail had treated him.

"By the looks of him, not well. He's quiet, very quiet, and he's a big lad now."

"He's always been quiet," I stated.

"Aye, but he's different. He seems like he's contemplating suicide every time I see him," a quiet pause between us, "they let him out early."

"Why?"

"On a technicality or something. Rumour is, he done over the governor in an act of revenge."

"Revenge for what?"

"The screws beat him constantly for two and a half years. The boys in blue let him off. I think they felt sorry for him."

"The governor beat him?"

"Don't know. They say Max stabbed him with a pair of scissors and it took four screws to haul him off."

"How do you know this?"

"I only know what rumours I hear and what Ringo tells me."

"What's he doin' wi' Jack? Has he no' figured out Jack put him in there?"

"No idea, do you want me to have a word?"

"No, leave him to walk his own path. He'll figure it out eventually."

Building my retirement fund was all for him, well mostly. One day, we'd be reunited and I could give him more money than he could count, but until then, I had to keep making the coin.

So, he'd killed a man, I hope the governor deserved his end. He'd been beaten and it was because of Jack and his sordid way of dealing with people who crossed him. Max would figure that out eventually, well I hoped he would. Once you take a life, it's hard to recover. It scares you because there's always a piece of you that knows what you're capable of. There wasn't much I could do for him, stuck in this black world of death.

All I could do was keep tabs on him and hope Jack didn't use him for his own malicious benefit.

Chapter 39

Fishing Trip:

The last delivery I made before Millacky's day of devastation was a shipment to England, two weeks prior, using Rankin and his plane, landing a load of AK47, M16s, 9mm handguns, stun grenades, high-velocity sniper rifles and scopes, bullet-proof vests and hundreds of rounds of ammo. It almost cleared out the arms bunker on top of the other guns delivered before that date.

Every worthwhile piece of equipment was taken from the bunker and delivered to one man called Eclipse, who would disperse them to specific locations around England. Eclipse was a hired man, a mercenary for the IRA. All he cared about was himself, as he didn't stop to wonder if what he was doing was wrong or inhuman. His personality was an uncaring one, even more so than Millacky and The General.

Not one soul outside the IRA knew about the havoc that would strike on November the 8th, which was the scariest thing about carting that consignment across sea and air for the upcoming attack. It sickened me to think about the devastation that would occur. I passed on six hundred pounds of Semtex and bomb-making equipment to Eclipse who relayed it to a source in London. The amount of weaponry that was transported across the sea was enough to furnish a small army.

Once the drop with Eclipse was done, I headed back to the safe house for a meeting with Millacky and The General. We had our usual seats around the table only days before the attack.

"After the 8th The General and I will be disappearing for a while, a long while, and you'll be a quiet man. I suggest you leave the country for a time, get yourself some cocktails and sun." I partook in the meeting with a glass of whisky by my side.

The other two didn't drink.

"I'll consider a little fishin' trip somewhere," I answered.

"Here's your pay for the faultless job you have done for us." The General slid the standard A4 sized brown envelope across the desk. I picked it up and placed it to my side.

"You usually look inside Davie," Millacky pointed out.

"Na, it's okay, I know what's in there."

"You never know who you can trust."

I turned my look to his, "If you wanted to rip me off, you would've done so by now."

"Maybe so Davie." Millacky slid his hand inside his blazer pocket and pushed a phone across the table, "Turn this phone on every morning after the eighth at 10am sharp. Leave it on for ten minutes then turn it off again. Despite us being 'on holiday', we will still need to keep in touch."

To me that meant something, something different. Previously he stated my position would be known every minute of every day. Now he suggested that he would only know where I was if I answered the phone, or it could mean another thing? What if he tracked the phone to find my position? Either way it sounded dodgy. It could have meant he was going to do away with me, my services not required after the completion of the attacks.

Would he have the chance though?

Chapter 40

Flat Down On The Ground:

Millacky's date with destiny, the eighth, arrived. Inside the bedroom of the safe house, the telly was on, as I waited for the news to air. It had passed the time Millacky said the blast would go off, but I'd heard nothing. Impatiently, I listened to the news, mainly interested in the death-toll, praying it would be zero. Pacing across the floorboards, smoking too much and constantly re-filling my glass, I was aware my conscience was struggling to stay calm, thinking the bomb would wipe out all the barracks with undesirable repercussions. I was no killer in this trade. I was a man on a mission to become rich.

Into the afternoon, still nothing and I began to think that the destruction would be too shocking for the public eye. I started flicking through all the Irish channels, but still nothing. I all but gave up hope, tuning into an antiques programme when it was interrupted by a news bulletin:

"We interrupt this programme for an exclusive breaking story." (The background brought up a picture of IRA men lying flat on the ground with their hands tie-wrapped behind their backs.) "This morning, a joint operation by the MI5 and the SAS infiltrated a combination of terrorist attacks on three different army barracks across England. Early reports suggest that the Real IRA are responsible. A total of twelve members of the IRA have been shot and killed and another twenty-six have been arrested, including

Conner Millacky, nick-named C4 Millacky, the head of the Real IRA."

The news reporter carried on relating the story then stopped in mid-sentence.

"Just a second…some new information is coming across. The intelligence gathered by MI5 for this mission is thought to be down to an informant inside the IRA. Sadly, he was gunned down in the attack and moments ago, died of internal bleeding." (Instantly, he was being heralded a hero by the British public.) "The hero's real name is Micky Macabrely, known inside the Real IRA as The General."

I spat out a mouthful of ale all over the telly. The General was the informant! Unbelievable! To me, he was as cold-hearted as any other I'd met inside the IRA, but the news report indicated otherwise and why lie about something like that?

The report went on to say four members of the SAS were injured and hospitalised, but it was thought they would pull through. I breathed a sigh of relief, expecting to witness mass-murder of innocent people but the results were good, considering. I sat down and absorbed the rest of the story. It was at least twenty minutes before it dawned, I no longer had an employer. Immediately, I became aware of the benefit of my freedom but of course, on the other hand, I had no employer. I had nowhere near the amount of money needed to make an exit, even though this was my best opportunity to vacate with the boss in jail and The General dead.

As I mulled over the options, I heard a car pull down the track road and come into the drive. From the window of the bedroom, I peeked through the curtains. Again, I didn't have a fucking gun on me and I was a gunrunner! The car crept closer, a black Volkswagen Golf I had no recognition of. It pulled up as I switched sides at the window, pulling back the screen to see who exited the driver's door, to my utter relief, it was Rankin.

 I returned to my seat on the bed, listening to him enter the back door and tiptoe through the house until he arrived at the bedroom door.

 On kicking the door open, he burst in with his handgun pointed.

 "Fuck, it's you!" he exclaimed.

 "Nice to see you too," I responded, trying to appear calm.

 "What the fuck you doing here?" he asked, lowering his gun.

 "Probably the same as you, lyin' low. Is it true?"

 "Is what true?"

 "You haven't heard?" He pulled his neck back, "Look at the telly Rankin."

 He walked around the telly, sat on the edge of the bed, and watched the news on repeat.

 "Holy shite! What's happened?"

 "What do you mean, what's happened? The attacks went up in smoke."

 "What attack?" He didn't know. I thought all people would've known and especially the most reliable man in the division. I went on to explain what had happened, Millacky's plan and The General being an informant.

 "I knew Millacky had something planned, but I had no idea it was something of this magnitude." He seemed as passionate an Irishman as the rest I'd met, but his lack of knowledge seemed genuine.

 "How could you nae know?"

"I'm a middleman Davie. I fly planes, forge documents, make contacts. I'm not taken with the violent side of things. I do my job and make my money, that's it."

As ideas go that I've had in the past, this one was up there with the best.

"How do you fancy makin' some real money, cut out the IRA completely, and become rich men?"

"You're reading my mind, Mr Rhodes."

Chapter 41

Missing Locker:

"So, what's the first move?" Rankin asked.

"The first thing we need to do is empty what's left of the arms bunker and obtain a new one." The arms bunker was low in supply and the sensible thing would be to move all the merchandise to a new location. It would be the perfect time; the authorities would have their hands occupied at that moment.

"We're moving all the weapons away from the two bunkers?"

"Two?"

"What?" he countered with a question of his own.

"You said two. I only know of one," I cross-examined him.

"The one beside Donegal and the one in Belfast."

"Belfast?" It seemed Millacky only told certain people in his regime certain things.

"The one below the church, off Falls Road."

Instead of asking more about this bunker, I needed to know what was in it.

"What's inside?"

"I've never been inside…I've no idea," Rankin shrugged, and opened his palms towards me.

"We'll head there later, but first we need a van, a big one."

"I'll get a van," he assured me, and immediately left.

I packed up my stuff into a big holdall, waited and planned my next moves.

I continued to watch the news. Millacky was about to be charged with all kinds, mass-murder, directing the activities of a terrorist organisation, conspiring unlawfully and maliciously to bring explosions and carnage to the United Kingdom.

It also went on to explain the Real IRA had six men who had enlisted in the British army, having been enrolled since they were sixteen. Two in each of the three-targeted barracks. On the day, the undercover soldiers had planted C4 bombs with timers to go off at 10.43am, next to explosives like a gas tank or a chemical lab. The timers were disconnected due to the intelligence source that was The General. The bomb was planned to create carnage, while a team of IRA members, blending into the background as pedestrians and road sweepers, hiding inside the back of vans, were to storm the gates with heavy vehicles and set off another three Semtex charged bombs. After that, the IRA foot soldiers were to storm the barracks and kill as many as possible, but every member was caught within a couple of hours and locked up. All members of the elite Real IRA were doomed. As far as I was aware, Millacky had used up his collection of loyal men for the job. That gave me free reign. I had been getting used to the loneliness and life in the shadows, now it was time to take it a step further. Unknown to Millacky, I had collected a note-book of phone numbers and contacts. That night he passed out drunk in the safe house, I had copied every number into my notebook, but all text was written in code. I had forwarded them to my phone to decipher later. Then there was Rankin, who like me, didn't care for the killing and only wanted to make coin. Two things we had in common and two things that would make us rich men.

I needed some infantry and that led to the birth of 'The Stable', four men, men who would know the delicacies of the trade and men who weren't fearful of capture. I had already thought of two.

Chapter 42

Time For Church:

Turk and Barb were right when they had said Millacky was on the way down, and down he sank to a lifelong sentence inside a maximum-security jail in Belmarsh Prison. That gave me a reassuring feeling of safety and a free rein. There was no empathy for the man, his fate was always going to be capture.

Turk and Barb were two men I could utilise to my benefit. But, getting a hold of men like that wasn't an easy task.

Me and Rankin emptied the arms-bunker into the van by the wheelbarrow and bag method. It was a gruelling task but we got it done, starting at 4am and working till 6.30am. Over the space of a few days and long trips to the van and back, the task was complete. We cleaned the bunker out dry, didn't leave an item inside. We also sealed the hatch more securely by rolling a heavy boulder over the top that nearly broke our backs.

As my aging body felt the pain of this, I had to remember the reasoning for it. It was the money, as I've said, but really, it was all for my boy I'd one day see again. It was a boundless feeling, knowing that I wasn't being watched and an even greater one knowing that finally, I became my own boss. Years of taking irritating orders from people I either didn't like or didn't understand were not to happen now.

As I drove the van, full of stock that could embed me and Rankin to the same fate as Millacky, I started to get that buzzing feeling that what we were doing was so off-scale it was almost incredible. The whole time I drove, Rankin attempted to contact Turk and Barb, with

218

little success. The paranoia levels throughout every IRA organisation in Ireland were on high alert.

As we loomed closer to Belfast, Rankin directed me to Falls Road. It was a republican part of the city, and I wondered if there would be any patrols going on since the failed mission. The murals of International Solidarity, revolutionary groups and heroes, painted proudly and masterfully on the sides of buildings, reminded every Irish man and woman of their country's past troubles. Heroes who sacrificed their lives, like Bobby Sands, whose mural was proudly showcased on the side of Sinn Féin's office wall. He was the leader of the Maze prison hunger-strike and died as a result of that very protest in 1981. That street gave you the chilling feeling that the war could ignite at any time and in Millacky's case, that's exactly what he had attempted.

"Carry on up this road and the church is on the left," Rankin directed.

"That easy is it?" I was being sarcastic.

"You'll be surprised how easy it is." I think he was referring to driving about Belfast's streets with an armoury in the back of a van, "See that red building?" he pointed, his finger resting on the windscreen.

"Don't point, man! We're tryin' to stay inconspicuous here," I whined.

"Settle down there! You're fine. Park up across the road," he persisted.

I mounted the pavement on the main road, outside a convenience store. The church was a dominating red-brick building that had been built in the late nineteenth century. It appeared to have two entrances, from where we were sitting, one down the side street and one that looked onto Falls Road. It had all the features a usual church would have, tall narrow windows, impressive architecture, with wide and high arched doors, the Catholic cross mounted with a statue of Jesus and two statues, one at either side of the main figure.

"Where is it 'en?" I asked curiously.

"In the basement. Come on, let's have a gander," he said casually, as he patted my shoulder with his hand and pulled the handle of the door.

"Wait, we can't leave the van here."

"Sure we can. It'll be fine. Lock the door." He came over way too casual with a gun reserve residing in the back.

"Of course I'm goin' to lock the fuckin' door."

Walking across the street, my head kept twitching behind at the van parked on the pavement. It didn't seem wise leaving so much money sitting there like that and inside a Republican territory too. I began to think Rankin had a few screws loose.

The interior of the church was as spectacular as the outside, as I walked in with my neck stretching towards the roof, admiring the construction. As I took it in, I slowed down and lost pace behind Rankin who absconded down the aisle between the pews.

"Have a pew. I'll be back in a minute."

He disappeared into the church confession box so I sat down, my heart thumping beats of adrenaline and excitement. My legs were restless so I distracted the discomfort by getting the tobacco tin out. While I made one rollie and started on another, a nun nipped past, glaring at me with disgust. I returned the tin to my pocket.

"Sorry sister." She passed and hissed as Rankin exited the confession box, a little grin on his puffy face.

"The priest will contact Turk and Barb, and I got these," he shook a set of keys hanging from his finger.

"For what?"

220

"The dungeon," he replied, as he hurried away like a teenager at the sight of free alcohol, and I followed.

We went out through a door at the rear of the church, behind the baptism bath, a maze of stairs headed downwards, a few more corridors and doors led to a solid steel door at the bottom.

"Holy shite!" I exclaimed, after Rankin turned on the lights. In front of me was a line of six locked medieval jail cells, the first three with their own collection of arms, the last three were empty.

"Not bad eh?" Rankin grinned from ear to ear.

"Who else knows about this place?"

"Well, let's see. The priest upstairs, and Millacky, I expect!"

It was a perfect place for storage, absolutely spot on. A couple of the cells even had beds, which had become a luxury for me over the years.

"Do you think we could use this place?" I asked Rankin.

"Possibly. It would be a risk." A risk worth taking with only the priest to keep happy.

"What's the story on the Priest?"

"If he thinks he's helping the war, then he should comply with a little payoff now and again."

"Good. Well there's no need to look elsewhere. We'll move the guns in here and you can sort out the priest."

Under the cover of night, the van was reversed into the back and unloaded into the church, before the tiring task of getting all the stuff downstairs. The priest arranged with the nuns to make us some supper and provide a couple of beds for the night.

It was bliss and a little surreal doing this under their noses, but it worked. If something works well, don't change it. I demanded and collected the only two keys for the door and kept them both. The priest came up

221

trumps with arranging a meeting with Turk and Barb at a safe house. I was to meet them the following day at lunchtime.

Chapter 43

Respect Needed:

Turk and Barb waited inside the safe house at 12 noon. I knocked on the back door. One of the twins answered, wearing the standard IRA military surplus, balaclava, patched jumper and combat trousers, holding a fixed arm and a handgun with a silencer attached. Why he was wearing a balaclava, I wasn't sure. The house was in darkness with the blinds and curtains closed. He pulled me inside the darkened kitchen with a firm grip on my bomber coat, and continued to point the gun at me with a solid arm.

"Fuckin' hell lad! I'm no' the enemy," I stated, with my limber arms relaxed.

"Pat him down!" Turk shouted, coming from the front room into the kitchen, as I realised it was Barb, the quiet one, who pointed the gun. Their hostility was acceptable considering the Real IRA had just been outmanned and taken out of service; yet these men weren't part of the Real IRA but the provisional IRA. The PIRA downgraded their pursuit of violence back in 1998 when they announced their disarmament.

Turk ploughed my face against the wall, spread my arms and patted me down from neck to ankles, checking for a wire and even poked the inside of my ear for a piece.

"Lads, I don't know what ye're doin', but we're on the same side."

They couldn't be sure as I was Scottish bred, not holding the same passion as they did.

"What're you here for?" Turk bellowed into my ear, the forceful loud ramble wasn't agreeing.

"I'm here to offer a proposal," I stated.

"What?" Turk yelled directly into my ear, pulling out his own weapon while his brother still pointed his, and flung me around until I faced him, holding his palm forcefully on my chest and gun pressed against my lung.

"Son, I'd listen well to what I'm about to say to you. If that gun doesn't remove itself from ma chest, one of two things is goin' to happen. One, it's either goin' off in ma face and that will be ma end and the start of yer destruction, or two, I'm goin' to retract that gun from yer hand while happily takin' whatever bullets fly into me and then pound ma fist continually into yer ribcage until I rip yer heart out and shove it back down yer throat."

What I meant was, I hoped Turk and Barb would figure out that a higher member in the Real IRA wouldn't take too kindly to my death under the present crisis, but it was a gamble, a form of deceit.

My composure of being under no threat from the gun in my face worried them; they were used to seeing fear and panic, but in me they saw nothing. It appeared almost as if I didn't care whether to live or die, but the truth was, I was shitting it. Turk looked at Barb, with an acceptance that I was no enemy and lowered his gun, placing it on the kitchen counter at the same time as Barb placed his down.

Turk held his palms out towards me in an apologetic gesture. They both removed their balaclavas, lifting the awkwardness.

"Right, is that you two kids finished? Now can we get down to business?" I showed my arm, leading them into the sitting room that was also darkened by closed blinds. I took my tobacco tin out on the kitchen counter and turned my back to them, looking over my shoulder, seeing both men watch me in return. I did feel a little flustered and it took the moment to lower my heart rate.

"Now, we are goin' to learn a lesson here." I stepped into the room, while Turk and Barb slid 9-inch-long fixed blades from their waist holsters. "I don't take to threats very well," I stated, while taking the lighter from my pocket and sparking the rollie.

Barb dropped his knife and fell to the deck, clutching his right shin bone. I turned the gun in Turk's direction, "I especially don't like being shouted at." A blow to his right shoulder sent him stumbling backwards onto the window, disturbing the blinds, before sliding down a wall, leaving a trickle of blood.

"Get away from the window Turk! Don't want the neighbours comin' round."

"You're a fuckin' prick!" Barb moaned, the first words I had heard from him, while sliding about on the bare laminate flooring.

"Aye boy, I might be a prick, but I'm the prick holdin' the gun and ye're the prick on the deck."

It wasn't Barb's first wound, but he made a lot of racket over it. I was more impressed by Turk's reaction. He grimaced in hatred, perched up against the wall, hand on his wound. It showed me he was already looking for revenge. That was the only occasion I'd ever use a gun.

"Now that I have yer full attention, I'm goin' to leave this house and return at the exact same time next week. You two will open the door and welcome me in wi' a smile and a cup of coffee, two sugars and milk, no decaffeinated pish. Alright? And we'll speak about this proposal."

Both responded at the same time.

"Aye."

Chapter 44

One Week Later:

I stood at the door at precisely 11.59 a week later and chapped again. When Barb opened it, he silently invited me in with a nod and a step backward. Turk stood in the kitchen stirring my cup of coffee. They bought a kettle, sugar, coffee, cups, spoons, and a pint of milk just because I asked.

"Fine day today boys," I was being sarcastic about the wintery day.

"It's stunning," Turk replied, in his own mocking manner.

They both seemed more eager to show me respect. A week before I had humiliated them and it seemed they had learned their lesson. I casually walked around the empty house without a care in the world, hands hanging loosely by my side. Barb limped into the front room, and Turk followed with my coffee, his shoulder-dressing evident by the bulge in his jumper.

"Nice coffee. What is it?"

"Kenco, just the normal stuff," Turk answered.

"You'll have to make the coffee more often, Turk."

Ignoring the lure of small talk, Turk got right into the business matter, "What's this proposal then?"

"Millacky is locked up, The General is dead." Mentioning The General seemed important considering he was the grass, "I'm takin' over and I want to hire you two to work for me."

They exchanged dubious looks with each other, but were eager to hear more.

"Millacky picked and chose who he sold to, I won't. We have the chance to make money, lots of money, and it would be easier if I had a stable of men to work wi'."

226

After another exchange of glances, then Turk asked, "how much money?"

That unpretentious question told me that they were my men.

"Well, that all depends how many contracts I acquire." Again, there was a little break in conversation, "I know you weren't big admirers of Millacky and you had the gumption no to get captured for the government heist he hired you for. That means ye're smart. How much did he pay you?"

"Considerably well, but it could've been better."

"Well, times that 'considerably well' by a large number and that's the kind of money you can make from me." I was making a false promise there, but I was taking a gamble in being able to secure some contracts.

"How's this going to work?" Turk asked, as he folded his arms in his patched jumper.

"I will contact you when needed, otherwise you have to live in the shadows like I have done. It's the only way it will work. Can't leave trails of where you've been. I operate in the black market of weapons so I'll supply identification, and means of transport. Provisions of weapons will come from me, yer job is to deliver the goods and ma job is to pay you."

"Where's the artillery coming from? As far as I can see, the Real IRA have been cleaned out and you're out of business."

"No, gentlemen, I'm just startin' business."

Chapter 45

The Hiring Of The Mercenary:

With the services of the first two stable members secured, a trip was arranged to secure the services of the next man. It was Christmas Eve, of all days, and Rankin flew me over to the same landing-strip he had picked me up from a couple of years prior. He hired a vehicle and we drove to the meeting place, a motorway services café, south of Newcastle. I didn't feel the need to go any further in the country, even though Max wasn't that far away. Me and Rankin were munching on a delicious full English breakfast when Eclipse entered and stomped over to our table, plopped himself directly opposite me and to the side of Rankin. He didn't disturb my breakfast enjoyment, but called the waitress over and ordered himself one. Unlike the other two stable members, Eclipse was a brute of a man, filling his space with a bulging chest that pushed the table out.

"So, to what do I owe this rare pleasure?" I had met Eclipse on three separate occasions while I smuggled the consignment of weapons to England for the failed terrorist attacks.

"Thought we'd fly over for a visit since it's Christmas, ma friend."

"Bullshit! Who's this?" he gripped the fork in a tight fist, pointed from the side at Rankin while keeping his stare on mine.

"This here is Rankin, an associate of mine." Rankin nodded as he continued with his food. Eclipse looked to the counter to see if his breakfast was near. By the look of him, he didn't enjoy waiting for food and probably ate more than the standard three meals, "I suppose you've heard Millacky's been locked up?"

"I know all about it. I watch the news." He glared at the counter again.

"Good, that'll save me time. Pass the salt would you?" I asked Rankin, "I'm looking for a man to hire from time to time."

"What you looking for, a gofer? Cuz this man to my side here," using the fork to point again, "would fit the bill better than me."

Rankin was an articulate educated man who by no means enjoyed confrontation, very non-aggressive, but he turned his head with a spiteful glare. Eclipse poked his chin out in Rankin's direction.

"What's wrong with you boy?" Eclipse asked, looking for a reaction.

"WOW! Calm down, who's ruffled yer feathers this mornin'?" I reacted as his breakfast arrived. It worked out well, kept him quiet. Rankin returned to his food and tried not to let his elbow brush his new-found friend.

"Listen, I'm lookin' for a body in England to run some merchandise when needed, just like you did before. Nothing fancy, will be pick-up and drop-off."

"When? I've got another job lined up." Couldn't believe the neck of this guy. You could hardly inform the boss in your other job that you needed time off to gun run to loathsome characters.

"As and when needed. I haven't got a work plan to look upon." He tilted his head to his shrugged shoulder, guessing that was a yes. We chatted until we all finished breakfast and me and Rankin headed off.

Once we were in the car, Rankin revealed his feelings about the man.

"You want that guy to run the consignments? You're crazy, disaster waiting to happen," he spouted off on a wee rant.

"I'm glad you have faith in him, cuz you'll be his partner."

The beginnings were all in place. We travelled home to start the search for our first drop. We contacted all the major players letting them know we were still in business. That would become my job, because I had to get used to the communication side of things. We sat down at the computer in the safe house in Carnagh. Believe it or not, there were actual web pages with 'Wanted' advertisements for arms all over the world and particularly in Europe, opening a whole new can of opportunities, but it had to be carried out illegally. Doing it in the white would mean paperwork and licences were necessary to cross borders, creating a trail, I didn't like that. Instead, we picked the most corrupt countries to start dealing. As far I as I was concerned, my time working for the IRA was over. I now had the ability to become a successful gunrunner, and that's exactly what I set out to do.

Rankin went on to explain that running arms across borders was no picnic and repeatedly, over the years, the IRA had failed on many occasions, especially consignments sent from Libyan leader, Colonel Gaddafi. The IRA were fortunate when Gaddafi donated boatloads of weapons in the mid-eighties, sympathising with their war against the British, but it was never plain sailing. Intelligence agencies and hidden informants would try to disrupt the flow and inevitably, many would fail to reach their destination.

The collection of the sympathetic Irish in the USA was another source the IRA counted upon in the past to seek out and flood Ireland with as much devastating weaponry as possible. A known gunrunner, George Harrison, emigrated to America for just that reason and sent back over two thousand five hundred weapons to the shores in the eighties. But it was never easy: often weapons would be transported in oil drums or container ships, hidden amongst ridiculous things like office equipment, food containers, fishing boats or anything that offered a legitimate disguise. The biggest problem when attempting to operate in the white area was paperwork. If you were transporting across land, each border would require a different piece of paper to confirm the entry or pass through of weapons. That was never going to work for our operation.

Part 3

The Swing Back Home

Chapter 46

The Money Flows:

In 2010, my sketch crept onto the MI5 'Wanted' list, labelled with a nickname, The Eidolon, translated as a 'phantom', and that's exactly what I had become. It laid the foundation that I was a known entity and being watched.

My loyal stable complied with my requests with the highest regard and with only minor hiccups, everything ran smoothly, too smoothly most of the time. I say 'minor' because there was one deal at the end of 2011 with a London crew, known as The Ghetto Gang, which caused a problem. The Ghetto Gang, a team of coloured men who dressed in a hip-hop style, wearing baggy clothes and funky hats, from the Brixton area in London. Dodgy characters, as most were in this world.

Eclipse and Rankin conducted the deal of twenty Berretta handguns and a dozen pump-action tactical shotguns with the usual high dose of rounds, shells and mags. The Berretta was a common request from the British Isles, but most of the time, people didn't care what metal work armed them as long as they operated and looked the part. The Eidolon name passed through the circuit, many divisions of the main cities gangs and gangsters required my service, and I was to provide.

On the back end of the deal, a heavily armed and professional SWAT team made a rapid entrance, seeing The Ghetto Gang arrested. Rankin explained that the raid was too specialised to be only police at work and they barely got away. I suspected it was MI5. My English Stable were able to make an exit, utilising their skills of desertion. A strange thing after the bust, no news coverage aired; usually, something like that warranted a headline story, but nothing. I always kept an eye on various web-sites, newspapers and international news channels for information on the European crime circuit.

The thing about dealing guns, if there are crimes, greed, quarrels and conflicts somewhere, there would be a need for weapons.

There was a detailed way to transport guns legally across borders with permits, end-user certificates, export and import licences, but I never succumbed to that itch. When crossing between the European Union countries, hunting rifles required an EPP, European firearms pass. Any other arms required an export licence issued by the Export Control Organisation, prior import consent obtained from the relevant authority in the destination country, and passing from a union state to a non-union state required authorisation of exports of non-military firearms in line with the UN Firearms Protocol.

Sure, I gave it thought, but it was a cluster-fuck of paperwork and licences, meaning I would need to create even more aliases and have to deal with airport staff, border security and departments of import and export. That would require me to show face, write signatures and indulge in small talk. That would bring an abrupt end to my secret operation. I preferred to find bent and deceitful people who would deal under the table and believe me, there were plenty of them. The Slovakian, Alexia Janko, to whom I dropped the consignment from Sweden, opened connections to south eastern Europe's organised crime gangs, like the sex trafficking gang in Chisinau, Moldova who smuggled Chinese and Thai girls across Europe. The Albania Mafia, who are more dangerous and powerful than the Columbian Cartels, needed an unconnected source to deliver large munitions of their own to connecting syndicates in Israel, Belgium and Italy. All this activity lead to gaining further connections with guerrilla armies, large and small. I had encountered a few desperate men in the trade, bold in giving their merchandise away for cheap, and my Swedish military contact had a habit of throwing out defective weapons with damaged components that were deemed unacceptable for use. Usually only one dysfunctional part in the gun like a faulty trigger, the release button for the mag, bent barrels, uneven lines of sight, dents or even heavily scratched, meant the guns with the faults were all discarded.

 Three times between 2009 and 2011, the Swedish contact requested I make the trip and pick up his profitable scrap. Needless to say, I accepted and transported the cargo by ship to the shores of Britain. They were transported in oil drums that were marked as 'consumable waste'. Inside the drum was filled with waste oil from the factory, provided by the Swede. The parts were thrown inside and the drum strapped to a pallet to reduce movement. The Swede would provide a shipping container with all the relevant in date certs for it to pass through Europe. I marked the drums and container with 'contaminated waste' stickers: who would want to open that and risk contracting a chemical disease? Everything was done in broad daylight by the Swede's factory workers while I chilled out at a nearby café, drinking coffee and catching up with the news on my tablet.

Once the container landed on the shores of Southern Ireland, I unloaded the consignment, ditched the barrels and scrapped the container. Transferring the load to the arms bunker, I had Turk and Barb construct as many functioning weapons as they could. Once done, any parts, surplus to requirements, were scrapped and the now fully functional weapons were scattered across Europe. It was beautiful.

The Stable of Turk and Barb took over my old job, overseeing the arms bunker under St Paul's Church. Instructing them I wanted the arsenal arranged, cleaned and inspected, they did a faultless job. As word spread of a gunrunner in Ireland who didn't choose sides, the orders and requests came in from all angles, but they were lacking somewhat. The troubles in Ireland were dormant and the Real IRA were all serving long jail-terms and that was bad for business, but random requests did occasionally filter across the desk from small outfits of rebels still opposed to British rule. Turk and Barb were my main men in Ireland, because, in fact, my time in that country became rare, choosing to remain outside most of the time.

They completed jobs to a firm set of rules I had laid down, talk as little as you can, keep heavily armed, always dress in black, wear gloves and keep the face covered. Once a vehicle was used, destroy it, and never leave a paper-trail. On jobs where money would be exchanged, they had to be paid first, as in the money had to be in their possession before the merchandise was handed over. In big operations, I was paid through offshore shell accounts. It was a necessity to be paid before the delivery. In some cases, I would be paid halfway through the transfer, depending on who I worked for.

We had just finished our biggest operation yet, when an enlisted government contract for arms appeared on a site named Euro Arms Contracts, and it was a little out of character.

'WANTED. 10,000 automatic and semi-automatic weapons for the Caucasian Emirate.'

The Caucasian Emirate was a militant Jihadist organisation, active in southwestern Russia, that used to be named the Chechen Republic of Ichkeria, the most hostile environment in Europe. After two wars with the Russian Federation during the nineties, the President of Ichkeria renamed the area as Caucasian Emirate, with the intention of eliminating the Russian presence from North Caucasus and establishing an independent Islamic Emirate in the region. The whole area had been engulfed in two separate Chechen Wars, and on 16 April 2009, it had all but ended, when another feud kicked off when a new warlord desired his own state. Arguments over religion and Caucasian men turning to fight in the Middle East, I could go on for hours about the politics, but the only thing I cared for was to arm this man and get paid. If I didn't arm him, someone else would collect on pay day.

The advert was brief, vague, and too short, with the lack of information leading me to believe it had nothing to do with the government.

Sometimes jobs like this appeared on that site. You needed an elite standing to be able to advertise on there, but on the odd occasion, someone would gain illegal access for a limited time, and it would include a phone number as it would only be a matter of minutes before it would be removed. It was only by chance that someone would pick it up and luckily enough that was me. All the other adverts included an email address for contact and a lot more information, but this one was just a phone number and single sentence. With myself in full charge of the operations, I was obliged to call, using a voice-muffler to camouflage my voice and speaking more proper.

"Hello!" a voice spoke in Russian or whatever lingo people spoke in southwest Russia.

"English?" I asked.

"Yes, I speak English."

"I'm calling about your wanted ad."

"Wanted ad? What do you mean, ad for new television or ad for 10,000 automatic and semi-automatic weapons?"

"I'm not in the business of selling electrical goods."

"Good, good," he said slowly, with a very deep mutter, "The name's Uri."

"Okay Uri, how can I be of service?"

"Can you get me these arms?"

"I could and I will, if the price is right Uri. What do you need?"

"The automatic M4 carbine with grenade launcher attachment…and the semi-automatic version."

"Five thousand of each?" I asked, the advert stated, 'ten thousand'.

"Yes, five thousand of each."

"Are you looking to start a war, Mr Uri?"

"No, end one." That was a lot of guns and not ones I could locate overnight. They were American guns and I would need to find an armoury.

America was deep in conflict in the Middle East and very paranoid about shifting weapons to foreign bodies, not to mention a Russian state.

"Give me some time and I'll get back to you Uri ....?" I was indicating that he should hand over his surname.

"Why do you need last name?"

237

"I need to make sure you're not a leach leaving a trail of slime. And if you don't inform me of your surname I'll be forced to put down this phone." These men were always desperate to get armed. It was like hanging a pair of succulent titties over a virgin's head, he'd be sure to take a grab.

"Very well. Popov, and yours?"

"The Eidolon, Mr Popov."

"The famous Eidolon!"

Firstly, I had to find out who this man was, the standard background check of any individual I took contracts from. That was Rankin's department.

"I have our next job," I said to him over the phone, "it's a big account but I need you to look over some files before I accept."

"Sure, I'll get on it right away. Send through the information, give me a little time to look over the file and I'll get back to you."

"Perfect."

I forwarded the information via fax. I always carried a laptop and requested a fax machine in my five-star hotel room. No more B&Bs and sleeping in cars for me.

While waiting, I ordered some room-service for lunch, instructing them to knock and leave the tray outside the door. I still believed in being seen as little as possible, even when in a 5-star hotel in a foreign country. By now, I had managed to almost hide my limp, but my leg still hurt like a bitch. I continued to devour strong painkillers but upped the dosage to prescribed ones, becoming immune to the weaker kind. Strangely, my drinking died down around that time but it was more to do with the perfectionist I'd become. The thrill of the game took over my need to drink heavily, but the excitement of the game wasn't all that it was made out to be. I was lonely and missed the touch of a woman. I could afford the good ones now and wasn't shy in ordering escorts to my room. Prostitution, the oldest trade they say, who was I to judge?

The incoming fax filtered through the machine.

A picture of an Islamic extremist came to my eye. He wore a Taliyah, the Muslim cap that's shaped like a bowl, with Maverick shades and a long jubba, an ankle-length robe-like garment.

Uri was one of the top men at the head of the insurgency movement in the Caucasian Emirate, opposed to the Russian hand of power. A vigilante who was building his own army to feed his narcissistic side of violence. He had mixed blood of Russian and Syrian, named by his father and followed his mother's muslim beliefs, since he had been raised in Damascus. He played the Bonnie Prince Charlie card, saw the Caucasians struggle and took many more extremists from Syria to fight the cause. It was thought that he was also a supplier of weaponry to the Middle East and I expected some of the order would make its way there. The file even went on to unveil his weakness: he visited swingers' clubs and had a fetish for dressing up as a woman. That's how good Rankin was - he could find out a man's most shameful secrets.

Heading into a deal of this kind is similar to having intercourse for the first time. You just didn't know how it would go. It could be awkward, rough, or even enjoyable, but one thing's for sure, it was scary as shit. But everything was going so well, I couldn't see anything going tits up, I had become untouchable. As long as I could gather the guns for the deal, I would only have the task of following through.

I proceeded to go through my diary, something that I carried with me 24/7; even while I was sleeping, it was tucked under my pillow. It held an abundance of

239

contacts, all written in code of course. It was completely necessary to hold such valuable information at close call.

I made calls to dictators, bent military men and even two African presidents, but I couldn't get any leads. I needed a connection to America. You'd think that would be easy, them being the most corrupt nation in the world and one of the biggest arms producers, but it wasn't.

On many occasions, I had to rely on Rankin for advice and this was one of those times. I gave him another call.

"I have a little problem wi' the account," I stated.

"What's that?"

"Well, the figures add up, but I'm having a little problem calculating which stock relates to what figure."

"Which stock is that?"

"Bike exhausts, 10,000 of them. I just can't figure it out," I said.

"Let me surf through the files and check."

We gained code names for many things over the phone in case there was a Peeping Tom, not only looking but also listening in. The carbine was translated as bike exhaust, car in carbine changed to bike and exhaust because a bine in Scotland is a cigarette. I had to wait some time before he faxed back with the detailed fake spiel and a message at the bottom, 'All looks fine this end, fall through with the rest.'

That meant I had to call him, from a random public line, to a number we kept for emergency use, preferably a good ten miles away. I travelled by metro until I found a public phone to use.

"Go ahead?"

"There's an American Quartermaster that goes by the name Dalton. He's tasked with disposing of out-of-date weapons and has the semi and automatic carbines available for sale inside an armoury on The USAG Grafenwoehr Army base in Germany."

"What about the grenade attachment?"

"He has them too and a stockpile of other accessories. Take as much as you can, he's desperate to offload them."

"How many carbines is he storin'?"

"Around the 15,000 mark."

"Jackpot!"

Chapter 47

Reputation Grows:

With the cash spilling from my pockets, I should have left the trade, but I couldn't, the thrill of being The Eidolon glued me inside. The reputation I had built, I desired to increase. All my life I had taken on other people's quarrels, paid jobs and orders; now, I was my own boss. My men respected me, were paid well and they followed orders. I was sitting at the top of the tree, travelled Europe and delivered countless consignments of arms. Only once had we become close to being tagged. That I thought, was a blessing. I lived on the road, on my own, and got used to the loneliness, but it sucked. When I wasn't busy, I thought of Max and how his life was. I cut contact with Donny, a tie to my past I needed to cut, but I always dreamt of being reunited with Max and killing Jack. I only had to look at my hands to reflect on the lifelong damage he had caused.

 The European market kept me busy. Most of the time I filtered around eastern Europe and the Balkans. Passionate warlords like Millacky fed their guerrilla armies with as many arms as possible and I was now the supplier. My contact list had built up so considerably that I could find any firearm desired. Every deal delivered, I hid from the buyer, whether it be under a dark corner wearing a balaclava or under the cover of another building, sometimes leaving recorded messages on top of orders with mp3 players or dictaphones. I'd survey the areas of the meeting points and drop the merchandise off hours beforehand, limiting the need for face-to-face conversation. In European deals, I was paid by bank transfer and as long as deliveries were to the letter, I could drop them off and make a rapid exit. They requested, I delivered, simple as. Travelling through airports would see me use different nationalities of passports and masquerade as different characters. I mimicked a musician carrying a guitar case, or a hippy modelling John Lennon shades, a head band with groovy clothing that suited my growing hair, an executive businessman holding a fancy briefcase wearing geeky specs, tourists in long shorts and Hawaiian shirts and I even made out I was ill once, requesting a wheelchair.

It seemed past lives in various criminal empires led to my success. My father had taught me to never beg for mercy. The Godfather taught me to be ruthless. My history as a fighter gave me a profound hardness. Jack showed how to run a calculated operation, even though I thought he was too calculating, and Millacky, he had taught me how to become The Eidolon and live in the shadows.

As far as I was concerned, I was a fucking magician, who could appear and disappear at will, leaving many people wondering who I was. I could've slipped into hell and toasted a whisky behind the devils back before he knew I was there.

Checking into hotel rooms with a false identity, I would be heavily disguised, and once it came to leaving the room or checking out, I would change disguise. My Stable never knew my location at any time, they never asked, it wasn't important but I wouldn't know theirs either.

The Irish stable of Turk and Barb kept the arms bunker in good order, I know, because I made random visits and checked from time to time. Many consignments that had to be sent to mainland Britain were sent through the Isle of Man by boats, or by Rankin's plane, and exchanged where Eclipse and Rankin would make delivery. The operations ran so smoothly I didn't have to lay out instruction.

As soon as I replaced phones, which was on a weekly basis, I would pick a select number of people I was 100% sure that were villains and text my new number with the initial E. If things were quiet, I'd switch on old phones and check messages, and people left messages for sure. The constant changing of phones was necessary because I knew we were being watched. On Britain's National Crime Agency's database, I sat at number seven between a man wanted for drug trafficking and someone wanted for fraud and stealing twenty-five million from a firm he worked for. Smart man him. The picture of me was a sketch, different from the one I saw when sitting in the pub in Rosslare with Brian Fitzpatrick. My hair was swept back in a bobble and my chin had a tidy beard. My eyes were peering under my brows, making me look more of a convict than I was. The description of me stated:

'This man goes by the name of The Eidolon. A known arms trafficker in continental Europe, the United Kingdom, and Ireland. He is reported to have connections with guerrilla armies in the eastern hub of Europe and the IRA. He feeds armies with small arms and high-tech weaponry on the black market. Reported to be an infamous character and a rare sight. If anyone sees this man, do not approach the individual and don't hesitate to call.'

On top of that, the same picture aired on Europol's most wanted list with the same description. But I was number five, not seven. I was on G2's most wanted list also, G2 being the secret service of Ireland, working closely with MI5.

Being so high on everyone's radar worried me somewhat but at the same time, I'd become a criminal of the highest calibre. The thrill of evading capture and conducting illegal deals behind the authorities backs gave me a feeling of unique satisfaction. I wanted more deals, to make more money, and to carry on being a ghost that couldn't be found.

I switched on an old phone and picked up a message from a couple of months past.

"I'm looking for The Eidolon and his toys." It was a Scottish tongue and I recognized it. I know what you're thinking, leaving messages for gun orders isn't exactly professional, but it was the way I operated. I'd considered using websites, blogs, auction sites or online advertisements, but that kind of trail could be followed by geeky IT experts, and that didn't agree with me at all. Phone conversations could be relayed in enough code to communicate and the conversation could be continued with a different line to any other number, simple. There's no way every line in the world could be tapped.

I called back from a public line, withheld the number and listened to the breathing on the phone.

"Hello," the speaker responded.

"You requested an order?" using the voice muffler, I was slightly aware this man might pick up on my Scots tongue, so I mimicked an Irish one for the conversation.

"The Eidolon?"

"Correct."

"How do I know it's The Eidolon?"

"Well, that's a gamble you have to take…Mr Dean."

"Ahh, you know me, that will save some formalities," his response wasn't one of shock that I knew the voice, only a satisfaction his name was known.

"I recognise the tongue, yes." I was trying to hide my Scots as much as I could. We had a slice of history.

"I hear you're a man that can get things."

"I can get you anything you like."

"Good, then I'd like some merchandise."

"And what kind of merchandise would you like?"

"Nothing decorative to a man of your calibre. Just a box of handguns, ammo and mags preferably." The usual order from the shore, handguns. That, I always had in stock.

The conversation continued as we discussed the novelty of numbers, dates and meeting points. It was a straight forward job. I instructed Rankin to smuggle guns to a landing strip beside Dundee. From there, Eclipse would meet him and deliver to a remote farm of his. Don't know what it is about farms and deals being made, but all the big guns in Britain seemed to have them. It was ideal for an exchange. Mr Dean kindled some memories of my heyday as a fighter and a fight that laced my legacy.

Chapter 48

Aberdeen 1987:

Back in 1987, I did something that sent me to the depths of despair. Even though I knew my closest pal at the time, Carl Jenkins, got what he deserved, I became burdened with guilt. He gave me no choice.

In Aberdeen at the time, I was known as a man who got things done and was often paid well to do so. A cousin of Steve Dean, a gangster from Glasgow, sent a job up the road to Carl. We paired up on many tasks and quarrels that needed sorted and this task was to locate two rogues who had stolen a considerable amount of drugs. Carl, a mid-twenties big-bellied man, seemed to be jealous of anyone who had more than him in life, held all the information; I only helped him in finding the individuals. He held a photo of them in his wallet the whole time, and I never asked to see it.

For weeks we were on the hunt for those men and for weeks we got nowhere. However, by utter coincidence, they walked into the Fountain Bar while we sat and shared drinks, having all but given up hope of finding them. The Fountain was a typical eighties bar of wooden panelled walls and sticky floors, mirrored whisky decals and cushioned seats around the edges. A place where the locals were prepared to back you up if there was trouble floating around and there was plenty of that in the Fountain.

The pay-day for the seizure of these men guaranteed two grand and being a bit dry at the time, I needed paid. When they strolled in, Carl nodded for me to join him in the toilet and hatch a plan.

"Those are the cunts we've been lookin' for!" he spat out quickly.

"What! That cunts that just walked in?"

"Aye, that's them. Listen, this is what we'll do. Keep an eye on 'er drink, when it's gettin' low, go outside and I'll stay inside."

"Aye, and 'en what? I take 'em both on? Don't think so pal."

"No, when they go outside, I'll follow 'em, you take 'em from the front and I'll take 'em from the back." Sounded like a decent enough plan.

They were both skinny runts. Mike was a flabby guy and I was well capable of taking both if needs must.

"Right, sound 'en. Grand each aye?"

"Aye, grand each."

The plan was sorted, vague, but that's how we did things in the eighties. We returned to our bar-stools and carried on as we were before we hatched that plan. The two runts had a few more pints before it approached closing time. Just as they had a quarter left, I gave Carl a wink; he nodded back and I went outside. It was baltic, the Aberdonian winter in full force, snow covered the ground and gusts of heavy wind blew it around. I didn't have a hat or gloves, so I froze my ass off waiting for them to appear. The only game plan I had was to halt their walk, stall them for as long as it took Carl to appear outside and take them down. It didn't quite go down like that though. I must have been standing there for longer than fifteen minutes. My body shivered and I'd all but decided to head home to the wife. Just as I took steps, the two exited and stomped right in my direction. I stood tall in the middle of the pavement under a street light and puffed my chest out, hands clinched by my side. They stopped a metre away from me.

"Got a problem here big yin?" one of them spoke in a Glaswegian accent, but I didn't respond.

"What's wrong? Got nae tongue pal?" the other taunted. Frozen and still faced, I waited for my pal to exit. It was at this point the guy on the left pulled out a kitchen knife as I studied his manner, the look in a man's eye tells all and he wasn't afraid to use it.

"I think yi' better get oot oor way pal." The man with the knife pointed the tip with a straight arm as I looked down the blade into his fierce eye, "This is yer last chance, pal!"

I looked towards the door in the hope of seeing Carl emerge, when the man plunged the blade right into the side of my stomach below the rib-cage. I grabbed his shoulders, trying to use his weight to hold me up but I slid into the snow. As I was falling to the deck, he had stabbed me five times. The blood rapidly soaked through my jacket as I slid my hands over it. Forgetting about the withering cold, I moulded into the snow, lying staring at the snowflakes falling from the fading sky, my body getting weaker. A thick gathering of blood ran into my mouth as I gargled, choked and spat it out. Blinking quickly became tiresome with the sky fading as I could feel the arrival of death. As I felt my body switching off, Carl walked into my blurring sight with a satisfied smile. That's the last thing I remember before waking up in a hospital bed with my wife and Joe by my side. That was the second time I'd cheated death.

The reasoning for Carl purposely failing to come to my aid was because he'd found out I'd been having a seedy affair with his wife for the past couple of months. I kind of gave him a slight dab of respect for having the balls to do that, but I couldn't let him off, as my moral code wouldn't allow me. It took me a few months to recover and offered Carl a fight to end the feud like men. Luckily the stupid cunt accepted and with the red mist catching fire, I maliciously beat him to death with my bare hands. Locals observed and even his brother, Mike Jenkins, was witness.

 The weeks after landed me at the bottom of the bottle, as I struggled to live with the guilt. I grieved for a friend I'd killed; it was a fucked-up position to be in. It was something that mentally tore me apart and changed me for life. The police probed the public about the suspicious death but as everyone knew in that world we lived in, it's not to be spoken about and you don't grass. If you did, you'd be singled out and probably beaten. I was questioned by a detective Magill, denied any knowledge of the event and used my wife as an alibi. In the pub, people wouldn't take me on and that sickened me. I took the frustration out on my wife and Joe, making them hate me as well. I was a social drinker before that time and not particularly violent at home, but I took my frustration out on the ones who loved me and sparked an addiction to alcohol to relieve the pain I tried to bury. Once you kill a man, you'll never be the same again. I would sit and stare at my hands and wonder what I had turned into, which only led to the opening of another bottle.

 The aftermath of that fight sparked rumours throughout the underworld's fighting community and eventually Steve Dean contacted me, a young narcissistic man on the rise with a love of flash cars and long coats, expensive pencil cigars and wads of cash. From the dull city of Dundee, he managed illegal fighters of all varieties and it reflected in his arrogant one-word answers to questions. From the weak to the strong, he used them for profit. As my name came to his attention, he would use me for his own benefit and offered me a contract for one fight, the biggest one I'd ever be in, and I accepted without thought.

Chapter 49

The Birth Of The Legacy:

His name was Cluster Sands, the top scrapper in the country. A London man who was at the top of his game. He wasn't a man confined to a dishonourable life like myself and many others in the trade, holding lawful employment in a scrapyard, fighting for the addictive adrenaline rush of the bare knuckle. His fights didn't go the distance: none of his bare-knuckle fights did, and no bare-knuckle fights in general ended within a time scale, leaving the man standing at the end as the victor. He was a mountain of a man, six feet six, who could flatten a building with his fist, and had the reputation of fighting like a brute, accomplishing the job in rapid fashion. If there was a man you could describe as being built like a bear, it was him.

It was April 1988, the rules were last man standing. If you got propelled to the ground, you were given a minute to stand; if you couldn't, you were toast. The fight was fought at a neutral venue in the basement of an abandoned building on the banks of the Clyde in Glasgow. An arena that if it could speak, could tell the most brutal of stories. That basement, that night, will be one of the last things I remember before I get the chance to meet the Devil.

Cluster was a man taller than me, freakishly white, with small curling bushy black hair and a bumpy face masking many punches taken. A vast solid belly that only added to his power, bulky arms through heavy bag work. Viking-sized hands and shoulders from his training of pounding cars with a sledgehammer until they were compressed to a shell and unrecognisable. The sight of him, standing across the gravelly ground

251

opposite me, embedded me with my first major dawning of fear in the fight game. He fought in blue joggers with white stripes and carried bomb like power in his fist. The stakes were simple: win and you receive five grand, lose and you receive nothing. The arena lit by floodlights tied to the tops of pillars only enhanced my inadequate loneliness.

At that moment, as his hollow eyes burned a hole through me, I filled with unwanted distress. My hands moist and trembling, my jaw biting down, I thought I was in too deep. All the other fights I'd had up until that point were low key affairs, £500 being my biggest purse. I had a feeling of uncertainty, thinking I'd maybe taken a step too far. This man had travelled from the great city of London, and I was only a mere random soul from Aberdeen. Questioning why I stood there, the only reason I could give myself was the money, but it wasn't. I was born for that moment, my gritty journey through life landed me there.

I didn't know if Mr Dean held faith in me, but I agreed to the fight and my destiny was in my own fists. Mr Dean was by my side at the beginning, looking through his tinted glasses without a hint of hesitation. There was no advice, I was on my own, but I was used to that. I tried to reason that Cluster would feel the same pain as me, but it did little to help my fragility.

Mr Dean turned his back and nonchalantly walked away from me, holding an impassive look in his eye. When I knew it was time, I turned around to see Cluster gallop towards me like a rhino then stop just outside punch range, running his hands around in mini-circles like a fighter from the nineteen twenties. I analysed his moves, shadowed him and tried to figure him out. He rolled his hands then dropped one to his waist before firing it at my face, followed with a bulldozing right hand that shook me to the core as I hit the deck, and I remember thinking that was the most powerful punch I'd ever felt. Oohs and ahhs filtered from the sadistic crowd as I felt the full weight of his hundred and twenty kilo frame. I had a minute to recover. The speed for a man of his size was frightening. I lay on the ground and debated if standing up was worth five grand. Cluster waited for someone to shout the minute was up before coming again.

When I heard a shout of five seconds to go, I stood and without hesitation he approached and stalked me again with the same circular movement of his hands. We locked eyes and I waited for him to make his move. He bounced forward and jabbed me again, then leapt out of range with a revolting grin on his face. He did the same again before I could register the punches, the blood leaking from my nose already. Again, he came forward with a torturous right uppercut into the base of my chin, lifting me off my feet and back on to the gravelly ground. As my head was trying to register the stupidity of my commitment, I rose to a kneeling position, keeping my back to him. Killing Carl had changed me, it suckered me with apprehension, I was scared that it would happen again. I wasn't right in the head. I rose as the minute timer ticked. I looked at Mr Dean, his hands in his coat pockets and head tilted back almost pleased at the lacerating beginning to the fight.

Cluster came again. I'd been down twice and I hadn't even hit him. His reputation at ending fights in rapid motion became oh so apparent.

"Come on 'en," mocking him, I stood tall, full of guts and not willing to admit he was getting the better of me. He galloped into my range again, as I flung a flat fist into his heart, causing him to suck in his breath. Continuing the onslaught, I landed four desperate straights to his face, his eyes blinking and legs jolting. Without delay, he countered blows onto my chin that sent me on a side shuffle but determined not to fall again, I didn't. His nostrils flared and face scowled as he ploughed into me, uppercut into the ribs then a downwards head-butt into my nose which crumbled my body with a shiver of pain. He held no mercy and came again. We stood toe to toe, like warriors, and exchanged hurting blows, my feet always taking steps backward and fearful of his power. He was filled with anger, not willing to give up his crown. As we were in a clinch, our chins rubbed our chests and elbows interlocked; he placed both hands on the back of my neck, pulled then pushed his weight down and his knee thrust into my face. I collapsed, face down onto the ground and lay there, my arms light and brain confused.

I tried to rise but slid across the jelly surface, rolling onto my back, my eyes blinded by a floodlight as I tried to lift my body up, but only my neck would lift. And, I noticed Mr Dean accept a wad of cash from a deplorable man stood beside him.

I struggled with the lack of coordination but made my way to my feet as the minute was ending, the minute that I had to stand, the minute where I realised Mr Dean had brought me there for his own benefit. With only seconds remaining, I stood, absorbing a look of annoyance from Cluster. He made a mistake and bided this time. I took advantage and walked in a wide semi-circle, wishing my senses to return. I reminisced about the life I'd led, I'd never given in, never said mercy and this fight would be no different. My nose was mush, my head scrambled but I hadn't begun yet. Cluster hadn't faced a man like me before, a man willing to die before giving up.

I swaggered towards him as he switched his look from his entourage back to me and I went to town on his face. Blow after blow collided through his slack low guard and barraged across his face as he turned, stunned at the size of my heart. Realising the bombardment wasn't to stop, he countered with his own punches that now bounced from my face as if a toddler was striking me. The pain no longer registered. His head took the blows like the champion he was, but he slowly weakened. My heart beat so fast it controlled my rage. Not stopping, I continued to attack as his will broke and eventually he took a weakened knee to the ground, almost begging at my feet.

Usually I respected the rule that once your opponent hit the deck, you must let him stand, but I was a changed animal after ending Carl. I kept going. He knelt with his side facing me as I re-paid his knee that flattened my nose, four times, until he slumped down to the ground like the giant falling off the beanstalk. If you can dish it out, it doesn't always mean you can take it, and Cluster showed he didn't have the heart to take it. All other men before him fell, yet I stood above him, chest filling with air, spluttering the blood that ran from my nose out of my mouth, holding my fists in a clinch. I turned to look at Mr Dean who had his hands out of his pockets, swiping his glasses off. It could've been shock, but I caught the fear in his eyes. I turned back to bask at my foe, defeated on the ground.

His palms were scratching across the ground as he tried to find the will to stand, but he was finished. This was the point where I understood I had to stop. It was within my arsenal to end his life but the vision of Carl's face had entered my mind and that was the stopping point. Scowling back at Mr Dean, I galloped over to him. The closer I got, the more I could see his anxiety increase, thinking I was about to beat him.

"Where's ma siller?" I demanded. Without an answer, I grabbed his glasses, snapping them like dried twigs and dropped them to the ground, as I had dropped Cluster.

"I'll have mine too?" the deplorable man, from whom he had accepted money, asked.

Mr Dean's hands reluctantly slid between his coat, into his inside pocket, handed me five grand and that deplorable man who was a young Jack Gallagher, snatched the rest from his hand. I grabbed my money and walked out without looking back.

I was an underdog who had become number one on the list of hard men in the country in a brutal fashion, but as I had fought numerous solid men over the years, I found it was the brutality that separated me from the rest, that made me the legend I became. I would go on to fight the best, all over the country, have countless soul-sucking fights, but I always knew where that step too far was. I didn't want to be punished with same feeling I got from killing my friend Carl.

Mr Dean was a deceitful man who only looked to benefit himself financially, however it would be, by setting someone up, as he had tried with me, or finding killers who would de-throne the best.

That fight, he had made a mistake, and I would never fight for him again.

Chapter 50

Cash And Scars:

 Rankin flew over to a retired air-strip in Errol, Scotland, between Dundee and Perth, with the consignment for Mr Dean. The guns were hidden inside loud speakers and tapped to the side using duck tape. There, he met Eclipse and they waited until dark to meet Mr Dean at his requested location, a farm in the country side near Dundee. I instructed them to follow the usual rules, keep appearances hidden, be professional, and make no exchange until the payment was in their hands. This deal was being paid for in cash and it was a relatively small amount compared to the other European deals I was used to. I told the men they could split the cash between them. Kind of a bonus for them being comfortable with that arrangement. It was a random selection of handguns, Brownings, Walther P5 compacts and colts. They were all out-of-date nineties guns, not in good condition and none better to be off-loaded to than Mr Dean.

 The Stable approached the farm in their box van. Mr Dean, smoking a skinny cigar, waited in a long ash coloured duffel-coat, and his accomplice Lukas, the Hungarian, who had served in a secret division of the police force was beside him, hands crossed behind his back and dressed all in black as he always was.

 The Stable, dressed in dark combat trousers, skin tight gloves, and balaclavas to conceal their identity, exited the van. No words were spoken as they walked to the rear and opened the van doors. Eclipse, a much more intimidating figure, stood, legs widely apart, arms floating to the side by the door, looking straight onto his customers.

"Evening gentlemen, looking subdued tonight," Mr Dean referred to their disguise.

Eclipse turned to Rankin to continue the deal.

"Let's not waste time chit chatting. Money, Mr Dean?" Rankin demanded.

"I take it neither of you two is the infamous Eidolon then?" Mr Dean asked, as Lukas impassively eyed Eclipse. He could see Eclipse was there for intimidation purposes.

"Where's the fucking money?" Eclipse growled, taking a couple of steps forward, disliking unnecessary questions. Rankin was much more tamed and spun his neck at his quick temper.

Mr Dean didn't like not knowing their true identity and didn't like dealing with The Eidolon, again because he had no idea who I was. He tried to stare them out to gain advantage.

"Lukas, grab the cash will you?" Lukas walked to Mr Dean's green Jaguar and opened the back door. Grabbing a holdall full of notes, he handed it to Eclipse who passed it to Rankin.

Rankin turned his back on everyone and counted the cash over the edge of the back door while Eclipse stood guard.

Everyone stood in silence as the money was counted. Eclipse spun his neck back to Rankin who met his look and rolled his eyes.

"I'll have the guns please, if you don't mind?" Mr Dean demanded, as Rankin turned, leaving the money in the van.

"It looks like it's all there. It's a shame it's fake though."

Mr Dean and Lukas glanced at one another before Lukas made a grab for his gun. Mr Dean dropped his cigar, Rankin picked up a wheel wrench from the back of the van and flung it towards Lukas. As it thundered into his face, knocking him back a few strides, the gun landed a few metres away. Eclipse saw Mr Dean slipping a knife from his trousers, sprinted over, lifted Mr Dean from his feet and bulldozed him to the ground. Rankin picked up the wrench and spattered it into Lukas until he ceased moving. Eclipse wrestled with the older Mr Dean, who was too weak to handle a brute like Eclipse, and taking control of the knife while it was still in Mr Dean's hands, he twisted it towards his face, piercing his skin at the ear before dragging the point across his cheek, parting the skin to the mouth, leaving the wounded man with a hollow whine.

"Get in the van! QUICK!" Eclipse shouted.

I lay in the bushes, watching it all unfold, knowing Mr Dean would try something deceitful, now he lay on the ground wishing he hadn't bothered. I got up and sneaked over his way, intending to gloat at the sight, letting him know his old friend was responsible.

As the lights of another vehicle approached, I backed off and ditched myself back into the bushes again. It was a black Astra, standard unmarked police car, from which emerged two official looking men wearing bullet-proof vests over formal shirts, with radios clipped to their waists. They helped Mr Dean into the back of the car as well as the unconscious Lukas, before speeding off.

The whole deal was a potential scam, a set-up, dirty bastard. I was maybe too unaware of how many bodies were now watching me. I would have to be extra careful from now on.

Chapter 51

Extra Caution:

That deal brought a halt to the operations of The Stable for seven months. It was smart considering the growing heat. For The Stable, they welcomed it, seeing it as a long vacation and chance to re-charge. For me, I carried on building the legacy and rose higher on the 'wanted' lists. I didn't know how to sit and do nothing. The festering of thinking I couldn't control, alone with thoughts of the past, I needed to be busy. Always thinking of ways of topping up the accounts and deceiving the authorities. It was the only way for me to live. I had to grow an eye on the back of my head, on alert 24/7. I also had a collection of motors stocked across Northern and Southern Ireland, Belfast, Dublin, Crossmaglen, Rosslare. These were cars I purchased from Millacky's contact at a scrapyard that couldn't be traced because they were marked as scrapped, having unique number plates, registered to fake identities. I parked them in various places from streets to parking complexes. The keys for these motors were all hidden close to their locations and if I was in the area, I'd give them a run around for half an hour to charge the battery. I began to think the worst and stashed cash in various places. In the old arms-bunker beside Donegal, I stashed five grand and a passport inside the maintenance cupboard. In the arms-bunker under St Paul's Church, I placed five grand and a passport inside a locked money-box. I filtered money through shell accounts across Europe until it landed in a Swiss one, another tax haven like Luxemburg. Moving to these countries after retirement wasn't an option, too close to the people I worked for, or with. I researched the most corrupt countries in the world for when it came to tax avoidance, and Panama came up the best option. Miles away from anywhere in Europe, in Central America, and few chances of banking officials and authorities asking questions. I thought it was as good a place as any, but I didn't care where, as long as it was outwith Europe and Max was with me. There was another option for me, a very lucrative one. Inside my old flat in Liverpool was a stash of over a hundred grand, earned from deceiving Jack, and still hidden under the cupboard floor.

I had various unused passports including British, Slovakian, Russian, French and Irish, and I still had the one related to my account in Luxemburg. These were inside the safe house in Carnagh along with another stash of ten grand.

I cut communication with The Stable and spent some of the time at the arms-bunker in the church basement, taking stock of what we had left. It was a mishmash of out-of-date guns and I had to make a point of getting rid of them. A run to Sweden saw me pick up a load of AK5s and dysfunctional parts. Automatic carbine assault rifles, weapons adapted for the subarctic Swedish weather. This latest version had a mix-up of parts from the last to this, so it left a load of spares that could be moulded together. The Swede gave me the contents of around forty guns, for a knock-down price, with attachable red-dot sights.

He also offered me a couple of other weapons for a third of the price. Eight light anti-tank weapons that could be fired and disposed of after use. A short-range fire-and-forget anti-tank missile. He also sold me ten mortars and three times the amount of shells. I didn't have a clue how I was going to shift them at the time, but the offer was so cheap, I couldn't refuse.

I flew across, drove to Denmark on the way back, ferried to England before driving to Pembroke and ferried to Rosslare. That kind of journey fatigued me when I'd broken into my fifties. The guns were concealed inside drawers of old furniture, and stacked roof high in the back of a heavy-duty truck. The boxes of anti-tank weapons and mortars were hidden at the front, inside their manufactured heavy-duty plastic boxes, behind big wardrobes and tall sets of drawers. I impersonated a private delivery driver, picking up the job from an auction site and travelling with an Irish passport. It was easy to pass through borders of European Union countries; no visas were needed. When passing through land borders and checkpoints, I appeared in disguise as I knew my appearance was on the wanted lists: as a result, I tried to give nothing suspicious away and complied with any requests without seeming hesitant, as I did when Customs officers at the ferry in Denmark asked to check my load. There was so much stacked furniture in the back, all covered over with bubble wrap and taped up, it was nearly impossible to step into the truck and all the furniture at the rear was empty of guns. One of the Customs officers stepped into the truck and opened a couple of drawers, then gave the rest of the stock a shy glance and couldn't be assed looking further. It was mint, a complete rush knowing I had deceived them, well-practiced over the years. I lived on the fact I always evaded jail, thinking it was a gift, something I was born with, like a talent.

When I returned to Belfast, all the guns and boxes were transported into the basement which was no picnic. I had to haul them down the stairs on a sack barrow one by one in the dark of night. The back door to the church was sheltered from the roads around, so it was no problem being seen.

Another hard trip and hard night's work, I was getting too old for this. There was only one corner of Europe where I could shift the heavy artillery, and that was in the south west.

I decked out on one of the cell beds and slept for about fourteen hours, waking fresh and ready for another hard day's work constructing the AK5's. It was my life, working hard so I could make money, all the time thinking of Max and our future: living in Panama where we weren't known and could live a normal existence, get wives and be content. If I deserved a wife, I didn't know, but Max did. It was fundamentally my fault he was locked up, punished, and I needed to make it up to him.

Approaching early summer in 2013, it was time to get back to work. The usual text messages were sent out to the loathsome world of men I now knew. A rare order from a gypsy came in, requesting shotguns. Shotguns were okay, we had six lying in the bunker and it was a short drive to Tuam, in county Galway, to deliver them. Nice and easy, and I thought I'd do this deal since it was low key. We'd never had a request from a gypsy before, but his money was as good as any. I still had the truck in storage and took full advantage of that. I changed the Swedish plates for Irish ones to distract un-wanted attention and it would be scrapped after use.

The delivery was being made in the late hours of Saturday evening. I packed the usual, balaclava and a burner, dressed all in black and put a woolly hat on. This was the only time I contacted Rankin in his time off for the standard background check and it came up blank. The person who went by the name Paddy was a dead source. It happens from time to time. Some of the collection of people we dealt with didn't want to be known and therefore, wiped the record of their name. Paddy was a gypsy, probably born without a birth certificate and therefore an unknown entity. The last people on this planet to work with authorities would be gypsies, so I felt safe with the deal.

I loaded the truck which was parked at the rear of the church, thinking that it would be a normal night and took the four-hour drive, late Saturday afternoon, arriving at nine o clock. I grabbed a takeaway for supper, then napped in the van for an hour. Waking after ten, I made my way to the address, a circus tent in the middle of the town, mounted on a level patch of grass with a small fun-fair being assembled to the side. I saw lights inside the tent, parked the truck among a collection of cars in the parking lot, and decided to have a nosey around.

As I approached the tent with the balaclava on, I heard a commotion of noise, cheers, oohs, ahs and the odd aggressive spout, when all of a sudden, it went dead quiet. I sneaked under the canvas flap of the tent, making my way to the gap in the stadium seats that formed a half circle around the stage area, looking onto a sandy centre. A gathering of around twenty men stood outside the pollard. They were blocking my view of who they were watching. I ran my eyes around the men until they stopped at the sight of a mane of jet-black hair, ending at the shoulders, over a waist cut duffel coat. There he stood, Jack Gallagher, blank faced. What the fuck was he doing here? Some of the men who were gypsies walked into the circle and stood over a huge hairy chested body, which lay dormant on the ground like a fallen gladiator. One man checked the victim's pulse, and shook his head at his friends. Jack now stood on his own when another muscled heavy came into my

264

vision as the bodies parted, swaggering over to Jack. Then I realised who it was - Max! He had just taken the other man's life in a fight with no remorse. Jack picked up a hoodie and handed it over. Max slipped it on over a body that was devoid of fat.

The muscle mass on his frame was that of a bodybuilder, sculpted abs, rock-hard chest over a wide stance and his hair cut in an army style. He flapped the hood up and strolled out as if it was an everyday event. Jack walked over to the circle of men.

"Danny, my condolences," he said, with his hands tucked in his waist pockets, before turning to follow Max out of the tent. I went outside and shadowed them behind the amusements as they walked across a patch of grass on the way to the car park, staying far enough away so I could be unseen in the dark night. Max dawdled along and didn't look back at the tent, unfazed at taking a life, he was a monster. He had become a fighter, like his dad. What had I created?

Chapter 52

Monster:

I had created a monster and Jack had turned him into a fighter, or should I say, a killer. Now I thought I should have kept contact with Donny, who could've kept me up to date with Max. There would be no going back for him now. He had killed the governor of the jail and now he'd killed a gypsy fighter. The deal afterwards was a quick exchange of cash and little conversation. That suited me. If they had any inkling that I was his Father, I don't know what their thoughts towards me would have been. I'm surprised they let Max and Jack walk out of the tent unharmed. The following few days left me with the regret that I didn't evade Jack's capture sooner back in Liverpool. I could've given Max a better future, but I still had a chance though. I still wasn't at my money target yet, but it wouldn't be long. I had to leave Max to whatever journey he was on and find out the whole story from Donny with the standard call to him from a phone box.

"Hello, Devils," somebody answered.

"I'm looking for Donny," I said.

"He's busy just now. Who is it?"

"Tell him it's his crippled friend. I'm sure he'll have time to talk."

"I'll pass on the message." The phone was bunkered and I assumed the guy went off to fetch Donny as a minute or so later, Donny responded.

"What a pleasant surprise! I thought you'd forgot about me."

"Never brother. How's life treatin' you?"

"Good mate, never better except for something you can help me with…"

"Go on," I answered, but already knew what he was going to ask.

"The scum raided my gaff a couple months ago, had to ditch a load of guns in the Mersey. Can you stock me up?"

"I could, aye. I've got a load of random guns, Glocks, service pistols, old Webleys, .32 colt model Brownings, that kind of mix. I'll throw in a few accessories and do you a good deal since it's you."

"Sound mate, sound."

"Have you seen ma boy lately? I hear he's a scrapper now."

"Your boy is a beast. I've watched his fights down at the warehouse. Every night, he's walked the line." Walking the line meant taking on ten men in a row and beating them all. "The last time I saw him was around a year ago, the last time he was at the warehouse. No one would turn up to fight him, so Jack's started to take him on the road."

"I know, I saw."

"Where?"

"Tuam, in Ireland. He killed the bloke."

"We heard yesterday when Ringo came in. You do know who that bloke was?"

"Who?"

"The king of the gypsies."

The king of the gypsies, whoever he was, was always avoided by everyone in the game. He was around in my time and I'm not ashamed to say that I'm glad we never crossed paths. He must have been getting on though, but by the stories, he was portrayed as the most ruthless man on the circuit. Never suffered defeat like me. It took death to stop him and that tells what Max was capable of.

We chatted for more than ten minutes with me filling the coin slot in the phone box. The temptations of visiting my son were high, but I left Eclipse and Rankin to deliver the goods to Donny.

Chapter 53

The Great Scottish Hope:

Business went back to normal, we dealt guns and made money, but I became increasingly paranoid with every deal The Stable conducted back home, whether they would return. I offloaded the tank missiles and mortars to Uri Popov of the Caucasian Emirate in south western Russia, and housed myself on mainland Europe, making new contacts. I hooked up with a gentleman gunrunner in Croatia in late 2013 and split business with him, having me escort arms on his behalf from Croatia to Turkey, all by the book. Mislav Babic was a man who liked the finer things in life, having a personal driver and a stern but alluring right-hand woman as a PA, who followed him unquestioningly. He always dressed elegantly, with thousand pound, slim-fit, Italian Dolce & Gabbana two-piece tailored suits and smoked his cigarettes through an ivory holder. The Croatian was a different mould of gunrunner, working mainly in the grey area of the arms trade. He slightly bent rules to get across borders, but tried to stay within the law and comply with the World Trade Organisation rules, on most occasions. He transported heavy artillery inside cargo planes, like the Croatian M-56 howitzer artillery guns he supplied to the middle eastern conflicts, Japanese built tanks he sent to the Latvia and Lithuania military, attack choppers bought from Russian reserves and sold onto warlords in Lebanon to fight in the civil war, plus mortars and rocket artillery to the Africans. Small arms weren't his thing and as he'd heard I was mingling around Europe, he hired my services, but that was as a consequence of me revealing my real identity. It was his only request, explaining he didn't deal with fellow men unless he could meet face-to-face. He set me up on legit road trips, with counterfeit passports, licences, and permits, to pass through every country on the way. While he dealt with the logistics of paperwork and fake identification for delivery, he housed me inside Zagreb's most luxurious hotel, Esplanade, and booked me into the presidential suite on the top floor, all paid for, of course. Remaining in the room for ten days with on-call masseuses, room-service, pay-per-view TV, minibar and what I enjoyed most, the exotic women he sent round at nights. Those ten days I lived as a King, soaking under a drench shower in a marble tiled bathroom, lazing in a bath with scented candles and being bathed by the striking hotel staff, then having the convenience of drying off in a two- seat sauna. Dining at my leisure, with full breakfasts in the morning and luscious steaks at night, lazing about the room in a silk robe with the comforts of heating control and air conditioning, drank free ale and dined when it took my fancy. It felt as if I'd made it in life, from the grim streets of the Gorbals to a five-star presidential suite. But as all good things in life, it ends, and I had to leave when the consignment was ready to be transported to Turkey. There, I befriended a radical extremist, who was building a division of mercenaries to fight the war in the Middle East against the Americans, and he opened doors to a warlord in Ukraine. The Swede kept supplying us, and I organised the shipments back to Ireland where Turk and Barb would pick them up.

 I'd spent over a year on mainland Europe, hanging out with bent military men, extremists, warlords and leaders of guerrilla armies. I made so much money I didn't know what I was going to do with it all. One day, I counted my entire worth and it was £1.7million.

Living on the road as I did was a total rush. I lived this life to make money, for Max's future. I couldn't go everywhere in disguise and had to reveal myself to many people. I was treated as a lord, given 5-star hotel rooms and exotic escorts and whatever drink or drugs I sought.

I managed to control The Stable from wherever I might be and the shit worked. Certain checkpoints and border passes in south east Europe, I was able to glide past. Strings were pulled for the men I worked for and bribes taken so I wouldn't be checked. It was like living in dream-land. As long as I turned a blind eye to what happened around me, I could live without a heavy conscience, but it wasn't easy. There were some awful sights I had to witness on the road, like in 2014 at the beginning of the Russian military intervention of Ukraine. I delivered a consignment of anti-tank weapons and boxes of AK-47s to south western Ukraine, to a warlord of pro-Russian forces that weren't connected to the Russian military. A guerrilla army basically. The area of Donetsk was heavily attacked before I arrived and while there, I became trapped in a warzone for a week-long battle between Russian and Ukrainian forces. Luckily, they agreed to a temporary cease-fire and I was able to flee the country. The standard of living was atrocious. While the fighting continued, kids walked around with guns as if they were holding toys and homeless youths scavenged for scraps, looking for warmth.

Before leaving the area, I picked up a flock of six homeless kids, sitting in the shade of bombed buildings, manky with blankets wrapped around them, and a fire ablaze for heat. I visited a shop and bought some comforts of hot food and water then managed to persuade them into the car, showing them pictures of a hotel from my phone, miles away from the destruction they sat in. I booked a room and paid extra for food and new clothes to be delivered, so they could be fed and bathed, allowing them to stay for two weeks until I fathomed out what I was going to do with them. I managed to smuggle them across the border into Russia and dropped them off at a hostel, specifically for war refugees, and they were welcomed in with open arms by nice people. What happened to those kids, I don't know, but I hoped there would be some kind of future for them.

The Caucasian area of Russia was no better, as I witnessed many people who had lost limbs, bombing scars, and no hope. This played games with my conscience. Every now and again, I'd try and do nice things, feed the homeless, buy them clothes, water, food, supply them with blankets, pay for medical treatment. I did whatever I could do to help on the occasions I could, meaning I couldn't help them in the middle of hanging around with war lords and guerrillas. I kept quiet and laughed at their jokes. One of them called me 'The Great Scottish Hope' because I always delivered on time and heavily stocked to their requirements. They thought I was a legend and I lived off it. The legacy I built was huge. Turned out Millacky created a perfectionist, and because of his dedication to a violent rebellion within Ireland that was never going to transpire, he was rotting away inside a cell.

Chapter 54

Ignorance:

I received the latest request from the Swede, early 2015, and it was time to head home. I needed to step away from the sights of devastation I had lived with in Europe. Entering Zagreb airport, I found it to be a disorganised mess of a place, with people criss-crossing checkout lines and arguments erupting with staff. There were armed police security guards keeping a loose survey of the area. The outside looked more like a neglected bus stop with dilapidated advertising boards, flakes of plastic drifting off. The 'B' in the Zagreb sign dangled and blew around in the wind. It was like something from a Communist past. Travelling light as usual, only carrying what was in my pockets, painkillers, diary, passport, cash and a couple of phones, I wasn't in heavy disguise, wearing a thick coat and Russian winter cap, gifted to me by the Russian warlord in Ukraine. I queued for over half an hour checking in, and as I turned to leave the desk, I caught someone taking rapid pictures through the low glass windows from outside.

As soon as I clocked eyes, he pretended he wasn't watching me and I carried on as if I hadn't seen him. He was dressed in a long, thin, tortilla coloured trench coat, indistinguishable between a tourist and a photographer, with the strap of a laptop case over the middle of his chest. He shadowed me, his head to the ground, as I followed the signs for the departure lounge. I continued to watch him from the corner of my eye. I stopped and played around in my pockets and he copied, pretending to do something on his phone. I took my boarding-pass out, pretending that I had found what

I was looking for. I continued to walk and he continued to follow from outside the windows. I ignored my stalker until I turned the corner and caught the peer of his eyes, confirming what I already knew. I continued my walk until I became invisible from his line of sight. Now there needed to be a change of plan.

I found an expensive clothes shop, bought a smart outfit of dressed trousers, plain t-shirt, blazer, trilby hat and a pair of shades that my level of paranoia required. The ticket for Stockholm was binned, and I returned to the check-in area where there was no sign of my stalker, left the airport and caught a bus. Flying anywhere was off the cards now. I would have to make my way back to Ireland and suss out what my next move would be. I took two buses that day, until I made it to a train station and skimmed across Europe, first through Slovenia then across Italy, through Milan, into Switzerland and finally to Paris. There was no hint of anyone on my tail. I checked every bus seat, carriage, train station and toilet I visited, but there were no repeat sightings of anyone stalking me. I stayed off the phone lines and knew my time had come.

If I was being watched, why had I only caught one person spying? Around Europe, I lived on the other side of the law; the areas I housed in, law seemed like a horrific fantasy. People were able to live by their own heartless ways. Were the authorities afraid of wiping these men from the map?

I had spent far too long revealing myself across Europe that past year, but didn't get the feeling anyone was on my tail; if they were, I would've hoped to have spotted them before now. Far too many people knew my face in Europe now and there was always a snitch somewhere. I conducted gunrunning as business-like as I could, trying not to offend anyone, giving no reasons to grass on me. I bailed out on the Swede, couldn't trust him now. All I had to do was think on the way back, conjuring up an escape route to a peaceful life. Passing on my operation to Turk and Barb seemed the logical thing to do. They were the most professional out of the lot, having the qualifications and experience required to run the operation. They knew the complexities of the trade, having been around firearms from a young age. They were also cautious of people they dealt with. Eclipse was still too young and way too reckless. Rankin was the middleman and placid when it came to dealing with loathsome men. He fitted the role as middleman perfectly with his ability to do background searches and gain contact with people I couldn't.

I only needed that little bit of time to arrange my exit, a few more deals around Britain and Ireland and that would be it. I could reunite with Max and live as a rich man.

Before that, I had to visit Vogue, the head of the French Hell's Angels. I needed an entry into Ireland without informing anyone of my return and since he was in France, it seemed logical to ask for his assistance. As inhumanly vile as he was, he seemed proficient in his trade and held the connections needed for a safe passage.

As I boarded another train and two buses, still dressed suavely, I arrived at the gate to his estate. There I had a problem as the gate and wall were way too high to climb over. Being worn out, I plumped to the ground and leaned my back against the gate, thinking I'd have to wait for someone to appear. Leaning back and closing my heavy eyelids, I became aware of the gate opening and I hit the deck. A biker drove down the track and met me, stopping right in front of my path, spun the bike around and told me to get on. He drove me up the track road, past his cattlebyre and between the four narrow slatted-roofed buildings and onto the drive of the eighteenth-century mansion. The outside had an elegantly designed Italian courtyard with water fountains and cedar trees to the side of a drive that looked as old as time.

 My escort stopped outside the grand entrance, a high turn of the century carved door, "Go in, he's expecting you."

 I can only imagine that Vogue had cameras at the gate and had spotted me as I tried to enter.

 I stood at the heavy door, preparing to knock when a butler opened it and invited me in, leading me across the open lobby, a white marble floor and half spiral staircases on either side. I followed him into a glamorous living-room. Sophisticatedly decorated with cathedral ceilings, bleached wheat in colour, with heads of hunted animals mounted on the walls, a commanding fireplace with the fire ablaze and two sparkling chandeliers.

 "Mr Rhodes." Vogue startled me as I was in awe at the decoration. He carried a ring-binder under his arm, "Looking fashionable. France has surely revealed your elegant side."

 "Somethin' like that."

 He walked to a stand with the top shaped as a drawer, where an abundance of expensive alcohol and crystal glasses were displayed. He poured some sherry into two glasses with the binder still tucked under his arm. I didn't care for sherry, but any kind of drink was needed after the two-day journey I'd undertaken.

 "Have a seat," he insisted, and guided me between two white sofas and a glass table sitting in front of the warm fire. Placing the ring-binder on the table, he handed me the sherry, "What can I do for you?" Nothing like getting to the point.

"I'm in a bit of bother," I said, as he shook his head at the end of that statement.

"Go on, I can't help you if you don't tell me your predicament."

"I need safe passage to Ireland." He took an elegant sip of his sherry, raising his pinkie. My drink was already gone as the butler entered the room, picked up the bottle and re-filled my glass. Vogue didn't hesitate to carry on.

"I could do that David, no problem. But, if I do something for you then you have to do something for me. Is that not how it works?"

"Look, I'll owe you. I supplied you once without repercussion and hopefully you know I'll pay back this favour come time."

"Don't panic. It's all in hand and I already have a favour to be paid back." I wondered what the favour could be, "I see you've been making quite a name for yourself, David, mingling with all kinds of creatures across Europe, while your predecessor has been wasting away in jail." He leaned forward and placed his glass on the table. The butler stood by the open doorway, awaiting instruction.

"Well, you have to make money in this world."

"Yes, that's very true and I'll tell you the secret to that. It's staying one step ahead of your opposition."

"That's why I need to get back, the opposition's making my head hurt."

"Ahh David, so blind to what's right in front of your nose, you can't see it for ignorance."

"What?"

"What if I could tell you who your opposition really is? Do you think that would make a difference?" He placed his palm over the top of the folder and slid it across the table.

"Why don't you scan through this, see if you find anything that takes your liking."

He clicked his fingers to the butler who filled the glasses again. I opened the binder to a large file. Turning the page to Uri, The Islamic extremist, head of the insurgency movement in the Caucasian Emirate, to whom I had delivered the carbines, bought from the American Dalton. Nothing unexpected, just a list of his crimes and so forth. I turned to the next body. Uri's right-hand man, an informant for the KGB, feeding information, and the cause of busts, jail sentences and deaths. I moved onto the next. In Turkey, I befriended a radical extremist who was building a division of mercenaries to fight the war in the Middle East against the Americans, but in his group of mercenaries, there was an asset from the Israeli army, who fed information back to a source, which had seen them all ambushed and killed. The Swede, a disloyal member of the Swedish military who grassed on anyone he dealt with and that linked me to the guy taking pictures of me at the airpot. My eyes opened to a pattern forming. I flicked through the pages to all sorts of people I'd met on the road. The Ukrainian leader of the insurgency Russian forces in Ukraine, the Croatian gunrunner who hired my services to deliver small arms, and his lady PR who was an embedded spy. They were all informants or had spies embedded in regimes and illegal wars. My eyes lifted to meet Vogue's.

"You see, nothing is as it seems in this world. You have been used as a puppet to unravel these people. You have been watched for many years and your time is running out."

The file was a collection of people across Europe who were all connected to illegal and legal arms deals.

When I returned to examine the file, I came across Mr Dean from Dundee, and that made instant sense because of the officials who had picked him up after Rankin and Eclipse had tried to exchange an honourable deal. Deceiving wretch. Then the section for the IRA: Millacky's file had the usual information, 'terrorist' was the headline. The General's file consisted of nothing that made him out to be an informant in the IRA. Rankin's file as an information asset for the Real IRA. Turk and Barb's file as ISU members for the Provisional IRA.

Then there was my file, with my birth name 'Davie Rhodes' attached. The file was constructed before my alias of The Eidolon was created. It did however have my life's work attached, the history of my family, my history of being a drug runner and bare-knuckle fighter. The file knew my whole life. Then another very handy piece of information - the mysterious five other members who formed the IRA's head table, all scattered across the world.

"What you don't understand David, is that there is one man pulling at the cord and the last page in that file tells you all about him."

I fast forwarded to the last page and a file under the name 'Lucille': no picture of the man who pulled the strings, but a host of information of how he hired people to collect arms and drop them off, including everyone I'd worked with. I scanned through the information until I got to the main piece.

Lucille was an unknown identity hired by spy agencies across Europe to plant informants in organisations. He was the man the collection of rats reported too, and then sold the information back to governments and spy organisations. To fix up and capture insurgency movements, guerrilla armies, Islamic extremists, dictators, warlords, terrorists and last, but not least, gunrunners. Along with that, he controlled the flow of arms across Europe and made a vast profit.

 "Why are you givin' me this information?" There had to be reasoning behind it and I had to ask.

 "You see," he leaned his elbows onto his knees, "your old boss supplied me with quality arms and handy information over the years, I've passed on this information to a select number of people and so far, I've shot blanks. Do you remember that member of my crew that I killed when you delivered to me?"

 "How could I forget?" He talked about the man hung from the hook and dripped blood from his slit neck until he died.

 "Well, his name is in that file, a double agent for the renowned but stupid French Secret Service, hired independently by this Lucille character and it took us three months to beat the information from him. Eventually he gave me a number to a safe deposit box." He folded himself back into the sofa and shook his head, "Stubborn fool he was, anyway, we still had to find the bank and it wasn't easy, six banks we had to raid, all on the same day. It took over a year of planning, but we got it and by the time we did, Millacky had already been caught." Vogue continued, "I knew our paths would cross again, and now I can repay the favour to your old boss. That is a copy and you're welcome to keep it."

 "Aye, think I'll hold onto it." That file was the one piece of evidence to uncover the identity of Lucille, located inside a safe deposit box of a bank in Paris which Vogue had raided, using the shipment of guns supplied by myself.

Chapter 55

Return:

 To my relief and gratitude, Vogue had me smuggled back to England through the Channel Tunnel, in the back of an artic lorry, then drove me up to Newcastle where Rankin waited at the air-strip. I entered the same gap in the fence Donny had created all those years back when I flew over to meet Millacky for the first time. Once again, I needed to get out of the public eye, and especially after scanning that file. Lucille was a hidden rat and who knows who he, or she, was. All I had to do was stay out of trouble and I was good.

 When I entered the hangar, I spied Rankin standing beside his plane with the usual set of shades and untidy shirt, half tucked into his trousers.

 "The traveller returns."

 "Aye, I'm back," I said, storming over.

 "What happened to the Swedish pickup?" he asked.

 "Caught a tail at Zagreb airport, couldn't risk it."

 "What kind of tail?"

 "A fuckin' squirrel tail, what do you think? Someone takin' pictures, looked spyish."

 "Spyish? Like suit, hat, long coat kind of spyish?"

 "Aye, wi' a fancy camera."

 "Sure it was you he was taking pictures of?"

 "Well it wasn't the fuckin' scenery." Rankin realised I was well miffed by the affair and let me ramble.

 "Have you got any pills?" He knew I meant painkillers and luckily enough, he did.

 "I've got some good ones for you, Tramadol."

 "Right, let's get the fuck out of here." We clambered into the plane and as he did his usual pre-flight checks while I started to make a rollie.

"You can't smoke inside here!" Rankin spouted.

"I'll open the window."

"If you want a smoke, you'll have to have it before we leave, outside."

"Fuck me, ye're a right fanny sometimes."

"Hey, this is my plane, bought and paid for, my rules."

"Fuck it, just go!"

Once in the air, the relief shuddered through my whole body and the Tramadol took effect. I told my vacation story to Rankin, what I'd been up to in Europe. He couldn't believe the people I'd met or the places I'd been. But I didn't boast, the places I visited were bomb-riddled shitholes most of the time. It was enough to make you forget about the five-star hotels, free drugs and loose women. I decided on the plane ride that my time was running out. I didn't want to be a man who got too greedy in his trade, to be caught like Pablo Escobar, who could have run away with his wealth and lived a long life. I wanted to be on that unique list of people who fled and was never found again, but that plan would be scuppered after I got back to Ireland. I kept the knowledge of the file to myself and had it posted over to an address in Ireland where I'd pick it up on my return.

"I've had some contact from an ex-RUC Special Branch officer, someone I knew back in the day from Belfast," Rankin said.

"What's he after?"

"All he said was he was after automatics and handguns, usual stuff."

"What for?" I wondered why an ex-member of the police service would want arms.

"I'm not sure. I looked up his file and found he's as bent as they come. Fed the IRA information for years and four years ago, stole six hundred grand from a

282

government account. They can't nail him with enough evidence to send him down and I suspect he wishes to spend some of that money. About a month ago, they released him and he's looking to be fitted up."

"Aye? Well we're goin' quiet for while so we'll set up a drop for later in the year." Rankin didn't know my desire to get out and it would stay that way.

"I think the man's in a hurry," he said.

"I couldn't give a flyin' fuck if he's in a hurry. He'll have to wait."

"I'll pass that on. Do you want me to deal with it?" Rankin asked, coming across keen to help.

"No, pass the contact details, I'll handle it."

My main goal now was to get out and I wouldn't be informing Rankin until the last minute. Turk and Barb would be told earlier, for they would inherit my business. It didn't matter how easy gunrunning was and trust me, it is, I just had to do the sensible thing and vacate. I'd made my money, built my legacy, risen to number one on the 'wanted' lists and I knew it was a matter of time before I'd be caught.

I laughed at the authorities. I always had a picture in my mind of them sitting behind desks, trying to follow my breadcrumbs to capture me, but I was only a puppet, dangling on Lucille's strings.

Chapter 56

Things You're Not Prepared To See:

 After Rankin landed, I had him give me a lift to the safe house in Carnagh, and strange as it sounds, it felt like home. Once again happy, being hidden from the public eye and ready for a proper sleep, after I'd checked my stash of emergency money and passports. It was all there. I went to the cabinet in the meeting room for a little night-cap and then lay on the bed with the TV on, exhausted. My aging body couldn't keep up any more, my knees were becoming more brittle and stiff, my head was tired from living a shadowed life, and all I wished for was a humble end. I'd settle for a simple life of being a handyman like Brian Fitzpatrick. I was sick of the sight of firearms and the characters I'd mingled with over the years, it wasn't for me anymore. But my journey wasn't nearly finished. I had acquired more than two million, nestling in an account in Switzerland, but I wanted more before I finished up in the trade, capitalise on the stock I had left.

 After a few thankful days of R&R, I got back on the job, feeling the need to check up on the arms bunker, but then I realised I didn't have a motor. With growing paranoia, I didn't want Rankin to know my position. Although back in Ireland, I still had to watch my back every second. I headed out to the back shed where the Ford Cortina was parked. The keys were hidden inside a rusty box filled with nails and screws. I tried to fire up the Cortina but she was dead so I popped the bonnet and noticed the battery was disconnected. When I re-connected it, an alarm started blaring to high heaven. Luckily, there was no other hint of life around the area, as there never was, and I turned the key in the ignition.

I revved the engine and it purred like a beast. I slipped my shades on, even though the sun wasn't out, and gunned out the garage like a Formula One driver.

I roared around the country roads feeling free. The drive made me forget about my fugitive problems and I enjoyed every second of it on the way to Belfast. It gave me a glimpse of a life I could lead somewhere else. I only needed Max as a passenger to complete the journey. I took time to stop in a lay-by and savour the moment when I realised I had left my tobacco in the house. I needed painkillers, but they were missing too. Two things I'd always carried with me, but worrying about Lucille had knocked me off centre.

Getting into Belfast, on the way to the church, I decided to take an out of the way route instead of driving down Falls Road. I parked the car off Shankhill Road and made my way down back streets to the arms bunker. The withdrawal of painkillers caused a jittery shake throughout my body and I needed painkillers and a smoke to stop it. Before I went into a convenience store, I folded my balaclava into a hat shape before setting it on my head. My pony tail was already tucked down my back and I kept my head down while approaching the counter, looking down at notes in my hand.

"Packet of Golden Virginia and the strongest painkillers you have, please."

Standing outside, I ripped the pouch open and made a smoke. I lifted the paper to my mouth to seal the rollie, as traffic stopped at a red light. A Vauxhall Vectra was first in the line with the driver gripping the steering wheel tightly, eager for the lights to change. I looked down to my pouch, closed it and slotted it into my pocket, taking out my lighter. As I lifted it towards my mouth, I froze, letting the flame burn in the air. I looked to the car again as the lights changed and there he was. Joe! He was driving the Vauxhall. My face flattened and the rollie fell from my mouth. I scanned the car as it drove away in a rush, as if he was trying to follow someone. The red light held for more than a minute. It was definitely him. There was no doubt in my mind, or was my mind playing tricks? I had no time to waste; when a taxi approached, I ran onto the road in front of the motor making the driver slam on the brakes, and leapt in.

"What the feck you doin', you feckin' idiot?" the driver shouted in annoyance.

"Shut up! Here's a hundred quid, step on it, we're looking for a white Vauxhall Vectra." The man still didn't move, "Look, here's another hundred, fuckin' move!" I yelled through the perspex partition, and he took off.

"Speed up man!" The next set of lights were at red; as we sped closer, the Vectra waited in the middle of a stretch of cars.

"Right, don't make on ye're followin' him." I settled down in the back as the taxi stayed behind.

We followed for ten minutes before I spotted Joe was following another car. As the shiny V6 Golf stopped outside a pub, so did Joe. The taxi stopped further back. A scraggily dressed man wearing baggy jeans and an over-sized baseball cap left the car and entered a pub. Joe was on the phone to someone and within a couple of minutes, the man returned to his car and we were off again.

We continued on their tail for another fifteen minutes until the shifty character stopped outside a house in East Belfast. Joe pulled off a street further up and parked his motor at the back of a derelict housing scheme. We drove past, watching Joe hurry down some steps and into the back of the redundant block of terraced flats.

I left the taxi and followed on foot with caution to the door, pushing it open as quietly as possible. Inside the entrance hallway were two doors to flats, and a stone staircase in a building that was obviously abandoned. I tiptoed around to check the doors, both locked, and I moved to the next floor. Above my head, I heard a voice from the top floor. I crept upstairs and saw a door slightly ajar.

When I peeked in, I saw Joe sitting on a fold-out chair, peering through a gap in the boarded-up window. Piles of rubbish and fag butts strewn on the floor with binoculars and a notepad by his feet. Joe was on the phone.

"Aye, no' much yet Steve. He just leaves the house to do a bit o'dealing, or clean his car." He waited for his caller to speak as I wondered who Steve was. "No Mr Dean, me and Micky will stick it out."

Mr Dean? He's on a job for Steve Dean. Why the fuck is my son working for Mr Dean? Joe stood up from the seat after his conversation, with his face concentrating on his phone. His face was less innocent than I remembered, a hardness about it. Hair really untidy and his body much more filled out. His shoulders were huge and his chest broad.

I wanted to open the door, confront him, but decided to find out what his motives were now he was here in Belfast.

I made my way to the arms bunker under St Paul's church.

Chapter 57

The Return Of Joe:

"Hello, who the fuck's this?" Donny asked angrily. There was an option to ask Rankin, to attempt to gather some information, but I was keeping the channel of contact between us closed.

"Donny?" I said.

"Aye."

"It's yer crippled friend."

"Ah Davie, what's the crack?" Fuck sake, he uttered my name, he was pissed.

"I've got a wee job for you."

"Make it quick. I've got three naked birds, a collection of the finest lemo and a major hard-on here."

"Is there a mobile I can call? Give me one of yer birds' numbers." The girls in the background were giggling and singing along to some music.

"Jesus, hold on," Donny slurred a number down the phone and I called back.

"Listen. As usual, this conversation goes no further. I saw Joe in Belfast the other day. I need you to find out why he's here and no half stories, I need to know everythin' Donny."

"Your kid from Aberdeen?"

"Aye, ma kid. And he's over here on a job, for Mr Dean."

"That Scottish twat." He noisily burped into the phone as he referred to Mr Dean, "The one from Dundee?"

"Aye him, and Donny, this is more important than bangin' lemo up yer nose. Do it fast as I haven't time to waste."

"I'll get on it the 'morrow."

"No! Now, Donny!"

"Fuck me Davie, did you not hear me? I've three naked bitches."

"Fuck yer bitches, get on it. I expect a call sooner rather than later."

My mind became overworked, the paranoia from Lucille and the mystery about Joe. There had to be a chance he was in the country looking for me, wasn't there? On top of that, I had to arrange my exit, but I wasn't going anywhere until I found out why Joe was in Belfast.

I woke the next morning, starving, cold, lonely, and no call back from Donny. I waited impatiently all day, still nothing. I didn't dare leave the arms bunker and called Barb and Turk after a couple of days to pay a visit.

"I'm done in this game." They sat across from me on top of a bed in one of the empty cells. The only time I could tell the twins apart were when they spoke.

"What do you mean 'done'?" Turk asked.

"I've a few things to arrange, 'en I'm out."

"So what happens to us?" Turk asked.

"You inherit everythin', ma contacts, the stock that's left once I offload some more, it's yours. I'm too auld for this shit. If I go much longer, I'll get caught. MI5 are hot on ma tail, I'm bein' followed all over the place. It's only a matter of when and no' if."

"If they're hot on your tail then they won't be far behind ours," Turk stated, as Barb was his usual quiet self.

"Aye, that may be true but you can re-group, start fresh somewhere."

"So, when are you out?"

"I've a few loose ends to clean up, shift some stock and that's it. Maybe a couple months, it's yours."

"How will we know when ye're out?" Turk asked.

"You'll know, but as far as I'm concerned, this will be the last time we see each other."

The only loose end that needed tied up was Joe and while doing that, I'd take on low-key jobs, twenty grand here, a few grand there, that kind of thing, hoping I would stay out of Lucille's sight in the meantime.

The sight of my forgotten son made me wonder if my past was going to bite me in the ass again.

Donny, having had to do some digging, finally got back to me after four days and came through with some info. Joe had turned to bare-knuckle fighting and had gained a reputation for himself in only a couple of fights. Joe, the man without the killer instinct, had found it, and I was the reason. The past he couldn't forget, and I wondered if he was on a quest to reunite with his estranged Father. Like father, like son, they say. Joe now lived in the same world I was housed in, walking the same path, on the same mission I had completed years before. He'd beaten a Polish man called Warsaw and a vindictive character called Skinner, whom I'd heard of. A master in the counterfeiting trade, keeping strong ties with Mr Dean who had befriended my son, hiring him as his enforcer it seems, and sent him on a job to Belfast, although Donny wasn't able to come up with all the information relating to the job.

After hearing that news, I left Belfast and gave myself some thinking time to figure out a few things before I could reunite with Max. I continued to keep my ears open as to what Joe was up to for the next few months. In that time, I dawdled between a few subdued places in Southern Ireland, including the safe house and old arms bunker in Ards forest. I also took myself fishing for a couple of months in the far west of the country.

Mr Dean contracted Joe for his fighting services, having another couple fights under Mr Dean's name, beating men called Tommy Masson and an ex-professional boxer, Matt MacGregor.

Then Donny told me some sickening news that further aroused my anxiety: my blood had to come to blows, my two estranged sons were on a path to meet, in the basement on the banks of the Clyde, in Glasgow. The nauseating reality of this situation took its time to sink in and turned my stomach, providing my mind with something else to ponder, something beyond belief.

On one side, there was Joe, a man wrecked by the suicide of his mother, my ex-wife, who killed herself because of the wrath I inflicted upon her. It brought back the unwelcome taste of guilt I'd forgotten over the past fourteen years. He didn't have the killer instinct as a youth, but he'd found it from the pit of his soul and I suspected the reasoning for that was me! I was convinced he was on a mission to rekindle his detestable love of his Father, or even kill me. That was a chilling reality.

On the other side was Max, nicknamed The Reaper, through his barbaric approach to fighting and taking the lives of two men, the governor of the jail and the gypsy king. He was a ruthless man, bent from the suffering of his upbringing and term in jail. A man who was ferocious with his fists and surely destined to beat Joe. A brawler of the highest calibre who could take on a bear in a fist fight and be victorious.

And then there was me, the man responsible for both these men's journeys of destruction, watching over them to see how their lives would pan out. On one hand, I wanted Joe's forgiveness and on the other, I wanted Max to end him so I could avoid his retaliation as a result of his mother's death.

Max was my protégé, I admired the man he had become, but his ferocity and anger made me wish he'd had a different path in life. I wanted to take him away from that path but it seems fate had different ideas. I could have stepped in to stop the fight, but there was curiosity in me that overruled anything else. Two men, bred from the blood of the great Davie Rhodes, would meet in a battle to be crowned the most vicious beast in the country. If anything, it was something to be proud of. Once I held the title as the hardest man, and my name mentioned in the fighting circle would see me talked of as a legend. Now, both my sons had built their own reputations, and that I had to see.

The couple of months before the fight were spent overthinking the inevitable and keeping a close eye on my back. I drank heavily, trying to forget my past and the sights I had to witness in eastern Europe, but it didn't matter how much I disposed of the whisky, I couldn't forget. I had to live with what I had become. Sure, I was proud to be the most wanted criminal in Europe, but all I longed for was a normal life. To wake in a bed and spend the day reading papers or watching TV, is that not normal? It seemed my life had never been referred to as 'normal', and it never would.

Along with the fight, there was a gun deal requested by Bobby Munroe. He required a collection of weapons and I was keen to offload them.

Bobby was the reason the connection was made to Sam Bryson and my torture episode. I debated the deal, but it was a payday. I'd send Turk and Barb and I'd witness the fight for myself. The thought entered my mind to deal with Bobby Munroe, but there wasn't the time. It would be my penultimate deal in the trade. Seventeen grand in my pocket, less three to Turk and Barb. I arranged the deal for midnight, leaving plenty of time for the spectators to squander their money and time for myself to finish something else off.

The day before the fight, I found myself back on the mean streets of Glasgow, walking through my old neighbourhood of Cavendish Street. I would never return to Scotland, or so I thought at the time. The area held memories I didn't want to relive and had changed dramatically since my youth, with my old housing terrace replaced with blocks of flats. The lorry depot yard I fought The Turban in was also gone, replaced by a supermarket.

The stench of disgust in the air still lingered, and instead of kids out playing hopscotch and football, the streets were dead. My old generation had vanished and all that was left for me were unhealed scars. Ever since those days, I had wanted a better life. I tried and failed many times to fill my wallet and gain enough respect. Now, I had the reputation and a bulging account, but there wasn't the feeling of satisfaction I thought there would be.

I was desperately lonely and something was missing in my life and as I reminisced about my mother, I knew what it was, love. I'd been feared most of my life. Respected? I didn't think so, I had no-one. The vile creatures I mixed with over my time would live and die heartless men. I didn't want that. I still had Max, my last chance of happiness.

The night of the fight arrived. I approached the brown cladded fabrication shed at the docks. A host of vehicles parked in the carpark, but the fight would take place in a building to the east. Under the fabrication shed was the tunnel, named the Walk of Death. Back in the day, fights would begin around the hour of ten, so I waited till much later to sneak in quietly once the crowd had gathered.

Chapter 58

The Beginning Of The End:

Many men had taken the fearful walk into hell down this abandoned gritty tunnel before, with their only intention being to inflict pain. The steps seemed to vibrate through your body and echo off the walls as your mind ran through the up-coming event, with fear controlling your thoughts and un-controllable nerves churning your guts. The times I walked alone down that tunnel, defined my future: in the past, I had told myself it was greed which took me there, but it went way beyond greed. It was for the crown of being the hardest fucker out there, the meanest man in the country. The hard man, it's who I was, it's who I still am, but now beyond my time. That time now belonged to Max, who had earned the name The Reaper through the barbaric carnage he would inflict when his fists flew through the air like a wild beast's. Damaged by his past, for which I took full blame. I'd created a man I thought I wanted as a son, someone to carry my name, but in the sickening reality of that walk, it occurred to me that I'd made a terrible mistake, but the end of his journey of destruction was near.

The closer I got to the entrance the louder the applause in admiration of the show, that told me the fight was being heavily contested. The light filtered into the tunnel from the alcove entrance. The crowd of peasants cheered and roared. I slowed my pace and shuffled my shoulder against the alcove gateway wall until I could peer around the corner, sneak into the rear of the crowd, and stand in the shadows of deplorable men. Mr Dean was only metres away to my right, eyes engrossed on the show. Jack Gallagher stood impassively, sure of

Max's reputation; his son, Ringo, my old friend, Eiffel, and a collection of men stood at the rear of the room between two pillars. The rest of the room was filled with the city's top gangsters and gangs. Then I spotted Donny, one of only two men that knew my identidy in the room, standing directly across from me, in his club cut with a few of his other recruits, including Fiddle.
 Under the bright lights, I could tell the fight had been a long war already as both men were heavily marked with wounds, and there he danced in all his glory, Max, grunting and growling, pounding Joe with as much thunder as he could muster. Joe tucked into a shell taking a savage attack. Max's lips had been burst open, blood spewing down his chin, his bodybuilder frame of huge chest, massive arms and commanding shoulders, were bursting with fury. My pitiful son, Joe, looked out of his depth, a smaller man in height and width. Max was making a heavy assault, bombarding Joe, and fired an upward elbow into the base of Joe's beak. The crackling crunch of cartilage could be heard through the groans of the crowd. With his nose crumbled under his eyes, Joe took a few steps back, rooted to the spot, licking the blood from his lips. There, the killer instinct showed from his aura like a wounded animal. Max stood adjacent, open-eyed and out of breath, observing Joe arrogantly lick the blood from his lips, dumfounded that Joe wouldn't fall and continued his attack, throwing fists and head-butts, filled with possessed rage. The onslaught was frighteningly barbaric. Joe could do nothing but take the blows, shuffle away and stand his ground, protecting himself in a shell and not a fist flew back. Joe's ragged hair dripped with stained sweat, one eye distressingly swollen and face covered with awful shaped lumps. The battle was gruelling and the crowd only stood in awe at the heroic nature of the

warriors. My connection to Joe wished him to take a knee, give up, but that was never Joe, he wouldn't surrender. What had he become? More balls than the men that ran out the landing crafts on Dunkirk beach. Max continued his attack, his pace slowing with fatigue after a monumental battle, but he continued, and Joe took it all without showing weakness. Time seemed to stand still for me, watching my blood beat each other gave me mixed emotions. I wanted Max to win, but in that moment when a tingle of sympathy sunk into my heart for Joe, I didn't want him to die in the process. I glimpsed at the back of Mr Dean, sure he was setting Joe up to fall. He was a man who profited from the weak, or people's need to earn money.

The fight continued as the pace took its toll on Max, slowing and grunting less until he stopped, dropped his tired hands to his sides and started walking around Joe, confused and weakened as to why he still stood. His lip hanging off the edge of his mouth and eye half shut. Jack Gallagher, now standing unsure with his entourage, as Ringo edged closer from the circle of gangsters and men around the room, wondering why The Reaper had not finished him yet. No man The Reaper had faced had lasted this long, they all fell to defeat time and time again, but Joe was prepared for the march into hell and he wasn't afraid.

Joe retreated from his shell and dropped his hands. For a moment, when he glared at Max, there was a unique feeling that they knew they were connected to each other, as if that chilling moment was already written in time. Joe gave his brother a cocksure wink before mounting an attack that sent Max back on his feet. Physically exhausted and weak, Max couldn't fight back. Joe continued, fist after fist wrenched into Max's face and any unprotected part of his body, watching him wince and bend from the waist. Joe took the barrage for one reason, to tire Max out. He used his brain, I used to tell him that all the time. Your brain will win a fight way before your hands will. Joe twisted power into every shot as if his life depended on it, his talented boxing ability on show.

 Max was a brawler of the highest calibre but too tired to fight back; this battle had been going on too long. The battle Max fought with his whole being was draining as his strength faded like a beaten warrior. A last barrage from Joe caused Max to bend over his waist, and when it looked all over for Max, he replied with a punch lifted from the bottom of his worth, clattering Joe across the jaw as his body followed, spinning him around in a half-circle. In that ferocious spin, Joe eyed me in the distance, catching my worried stare for a few seconds, as if I was a fictional mirage, then turned his attention back to Max.

 The ferocity of his punch left Max grounded on both knees with exhaustion. Joe lifted his fist, high into the air, and the sound in the basement went numb. I almost screamed out before Joe howled with terror as his wrath ripped across Max's face and his head careered to the ground with a blunt thud. I leaned away from the wall, hands left my pockets. I knew this moment well. Joe's boot lifted into the air and stamped over Max's head several times before Jack Gallagher sent his entourage in to pull Joe off. With the upheaval, I couldn't see Max's body as Joe, whose rage gripped his insides, struggled to get near Max's inert body. Bodies parted enough for me to see Ringo hover over Max. Slapping, shaking, checking his pulse and then frantically pounding his fist over his heart in a desperate attempt to awaken the dormant body. The noise in the room faded as Jack still stood on the spot, white-faced. The entire room, silent, awaiting the words that would confirm what just happened. Ringo lifted his neck slowly towards his Father after he ceased pounding Max's chest.

"He's dead!" Ringo said, as my breath stopped and my heart hit the ground. My leg twitched to step forward for a split second, to gallop over and check the pulse for myself, but I couldn't, I'd be seen. My shallow worth as a Father dropped even further as I could do nothing to change the outcome, and I'd had my chance to do that well before the fight begun. I watched the fight for two reasons: one, the curiosity of my sons exchanging fists and the other was to whisk Max away from the world, make him a rich man, but that second plan died with Max, as did my soul.

Chapter 59

Grief:

 Hanging around in the basement wasn't an option. I had to be the first one who left, and stay hidden. I held my temper but the magnitude of what had happened left me in shock. Walking back down the tunnel, my legs had an uncontrollable tremor and I bounced against the walls to keep me upright. My head spun, and I couldn't accept the son I disowned had just killed my promising protégé. Ironically the words 'Walk of Death' seemed ever more appropriate as I tried to rush out the tunnel. When out the other side, I tried to keep my jaw clenched as my teeth offered to rattle together and I fought against the tears as my eyes glazed over. I stiffened up and compressed my fists as I tried to hold it all together, but it was hopeless. All my plans were fucked. The torture I had put myself through, by dealing guns, wasn't worth it now Max was dead. Exiting the shed, I shuffled over to behind a small electrical sub-station and kept out of sight, trying to pull myself together and think smart. I slid down the wall, hitting the cold deck and then I couldn't battle any more, trembling as I swallowed a mouthful of painkillers, almost choking in the process, while years of trapped emotion bellowed out. It was as if life had been yanked from my stomach, my heart crushed, mind angry and already thinking of redemption. I realised there was nothing left. The trickle of water running downstream in the black Clyde was the sound of the life that just left me. A broken man, I wallowed in my torment and had to remind myself who I was and how far I'd come in life.

I had to get back to the plan and Max's death had to be avenged. Jack Gallagher had to pay for this. Max and me were going to get rid of him anyway, so why change the plan? It was by his doing that I had been tortured by the Eradicator and in my mind, his doing that Max was dead. The only way I could deal with the grief was to blame someone else. As I calmed down, a slow stream of clear thought started to return.

Already, many bodies had left the shed, entering their cars and departing in the night, having witnessed the greatest fight that ever graced the musty grounds of that basement. I peeked around the corner of the wall until it was dead quiet, with only a small collection of vehicles left. No sign of the deceased, Joe or Jack. Arguments would take place on how to dispose of Max's body. No chance of him being buried in a cemetery.

Bodies from these events found their way to the bottom of a river.

The minutes passed as if they were hours as I tried to make rollies, unable to stop my hands from shaking.

Dead on midnight, I heard a van pull up. Rising to my feet, I checked to see who it was. Two men in balaclavas, Turk and Barb, drove past in a long white transit-van and were waiting for the huge roller-door to open. When it did, they drove in and the door shut behind them. I couldn't see inside, but only ten minutes passed before the door opened and they left.

Moments later, Donny appeared with three of his men carrying Max's torso to the car. Jack followed seconds after. They opened the boot and threw the body in, all staying respectfully quiet in the process.

"I'll take it from here," Jack said, while remaining soberly quiet and appreciative towards Donny. In all my time in knowing the pair, they had never seen eye-to-eye, but both held an abundance of respect towards the deceased. As the other men departed, Jack slipped his head and arms into the car boot then took a step back, as if he was reading the last rites to a dying legend, before shutting the boot to indicate the closing of life. He climbed into the driver's seat and sped off.

It crossed my mind to jump out from behind the wall, but then I'd run the risk of revealing myself and after all I'd been through, gunrunning, I couldn't do that.

Grabbing Jack at that time would be a mistake, since I was in no mental state to do anything smart and not only had I lost my son, I'd also lost a loyal stable member.

Chapter 60

Eclipse:

Max became a loyal son when he came around to my ways back in Liverpool. When he was released from jail, I was there to meet him.

Altcourse Jail, Liverpool: Mid-October 2008

The jail was a combined unit, with young offenders in one part and adults in another. Max had been put into the Young Offenders and that day, I waited across the road for him.

I watched him walk out of the gate, almost eighteen, with only the clothes on his back, gaze into the sky and even the dull English weather didn't take away his moment of new freedom, sucking in the fresh air, knowing he was free of the torture. He had grown considerably since I last saw him at the age of fifteen, filling out in his tight jumper. As his gaze into the sky lowered, he caught sight of me standing across the road and that swiped the look of relief from his face. With one leg on the ground and another against the wall, I waited for him. We fixed eyes on each other for a moment, before it dawned on him who he was looking at. He marched across the road in a possessed swagger, the top of his head landing just under my eye-level, he stared at me, with his deep darkened eyes that masked the full torment of pain he'd suffered.

"Good of you to come visit, Da'." I had to step to the side as I didn't care for his anger forced into my face.

"Couldn't son, too dangerous."

"What the fuck happened? More than two years I've rotted in there!" an aggressive bellow spat across my face, "How did it happen? Where the fuck did you go?" he was completely enraged.

"I know who put you in 'ere, son."

"Well, why don't you enlighten me cuz I've been raking my brains trying to figure out where the fuck you went!" His head shifted from side to side, edging closer, spitting over my face.

"It was Jack. I slipped up son, I'm sorry. This was never ma intention for you," I was genuinely repentant.

"Jack! What?"

"That gear I was shiftin', most of it I skimmed off the surface…"

"You mean, the gear I shifted for you Da'?" I realised at that moment I had lost his trust.

"Aye, that gear Max. I had a plan to do a runner, get us away from this life, but I fucked up and Jack caught on."

"So, where the fuck have you been, cuz I've been in there?" he pointed towards the jail, while maintaining his look of fury, "getting the shit beat out of me, starved and fucking abused!" I quickly realised that deep dark stare he had as a teenager had turned to something very unforgiving.

"It was all Jack son. You weren't the only one, look." I showed him my deformed hands but staring at them, he showed no sympathy.

"Was there not a time when you told me to never show pity, Da'? Why shouldn't I just do you right here old man, why not?" His breath filled my face and thought I had to take him back to reality. I gripped his throat with my deformed hand and squeezed, listening to him gargle for breath.

"Look boy! I'm still yer old man and you better remember what I'm capable of." I turned him on the spot and planted him against the wall, "I've come here

303

today to make things right, but it'll take time, you hear? A long time." I buried my look into his soul, "We have to be smart. In time, we'll take care of Jack but for now, we'll have to play smart, the long game." I could see in his eyes that he was listening, but I also saw a monster who was enjoying the struggle. It made him feel alive, "Alright?" I finished my say and loosened my grip as he kept his back firm against the wall. "Ye're going to go back to Jack's and start workin' for him, get to know him and one day, we'll take everythin' he has."

"How the fuck can I work for him? If I'm going to do anything, it'll be killing the spineless cunt!"

"Look son, sometimes it's better gettin' even by being smarter, and I know ye're smart boy."

He began to calm down and his brain started to reason.

"What am I supposed to do? Act as if nothing's happened?"

"Aye, exactly that, and in the meantime, I have a job for you."

"Using me as a puppet again? I don't think so Da'."

"You need to make money and we need to stay in contact, so don't be a pussy and take the work."

"What fucking work?"

"I work for the IRA, for a man called C4 Millacky. He's plannin' somethin', and I make deliveries for him."

"Deliveries of what?"

"Guns."

I spent the rest of that day in his company while he vaguely filled me in about his horrific time inside. The screws abused him, starved him for days at a time, beat and humiliated him. He didn't have anyone to confide in and no one was willing to take him on because the screws made it so. His torture was partly down to me and I'd have to make that up to him but mostly, I held

304

Jack to blame. I filled him in on the drops I wanted him to carry out, prior to Millacky's terrorist attacks on the barracks and gave him the code name Eclipse.

The Roadside Café: The End Of 2008

The days after Millacky had been locked up, I was having breakfast in the café with Max and Rankin before fully hiring Eclipse to be my gunrunner in England.

After only seeing him a few months prior, I thought he would have calmed down a bit, but he was a maniac. He thought the entire world was against him. As we shared breakfast together, I explained the consequences of Millacky's actions in the failed terrorist attacks and the plan I had of taking full control of his gunrunning operation. Rankin knew full well who Max was; he was Millacky's information asset and if Millacky knew of my past, then Rankin probably sourced all that information.

"Listen, I'm lookin' for a body in England to run some merchandise when needed, just like you did before. Nothin' fancy, will be pick up and drop off," I explained to Max.

"When? I've got another job to start." Couldn't believe the neck of this guy. You could hardy inform the boss in your other job that you needed time off to gun run for loathsome characters.

"As and when needed, I haven't got a work plan to look upon." He shrugged one shoulder and tilted his head. I guessed that was a 'yes'.

"The drops you did went well." He ate his food at a rate of knots and held onto the plate with his arm stretched over the front as if he guarded it, leaving Rankin squashed between him and window, something he probably picked up in jail, "I will have nothin' to do with the IRA now, and I'm only interested in makin' money. I have two men workin' for me in Ireland, who you will meet from time to time when swappin' loads over. You will be based on the mainland of Britain and in charge of the drops here. Okay?" He still swept through his food as if it was his last meal.

"Aye, sounds fine," he replied, through a mouth full of sausage.

"Rankin, can you give us a minute?" I asked, as Rankin looked at Max thinking he was a Neanderthal who hadn't seen a meal in some time, waiting for him to shift before leaving and he didn't care to leave his plate. His hunger was caused by the high dose of steroids he was on. I could tell by his trapezius muscles, which looked like mini hill peaks and his arms that were bursting through his t-shirt.

"What's happenin' wi' Jack?" now that Rankin was out of the café, I could ask.

"I'm getting my foot in the door still."

"What do you mean, foot in the door?"

"I'm going to fight, win, and he'll see the potential to make money from me. That's my foot in the door." That's exactly what he did: there was a warehouse by the Liverpool docks that hosted fights where random people in the crowd would take each other on and, from day one, Max walked the line every night he appeared. That got Jack's attention and the rest was history.

"You sure you want to do that? It's no' pretty." His other job he referred to was training to fight, but a man like Max didn't require training as such, it only added to his arsenal.

"What! You concerned for my safety, Da'?"

306

"No' yer safety. The safety of whoever is on the other side of you I'll be concerned about." That seemed ironic as he was on a path to fight his own brother.

"Who's that tit?" he nudged his head to the empty space where Rankin had been sitting.

"That 'tit' will be yer partner from now on."

"No, I work alone. What is it you used to say…you can only count on yourself."

"Aye, that's true son, but in this game, you need a backup."

Over the years we met on many occasions and conjured up a plan to dethrone Jack from his chair. But, there was one thing that kept him in Liverpool, his will to fight. He was possessed, thrived on it. It made him forget his past and he wanted to be the best, just like me. All he did between secret gunrunning missions was train and eat. When rumours of a prospect from Aberdeen was on a mission to take over Max's reign, there was no talking him out of it, and I tried. Two weeks prior to the fight, he travelled over to Ireland to discuss our plan to dethrone Jack.

Safe House In Carnagh: Two Weeks Before The Fight

"Max, is there really a need to have this fight? I've got a bad feelin' about it." This was my last hope to get him to pull out, but it had the opposite effect. I was only interested in leaving, but I had to wait for Max and he wasn't willing to leave before the fight.

"What?"

"There's no need to take this on. You've proven ye're the best, untouchable. We could leave right now, jump on a cruise-liner and be out of here."

His head turned to me and then he stood up, showing his massive frame spread wide as his soaring addiction to steroids was on full show. He took a couple of intimidating steps towards me.

"This is what I do. If this cunt from Scotland thinks he's taking my crown, he's mistaken. I'll squash him like I've done every other prick who thinks he can beat me." The anger that he held inside made him an animal and even I was Intimidated by his rage. When I was young, I was angry at life, but Max took it to a whole new level. Fighting set him free.

"It's up to you son, but be wary." Telling him that he was about to trade punches with his brother would only heighten his need to take the fight and even if he knew, it wouldn't change a thing. He held no remorse for any of his opponents. I think the main reason I never told him was my selfish curiosity to see who would be victorious. I moved onto a plan that we had fabricated to dethrone Jack from his chair. It had been in planning for years and finally we'd both get our redemption.

"So, the legal documents sorted?" I asked.

"Aye, everything's in place," I left Max to procure the legal documents to transfer all of Jack's properties over to his son, Ringo. Max paid a bent lawyer to construct the document and forged Jacks signature. Max had seen Jack's signature so often over the years and he had practised it until it was a perfect copy. Ringo receiving a beating that nearly killed him was a burden I had carried, and this decision would make things right. After Jacks death, we were going to plant it in Jacks office and Ringo would have the common sense to sign it.

After the fight, Jack would take Max back to his home and in the middle of the night, Max would leave one of the doors open and I'd sneak in and kill Jack. Sounds simple but it never is, pulling the trigger, and believe me, I'm no killer at heart. Holding a gun to a man's face and pulling the trigger isn't easy, that's why I intended doing it while he slept. The main goal here was extinguishing ties to the past, before moving on.

Max would deal with Joe and I'd deal with Jack. Jack had treated Max as a son over the years and that's exactly what I hoped for. Max had to hold his wrath towards Jack, all the time thinking of the long game and I was proud of his patience. But the plan went to shit after he died.

He became a man of few words towards that time. Fighting for the legacy he built controlled him. That was another reason I wanted to take him away from the scene. I kind of thought if he didn't get away, he'd end up a corpse, and I was proved right.

Chapter 61

Jack's Fate:

 I spent the next three days in my car, hovering around Glasgow, letting the festering grief take hold of me. Bottles of whisky were drunk like water and smashed off walls. I'd wake in the morning, frozen, outside somewhere, lying in a puddle of my own filth or sick, always with a bottle nearby. There was no consideration of being tagged, identified by a random on the street, or being spotted by a street camera. My motivation to stay concealed now wasn't important to me. I became a man in my fifties with nothing to show for my life, well, nothing to be proud of. My future plans for retirement were fucked. Thoughts of redemption ran around my head, with the standard images of revenge, Jack sitting on his office chair in a bullet-ridden mess, pictures of Joe struggling for breath, weakened in my sight. Seething with anger, I realised there was no other option but to pay my old friend, Jack Gallagher, a visit. The only way to help the process of grief.

 After the fifth day, I laid the drink to one side and calmed down enough to end my feud with Jack.

 I found myself back in Liverpool, back to my old life. There was no easy way to sneak into McCartney's, Jack's beloved establishment. I strode down the eventful Hope Street on a busy Thursday night, dressed in jeans and black bomber jacket, a disguise was unwarranted. A reckless move, but I only wanted to kill Jack in his chair, ironically with a Walther PPK, his favoured firearm and convenient as it fitted into my fingerless hand.

In all the years as a gunrunner, this was the first time I had carried a gun.

I thumped up the darkened wallpapered stairs, hearing music from the Beatles. I kicked one side of the double doors open, not bothering to look through the glass to see if there was anyone on the other side.

The payment clerk shouted, "hey you, stop!"

I slipped the PPK from my jacket pocket, looked into the busy bar, turned a corner and burst through the office door, pointing the gun at the back of the seat, at the same time turning the latch to lock the door. The payment clerk was right behind me, shouting, "you can't go in there!"

The chair was still facing the wall.

"I bet you never figured you'd see me again, Jack!"

The seat swung around, my finger nestled on the trigger, my desire to see the dumfounded cast of Jack's lumpy face.

"Davie, what the fuck are you doing here?"

"Ringo!" he was exactly as I remembered, still with the long ash brown hair and welcoming smile. I lowered the gun to my waist, "Where's yer old man?"

"You're back!" he said, as a spring in his body rocked his reclining chair.

"Aye, I'm back." The last person Jack would ever allow to sit in his seat was his disowned son, "What you doin' in that seat?" I lifted the gun again.

"Put down your gun kid!" Ringo said, as the clerk knocked on the door.

"Are you alright boss?" the voice at the other side of the door asked.

"I'm good Bert, get back to work."

"Where's yer fuckin' dad Ringo?"

"He's gone Davie."

"Gone fuckin' where?" I shouted, taking a step right into the desk frame, "On holiday?"

"No, he's gone, as in dead!"

"Dead?"

"Had a heart attack three days ago, passed away."

"A what?"

"Too much stress and Japanese whiskey."

Jack was always so calm, I had never thought of him as a man who suffered from stress.

"It was you who killed him, you know?" Ringo stood and poured a whisky from the drinks cupboard, behind the desk in the corner. I lowered my gun again.

"After you left, he turned into a paranoid mess, thought you were going to catch up with him one day and after Max died, well, that tipped him over the edge." I couldn't believe the chances. I was two days too late. "Do you want a drink?"

"Aye, a large one." I took a seat across from him, not knowing if I was disappointed or glad. Nevertheless, Jack was gone.

"I take it you know about Max?" he said solemnly, as he placed the drink on the desk in front of me.

"Aye, course I do. Why else do you think I'm here?"

"He was a good friend, Davie. Running this place is the only thing keeping me occupied at the moment."

"Jack left you this place?"

"Not entirely. He didn't leave a will. Mom said I could have it, all his properties, as long as she kept the money that Da' had." That was ironically convenient for Ringo, considering he was about to inherit all Jack's properties anyway. It was supposed to be repayment for the beating he took after I was captured. It was my way of paying him back. I was responsible for the beating. Seemed I was responsible for a lot lately.

"Lucky bastard!"

"You could say that, but I think it's a decent bit of karma, that beating I got, after you disappeared, nearly killed me. I'm lucky to be sat here."

"Ringo, I never wanted that for you."

"Ach, it's in the past, I don't want to be like Da' and hold grudges. I just want to enjoy what I have. You know, he hired a bodyguard after he found out you weren't dead."

"I heard. That Eiffel guy?"

"That's the one, big rude bastard he was."

"Where is he?"

"Eiffel? He left, nothing here for him now." A silent pause made me think about what Ringo was saying. It was all down to karma. With a shy grin, I had a wee chuckle to myself.

"What's funny?" Ringo asked.

"Nothin', just thinkin' of yer Da', flappin' around like a fanny." Ringo joined in the joke, "So what did they do wi' the body?" He knew I meant Max.

"Same as they do with all the bodies, bottom of the Mersey."

We shared stories of the past, some memorable, some not so much. Ringo explained he was living a straight life. No drugs, no crime, and honest money. But he still had a weakness for a piece of skirt, and wasn't shy in sharing stories of his conquests from over the years I had been gone. It was a strange thing, watching him sit there at that desk, the maverick I remembered now looked like an organised business man, just like his dad. Then he told me something I didn't know, which wounded me. As his Father, he should have told me.

"You do know you're a grandad now?"

"No!" For a moment, I thought he was referring to Joe, but no-one down here knew Max had a brother except Donny. I was puzzled as to why Max had wanted to leave a woman and a kid behind to run away to Panama with me. It seemed not only did he carry the Rhodes blood with the use of his fists, but I'd passed on my uncaring nature when it came to family morals.

"He was born the night of the fight…she named him Max." I was speechless.

It took a few moments before I could reply, "what's his mother like?"

"She's a diamond Davie, a real gem."

"Good. Is she stayin' at ma old flat?" I knew that because Max told me Jack had given him the old flat to stay in.

"She is, why?"

"Could you pass on a message?"

"Sure, anything."

"Under the floor boards in the bedroom cupboard, there's a plastic bag. Tell her it's a present from me to young Max." I wasn't sure if that bag of cash would still be there and I once had intentions of checking but there wasn't a need now, without Max.

"No problem, I'll pass it on." Ringo wasn't like his dad in any deceitful way. I knew he'd make sure she got the message, and the cash.

"Ringo, I can't stay. I shouldn't be here in the first place."

"I know kid, I know." I leaned over the table and gripped his hand in a conciliatory shake.

"You look after yerself Ringo."

"You too freind."

"Good to see you doin' well, keep it up. I might catch you again someday."

He nodded his head, winking as I left him to his new life. I would never see him again; we both knew that. Now I had to get back to Ireland and make some arrangements.

Chapter 62

The Last Deal:

I couldn't help myself, even with the mysterious Lucille out there. I could have walked away but I wanted one last deal, a final farewell to the trade. It was for old time's sake, like a boxer who knows he's past his prime, but can't resist that final fight. I needed that 'one last time', that final pay day, the last rush of being The Eidolon.

The ex-RUC officer, Mr Farrell, continued to pester me for a collection of firearms, even after already waiting a few months. It would be my last showdown. There was no significant request for any specific arms, only asking for a supply of guns, and that suited me. I travelled to the arms bunker and grabbed a collection of thirty guns with a sufficient number of mags and rounds, being generous in my last deal. I could've handed it to Turk and Barb, but I was compelled to make the last drop: my greed for adrenaline and the extra slice of siller, bringing in over twenty grand could be my undoing. Before leaving the bunker, I left an empty gun magazine and a two tin's of export, sitting on top of a wooden create, with my diary beside, a book that contained contacts for every degenerate outlaw across Europe worth their salt. That was my message to Turk and Barb that I was out. Being paid in cash was something that didn't fit well due to the confrontation with the buyer but fuck it, one last time, and the twenty big ones in my hand could be used as walking about money.

I picked up the Cortina for the job, wanting my last job to be done in style, and the car oozed it.

A quick conversation with Mr Farrell was had, instructing me to meet him at a portacabin office on the Belfast docks.

It was 2am on a quiet weekday morning when I idled along the dockside and already something didn't taste right in the eerie silence of the area. I approached a heavy fenced galvanised gate with a run of barbed-wire across the top. I got out of my car and typed in the key code, supplied by Farrell. The gate opened very slowly, causing a creaking noise over a dead silence. I drove the car forward and stopped, leaving it in a position where the motion sensor wouldn't close the gate. I slid out and sniffed. It wasn't right, the odour was wrong.

Dressed in black, I slipped the balaclava on and locked the door. I followed the narrow entrance road, a red-cladded warehouse on the right and the waterside on the left, stopping before the space opened to a large expanse of tarred ground, exposing the harbour. I hid behind a crate of blue plastic drums filled with industrial disinfectant, peeping my eyes around the corner. I could see a waterside crane that ran along rail tracks, and stacked containers in the far distance. The building was lit by floodlight's fixed on poles, which didn't help my need to stay hidden. Around the corner was a giant forklift and in front were pallets full of sack bags. I approached the forklift for cover but with my head high, I thundered my bad knee into it. Biting down on the pain, wondering why a man of my age was doing this; but as my heart raced, I knew I'd miss the feeling. The impact made me unable to straighten my leg. I popped some pills and waited for the sensation to return. Now, I limped towards the pallets of sacks from where I noticed a square covering of light, moulding into the tarmac. Sliding across the edge of the pallet, I spotted the portacabin, sitting in a recessed area of the warehouse.

Farrell sat at an office desk, his left shoulder exposed to me. He hung up a phone and shifted through some paperwork. I scanned the area, void of any movement. There was nothing suspicious that I could see, but why take a call at two in the morning? Maybe my paranoia was taking control of my head, a case of overthinking. I shuffled back across the pallets, heading for the car, easing past the forklift and swore in annoyance under my breath.

As I was about to head around the corner, a red-dot flashed across the ground in a diagonal line from the position of the crane. Stupidly, I stopped; I should have kept limping. Moving my leg to step forward, I heard a clink of metal echo across the open area. I picked up pace, my knee aching, dragging my feet as fast as I could. Once around the corner, I was clear of the shooter and kept pace, but outrunning anyone wasn't possible, then rapid footsteps sounded from my rear. Realising I couldn't outrun them, I had to get to the car. I struggled to take the key from my pocket to open the door. A spread of vehicle lights illuminated the area from a short distance away, highlighting a small extension under construction.

Moving fast, I slipped around the end of the site fence, scraping across the harled wall. The shuffling of rapid steps got louder, the lights got closer, I couldn't make it to the entrance of the extension building as planned, so leaping into a sand-bag was the only option, and I landed quietly and waited motionless. Hearing the bodies run past, I couldn't help myself and lifted my eyes over the top, seeing the backs of three men dressed in SWAT uniform, wearing night-vision lenses fixed to their helmets, tactical vests, and guns around their shoulders. They ran straight into the lights of the car and were dumbstruck as to where I had gone. Over the side of the sand-bag, an empty one lay on the ground. It was a hefty risk, but I pulled it up and covered my body. Lying as still as a corpse, not daring to move. My breathing bellowed, the covering of the sack blowing in and out. The body of men walked back in my direction. "Check the car, see if the guns are there," I heard one say in a proper English accent, "You two, do a sweep of the area, he might still be close. Baxter, get the rest of the crew and survey the water, he couldn't have got far." Whoever he was, he was in charge. The plodding of heavy boots lingered around with little communication. I could make out torch-lights shooting across the area, their movement around for some time.

As I calmed my breathing, I heard two sets of steps edging closer, both walking straight past and up the ramp of wood entering the extension. It turned quiet for a moment, then the sound of footsteps came towards me again. I held my breath. My heart pumped through my chest as a shadow rotated in a mini-circle. I was so aware of any movement, I still held my breath when the engine of my car fired.

"Right lads, spread out in formation, he can't have gotten far. Jones, search the car, don't let this target get away. Barns, get on the radio to the chopper, tell them the target is loose. We don't leave this area until we have him."

That was too close for my liking and I still didn't dare move. They hustled and searched the area for over an hour, passing the sandbag too many times. I could hear a low flying helicopter circling the city and constant radio communication between them and the ground squad. Eventfully they'd stopped and were in a heated discussion. The man in charge reluctantly shouted,

"Right, keep the chopper in the air and let's move the ground search into the city."

Shouting they were headed off could've been a trap and the chopper was still circling. I had to stay where I was.

A site-worker woke me at the crack of dawn when he pulled the empty bag from me. Casually, I thanked him for the wakeup call and swaggered off with my knee in agony, thinking my gift of avoiding jail was still burning.

I was sure I wasn't being watched as I left the dockside. Mr Farrell must've been working with the authorities, bribed into setting me up, to reduce a sentence he faced, or perhaps it was enough to get him off the hook completely.

My quick thinking and God-gifted luck had been enough to keep me free. It was now time for me to get out.

Chapter 63

Headlines:

Back in the safe house in Carnagh, I hooked up to the internet while listening to the Irish news on TV. I needed to book some tickets, check my funds online, and transfer it all to a shell account in Panama, the most corrupt taxing nation on the planet. Everything was sitting in my shell account in Switzerland, under an import and export business account. My plan was to emigrate to Panama because of the slack tax laws and the fact it was a completely random place where no-one, especially this Lucille character, would think to find me, and I was a hundred percent convinced it was him behind the botched Farrell deal. Logging in and waiting for the page to load, I was kind of humbled I'd made it this far, and grateful I was within spitting distance of the exit. I was so naïve to want one more deal out of this trade, and I'd almost paid the formidable price. Years back, I had planted stashes of emergency cash and passports that Rankin supplied. I also got two of my own made by Mislav Babic, the Croatian gunrunner. Those passport's no-one knew about, except him. One was in my birth name of Davie Rhodes and the other was an alias. The alias was the passport I'd use to get out of the country, taking two cruise-ferries on the way to Panama. I daren't go near airports, much too risky, with cruise-liners and ferries more relaxed. The Davie Rhodes passport was used to open the account in Panama. It was smart. After all the aliases I'd used in my time, who would think I'd use my own name?

The Swiss account loaded on the screen. Empty! What the fuck, empty? It had to be a computer error. I refreshed the page, still empty! Then I logged out and logged in again. Still empty!

Panic stations! I'd been done over, but I couldn't understand how that was remotely possible. I had never repeated the password to anyone. I sat back on the seat, slapping my palms on my face. "Nooo!" I yelled in anger. This couldn't be. I had transferred money around many foreign accounts under lots of aliases and in case I was losing my mind, I started to check them all. They were all empty, every one of them! I'd forgotten about the ten grand in the Luxembourg account, the one I opened on the very first trip to Europe. To my relief, there was still money in that account. I was sickened with horrific disgust and in panic mode. I'd been fucked over bigtime, and I didn't have the foggiest idea who was responsible. As I did with any other precarious situation, I opened the bottle.

I stomped around the safe house trying to fathom out a credible reason. Maybe it was a bank error - a lifeline, I thought. Immediately I got on the buzzer and after an automated line, conversations with three different people, including the top dog in the bank, it was concluded the cash had been transferred the night before. I enquired as to the identity of the transfer and after the top dog opened the file, a virus flooded his system and shut his bank down for the day.

My life was now fucked! I'd lost Max, killed by my disowned son, and my worst nightmare was coming true. I was skint and up shit creek. To add to the nightmare, a news headline flashed on the screen along with the face of a man I thought I'd never have to see again.

Breaking Headlines:

"IRA's C4 Millacky last night escaped from the maximum-security prison in Belmarsh, South London." By what was being said, it was a professional job. It's thought he is to unite with this man, The Eidolon," My face flashed on the screen, "an infamous gunrunner and number one on wanted lists throughout Europe. A nation-wide manhunt is in progress."

Now I knew who it was. It was no coincidence that the day after he escaped, my fortune had disappeared. This was bad. Now I had to shift gears and shift quickly. The first thing I grabbed was the one gun I had, the Walther PPK, then cash, two passports, hat and gloves, and filled my pockets with my essentials of tobacco and painkillers. I ran out the door and into my car, but I'd left the keys inside. I ran back to the door, but it was locked. Shit. Panicking, I had to move and do so on foot. Jumping over a ditch and into the field at the rear of the house, I heard a motor's engine on the road behind the hedges, and rapidly dropped into a mini-bog then rolled out of it. The car turned into the cottage road and when hidden by the building, I returned and flung myself into the ditch. I fumbled for my gun, took it out and poked my head over the verge in time to see Millacky get out of the car, dressed in a suit of all things, with a pistol in his hand.

He left my sight as I heard him boot the front door in, followed by the inside doors being booted. He'd made it from England to Ireland overnight. I knew he was looking for me. I tried to see the driver, but the light from the sky reflected on the car window and I couldn't tell who it was.

I didn't dare move. I could've gotten up and went out on a blaze of glory, but that wasn't my style; besides, I was no marksman, gunrunner or not, I'd only fired two bullets in my time. Millacky left the house and stomped around the area until he got to the shed. "He's taken my fucking car!" he bellowed, "Rankin!" To my amazement, Rankin stepped from the car, looking scared out of his wits, dangling his arms by his side with his head afraid to meet Millacky's furious look as he stuck his face into Rankin's.

"You've been working with him, where is the man?" The barrel of his firearm pushed up into Rankin's chin.

"We could check the church," panicking, he looked like he was going to wet himself.

"Get in the fucking car, you wretched cunt of shit and drive me there!"

I lay in the ditch somewhat disillusioned as to how things could've gone so tits up in the space of a day. When the car was way out of sight, I headed back into the field and started walking. As I continued to walk, I considered myself doomed: not only was Millacky after my blood for inheriting his empire, there was a nation-wide manhunt on my back.

'Be one step ahead,' I reminded myself, but I'd run out of steps, or so I thought…until it dawned on me where I could hide.

Chapter 64

Brian's:

He had the decency to help me before, Brian Fitzpatrick would have to help again.

Setting off on foot through fields, ditching myself when traffic passed, I came to the first house in the countryside and grabbed a scarf from a washing line, wrapping it around my neck and mouth, attempting to keep my face hidden as much as possible. I changed out of my bog-covered clothes and took what I could from the line, a pair of corduroy trousers and a parka jacket with a heavy hood. I walked south on foot for eight miles, through fields, crossing the border to Southern Ireland where I came to a main road. I flagged down a bus en-route to Dundalk, in the north-eastern tip of Southern Ireland. When boarding, I kept my head down, pretending I was nearly deaf, confused, and a demented old man who had become lost. I padded to the back of the bus past fourteen passengers and shuffled into a seat, avoiding the driver's eye in the mirror.

In Dundalk, I waited half an hour, pretending to sleep on a bench outside the station, hiding my eyes under my hat and heavy hood with the scarf covering the bottom of my face. The bus to Dublin arrived. Getting to Rosslare was no easy feat, especially with the paper stands outside newsagents with Milacky's and my name, plastered over them. Our identities were shown on every news channel and newspaper in Great Britain and Ireland.

Once I got to Dublin station, my paranoia heightened. Stepping off the bus, I was confronted by 'Wanted' posters, like gunslingers from the Wild West, stuck to

the walls. Outlaw, that was a good synopsis of me. I
had to abort my plan of purchasing a ticket at the office
and hoped I could pay the ticket once on the bus.
Standing in the queue for the bus, of around twenty
bodies, didn't help. Trying to appear I had a pained
neck, like a veteran, with my head to the ground, I only
needed to get on the bus and luckily, I did. My gift of
avoiding capture for my crimes was still alive.

The bus left the station and I could breathe again. It
travelled straight to Rosslare.

Brian's house was a couple of miles from the town and
I started my walk, but by now my knee pain so bad I
could hardly walk, and I'd run out of painkillers again. I
had a motor stashed in Rosslare, but getting to it and the
risk of it not starting wasn't worth it. The hard road
made each stride hurt badly, but I pounded the tarmac
as quickly as I could, a sluggish pace for a man on the
run. Some passers-by peeped their horns but I wasn't to
curse, hoping they thought I was a silly old man,
walking on the side of a main road.

An hour later, arriving at Brian's detached house, I
discovered he wasn't at home. I checked under every
stone and ornament, but there was no key. I broke in
through the back door, headed to the sitting room
overlooking the road, shut the curtains and collapsed on
his one-seater, feeling the pounding beat of my heart
and the pain dissipate from my knees.

Once rested, I checked his cupboards for whisky,
poured a stiff glass and lit a rollie. In front of the telly, I
waited for the news to headline my name. I had been
spotted in Dundalk, early in the morning around 10.45
am by a passer-by. If a passer-by had spotted me, then
plenty others would have too.

For the time being, I was confined to the house. The
panic subsided and my head started to function as the

325

whisky calmed me. Millacky had turned up, and my money had vanished. His break-out must have been expertly planned, but a man of his calibre, even inside a maximum-security prison, would have criminal contacts to count on.

The front door opened late into the night and I heard Brian swear as he stumbled in, drunk I thought. There was a dimmed lamp on and the ashtray filled, whisky was finished and I was nearly asleep on the chair. The door was flung open.

"Be Jesus man!" He searched the area for a weapon and grabbed a homemade baton, holding it above his head, "Davie, is dat you?" he slurred.

"Good shift at the pub Brian?" it was a rhetorical question.

"Aye, it was dat. I wondered if you might pay a visit again." He flopped onto the sofa.

"No' shocked to see me?"

"Well, you could say I am, but when a man needs ti hide, he goes where no-one will know where he is." Still in his work dungarees, with beer staining his wild beard, his body folded into a comfortable position on the sofa with his feet resting on the coffee table.

"Let's hope no-one knows where I am 'en."

"You'll be safe here, don't you worry. I've been safe here for many a year," his palm opened to me as he repeated himself, before dozing off, and I followed suit.

The next morning, he woke me with a strong coffee after watching me twitch in the throes of a nightmare. Joe was standing over my dead body, that's when an inkling started to brew.

"Morning Davie, good sleep was it?"

"What's the time?" I jumped up.

"Relax man, you're good." As the nightmare subsided, I focused on the morning and the horrible pain.

"Got any pain killers to go wi' that coffee?"

"Aye, I'll get you some." He came back into the room, handed me a packet of a supermarket brand and sat down on the sofa, "It's gone eleven by the way."

At that moment, I truly felt my age, all fifty-four years, no money, no escape plan and no fight left in me.

"You've been out?" I asked, noticing his boots were damp.

"Been down ti the shop for a paper, t'ought you'd want a look." Millacky's story occupied the front-page, with my picture tucked in a corner. A six-page spread told our stories. The paper had us as allies, partners in crime. It even had me suspected of aiding his break-out. The detailed articles explained Millacky's life in the IRA with me as his gunrunner and now top of the 'wanted' lists. Money was offered for information on our whereabouts, and we were not to be approached under any circumstances. It made me out to be a monster, but it was Millacky who was the monster.

"Is it true?" Brian asked.

"Which part?"

"Any of it?"

I didn't see the point in withholding information. If he wanted to grass me up for the reward, he would've done so already. I told him my story of working for Millacky and then taking over, my European travels and the stolen money. Told him everything, from day one to that moment. Even about Lucille. We spoke for hours about the men in the trade and in return, he told me his story. He was a bomb maker for the IRA, at the height of the Troubles in the seventies and eighties.

"So Millacky broke out fir your blood?" he questioned.

"Aye, and he won't stop until I'm found."

327

"Millacky's an evil man, the t'ings he will do ti you if you're caught aren't worth the t'ought. IRA have a stern policy in dealing wit' dere un-loyal."

"You know him?"

"Aye, ti be sure, I'm afraid."

"Until I can figure out what to do, I'll be hidin' here, the ritual of the IRA torture process doesn't float well wi' me."

"You're welcome ti stay as long as need be."

"Good, I don't intend on venturin' out. How long you been out the IRA?" I asked.

"You can never leave the IRA. Once you're in, dere's no getting out. I've known men who have tried 'n' failed." His manner turned despondent as he battled himself to hold something in, "You see, I'm down here cos…cos I done somet'ing terrible, somet'ing dere's no forgiveness for." He stared at the blank curtains and held his head as still as time, "I don't deserve any. I used ti be a passionate Republican, since my birth, till somet'ing changed me." His eyes glistened and he turned quiet, before a lonesome tear dripped slowly down his cheek and into his wild beard, "T'ree girls, Davie, t'ree innocent goddamn kids, all under eight, and dere mother." His chin agitated and cheeks fluttered as a river of tears battled to get out, "All cos I set the timer wrong." I looked at the whisky bottle, hoping I could pour him a drink, but it was empty. I placed my hand on his shoulder, gripping with my thumb and fingers.

"It'll be alright Brian."

Chapter 65

Reality:

 This is what my life had come to. Too much greed had led me to become a recluse, too paranoid to leave the house. At Brian's, I never left the comfort of indoors, not once in the first five months, sitting with the living-room curtains drawn and wary of standing at open windows. The road outside was the main drag into Rosslare with plenty traffic passing each day. Was this really what my life had turned out to be? Many years ago, when I stayed with Brian, I wondered if I'd end up a lonely old man like him, and that's exactly what had happened. Left with nothing but thought and regret from my life. The one person I loved was rotting at the bottom of the Mersey and there wasn't a goddamn thing I could do about it. I had become greedy, paid the formidable price of loneliness. I always gave thought to withdrawing that ten grand from my Luxemburg account, but even logging in to it could uncover my position, so I left it be. I kept updated with the headlines and newspapers every day and sure enough, the publicity died down.

 I checked the 'most wanted' lists and I'd dropped down a few places, due to my lack of activity, but I knew I'd never be forgotten, not by the IRA anyway.

 Brian and I became good pals, shared stories of the past, I told him everything about my upbringing, Jack, Joe and Max. The stories filled time and there was plenty of that. I became gaunt, white as a vampire and depressed. The hardship of life caught up with me and I couldn't get over my downfall. If I hadn't been so greedy, I could have been living my dream in Panama as a rich man, blessed with cocktails on the beach, hot weather and foreign beauties. Max could have been by my side; we could've been happy men. But Max was gone, killed by my forgotten son and that's something that plagued my mind every day.

As Brian was a big smoker of grass, I succumbed to the habit too. It helped ease my physical pain and at times, it would mentally chill me out enough to forget, relax, but other times my mind wandered to who stole my money. Max had been the closest person to me and the only one who knew my money plans. Rankin knew nothing of my accounts and if Millacky tried to reach out to him, I'm sure he would've let me know, since he was as deep into deceiving Millacky as I was. I always dealt with my own money transactions, can't trust others with your income.

A niggling thought chipped away like a woodpecker pecking a hole in a tree. My account was dried, but by whom? The idea that Millacky was to blame just couldn't stick; sure, it was convenient he appeared and the money disappeared, but was it him? It kept running around my head like a Nascar race that never ended. It had to be Joe. Who else could it be? But the more I thought, the more it couldn't have been possible and the more I dismissed the idea, the more I went back to blaming Millacky.

Maybe it was the paranoia from smoking Brian's grass in conjunction with heavy drinking and painkillers, but it was a continuous niggle and I could never make my mind up.

After five months, the itch to go outside got the better of me and taking a chair, I sat in the pouring rain, in my t-shirt, one morning, smoking a joint. The rain didn't bother me, the countryside filled my lungs with fresh air. Being so paranoid before that day, I didn't dare open the door. Sitting in the rain, I wondered what the fuss had been about.

 Outside, I was relaxed and calm. I swivelled my gaze to the mess of Brian's scrap-ridden land. A couple of acres of rust and disorganisation. Without his permission, I began to clean up. The hard work, sweat and dirt made me feel normal again. Each day after, I rose, made a coffee, rolled a joint and for months I worked on that mess. Moving cars, farm machinery and boxes of scrap with his telescopic forklift into tidy organised piles, like when I tidied the arms bunker in Ards forest. I ransacked his three large wooden sheds and a couple of smaller, garden ones. Brian never once questioned my activities; just like him and his past, I wanted to feel normal again. I let my beard flourish and kept my pony tail cut at below shoulder height.

 After the land was tidied, I became depressed again, especially when the heat of summer arrived.

 All day and night, I didn't see the point in life, what was I doing here? Brian made me a welcomed man and I'll always thank him for that. In theory, he saved my life. If it hadn't been for him, I'd be decomposing in a jail somewhere or a torn-up corpse, the result of Millacky's wrath. He was still on the run, but I knew he was at peace with that. It was a soulless life he lived.

 The time ran on and a couple of years passed. Once upon a time, I had been a brutal fighter, the best in the land, feared by most and now, I was a frail man, defeated by the memories of my past. My whole life I wanted to be that famous criminal and I did so as The Eidolon, an infamous gunrunner, top of the tree, and now I was nothing but a shell of my former self. I'd been on a mission to reunite with Max, and that had been yanked from my heart. I became everything I desired to become, and bow there was nothing but my own thoughts to ponder.

Waking up one gloomy day, as they all were, I made my coffee and sat outside in the brisk morning. I stared at the green surroundings and looked to the sky, again with the same wonder of what my life had become. A low-flying propeller plane swept above my head, reminding me of all those illegal border crossings with shipments. That was the moment of clarity for me. A dawning of clear thought awakened me like the light at the end of a long tunnel. There was no way I could live the rest of my life as that frail man with unfinished business, casting regrets. It was time for change.

As I looked at my reflection in the mirror of the bathroom cabinet, my hollow eyes were devoid of life, surrounded by ageing wrinkles on the same hard-skinned face I always saw. My scraggy beard and receding hairline as grey as the life I now lived. I opened the cabinet, grabbed scissors, a razor and shaving cream, and proceeded to chop off the beard, feeling the smooth chin I always preferred. I trimmed my side-burns high, cut the hair running from my nostrils and tidied up my eyebrows, until I presented an image fit enough for a job interview. I showered and scrubbed everywhere. The cluster of random clothes Brian had bought me were washed, dried and ironed. I picked the best outfit I had. My eighties look of pale-coloured jeans, plain black t-shirt and the black faded bomber jacket I'd had since the day I fled Aberdeen sixteen years earlier. I dressed and fitted my hair into a black bobble. Pouring a whisky, I also made a stock of rollies, humbly smiling as I sat in Brian's chair in front of the telly, waiting for my friend to return from his daily jobs.

He walked into the room, shocked, while I'd just hung-up the phone on a very important call.

"Be Jesus man, check you fella! Going out are wi?"

"Aye, we both are, to the pub!"

"You've t'ought this t'rough?"

"Every single day I've been here."

"Well, better get in the truck then."

"I'll be drivin'." He threw me the keys and with him still in his dirty dungarees, we were off to the pub.

I grabbed my two passports and the money I had left from the five grand hidden in the safe house.

The brisk feeling of driving with my rollie in my mouth and the wind wafting into the truck was the best I'd ever had. I didn't care if I was seen, I really didn't.

"I'll get these," I said to the big bellied barman who recognised me straight away, "A Guinness, export, and two whiskies please."

"Feeling flush are wi?" Brian asked.

"Na, just grateful." Sitting at the bar with five others, the same five who sat there the first time I visited Brian, I was happy, my manner said so.

We took the piss out of each other, laughed and shared rounds. Everyone knew my real identity but it was never mentioned, not one little hint.

Three hours and lots of drinks later, I stopped laughing and spoke straight up to Brian as the others held their own conversation.

"I think I've got a bill to pay, Brian."

"Ye're alright, I'll get the next wan."

"No, for ma lodgin'."

"Davie, I don't want your money."

"It's nae money I'm givin' you." He waited for me to explain as his expression changed, "Beside Donegal, at these coordinates," I handed him a piece of paper and the padlock keys, "there's a fallen broken tree, you'll see it, it's obvious. There's a large boulder in line wi' the tree. Under it, is a closed hatch and a bunker. In there is five grand."

"Look, I don't want your money," Brian repeated.

"No, listen. There's a copy of a file, a file you can use if ye're ever in trouble, inside a small cupboard by the door. If someone comes askin' about me, use the file for yer own safety, you hear?" He nodded in acceptance, "I'll be goin' away for a long time and if you ever hear of somethin' happenin' to me, I want you to contact these people." A piece of paper with a list of names passed across the bar. A list of men I'd dealt with across Europe, with addresses and phone numbers, who'd be happy to know about the operations of Lucille.

"Aye, consider it taken care of," Brian answered formally.

"It's been a real pleasure Brian. I thank you for what you've done for me," I stated.

"Pleasure's been mine, Davie."

That was the end of my time with Brian. I was off to fetch the motor I'd stashed in Rosslare and sort out some unfinished business so it couldn't bite me in the ass in future.

In the past, I'd been bitten hard, from Sam Bryson and Jack Gallagher. They were both dead and that left Joe. That niggling thought he had something to do with my money just wouldn't leave me alone, and the need to rally some redemption for Max's corpse made my decision for me. Although Millacky was a tie I couldn't cut, yet, it would be unwise, if not suicidal, to attempt to locate him.

Chapter 66

Cutting The Last Tie:

The wait was over, the moment had arrived.
I stormed towards the door with my sleeves rolled up,
tingles of nervous adrenaline pumping. Preparing to do
the unlawful, my heart beating like a possessed wolf
with a desire to bring a terrible end to him, my own
blood. Keeping calm before one last violent eruption, to
neuter that pathetic cowardice he had as a weak child
and watch him whimper in my sight. The prolonged
build-up to this moment made my nostrils flare and
images swirled through my head like a hunter sniffing
out his prey, wondering what I was willing to do when
we exchanged uncontrollable looks of disgust. Would I
kill him? I didn't know. Was I prepared to? Fuck, yeah.
All I wanted was to escape from a world of solitude I
became trapped inside and that's what brought me
within moments of my disowned son's door. Sixteen
years ago, inside the Fountain Bar in Aberdeen, his
vengeful eyes longed to tear me apart; now the feeling
had rebounded. The last time I saw him, I helplessly
witnessed him viciously kill The Reaper, my protégé,
his brother and the only son I held pride for. That
chaotic night punctured a hole in my soul and left me
with unfinished business. My sons didn't know they
carried the same blood, brought together on a bitter
night by the law of fate. Ending up in a colossal battle,
in a fight laced with a legacy that would never be
forgotten by the gathering of deplorable men who
watched in admiration. Two men who were on a
steroid-fuelled quest to be crowned the greatest bare-
knuckle fighter of their generation, as I was, once upon

a time. Men who lived distant lives from each other, but so closely bound and so unaware of their connection.

This corner of Scotland, I doubted I'd ever visit again, but needs must, and my connection to Joe was the last tie to my past, and the only dangling branch before my exit. I was so blindly close to getting out of the game with more siller, hard cash, than I knew what to do with, but my fortune suspiciously vanished and somehow, Joe was to blame, I knew it.

Usually I stuck to a compact set of rules, rules that kept me alive, in the shadows and free from jail. Being at the top of Britain's most wanted list has that effect. I'd be breaking the rules by visiting my past but fuck it, it had to be done.

As soon as I made him suffer and harvested some answers, the first ferry out of the country was my next port of call. Airports were too risky. A ferry, I could drive in by car in disguise using one of only two passports I had left.

There was a collection of people burning to bring me down and end my reign, authorities that wouldn't rest in their quest to get me behind bars for the rest of my ageing life. And I wasn't prepared to be thrown into the IRA's torture process, before the standard bullet in the back of the head finished me off. I always told myself I'd get out on top, but I'd gotten too greedy and paid the formidable price. Getting out on top now, meant escaping with my life.

The long festering pain of regret and grief I'd dragged around was about to end as I quickly made my way towards the door. Years of selfish, abusive living had been brutal to my body, the torturing pain I carried in my knees had run me down and could be seen in my scowl that always had an aggravated look. The bones in my hands were brittle, my skin hardened, my head overworked and pounding with my serious addiction to painkillers.

With both fists clenched tight, I psyched myself up and remembered The Reaper's death. The anticipation of seeing Joe's pitiful face conjured up hatred that swirled like a whirlpool. My jaw bones clenched, goose bumps ignited and nostrils flared, the forthcoming confrontation pictured in my mind. His weakened body beneath my stance, his face mauled and begging for mercy. After I left his life, he became a hardened man, feared and respected by tough criminal men, but the fear he had for me would always swill around his brain like a sieve that wouldn't drain. His abhorrence for me would cause his belly to weaken and turn gutless. My face in his would be the last thing he'd expect.

I kicked the low gate off the hinges and ran over the footpath to his door. I used the side of my fist to pound two intimidating knocks. I waited. No answer so I pounded again. My paranoia made me gander over my shoulder, onto the street. Checking my back, as I had to, every minute.

The door opened. Joe answered with a jubilant face, looking like he was enjoying his late Sunday afternoon. Wasting no time, I stepped in and gripped his throat, lifting him onto the tips of his toes and backwards till he slammed into the banister. His stupid, happy face turned to terrified panic as he realised who it was.

"Alright, boy." His eyes burst open and his mouth gargled as he struggled to speak and breathe. I could smell a barbeque, and hear sounds of laughter and chatter from the back of the house. I squeezed harder while his hands gripped my forearm, looking for that strength to break free. I gripped even more tightly, watching his face turn purple.

"What's wrong? Nothin' to say?" I laughed at his weak struggle.

 I relaxed enough pressure so he could answer, but kept enough so he couldn't break loose.

"What the fuck you doin' here?" he gargled, unsure if his eyes were telling him the truth.

"Came to say hello, son!" His whole body squirmed with fear and rage, his girlish grip on my forearms mustered all the strength he had, as all he wanted was to lay his wrath on me.

"Seen yer last fight boy." He began to stop struggling and the rage appeared to turn to shock as he looked at me dead-eyed.

"What?"

"I was there, watchin'." Now an irritation flooded his eyes. "Fuckin' prick!" he replied.

"That's no way to speak to yer old man," I said sarcastically, knowing that would anger him more, "I never did get the chance to tell you about yer brother."

"Who?" Joe asked, as he attempted to pull my hands away.

"He used to be a fighter, like you. We called him The Reaper." His body turned limp, his eyes turned stony and broke contact as he gazed past my ear, onto the street outside, attempting to work out how that could be possible. A few seconds of stillness passed before he got some inspiration.

"It's you who should've died, you pathetic cunt!" His revulsion at his own hopelessness to free himself made his aggression levels rise again, as a stream of saliva rolled from the side of his mouth and spit spluttered into the air. I pulled my Walther PPK from my jacket pocket and jammed it into his eye as he stared at my mangled hand with missing fingers.

338

"Ye're a fuckin' coward, you always have been son. Who's out the back?" I asked.

"I've proven I'm no coward. You're the one that ran, you fuck!"

"Less of yer backchat, boy! I said who's out back? And don't make ma ask again. You know what I'm capable of wi' ma finger restin' on the trigger."

"You can pull the trigger if you want, but the man behind you might pull his."

I heard a gun cock and press into the back of my head.

Chapter 67

The Outcome:

"Mr Rhodes, or should I say The Eidolon." His tongue was Irish, "Now if you make any sudden movements, a bullet will enter that deceiving brain of yours."

"Don't worry, I'm no' movin'." I shared a bewildered exchange with Joe as he got his breathing back to normal while rubbing his neck.

"I knew you'd come back here one day, and I've been waiting."

"Hope it's no' been for too long," I answered politely and slightly coy.

"Mmh, long enough to enjoy this moment," he replied.

"Who are you?" Joe asked, his stunned eyes looked towards the man with the gun embedded in the back of my head.

"I'm just your neighbour, Joe."

"Ahh, you've moved into the neighbourhood, have you?" I asked.

"Been here for more than a year Davie, I kind of like it around here. Inverurie's a nice place, shame about the neighbour's family though." Joe didn't know whether to hit me, or the guy holding the gun.

"Here Joe, catch!" A roll of duct tape was thrown into Joe's hand.

"Who the fuck are you Ben?" Joe asked the man behind me.

"Haha, Ben, is that yer alias now?" I spouted and laughed at such a petty name.

"While I'm up in these parts it is, but thanks to you, I won't be any more. Joe, get rid of whoever is out the back." Joe's long face crossed between us, "Joe, if you don't want your kids to hear gun shots, I'd suggest you get them out of here. Mags and Tim too." Without words, Joe idled backwards through the tight lobby and opened the kitchen door.

"Put your hands behind your back?" What choice did I have? It was either that, or getting shot. The silencer on the gun that I could feel bed into the back of my head would lessen his hesitation to shoot. He placed a set of handcuffs on, without moving the barrel away. "Now walk into the sitting room, slowly Davie. I know you've got a habit of brushing death to the side. Now take a seat. Be as well to get comfortable before your taxi arrives."

I sat down on the edge of the corner sofa by the door. Seeing pictures of my grandkids hanging on the wall and a wedding photo of Joe and his wife. It looked as if he was living a pleasant life.

"What took you so fucking long to get up here? I was getting impatient waiting."

"Well, I was kind of re-thinkin' life, you know how it is. Took me a long time to figure somethin' out," I answered.

"I thought you would've got out the country, spend that retirement fund you've had tucked away."

"Don't play smart wi' me. You know ma account's been emptied." His expression came across snide.

"Yes it has and that cash will nicely top up my account, a little compensation for the time I've wasted up here, I'd say."

"Ye're a treacherous bastard!"

"I needed to bleed you dry, flush you out so to speak, take you out your rhythm. I almost gave up and pissed off. So glad I stuck around for this family reunion." That was my suspicion confirmed.

"I presume the IRA treatments comin' ma way."

"Ohh that's a certainty Davie, Millacky will take great pleasure in organising that. I can't wait to tell him the news."

"I don't think that's a very good idea," I stated.

"Why not?"

"Because Rankin, I know who you really are."

"Really, I'm just the middleman Davie, you know that."

"No Lucille, I know different."

Chapter 68

Lucille:

When the plane had flown overhead, as I had been sitting at Brian's back door, my head cleared as to who Lucille was, and everything made sense. The very first time I had met Rankin and boarded his plane, inside the hangar, a man was polishing the logo of Rankin's plane, the picture of a woman in a bikini, and indecipherable writing underneath with only the initial 'L' readable from the word, Lucille. I'd been on that plane countless times and why it took me so long to figure out, I don't know. Probably the worry over my two sons fighting and after Max died, it clouded my thoughts. On top of that, I was trying to get out of the trade and figure out where my fortune had disappeared to.

Lucille's background, as it said in the file, was as a member of the Army Ranger Wing, the elite special operations of the Republic of Ireland Defence Forces, and he'd been enrolled since 1984 where he got scouted from the Air Corps. His speciality was counter-terrorism and intelligence gathering that led the Army Rangers bedding him inside the IRA's operations and ever since then, he had become a double agent, deceiving both sides for his own financial benefit. He managed to cultivate a close relationship with Millacky, and since the late nineties, went rogue from the Rangers, changed his appearance and teamed up with Millacky, when the IRA split from the Provisional IRA, cultivating in the division of The Real IRA forming where Millacky sat at the top.

It all made sense really, the information asset who could unravel contacts and reveal efficient background checks, mould counterfeit passports, and had a depth of knowledge of weaponry for sale. Then he happily sat on the fence while I gallivanted around Eastern Europe earning a fortune. All the time keeping tabs on my location, when he could.

 The day he turned up after Millacky's failed terrorist attack and arrest at the safe house was not coincidence; he had been following me from day one and when I insisted I'd take over the gunrunning, I fell hook line and sinker into his lap. The arms bunker under St Paul's church was his old base where he kept tabs on the arms trade, myself and the rest of the IRA. The story that Millacky had two arms bunkers was a croc of shit. He got the priest, who was well in bed with Rankin, to clear out the cells while we transported the arms from the underground bunker to St Paul's church. Because of Rankin's connections, he could fill the cells with a collection of arms from somewhere, setting the trap that I'd use it as storage. The priest never asked questions, which I thought was strange and explains why the comings and goings of myself, Turk and Barb, were never questioned. The sketches of me that made it onto the news was his doing. Planting a seed as to who I was, but the authorities had no intention of taking me in at that time because Rankin insisted I'd open up many doors to the European arms trade. It was only a ploy to keep me on my toes. He then used me to gun run across Britain and Europe, gain intel on regimes, organised gangs, dictators, guerrilla armies, Islamic extremists, and sell that intelligence onto governments and spy agencies. He controlled the flow of arms across Europe and controlled me from day one.

 The easiness of running guns across borders in eastern Europe was down to him. He was the henchman who controlled everything, setting up arms contracts so intel could be gathered, like the time the ghetto gang from London got busted after Eclipse, who was Max, and Rankin himself were present. That explains why they could get away. That was Rankin's strategy to have the Ghetto Gang busted. Another drop he was present at was when Eclipse opened up Mr Dean's face, and soon after, the CID stormed in, but I couldn't figure out how that would benefit Rankin because he was present at that deal and surly risked his identity being uncovered. Mr Dean was certainly plotting with the police, for whatever reason, to have both Rankin and Max arrested. Mr Dean, as the file explained, was a wretched informant. The RUC man, Mr Farrell, was supposed to be my final nail in the coffin. Rankin decided I'd become too greedy and had a long enough run. That's what he did, let the arms flow for a while and then kill off or lock up the gunrunner.

The entire legacy I thought I'd built as a gunrunner, was false.

I look back now and think of the easiness of how he was able to gain contact with the people I couldn't. The American, Dalton, who I picked up the carbines from at an American armoury in Germany was an example. You couldn't just come across a contact like that on the black market. He had intelligence agencies and sources to fall back on for information.

The ring-binder was a classified file that found its way into a safe-deposit box in a bank in Paris. Once upon a time, Rankin was part of a duo and his sidekick from the French secret service was embedded into Vogue's operation, like Rankin, who embedded himself inside The IRA. The man was unravelled by Vogue and torturing him filtered out the information about the file, but all the pieces of the puzzle weren't entirely there. The mole from the Secret Service created that file just for a rainy day, and surely he was looking for a way to survive and stop the agony of the beating by informing Vogue of the file. It didn't work, he was killed anyway. Vogue then had to decipher what bank the file was hiding in and plan six different robberies on the same day, that took some time to arrange. If anything happened to me, Brian was my insurance policy, who would leak the information of Rankin's true identity. Even living a lonely life and detached from the IRA, I knew any news of my downfall would somehow filter back to him. Vogue was one man who would receive the information. The piece of paper I slid across to Brian in the bar had the simple headline written at the top:

'Rankin is Lucille.'

Chapter 69

Back To The Sitting Room:

Joe got rid of his barbecue party and returned.

"Joe, take a seat," Rankin insisted, and Joe sat opposite the corner sofa. Rankin floated the gun between us both.

"You can't kill me Rankin," I said.

"Sure I can."

"If anythin' happens to me, there's a file that explains yer real identity and it's goin' to find its way into many people's hands. People who won't be as kind as me."

Joe was shocked and silent, trying to figure out who his so-called neighbour was, and what I was rambling on about. Rankin had moved next door to Joe for just this reason, waiting for me to appear. It kind of worked out well for me that he did.

"What file?" Rankin queried with a laugh.

"It came from an old friend of yours, contains all the information about how ye're a dirty rat for intelligence agencies."

"Davie! You really think I'm that gullible?"

"Kill me and find out for yerself."

Quietly he pondered the threat while I butted in with a query.

"Tell me, there's a couple things I don't understand. What happened at the deal with Mr Dean?"

"That deal was supposed to be a set up to have your boy nicked. I couldn't stand the sight of the cunt. A total unprofessional liability in my opinion, so in truth, I'm glad Joe here done him in." That was it, a set up that went wrong and explained the fake money, "I think he inherited that annoying trait of survival of yours, pain in the ass he was."

There was still something I needed to know.

"How did I acquire ma name, The Eidolon?"

"You became a very hard man to track. I had to use all my resources to find you at times, hence why I planted the name. I had to call you something, every criminal deserves a nickname."

"So, are you goin' to use that gun, or is it just an ornament?"

"Killing you is not my plan. You'll be handed over to Millacky who will deal with you as he wishes but maybe I could kill Joe." Now the gun pressed into Joe's temple.

"On you go, I was comin' here to do that anyway."

As Joe absorbed the information that he had killed his brother, and now this altercation inside his sitting room in the humble town of Inverurie, with a gun on his temple, he was in too much shock, unable to speak, open-eyed, staring at me, not able to understand my vindictive nature. I continued to play my ace card.

"Millacky will be one person who will receive this file. You know he'll never quit in his search for you. The IRA torture process is pretty severe I hear."

"Joe, tape his mouth shut, now!" I'd said enough to keep me alive. Joe stood, Rankin stepped out of his way. With Joe's back to Rankin, he tore a cutting of duct tape with his teeth, approached me with little love in his eye and stretched the tape over my mouth before walking back to his seat.

"We will just have to wait for your taxi to arrive," Rankin said, as I arrogantly leaned back into the couch and put my feet on the table.

"Who are you?" Joe asked Rankin again.

"I won't go into details, but I'm not just your neighbour Joe. I was ordered to move up here and wait for your Father's appearance."

"Who's Millacky?" Joe questioned.

"Your dad's old boss, and he's not what you'd call a happy man." Rankin turned his attention back to me, "Millacky's waiting for you Davie, he has been for some time. The IRA like to take their wrath out on the next of kin if they can't locate their target, so I had to persuade him otherwise and transfer me up here to this shitty town in case you showed face. Of course, after this indication that you have a file on me, has come to light, I will have to do away with you myself." He lowered his gun and started to relax a little, but he continued to spout his mouth off. "I've been a double, no wait, a triple agent, for many years, and I had to see to your capture before I myself do a runner, with more cash than you'll ever know of. Cut ties to the past, so to speak. You know the feeling Davie, after all, you came here to kill your own son."

As victory speeches go, this one was rotting my eardrums, but he wasn't finished.

"Remember that painting, the heist Millacky hired Turk and Bard for?" I didn't acknowledge him, "I hired Millacky to do that, made twenty million from it, sold it to a wealthy Arab. Can you believe that shit?" I still didn't acknowledge him.

Joe seemed to get frustrated and attempted to rise, "Sit, Joe, I'm not finished yet. Another thing I don't understand though, the flawed attacks on the barracks, I knew nothing, nothing at all about it! Millacky didn't involve me nor mention anything, and The General was no grass because I planted that lie, so who was the snitch? Was it you, Davie?"

This time I did acknowledge him with a nod of my head.

I couldn't let Millacky kill all those men, it was heartlessly evil. I had to stop it, calling one of the

349

barracks a few weeks prior to lay the seed. The story of The General being the informant was a complete hoax. That's why my coffee was spat from my mouth at hearing the news inside the safe house. It was always my plan to take over his gunrunning operation.

"Well well, Davie Rhodes, the great hero. Shame no-one will ever know, except your son here." Rankin moved to the window at the sound of a vehicle approaching, "Taxi's here," he smiled, "Well Joe, it's been a pleasure knowing you but we've got to shift, the meter's running."

Rankin lifted me up by my arm pit as I gave Joe a finial dagger but he didn't respond.

Outside was a blacked-out Range Rover. In the light of the day, Rankin marched me from the house, his victory speech finished. Before he opened the car door, I glanced back to Joe who postured with his arms folded, leaning against the inside of the door frame, with a coy half-grin on his face. Manhandled out of the house in broad daylight, handcuffed and gagged, I was smiling under the duct tape for very good reason.

This was about to be a moment of pure joy. Rankin thought his taxi was being driven by one of his goons, but it wasn't, it was Millacky! The phone call I made before I left Brian's was to Millacky. An emergency number he gave me many years beforehand, that he insisted I'd always be able to contact him on and sure enough, I did. I explained who Rankin was, informed him of the file that Vogue had passed onto me. All the details inside, and that it was Rankin's fault the barrack attacks was flawed and he was jailed. Even though it was myself who had thwarted that plan, it was the level of deceit I had to use to even us out. We agreed the information would settle our debt and he provided me with some very valuable information, that he had moved Rankin into Joe's neighbourhood in case I would show face one day. That then got us talking, and we came to this conclusion of events. Millacky would get Rankin and do as he wished with him, and I'd get Joe and do as I wished with him.

Rankin walked me around the jeep to the rear passenger door. There was no need to struggle. Once inside, Millacky was waiting, and I hoped he was going to live up to his word. Rankin walked around to the other back door and entered.

"Right, let's get away from this monstrosity of a place!" A gun with a silencer attached came between the front seats, held by a hooded passenger. I looked at the back of the driver's full head of jet black hair.

Rankin lifted his head to the passenger and recognised him straight away.

"What the fu…?"

A bullet pumped into Rankin's heart and shut him up instantly.

The driver turned around. Jack Gallagher!

The shooter's hoodie flapped down as he swung round, "Hello, Da'!"

Lightning Source UK Ltd.
Milton Keynes UK
UKHW01f2044210618
324611UK00001B/10/P